# The
# Carbon
# Diaries
# 2017

# The Carbon Diaries 2017

Saci Lloyd

Holiday House / New York

Copyright © 2009 Saci Lloyd
First published in Great Britain in 2009 by Hodder Children's Books. The right of Saci Lloyd
to be identified as the Author of the Work has been asserted by her in accordance with the
Copyright, Designs and Patents Act 1988.
First published in the United States of America by Holiday House in 2010
All Rights Reserved
HOLIDAY HOUSE is registered in the U.S. Patent and Trademark Office.
Printed and Bound in December 2009 at Maple Vail, Binghamton, NY, USA.
www.holidayhouse.com
First American Edition
1   3   5   7   9   10   8   6   4   2

Library of Congress Cataloging-in-Publication Data

Lloyd, Saci.
The carbon diaries 2017 / by Saci Lloyd.—1st American ed.
p. cm.
Sequel to: The carbon diaries 2015.
Summary: Two years after England introduces carbon dioxide rationing to combat
climatic change, eighteen-year-old Laura chronicles her first year at a London university
as natural disasters and political upheaval disrupt her studies.
ISBN 978-0-8234-2260-9 (hardcover)
[1.  Protest movements—Fiction.   2.  Rationing—Fiction.   3.  Energy
conservation—Fiction.   4.  Climatic changes—Fiction.   5.  London (Eng.)—
Fiction.   6.  England—Fiction.   7.  Diaries—Fiction.]   I.  Title.
PZ7.L77874Cas 2010
[Fic]—dc22
2009020412

*This book is dedicated to the memory of*

Victor Hugo Daza, 17
Carlo Giuliani, 22

*And all the others who have fallen
in the defence of human rights*

## Author's Note

About three years ago I walked past a newspaper stand and the lead story in one paper was all about how we were going to fry, and in another how we were going to freeze to death unless we tackled climate change. I remember thinking, "Whoah! Which one is it?" before stepping aboard a roller-coaster research ride of heart-stopping bad news about how much we're messing up the world. But the strange thing was, the more I found out, the less scared I got and the more I wanted to start fighting for a future. Plus after all that doom, I wanted to have a laugh. As a teenager, I was always drawn to books that asked big questions about the world, but I also loved funny books, with lead characters who never wanted to teach you a thing: Holden Caulfield, Adrian Mole, Huckleberry Finn.

Laura Brown would be furious if she knew I'd published her secret diary. I ain't telling her anytime soon.

*Saci Loyd, 2009*

# FOCUS ON: THE GLOBAL WATER CRISIS. Is 2017 the year of

## USA: OGALLALA AQUIFER
Current Status: 5 years remaining.
Source of 1/5th of all US farm water.
Extraction: 12 bilcubic metres P.A.

Conflict status: Civil unrest/state
troops mobilised 4 times in 2016

## SPAIN: EBRO RIVER
Current Status: Lowest recorded levels.
Channel project completed in 2014 to
re-route water to Southern Spain has
brought region to crisis point.

Conflict status: Severe civil unrest/state
wide strike in Catalonia, Aragon/border
disputes with France.

## CH
Cu
42
Ch

Co
12.
Riv
pec

## MEXICO CITY
Current Status: Clean water
failure. Severe cholera
outbreak in 2015/16
City has sunk to extreme
danger levels due to over
pumping of aquifer.

Conflict status: Forced
evacuation of districts.

BRAZIL/PARAGUAY
ITAIPU DAM CONFLICT

## INDIA/PAKISTAN
GANGES RIVER DISPUTE

## ISRAEL/PALESTINE
Current Status: Sea of Galilee at crisis
levels. Israel's main reservoir now in
danger of complete salination.
Severe drought in Palestine & Jordan.

Conflict status: Massive civil unrest/
Israeli military strikes on Gaza strip/
escalating Jordanian border conflict.

## AFRICA
Current S
Nile at low
Intense co
Africa, Lak

Conflict s
Nile in 20
disputes.
Chad, Can
displaced
massive ri

## Water Stress Indicator

Low/Mid Stress          High Stress          Extreme Stress (Conflict)

## rst water war?

**YELLOW RIVER**
atus: Lower reaches dry for
eriod. Water table on North
n dropping by 2 metres P.A

atus: Forced relocation of
n people in Yangtze/Yellow
ect. Estimated 40 million
starvation levels.

**ZBEKISTAN/KAZAKSTAN**
**RAL SEA COLLAPSE**

**IRAQ**
**WETLAND COLLAPSE**

**AUSTRALIA**
**DARLING RIVER**
**CRISIS**

**E RIVER‚LAKECHAD**
evere drought in many areas.
els in recorded history.
tion for resources. In Central
is at 2% of previous levels.

gyptian military defense of
iopia & Sudan in border
gilante River Patrol in Niger,
. Estimated 150 million
g at starvation level,
egal entry to Europe.

# TEMPERATURES RISE AGAIN BY 0.35°
## CARBON RATIONING CARD TO GO GLOBAL

## Historic agreement reached today in Vancouver. 160 countries sign up to global carbon rationing card &trade permit system to set global limit for C02 pollution.

International environment ministers worked through the night to reach a dramatic 11th hour global agreement to lower carbon emissions on the last day of the Vancouver Emergency Climate Sessions. The agreement is in response to drastic new data, revealing that greenhouse gas levels in the atmosphere have risen to an historic high of 400 parts per million and average global temperatures have recorded their fifth annual rise. There are two main elements to the plan.
1) A massive new global infrastructure in which every citizen will be issued with a carbon rationing card to limit his/her annual carbon emissions according to internationally set targets. The system will be be based on the existing EuroZone trials.
2) A global limit to be be set for industrial carbon pollution. Permits will be issued to companies extracting or refining fossil fuels. Failure to comply will

# January

**Mon., Jan. 2**

So exhausted. My family is in a deathlike trance after the village New Year's Eve Organic Goose Fayre. After 2 days of meat-induced coma, I finally dragged myself out of bed and walked the five Ks into Abingdon to check out the sales. I'd just got to the market square when I heard this creepy jingly sound and a bunch of Morris men rocked up in ribbons and bells with little sticks and started dancing around like idiots. I observed them closely, with their piggy eyes and big bellies. City people, bringing back traditions that have died out because they suck; the country is full of them.

Dad was super happy when I got home. He saw me by the gate and opened the kitchen window.

"Mail from Kim. Come on!"

I crunched moodily up the driveway.

it's your world...

Hi guys⊃ quick mail before the power goes
Having such a blast here⊃ Last night we wen
to the opening of a new temple. We got there
on a bus with about 200 people inside and 300
hanging on outside. It was about 1 million degree
in there, everyone laughing and singing and
sneaking Thai whiskey in the back. They⁊⁊d set
up a screen on the roof playing crazy Chinese
music vids through 12 banging speakers. It was
so loud it⁊⁊s like when you go deaf. The temple
was massive and golden, full of monks, a sea
of orange robes and flower garlands and so we
bought our own robes for 30 bhat and circled
the wat 4 times before doing some stuff with
candles and incense. In the end we threw our
robes into a hole in the new wat and a monk
poured holy oil and set them on fire. The flames
shot up so high my mate John nearly lost his
eyebrows
Leaving town tomorrow, heading for the beach⊃
oh yeah

Love ya
K x

Later I lay in bed thinking and got dead mad. How does my sister
get that life? She left her old job as promoter for Carbon Dating with

Kieran last summer and got a job in Thailand working for an eco tour holiday company called LoveWorks, which basically charges € 5,000 to fly guilty white people out to Thailand to build bad log huts for skinny villagers in rain forests. So there she is off her head on 100% proof Thai whiskey and here I am, 18 and lying on a single bed on a farm in Oxfordshire. I was supposed to be up in Glasgow with Adi for a massive New Year's Eve party, but guess whose mum washed a carbon card on heavy spin with an old knapsack? I'm totally grounded till I get that puppy back on line. Money ain't enough these days. Got to have a card to live.

### Wed., Jan. 4
It's so definitely time to get out of here. I came downstairs this morning to find a local community farmer meeting happening in the

kitchen. I walked in as Dad was turning from his laptop to face the group. "I've got something I'd like to put before you. Many of us keep pigs here, but what if we were to extend our facilities—and, and . . ."—he glanced at Mum's face—"and start converting our pig manure into crude oil!"

Mum gave an involuntary jerk. "Jesus."

He pushed on. "Look, oil and gas prices are at an all-time high, oil is $250 a barrel—and it's only going to rise. This recession is biting deep; we've simply got to make our own fuel. They did it in the oil crisis in the 1970s, so the technology exists. Look . . ." Dad jabbed his finger at the screen and it sprang to life, revealing a weird-looking machine. The farming randoms muttered.

"All you need is this small-scale thermo chemical conversion reactor. It basically puts heat and pressure on the pigs' . . . doings . . . and that breaks the manure's long hydrocarbon chains down into shorter ones."

"What does that mean?" asked Daniel. He's the only one I know by name cos he's super gorgeous. He's an ex-city broker with curly chestnut hair and hazel eyes who lives in a cottage in a bog with a really bossy blonde woman called Rachel who breeds llamas with big teeth. (Her, not the llamas. They are cute.)

"I'm not sure of the precise details, but it says here that each 5-liter batch of manure converts to a liter of oil. With the right amount of pigs we'd be self-sufficient."

Big Teeth spread her hands on her llama-wool-trimmed leggings. "And how many animals would that take? A few hundred?"

Dad nodded. "Yeah, Rachel. Give or take."

Mum groaned. "Oh, Nick, no, tell me you're joking."

Dad stared back at her; the group stared. Not a smile between them. Big Teeth turned to Mum and spoke clearly, like to a slow learner. "Well, with the economy the way it is, the unemployment, the inflation . . . not to speak of the flooding and land prices rising because of everyone leaving the cities . . ." She checked Mum's eyes to make sure she was following. "Under these conditions I'm sure you'll agree we have to take every chance we can."

Poor old Mum.

## Thurs., Jan. 5

Got a replacement card today. Freedom. Not that I've got any points left for the month. I had to give loads to Mum and Dad to power up the van so they could move their farm shit around over Xmas. Santa had the right idea with those reindeer.

## Fri., Jan. 6

I sneaked out this afternoon to throw some spuds to Larkin the pig. (My life is a roller coaster right now.) Although as pigs go, he is an uber pig. What other animal could go missing for 2 weeks in flooded London and make his way home in such style? Anyway, I'd finished with the potatoes and was giving his ears a scratch when Dad suddenly appeared. "Fancy some company?"

I smiled sweetly, mentally counting the seconds till he said the P word. 1, 2, 3, 4 . . .

Dad put his hand on the swing gate. "So what do you reckon to my pig manure plan?"

Impressive. Not for the first time I found myself wondering if he's OK in the head. He gets fixated on things, like those autistic savants that only get little bits of light shining in their brains at any one point, 'cept their brilliance is usually piano solos or molecular physics where my dad's shiny bit is pigs, which kind of takes some of the style away. Nobody's gonna make a movie about him.

I glanced up at him. "Dad, if you want to start up an oil factory that's fine, but you've got to get the others to lay off Mum a bit. I mean the way old llama legs was talking to her was dead mean."

He bit back a smile. "I know, but . . . your mum just won't get involved . . ."

"Surprise, surprise, Dad. The woman doesn't want to spend her life rolling in hoofed mammal crap. Ever occurred to you she's the normal one?"

"But that's just it . . ."

"What?"

He frowned. "There is no normal anymore."

We stood there a moment in silence. Deep silence. Although I swear Larkin winked at me. Cheeky little porker.

## Sat., Jan. 7

I was packing my stuff up when Mum came in, sat on the bed, and reached for a sock.

"I envy you, y'know. Back off to London . . ."

Uh-oh. I folded a T-shirt in silence.

"Your father is completely happy, of course, buried in the country."

"How's your library job going?"

She balled up a pair of mismatched socks. "It's fine, I mean, really it is. It's not publishing, of course. . . . And I'm very grateful to have a job right now, but . . ." She paused.

*But.* Seems to me there's always a *but* in everyone's life. I was saved by a horn tooting from outside. Mum jumped up. "Oh, God, the work bus!" She hugged me super tight. "Maybe I could come down and see you some time?"

My eyes widened in alarm, but she just kissed me and shot out. I watched from the window as she clambered into a little beaten-up minivan, full of local people going to work. A man in the back row looked up and waved at me. It was like the special-needs bus at school. Heartbreaking.

## Mon., Jan. 9

Mum made a special farewell dinner last night and as a special treat, Dad uncorked a bottle of his vintage homemade carrot wine. He handed around the evil juice in 3 homemade pot vessels and then turned to me, his eyes all misty.

"So, off to the Big Smoke again. Well, here's to you."

Mum raised her goblet. "To our lovely girl," she quavered.

I didn't know what to toast to. Future pig oil success? The survival of their marriage? So I smiled and took a sip of wine. It tasted like what villains slip into goblets to poison people in Shakespeare. I stared hard at the table, willing myself not to choke, but when I looked up again they were both gazing at me so intensely that I had to say something.

I waved my knobbly pot. "To the future!"

"Don't!" Mum dropped her goblet (clever move, lady), buried herself in Dad's chest, and reached out an arm and hooked me into a ghastly group hug. I stood there, smothered in damp wool, and then a strange thing happened; my heart went all soft. I mean, they're mad and they're starting to smell funny, but they're all mine.

## Tues., Jan. 10

I fell into a dark mood on the way back to London. There's something going on with me and Adi and it feels like a long time since I spoke to him. The truth is I was glad to get away for Xmas. I can't work it out, I know I love him; I just feel like it's all a bit safe. I mean, we've been going out for a year now and . . . I dunno. He wanted us to move in together when we started uni back in September, but I'd already got a room in a house in Elephant and Castle and so I said it was too far for him to travel cos he's over at Queen Mary Uni in Mile End. I'm excited to see him, I really am, *but* . . . There's that word again.

Then my brain moved on to the band. On the surface it's going good, we're starting to get some hits on the *port*, the only music site that counts, and we've been gigging hard on the scene. In just the last 6 months, we've done shows at a bunch of universities—UEL,

London Met, Westminster, LSC, and Camberwell—but there's always loads of tension. I reckon Adi secretly thinks it's kind of stupid being in a band, like it was OK when he was at school, but now he's moved on, but he never comes out and says it straight. And on the other side there's Claire, who's gone all hard-line political since she started journalism at UEL. Stace just drums, so somehow it's always down to me to keep it steady. There was a massive fight over the *dirty angels* name at the meeting just before Xmas. Adi said it was dumb and that we came up with it when we were 15. "Times change, Claire," he said.

She eyeballed him. "Maybe you mean *people* change. I'm serious about this band, if you're not." She flicked a glance at me. "Maybe we *all* need to think about why we're doing this."

I threw my hands up. "All? Why am I in this?"

"Cos you two are such the little couple. Buy one get one free."

Her words've stung ever since. Sometimes it feels like we're married or something.

Anyway, by this time, the train was battering through the London suburbs. The place has changed so much, it's unbelievable. They're rebuilding the barrier, but there's always money and tech problems and so, basically a year after the flood, the whole city's under threat, big time. And the water keeps on rising. Last year, the Thames flooded 34 times. And each time it floods, more people leave. Property prices in the bad areas have dropped to joke levels. Everyone's fighting to live in the hilly bits, like Hampstead and Shooters Hill. A 4-bedroom house just went for 8 million euros in Bromley cos it's the highest point in London. We were pretty smart; Mum and Dad fixed up the house really quickly after the first flood and got the hell out of town. I stayed with Claire till May so I could sit my exams and then went up to Abingdon to join them. They didn't want me to come back to London to study, but the way I see it is this is my home. That was their decision to move out to the country, not mine.

Once I got to Waterloo, I decided to walk to my house. Turning into my street, I walked the 100 meters, took out my keys, and stopped dead. The front door and the windows were all blocked off behind heavy metal sheets. It took me a few seconds to take it in. And then I lifted my wrist and punched a number into my fone. It went straight to voice mail. I took a breath, shouted, "You bastards. You never paid!" and punched *disconnect*.

I turned and kicked the door. Solid. An emergency fone number for a company called Repossessions Solutions was pasted vertically down the length of the door. I dialed it. Voice mail again, this time one of those lady androids:

"*Repossession Solutions is unable to take your call at this time. Our office hours are Monday to Friday, 9:00 A.M. to 4:30 P.M. We apologize for any inconvenience this may cause.*" Click.

Inconvenience? I tapped my fone against my forehead, fighting down panic. Who could I call? I knew Adi was coming down tomorrow—but everyone else was still away on break. I shivered; it was starting to get dark. There was only one person.

Sighing, I dialed a new number. "Hi . . . it's me."

"Oh."

"Look, I know we need to talk and stuff, but can I crash at yours tonight? Those bastards, Lou and Greg, took off. My house is locked down."

A pause, then: "Sure."

Relief flooded through me. "Claire, you're a lifesaver."

She sighed. "I know. I'll meet you at Royal Albert station at 7. But don't be late, I've got a meeting later."


An hour later I stepped off the train onto the platform and total darkness.

"Claire? Mate?"

"Over here. Can you see the steps?"

I stepped forward and stumbled. "No!"

"Wait up."

Something soft brushed past my head and then a hand grabbed my shoulder. "Hey! I've got you. . . . It's harsh, huh? We haven't had lights here for months."

Together we crossed a parking lot before turning right along the waterfront, the Excel Centre a massive dark presence on our right. Then we ducked under a walkway before stopping outside a warehouse building where Claire fed in a security number and we went thru a set of double doors.

"This place is hectic. How d'you know where you are?" I asked.

She shrugged. "You get used to it pretty quick . . . nearly there now."

We climbed up a final series of steps before coming out on a walkway, banged together with bits of wood and railing onto the original balconies. It looked super sketchy, like a sagging wooden hammock. Everything was dirty and beat up, with windows all smashed and peeling doors half hanging. On every door there were nailed 5, 10, 20 eviction notices, all fluttering in the wind.

Claire glanced over. "They're from that Rebuilding London Agency. S'kind of a badge of honor: The more eviction letters you get, the longer you've faced them off. Anyway, who's gonna come here and move us? The place is total flood land."

"Don't they try? I heard there was some trouble."

"Nah, not really, and anyway all you've got to do is work it out with the squat committee and move to another empty flat farther down the block." She stopped outside a metal door and fumbled with a padlock. The door opened with a rusty whine. "*Voila!* Come on in . . . yeah, but wait a sec . . . they've cut the electric *again*."

Claire struck a match and suddenly light flooded into the room from a kerosene lamp in her hand. In the flickering light and long, shaky shadows, the flat seemed massive, bare apart from a stripped-down table and 2 leather armchairs, stained with water.

I gazed around the room. "Wow."

Claire put the lamp down on the table. "Yeah, tell me about it, these flats were going for 2 mill a few years back."

I looked at the table, imagining them before. Some up-and-coming couple, looking out over their city skyline.

Claire glanced at her watch. "I've got to go in a minute. You can crash for as long as you want, yeah . . . but what you gonna do about your stuff?"

"Don't know. The Repo company has left a number—all I can do is call them. The only reason I'm not completely losing it is that I left my bass and music files at Adi's over Xmas."

"Mate, I can't believe you're still paying rent when there's so much free room here. . . . All you've got to do is see Tano Adile in the London Partnerships Centre in Excel, and then have an interview with—" Her fone started to vibrate.

I poked her. "Who?"

Claire giggled. "You won't believe it if I tell you. Hang on." She flipped up the fone. "Oh, hi. Are you coming down to the meeting? What?" She turned sharply away. "But you promised, Jax. I mean you gotta be on it. The Dox is the most important thing going on right now . . . independent DIY media projects are spreading around the planet at unprecedented speed. . . . Triggered by discontent with the mainstream media, groups are creating their own channels of information and distribution in order to bypass the corporate media, y'know?"

And *that's* why I still pay rent. Conversations like that are way too high a price for a free room.

## Wed., Jan. 11

I got to Adi's by lunch. I knocked on his door and after a few moments the upstairs window opened and Nate's messed-up head appeared, followed by his trademark grin.

"Yo, Laur!"

"Is Adi here? I can't get him on his fone."

He shook his head. "Yeah, he's lost it. His mate called, said he's on his way, but still up north."

"What, he's not back down from Scotland?"

Nate smiled. "Nah, Tottenham is all. Said he'd be back later today. 'Sup?"

"Can I come in?"

"Yeah sure . . . but . . ."

"What?"

"No comments. A'ight?"

I rolled my eyes. "No comments."

Adi and Nate's room is like those health and safety campaigns about how bacteria can kill in the home.

A few minutes later, I was staring deep into Che Guevara's left eye on a massive poster on the wall, trying to keep my 5 senses from getting sucked into the piles of dirty clothes, broke bits of engine, pizza boxes, scummy plates, engine oil, stubbed-out cigarettes, oozing cartons, odd chips, etc.

I perched on the edge of Adi's bed. "So what's new?"

Nate ran his hand across a random piece of engine. "Not a lot . . . I've mostly bin workin' on my Chevy van, she's a purebred hydro now."

I hid a smile. Nate's been working on this van since when we were 15. "So I was down at the Docks last night."

"Uh-huh?"

"You lived down there for a bit, din't you? What are the people like?"

He fiddled with a switch, rolled his eyes. "Punks, scum, robbers, bums, wasters, tossers, speed freaks, Asian virus, goths, dickheads, piss heads, muggers, crims, serotonin freaks, rastas, wannabees, junkies, chavs, straightedgers, roaches, crystal methers, violent bastards, weirdos, critical massers, dropouts, grimers, acidheads, pigs, crusties, animals, indie kids, e-heads, terrorists, dopeheads, and Neil the Matrix."

"Who?"

"Y'know, dat fool in the long leather coat, from sixth form?"

"Oh yeah. But it's free, right?"

Nate lay back on his bed. "Well, yeah . . . but there's all those *activists*. I wuz down there for a party with these animal-rights freaks a few months back, a'ight? An there was, like, vegan chili in a bucket on the floor with sprung rats they wuz keepin' as pets, all running and divin' in it."

"How d'you know they were pets?"

"Collars. They'd these little collars on."

"You sure?"

Nate paused. "Nope. It wuz kind of a messed-up time for me back then."

The afternoon dragged on and on and still no sign of Adi. Nate disappeared at about 5 and then I must've fallen asleep. I woke up in the middle of the night and felt Adi next to me. I reached over, put my arm around him and felt safe, like I always do when he's near.

## Thurs., Jan. 12

Today I spent 7 hours on the fone, calling Repossessions Solutions, the council, the police. The U.K. is now run entirely by robots. I didn't speak to one single human being all day.

## Fri., Jan. 13

I worked the robots again. Nothing. I've only had 2 hours' sleep cos Nate brought a girl back. This afternoon I broke thru and actually spoke to a woman from the council. She listened to me for about 30 seconds, laughed dead loud in my ear, and tossed me back to the machines again. So much for species loyalty.

I hung up and dropped my head in my hands.

"I'm never gonna get my stuff back. Uni starts in 2 weeks and I've got nowhere to live."

Adi shrugged. "You can stay here as long as you want, you know that."

I rolled my eyes toward the bedroom. "No offense, but . . ."

"What then? You ain't gonna ask your parents for help, are you?"

"No. No way. There's only one way to go." I took a deep breath. "It's the Docks for me."

"You're joking, right? You'd rather go there than crash here?"

"It's only for a few months so I can save up to get a deposit together. My loan's not due till the end of the month and my carbon card's super low. 'Sides it's not that bad. I was down there a couple of nights ago."

"Fine."

"We've gone thru this before. It's not about me and you . . . it's just I'm not ready for us to live together yet." I slid my arms around his chest. "I'll get my own place; I don't have to go in the squat with Claire's mutants."

He pulled away. "Laura, you were there at night, you don't wanna see what daylight brings. That place is half underwater every time it rains or there's a high tide. It's like the biggest pile of shit."

"Oh yeah? Have you seen your room?"

His mouth turned up into a smile without him wanting it to.

"Adi, will you come down there with me on Monday?"

"Where?"

"The Excel Centre. Y'know, it's where they used to put on all those exhibitions and business conferences in London. Claire says there's a guy there called Tano something who can fix me up with a place."

He started to say no, then saw my face and sighed. "Sure."

## Mon., Jan. 16

A bad thing happened on Adi's street this morning. We were waiting at the bus stop, when out of nowhere a bunch of 5 skinheads appeared. They were strutting along the pavement, but when they got to an Indian film poster with some Bollywood stars on it, they

14

stopped and spit on it. One after the other. Like dogs marking their territory. Adi spat himself. "Nazis. The right is rising, Laur."

"Nobody takes them seriously . . ."

"I do!" Adi pointed at a swastika sprayed on the bus stop panel. "It's on these walls, in my face. There are streets not far from here where you get beat down if you're the wrong color—or the right color with the wrong accent. Those United Front bastards are stirring up all the projects, saying there's not enough jobs to go around no more. I mean, it's all right for you . . ."

"It's not all right for me. How can you say that?"

He held his hands up. "OK, I'm sorry. But there are some things you can't ever understand, not fully."

It was midday by the time we climbed the Royal Albert footbridge. We stood for a moment in the slanting rain, looking out over the Docks. Across the side of a crumbling block opposite the Excel Centre, in massive, oozing letters, somebody'd sprayed:

Adi took my hand. "Well, that's for sure."

We picked our way across the battered parking lot toward the Excel Centre entrance.

"What's that?" I nodded ahead. A rusting hull of a ship loomed up, half sunk in the water.

"It was a hotel I think. Yeah, look . . ." He stopped in front of a bulletin board. Under the scratched laminated board we could just make out a yellowing poster.

Adi angled his head to read the last few lines. "*With a host of leisure attractions just a stone's throw away, the guest could not be more ideally located.*" He flicked a glance around the mud and slime. "C'mon, Laur, what you waitin' for?"

We walked into the deserted, spooky Excel Centre. Where there once were stalls, businesses, and conference rooms was now a great echoing empty space, totally ripe for aliens and monsters to leap out. We kept to the left side cos there was a great sheet of water stretching out over the rest of the concrete floor, sloshing back and forth with cans, plastic, clothes—it was like some giant shipwreck.

I stopped. "This can't be right."

Adi pointed ahead. "Look—there's a light on in that office at the far end, where it's drier . . ." He squinted. "London Partnerships."

"That's it, that's what Claire said to look for."

After a few hundred meters of sloshing, I pushed the office door open. "Hi, I'm looking for Gaetano? Tano?"

A small, curly-haired man glanced up from his desk. "*Si,* that's me. Tano Adile." He motioned for me to come inside.

"Oh, right. I was told you could help me find a room in the Docks?"

He frowned. "How can I do this? All the flats here are privately owned or are in process of demolition."

I stared at him. "But there's the squat . . ."

He stared right back. No expression. "The squat is illegal, miss. This is a government-based housing advice center."

"Oh." I started to blush. "It's just that Claire said to—"

"Claire who?"

"Connor. From the *angels*."

A sudden shy smile spread across his face. "Eh, why din't you say so before? Claire say for you to come?" He grabbed my hand. "*Viene*, let's go to see the queen."

"Who?"

"Follow me."

With Gaetano leading the way, we stepped out into the freezing wind and walked toward a block of flats set back from the water. 2 flights of stairs and a walkway later, he stopped and knocked twice on a steel-barred door.

After a moment someone called: "Who is it?"

Tano pressed his face close to the metal. "Me. Got someone for you. . . . *Un amica di* Claire Connor."

I gazed at him.

He spread his hands. "Sorry. I say you are a friend of Claire's. I am from Sicilia, here 10 years, and still I speak this half-English half-Italian mess."

There was the sound of metal scraping against metal as the door bolts were drawn back. The door opened and a woman, early 30s, stood framed by the light. She was a weird mix of tall and slim, but also baggy and huge cos of her oversized khaki army pants. Her hair was longer than before, but still I'd know her anywhere. It was Gwen Parry-Jones, my old teacher and savior of our street during the flood.

She started to laugh. "Well, well, Laura Brown!"

I still couldn't speak.

Gwen glanced behind me. "Oh, and Adisa, too. Is this a social visit or are you both looking for a place to stay?"

Adi nudged me.

"Er, no. Just me," I croaked.

"You don't sound too sure."

Tano cleared his throat. "Well, it seem like you two are old friends, so . . ." He turned to Adi. "*Viene* or *va*?"

"Is *va* go?"

Tano nodded.

"Then *va*! Definitely *va*!" Adi flicked a laughing look at me. "I've got a lecture at 2:30 so I'll call you later, Laur."

I leaned over and kissed him. "Thanks."

GPJ smirked. "When you're ready, people."

The others walked off down the corridor and I took a breath and followed her inside, the door clanging behind me with a heavy thud. Gwen leaned against a kitchen unit. "Well, you can stop staring at me like you've seen a ghost. You don't hate me that much, do you?"

I laughed. "No, I don't hate . . . course not . . . I'm just . . . When did you come here, then?"

"Straight after the flood, really. I just couldn't go back to normal life, y'know, teaching again after that . . . so when I saw what state the Docks were in, I joined up with a group of people and . . . well, here we are."

"Wow."

"Yup, so what brings you down here? I heard your parents left ages ago."

"Yeah, they've got a farm in a village near Abingdon, but I came back to study. I never wanted to leave in the first place."

She smiled. "London girl, is it?"

"Something like that. But I've been chucked out of my house and—"

"Why?"

"Well, nonpayment, but it's kind of complicated. . . ."

GPJ frowned. "Not really. You're either a payer or a nonpayer. So which kind are you?"

"Uh?"

"You see I have to make a decision fast. In places like this, there are payers and nonpayers, givers and takers, and there's nothing you can do about it once they're in."

"Am I paying *you*?"

"No, mate, you're not paying *me*, although if it's something totally free you're after, then there's an anarchist collective in the old Harrods depot. We're more like a group that shares stuff, but we've got a committee to manage things, like gas, electric, water. . . . Some people get together to cook at the café, but you don't have to. Depends how much company you want, and . . . how much money you got. It's not much, maybe a chiller a week all in for the bills, cos they're always cutting us off. We're trying to get self-sufficient so we don't need those bastards anymore." She scanned me. "So?"

"I guess I'm a payer, then."

"You don't sound too sure. But I know enough about you to trust you. Got any politics?"

"I—er—I don't . . ."

She paused, looking at me like she was drilling a hole thru to the back of my skull. "You kids . . . Well you don't have to be active, but you've got to help out in some way. I mean, why else would you want to be here in the first place?"

The same question must have been stamped all over my face.

She grinned. "On the plus side it's good to have someone vaguely normal around—I mean at least you've got your own accent."

"Who else's would I have?"

"Are you joking? This place is swarming with lovely, caring, middle-class students and they all sound like they was born in a bucket in the East End."

I laughed, suddenly remembering that I liked her. "Like Claire, you mean?"

She raised an eyebrow. "Anyhow, all right. You're on a one-month trial, but you've got to help out. There's a schedule. Deal?"

"Deal."

She snatched up a set of keys. "Follow me, then. You can go in 31A. It's a first step."

"A what?"

"A *1/2* bedroom flat, perfect for that *first step* on the property ladder for your young city couple. It's a bit nasty in there, though. Monica was pretty mucky and she's been gone these 2 months. Don't know if she'll be back."

"Where is she?"

GPJ dropped into a mockney street accent. "Inside innit? 6 months for Wilful Damage on an Airbus. *Gatwick*."

The flat was high up on the 7th floor and it properly stank when she opened the door. My heart sank.

"Feel free to clean it up. We've sorted out the basics. Y'know, drilled the cement that the council poured down the toilet bowls, got the water and electric back on. It's a lot better than it used to be. Until 3 months ago we had to go to the swimming pool to get clean. Oh yeah, and there's a €25 deposit."

She saw the look on my face. "Give it to me tomorrow. Come on, girl, it's not as bad as it looks."

After she left I walked from room to room. It was like this invisible film of badness was stuck to everything, slippery to the fingers. I kicked at a pile of rubbish that was blocking the door to the balcony, yanked the door open, and stepped outside. The wind cut through me like a wire. Who could I ask for advice? An image of Kieran, my crazy gay ex-neighbor, shot into my head. He's always been a total lifesaver. I punched a number in my fone.

After 3 rings he picked up. "Kieran's House of Mirages."

"OK, Kier, it's me, Laura. I've been thrown out of my old place and all my stuff's been repossessed and now I've got 3 choices: A) move into the Docks and live there for free until I sort myself out, B) move in with Adi even though we're a bit weird, or C) be totally pathetic and ask Mum and Dad to bail me out."

"Hmm. The Docks as in that anarcho squat with those green rabids in stripey sweaters and bone skull piercings?"

I balled my fist. "Yes."

A long pause. The wind tossed bits of grit into my eyes. "Mate?"

"The thing is you don't have any choice, darling. You're not pathetic or needy so B and C are out. So A it is. You'll get some meaty band lyrics out of it, that's for sure."

I sighed. "I think meat's off the menu."

He laughed. "True. That's more like my girl. Come on, where's your sense of adventure?"

"Repossessions Solutions have got it boxed up in a warehouse."

"Bollocks. Go and have a laugh with the freaks—" He took a sharp breath. "Oh, God, is that the time? Sorry, I've got to go, Carbon Dating waits for no man."

"Where are you this week?"

"Scunthorpe. It's ghastly, but this boy's got to eat, y'know."

"OK, then, I'll catch you soon?"

"Course, I'll be back in London in a month or so. Oh . . . and Laura?"

"Yeah?"

"Happy New Year!"

He locked off.

I really, really miss Kieran. Since Kim's gone, he's hardly been in town at all cos he's had to take over running all the local Carbon Dating venues himself. I sucked in a lungful of dirty Docks air, turned and went back inside the flat, just in time to see a bunch of little black mice scamper down the hallway. Happy families.

**3 A.M.** Gwen Parry-Jones! Unbelievable!

## Fri., Jan. 20

I've spent the whole week pushing back the slime. My hands are now about 5 years younger than the rest of me, so many layers have peeled off with all the scrubbing. Claire's been brilliant. Day to day she's a living nightmare, but she turns into a really good mate when you're down. Together we raided a bunch of trash cans and charity shops. I now own: 1 sofa, 3 chairs, 2 sheets, 1 Scooby Doo duvet cover, 1 yoga mat, 1 wok, 3 plates, 2 cups, 1 can opener, 6 oranges, and 1 bottle of vodka. Even Adi's helped. He rocked up at about 5 this evening, just in time to help muscle the sofa up the stairs.

It's midnight now and we're finished. Me and Adi are flopped on the sofa like an old couple and are looking out at my new view. It's weird, there's sparkling lights over in Canary Wharf and then beyond, *nothing*. Just the darkness of the east spreading out.

Adi took a swig of vodka. "They've got this new chief of police. He says he talks direct to God."

"What made you say that?"

He shrugged. "Dunno, just thinking about him, maybe even now he's looking out of another window down at the city. Thinking he can clean it up in the name of the Lord. Mad."

When it's like this I want us to be together all the time.

## Mon., Jan. 23

3 bits of horrible news within 30 minutes of waking up. First I got a letter from the student loan company saying all their payments are delayed and my money won't be available till March 5. After reading it, I threw on some clothes and went down to uni to check my status. First I swiped my carbon card in the student union meter.

Aaargh.

Then I turned to the ATM and slotted my credit card in with shaky paws. €97.00 in credit. I've worked out it adds up to about 6 euros a day and 0 carbon swipe till Feb. After I'd counted it all up, I dug my fingers into my palms, fighting down cold fear. What did I even leave the house for? It felt like that old "Streets" song about messing up the day by just getting out of bed. Should have stayed under the sheets.

**Tues., Jan. 24**

All I ate today was a baked potato. I said no when the woman asked me if I wanted any filling and she looked at me dead kind and gave me double marge.

**Wed., Jan. 25**

Aargh, hunger pangs of doom. On my way back from the library, I walked past a fried chicken shop and stopped dead and sniffed the air like a wild animal. When I got back to the Docks, I found it'd all flooded again and there was a sort of wet black mist hanging over the place with the sun a hanging pale disk in the grayed-out sky.

I can't sleep, either, cos there's no carpets, no curtains, and I can hear everything from the flats around. I spent hours last night listening to people going to bed in other flats, grunting, whispering, shifting, and moaning. Even after I fell asleep, I woke up shivering in the

middle of the night, with the rain drumming on the windows, and just felt super lonely. A year ago I was living at home with Mum doing all my washing. Talk about childhood being over. Anyway, I'm not asking for help, not from my parents, Adi. No one.

### Fri., Jan. 27

Hunger has driven me into the arms of the squat. I woke up this morning so frozen and starved I didn't care anymore. I buzzed 4 times on the door of the Dox café, before banging on the door until GPJ appeared in a McDonald's apron.

"Buzzer's broken. So, I'm guessing you're here to help?"

I nodded and followed her inside. It was kind of punky in there, with broken chairs, school desks, and a poster of *The Clash* on one wall. A big sign was pinned up next to it that said: "*Wash up if it looks busy, you slackers, yes that means you.*"

Gwen waved her arm around. "Basically it's a veggie greasy spoon. After the first month we got rid of stink dogs and electro music, but we kept the politics. Everyone does one shift a week . . . and then we have a meeting once a month just to diss each other." She rolled her hands over her jeans. "There's not enough of us to keep it going all the time, but my problem is I'm too stubborn to quit."

She put me chopping root vegetables with a boy with red dreads who kind of flashed me his teeth as a greeting and went back to slicing. He was totally wired into his e-pod; I could just hear venomous Rust crunching out thru his headfones, so I was glad he wasn't a talker. "Together" we made parsnip stew with bread-crumb topping for 80. Desperate times.

After, I ate mine with angry little bites. If I ever see my ex-flatmates Greg and Lou again I will kill them. Slowly. With parsnips.

### Sat., Jan. 28

Rehearsal at Stace's tonight, down at her aunt's place in Bow in east London. When I got there, there was a 15-inch pizza box open on

the kitchen counter with a couple of cold slices inside, and my eyes keep swiveling over, like out-of-control supermarket cart wheels.

Claire looked up from her e-pod. "So, is everyone good for the next gig?"

I sighed. "I ain't even got any clothes to wear."

"I can figure something out for you," said Claire.

"But—"

"C'mon, Laura . . . it wasn't like you were exactly a fashionista . . ."

Stacey laughed. "Yeah, dude, I don't think I saw you out of your skinny black jeans once last year."

"Fine, Stace. I'll borrow some of your stuff." I flicked Adi's ear. "Thanks for the backup, buddy."

"Huh? I love those black jeans. What I don't love is our sound. That last gig we came off like shit. We got to get us some better amps and a sound engineer—"

Claire cut in. "Look, it's not about the sound—it's about attitude. Like McLaren said about punk, if it'd all been about the music, punk would've died after 6 months."

I looked down. Right now I've got as much attitude as a senior citizen. All I need for total happiness is a radiator and a microwave full of shepherd's pie.

Claire scrolled thru her calendar. "So they want us down at The Rose Club for the OUTSIDER night on Wednesday, Feb. 1. It's kind of a big deal."

Stace frowned. "The Rose down in Canning Town? That place is like out of a slasher movie. It's in a swamp, an' all the people around there've got lumps of rotting flesh falling off their faces."

"Ah, come on, don't tell me you believe all that media shit?"

Stace puffed her cheeks out. "That place is really, really lawless. People are getting shot, stabbed, on like a daily basis. My friend got beaten up really bad there."

Claire snorted. "I've been down a couple times. It's not so bad."

25

Adi crossed his arms. "What's this OUTSIDER crowd like any-how?"

"Used to be loads of local black kids, but now it's gone wide. It's like, the uber-cool place to go with white kids mixing in and girls, too. I mean, where else do you find girls actually allowed up on stage? The scene's gone so macho now."

"What's the venue size?"

"850."

Adi whistled. "Big."

"Course, I tell you I had to work hard to swing this one. . . . So are we up for it, then?"

I nodded and slowly so did Adi.

Stace rolled her sticks across her knees. "Well, if everyone else is, then I'll do it, but I'm telling you . . . I was there last summer and there was no bar, no toilets—and those white kids you're talking about? They were all rich kids from the City, y'know, slumming it in the flood lands."

"Kids like us, y'mean?" muttered Adi.

## Mon., Jan. 30

There was a knock on my door this afternoon. When I opened it, GPJ was standing on the front step with a heater.

"I found it in a trash can and fixed it up."

"But I can't use it. I've got nearly zero credit on my card."

She shrugged. "Who said anything about cards? We've got a little black market supply running, courtesy of our dodgy Sicilian."

"Who?"

"Tano, of course. He'd steal your mother off you if you left her unlocked on the street. Right now, he's hacked into the main supply at the Tate & Lyle factory. . . . Won't last for long, so use it while you can." She shot me a cunning look. "Just one condition, though, come to the meeting this Thursday in the Dox Centre?"

"Miss Jones, I'm so cold my teeth are grinding. This isn't fair."

She grinned. "Miss Jones? You're still a bit frightened of me, huh?"

"No!"

"Well, prove it then and come down."

I looked into her eyes. "Maybe, if I'm free."

"Atta girl." She handed me the heater and I ran inside and plugged it in and now, after 6 hours, I'm finally starting to defrost, like I'm some big old Xmas turkey.

Frightened of her? She makes my blood freeze in my veins.

## Tues., Jan. 31

I am a total lizard. Apart from a shift at the Dox café (stuffed peppers × 64) I have not moved from the heater bars.

# February

### Thurs., Feb. 2

Bloody Dox meeting tonight. I dragged myself away from the heater and followed a dodgy old dog with a bit of string around its neck to the Excel Centre, where I found the meeting room, a peeling ex-office on the ground floor. The meeting had already started, so I sneaked in and sat at the back. I guess there were about 500 people there. A scraggy man with cropped hair plus a *disgusting* rat's tail was going: "OK, so *Discussion Point 3* on the agenda. *What trends in the current political climate are ripe for exploitation for the revolution?*" He gazed around the hall. "Obviously at this time, with mass unemployment, the backlash against nuclear power stations, the recession, the failing New Green Deal initiatives of the government—all of these give us great hope to build a new future for the workers."

I glanced up quickly, expecting it to be a joke, but no one was laughing. The *workers*? *Revolution*? Red Dreads Parsnip Boy raised his hand. "With like . . . uh . . . all due respect—this kind of . . . sort of . . . talk at meetings is kind of like . . . uh . . . redundant. We gotta get . . . active. I mean I sort of . . . like to know how many of us are . . . uh . . . like supportin' the . . . uh . . . Workers' Walk from Manchester to uh . . . basically uh . . . London?"

As soon as he started speaking, I knew his accent wasn't his own. It was a kind of street London, but bits of posh kept sneaking through. Suddenly I became aware someone was looking at me. GPJ. She rolled her eyes.

After half an hour of drone, I slipped away. I walked quickly around the corner and leaned up against an old bulletin board and breathed deep. Why do I react like this? The thing is these are basically good people; they're not just sitting around on their arses. They've got a whole life going, making their own fuel, the Dox community, pickets, demos. Why do I think I'm better than them? It's something to do with their eyes . . . they love it . . . love the excitement of being part of something. That's it—they remind me of born-again Christians, a cult.

Suddenly I heard a voice. "I'm tellin' you, man, dis time is different. They hacked his hair . . . they drew a *swastika* on his body . . . then they cut his ear off, an' on a nearby wall they sprayed: *One down, one million to go.*"

I glanced along a row of offices, trying to see who was speaking. There was an open window about halfway down. A second voice cut in. "Well, you've got to remember what the Nazi Dr. Goebbels said: *Who controls the streets will win the final victory.* And right now the *United Front* controls the streets. The police sure as hell won't protect us."

The first voice again. "I can't back down no more."

"I agree, maybe it's time for us to get more *physical.*"

"I'm up for that, but I ain't doin' no bullshit, no waving banners an' that. It's gotta be hard core."

Suddenly a hand appeared at the window and a cigarette butt flew past me. I pressed myself back against the bulletin board.

"We'd better get back to that meeting."

"I don't see why we still goin' . . ."

"Because it keeps us in the heart of the action while we're still undercover. And besides . . ." The speaker mimicked Red Dreads Boy perfectly, "*We gotta . . . uh . . . be . . . uh like . . . uh . . . totally active.*"

I sneaked away and went back to the flat, super thoughtful. Who the hell were they?

## Fri., Feb. 3

I woke up to a monster fight on the walkway between Bob and Sue, this alky couple from two doors down. At one point Sue screamed: "Wha' we're fer anyhows? I can't stann'it no more . . . s'nuffin' but fights, drugs an' drink, doors kicked in an' winders smashed in. An' the dogs, look, look! Hundreds uv'em, wand'rin' all over an' crap ev'rywhere!"

I took a deep breath and thought about Kieran and *my missing sense of adventure*. What am I now, a Harry Potter book? Jesus. Ha, ha. The thing is, though, I just don't know if I'm ready for all this yet. Feels like I've checked into the London zoo—the nocturnal bit, where they keep all the animal crazies with luminous big eyes.

## Sun., Feb. 5

I hate giving up. In a bitter wind and falling flakes of snow, I plugged into my best doomy old skool P.J. Harvey tracks and stomped all the way around the Albert and then the Victoria Dock till I came to a footbridge. I climbed slowly to the top of the stairs and leaned against the railing, looking out over the crumbling Docks and beyond to Canary Wharf. It's no more than 5 Ks away, but it feels like a million and more to the mainstream. A half-submerged mass of abandoned buildings, a wreck of capitalism and greed grinning across the dark water toward the lights of the city. Suddenly I heard footsteps behind me and turned to see Tano looming up out of the twilight. He nodded as he was going past, then catching a glimpse of my face, he paused.

"Eh, Laura, how's it going?"

I shrugged.

We stood silent for a moment before he cleared his throat. "There's good people here."

"How d'you know . . . ?"

"Your face."

"Is it that bad?"

He gave me his shy smile. "You must find your own style, is all."

"But what if I haven't got a style to find? All I do is go around judging people."

He put his hand on my arm. "Because you are not just following, you work it out for yourself, where you fit."

"And what if I don't . . . ?"

"Fit?" He shook his head. "A person is not a . . . *figura mathematica*. It take time . . . and the most important thing is that we're free and our ideas, too, they are free." He looked out over the Docks, kind of sad. "It's so easy to forget how vulnerable and beautiful is our freedom. And soon maybe we must fight for it."

I didn't know what to say, it felt like it was an internal debate and he wasn't really talking to me. But now I'm in bed, writing this, and I feel better; like some kind of pressure's been taken off. Dad's right, normal's gone now and I never even liked it when I had it, anyway. This feeling's come over me, stronger than ever, we've just got to make the *angels* work. At least I've got my new carbon points for February today. Good news, I'm finally climbing up out of debt. Living here at the Docks is cutting my points big time.

## Mon., Feb. 6

First day back at uni and straight off we've been set our first project: to design a direct-action campaign to change how and why people drive cars. Yawn to the power of $n$ squared. The last project we did was cool, all about revolutionary slogans, but now they follow it up with this.

## Tues., Feb. 7

Adi called and told me a man from Repossessions Solutions has just banged on his door and left a letter. What did I give them the address for? If they find me they'll take me to court for nonpayment of rent. €2,566 plus €1,750 legal costs. Well, at least things are simple. It's stay here or go to jail for nonpayment.

Anyway, I woke up dead excited in the middle of the night. Gig tomorrow. Can't wait.

## Wed., Feb. 8

I walked down to The Rose cos it turned out it was pretty close to mine, but by the time I got there the band had already done a sound check. I asked Claire why they didn't wait up for me.

"Told ya, s'all about attitude. Sound checks are for straights, nobody cares about the sound." She tapped her chest. "In here's where it matters."

I sighed. Claire was definitely in militant mode, so I just let it go and went outside looking for Adi. I found him drinking a beer with Nate.

My eyes opened in surprise. "Nate? What are you doing here?"

"Your boy brung me down. Says I got to support da backlash, so what kind of tunes you all makin' now?"

I smiled. "You know our style, *rude bwoy*. Anyways, first, it isn't all white—there's loads of Asian and black kids here, too—and second, keep it down. Loads of those people come down to our shows regular."

Nate bopped Adi on the arm. "Yeah, Adisa, what is that about? Punk sound ain't from 'round here. Dis is Canning Town, not art school dropoutland."

Adi frowned. "Why you want to stereotype me? I don't care about all that black gangsta shit. Grime, punk, black, white—they all coming from the same place. The best music is always from the streets."

Nate rubbed his hands. "True, remember grime when it wuz good? I was a little kid back then but my brother wuz hard core. It was *the* music. Fused-up drum n bass, beats and garage, speeded up to 130 bpm. It was cold an' clean, the sound of our streets, not this white kid punk shit. They was talkin 'bout survival for real. I wanna stay true to Pow—"

"What! Lethal Bizzle? You talking proper back in the day."

"Don't matter." Nate jerked his thumb at a group of skaters. "What these boys and girls know?"

Adi turned to face him. "They know enough. Things ain't the same now, we're all in dis shit together. And, anyway,"—he grinned—"you ain't no gangsta. You studyin' political science, like me—and don't tell me u don't work in Foot Locker."

A second, then they both started to laugh.

Nate flipped his fingers. "Truesay!"

After Nate had gone I nudged Adi. "Thought you hated it down here?"

He flipped his beer bottle on its end. "Don't get me wrong, I still think it's dirty, but at least there's anger here. Real anger at the system."

I eyed him. "You're starting to sound like Claire, mate."

I expected him to laugh, but he just eyeballed me back, hard. Where's my boy gone?

Up onstage the lights drop. I roll in with a stripped-down bassline. Claire jumps up on the boards, goes, "Put your fists in the air!" and then Stace kicks in and the crowd roars. Later there's this bit in *stick it* where Claire paces up and down chanting:

```
Double digit inflation
Backsliding frustration
They've got you under control.

Imprisoned by destruction
And corruption
They've got you under control.
```

Until the whole place is shouting along with her. Sweat, blood, passion. You can't deny Claire, she's a mental bitch on stage. That's why I get so mad with her off it. It's like she loses the best, most ferocious part of her.

When we finish the lights go up for a few minutes, the music skids to a stop, and suddenly a load of black and Asian kids push to the front cos it's time for Predator, the headliner, a skinny, scared-looking

15-year-old kid from Forest Gate. I watch from backstage as he shuffles into the lights like a schoolkid. Then he opens his mouth and unleashes a torrent of rhymes, venom, rage. His voice cuts through the air like a saw. The art school kids further back go mental, too, trying to keep up with the words. The people at the front are unanimously mouthing every line along with him. The whole place is turning into a mass of random parts, kids screaming and diving . . . and then gradually the place starts to lose it, bottles, sneakers, spit flying about . . . it's like watching atoms splitting apart . . .

I slipped out thru the stage door, yanked open the emergency exit, and took in a big gulp of cold air. It felt kind of unreal out there after that sweat pit.

Somebody tapped me on the arm. "Wanna beer?"

I turned to see this guy, Sam, from my course at uni.

"Hey, what you doing here?"

"I always come down The Rose." He held out a bottle of Becks. I reached over and took a swig.

"Anyway, you were great, genius." His eyes were dark and shining with excitement.

I blushed. "Yeah, all right."

"No, definite. I play guitar for a couple of bands, but I'm looking for something more, well . . . don't suppose there's any space in the *angels*?"

"Well, no, Adi . . ."

He held out a hand. "Sure, sure. But you wanna hook up on the new uni project?" He smiled. "C'mon, you can't turn me down twice in one night."

Suddenly Nate appeared out of the dark and grabbed my arm. "You never guess wha' I jus' seen . . . a dogfight up on the roof of that block. Some kids took me up there. There wuz this big massive pit bull called Wolf an' a white Argentina dogo thing. They had to pull 'em apart with an iron bar 'fore it got too mad. This place is like the end of the world, Laura!"

I looked at him, then looked around the yard, and suddenly I got this wave of excitement, seeing it thru his eyes.

## Thurs., Feb. 9

Close to death. If I end up on the dark side, the coroner's report will show cause of death as either A) Toxic Death Hangover or B) MRSI Super Bug infection from Claire's kitchen from hell. We stayed out for hours last night before going back to her place, starving like wolves. The others went into the front room and started playing tunes, while me and Claire went into the kitchen. I'm not joking, her place is even dirtier than Adi's. She should be made to do one of those training courses they make new prison releasers do so they'll be able to cope on the outside. I scanned the dark corners before pulling together a pack of macaroni, 6 Laughing Cow cheese triangles, a bit of flour, and a battered carton of Parmalat milk circa 2008.

"All right! Cheeeeesy Pasta," cried Claire, grabbing the macaroni pack, which turned out to be open and all the bits tipped out across the floor.

I stared at them, settling down among the dirt. "No!"

She started to laugh.

I fumbled in my pockets. "We . . . can't eat that. Gotta getsomore from the 24 . . . Only go' 60 cents. You got s'thing?"

Claire giggled. "Nope. Don't besucha girl, anyway."

I bent down and scrabbled up all the noodles I could find before dumping them in the sink and running the hot tap over them.

"Whayoo doing?" Claire peered over my shoulder.

"Washin' the scum off . . ." I wobbled over to the cooker and tried to light the gas.

"Scumbum . . . Scumbum," chanted Claire. "Ooh, hey, Laur, s'posed to doothis?"

I put down my lighter and ran back to the sink. All the macaroni had melted into one solid white lump under the hot water.

I nodded. "Cool. Perfectolino." I slid the alien life-form into a pan of water. Then I kicked off on the cheese sauce and I was going good until Claire suddenly did a random karate kick across the room and my arm shot forward, whooshing all the flour into the pan. I swear I saw little bugs flying up in the dust.

"Whayou doin'?" I cried, desperately scooping it out, but it was too late.

Claire came close and stuck her finger in and licked it. "Hmm . . . wha' we got here, huh? Hmm . . . iss . . . iss . . . glue! Laura, youmake Cheesy Glue!"

I made everyone eat it, too. I am *so* my mother's daughter.

## Fri., Feb. 10

Talk of the devil. My fone rang at 3 this afternoon, but I was still so out of it I let it go through to voice mail. I've just listened to it now.

*Hello, sweetie, only me! Feels like ages since we spoke, we've got our own mini drama here, the village is all up in arms with the Thames Water reservoir, they're saying the wall is going to collapse and drown us all, but have you heard from Kim? I haven't and I'm starting to really get worried, I mean she's stuck all the way over there in Thailand and they're saying the U.S. is gunning for another oil war in Iraq. Thank God I can reach you if I need to but why on earth are you living at the Docks? And why didn't you tell us? I had to hear about it from Kieran . . . honestly. Anyway, please, pretty please call me as soon as you get—Beep*

I can't face calling her, and, anyway, I can't cos I've got no credit. Aha, poverty has its uses.

## Mon., Feb. 13

I've spent the whole day with Sam in the workshop at uni, working on ideas for the new design project. I had to agree to work with him, he wouldn't take no for an answer. He caught up with me at break in the corridor, dropped to his knees, and clutched his heart, going: "She rejec' me, she no love me, I a killa myself!"

Anyway, turns out it was the best thing I could've done. He's dead talented and he's *funny*. We did a bunch of drawings and got something worked out, it's gonna be like a joke anti-car kit. Sam did a mock-up of the box cover in Photoshop. I'm gonna start raiding trash cans and empty flats tomorrow. I might even get a good grade for this project after all.

### Wed., Feb. 15

On my way home I scored an armload of wire from a burned-out car. I was dragging it along my walkway when I bumped into GPJ. That woman is totally omnipresent.

She looked me up and down. "What's all this?"

"3-D project for uni."

"You should talk to Tano; he's working on a shallow solar boat, for the Thames and the Docks when it floods. It's brilliant."

I gave a tight smile. "Yeah, maybe . . ."

She put her hands on her hips. "But . . . you don't trust me. I know, you think I'm trying to brainwash you or something."

"I don't think that, it's just things aren't so black and white for me as you."

"How do you know what I believe? Get to know me before you judge me."

"Likewise."

She dug in her pocket for gum. "Look, I can't stand those Dox meeting types any more than you can. You're different from them, I see that, but that's not an excuse to be so . . . *passive*."

"Passive!" I almost spat the word out. "Have you seen the *angels* play?"

"Yes, once—and don't get me wrong, you're out there. But is it enough?"

I shrugged. "I'm guessing no, Gwen. What you want from me?"

She looked me straight up. "More. Come for one day down to the Dox Media Centre, spend some time, see what we actually do. Then say no."

I stared at her a long moment, bending a piece of wire between my fingers.

"That's a big silence."

I sighed. "When?"

"Next Saturday. It's a major day for us."

"I'll be there. But quit hassling me."

She smiled and turned on her heel. "Deal."

Oh, what the hell. She's crazy GPJ, but the woman's got a certain style. Plus I reckon I kind of owe her after she practically rescued our whole street.

### Thurs., Feb. 16

Claire banged on my door this morning with a rolled-up magazine.

"Gig reviews! You read 'em, y'know I get too nervous."

She tossed the zine at me and dropped down on to the sofa. "Page 12."

# Dead or Alive

The unlikely combination of Da Terminator, Predator and the *dirty angels* on Tuesday night at the Rose disturbed a lot of people, myself included. Such a mash up of musical styles and cultures, ranging from heart-stoping nu-grime to punk and beyond clearly set the crowd back a few paces too. For here, face to face, in Canning Town, the arse end of London, blacks and whites, straights and gays, goths and froths faced off and faced up to a whole new future together.

It's an experiment and it's a dangerous one. At one point I saw a knife blade flash as some pretty boy batted his eyelashes a little too close for comfort for the gangstas of the Town. But in the end it was the music that pulled it altogether.

Maybe the best way to judge a band is how much sweat they create in the atmosphere. Judged by these standards, the *angels* are way down on the barometer. And down is good, it's where the storms rumble and growl. Claire Connor is a beast possessed on stage. Her eyes bug out like out like she's being punched in the belly and she can scream with the the best of them. Plus she's got a glare on her like a prehistoric lizard. By the time the band got to their anthemic *messed up world*, the club was a seething mass of bodies with three hundred mouths singing along in unison. The only downside was the band's bargain basement sound system that practically made my ears bleed.

There was definitely tension as the crowd waited for the headliner to come on, with the artskool kids moving to the rear to make way for the local yout. Once again I saw knives, screwdrivers, but before anything could kick off, Predator, the fifteen year old phenomenon from Forest Gate swaggered onstage. He grabbed the mic and turned to a group of vocal girls, telling them 'not to write a check with your mouth that your arse can't cash.' The crowd rocked with laughter and with that the big phat beats rolled in like Atlantic breakers and soon

"That's good!" I cried. "*Claire Connor is a beast possessed.* Does this writer *know* you?"

"Shut up." Claire landed a punch on my arm. "But, yeah, good, we just need to build up reviews like this. But there's more, here's the big one . . . let's see what Suzi K says."

I gasped. "Suzi K came down? She's like a total—"

"Legend? Tell me about it. And super mysterious, the only way I knew she was there was cos my mate, Damon, recognized her."

"How's he know her?"

"Doesn't, but she's famous for always wearing this freaky pearl and bone earring in her right ear."

Claire flipped on her e-pod and while it was hooking up, my heart began to pound. Suzi K is this completely frightening super-influential journo from *most wanted* magazine—and the biggest bitch around. But if you can get her onside . . .

The screen flicked into life.

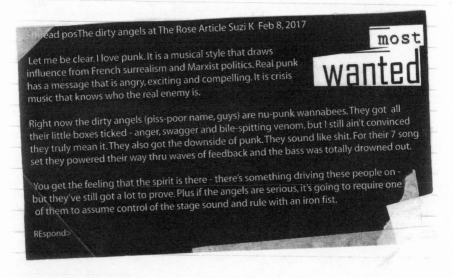

Thread posThe dirty angels at The Rose Article Suzi K  Feb 8, 2017

Let me be clear. I love punk. It is a musical style that draws influence from French surrealism and Marxist politics. Real punk has a message that is angry, exciting and compelling. It is crisis music that knows who the real enemy is.

Right now the dirty angels (piss-poor name, guys) are nu-punk wannabees. They got all their little boxes ticked - anger, swagger and bile-spitting venom, but I still ain't convinced they truly mean it. They also got the downside of punk. They sound like shit. For their 7 song set they powered their way thru waves of feedback and the bass was totally drowned out.

You get the feeling that the spirit is there - there's something driving these people on - but they've still got a lot to prove. Plus if the angels are serious, it's going to require one of them to assume control of the stage sound and rule with an iron fist.

REspond>

**most wanted**

I sank back down on the sofa.

Claire put her head in her hands. "She crucified us." Dead silence in the room and then she suddenly jumped up and pulled her jacket on. "Right, I'm going down there right now!"

"Where?"

"To *most wanted* offices. In Shoreditch."

I spread my hands. "You can't *make* her write a good review."

"Don't care, I've got things to say to that bony bitch." Claire snapped her e-pod shut. "This is an iron-fist job, Suzi."

"But, Claire—she's got a point. I mean, Adi's been saying we sound bad for ages."

"And?"

I didn't say anything. Didn't dare.

## Fri., Feb. 17

I waited until evening to hear from Claire, but nothing. So in the end I called her. "How'd it go?"

A long pause. "She wouldn't even let me in the building. Left me out there like I'm a complete nobody." Suddenly Claire's voice cracked. "I know I messed up with the sound thing, Laura, but this band . . . it's everything . . . it's from before when things were OK . . . I can't let it go."

And then she locked off. I called back, but it went thru to voice, and when the beep sounded I shouted: "Suzi's right, we sound rubbish so stop being such a stupid cow and get a sound engineer cos you're brilliant and we're brilliant and nobody's gonna stop us not now not ever!"

It sucks having no money. Adi asked me over to his, even offered to pay my bus fare, but I'm too proud . . . so here I am, freezing my tits off in a squat in the Docks on a Friday night listening to the *port*'s download top 20. This is not the life advertisers have led me to believe will be mine.

## Sat., Feb. 18

I woke up late and lay under the covers, looking out at the stone-gray sky. Tate & Lyle found out about Tano's electricity hack and so we're back to freezing again. I'm like a fox on the tundra now; I don't even feel my stomach gurgling anymore. Adi says the Repo man has been back twice, but he reckons they'll start getting bored soon. The downside is I'm never going to get my stuff back. I did a mental list of all the things I've lost. It hurts, but not as bad as it did a few weeks ago. Maybe these are my first steps on the road to Nirvana.

I was just getting ready to fall asleep again when suddenly it hit me. I'd promised GPJ to go to the Dox Media Centre this morning! Groaning, I slid out of bed, pulled my clothes on, and swallowed some coffee. The Thames has overshot its banks again; at the bottom of my stairwell I had to take my sneakers off and roll up my jeans to cross the courtyard.

It was nearly 2 by the time I got there. I stood in the doorway for a minute, unwinding my scarf, taking it all in. People were swarming everywhere, calling out questions, shouting answers, running around with bits of paper, swinging back and forward on chairs between beat-up workstations.

"Laura!" GPJ shot past, balancing a cup of coffee on the back of a bunch of files. "Come on, we're gearing up for live feed reporting on the demos today. What we got, Emanuel?"

I spun around. Red Dreads Parsnip Boy stood behind me. Emanuel? He counted off on his fingers. "Er, okay, uh . . . action against . . . uh . . . the energy minister in Ealing, er . . . coverage of the . . . basically . . . ongoing workers uh . . . march to London, um . . . action at the immigration center . . . near Gatwick. Oh, shit, man I got to . . . uh totally um . . . go. Bus leaves in five."

A girl shouted across the room. "Eman! Bus, now! Richie's stuck in traffic—Gwen, can you cover for an hour? Live feed, starts ten minutes?"

"Sure." Gwen glanced at me. "Up for it? Basically we listen to the reports sent in from all over the country—from fones, web, push, portal . . . whatever. . . . Cut them down to a few lines, then input them direct onto the *actions page* for the world to see."

She led me across the room.

I gazed around. "I didn't know it was this big."

"Uh-huh, we're getting about one million hits a day. Worldwide. Everything's donated, built, stuck together. Sometimes when the site traffic rockets, we try to lay on extra lines. We've got a backup generator, but still we get cut off a lot."

She nodded over at a couple of nerdy guys, swimming in wires and circuits. "We've got Jimmy and Luke working all the time to keep us open source. I don't want to sound like a crazy conspiracy theorist, but the gov would love to shut us down. Do you know how much control there is on the net already? So, that's Jimmy's job— hacking, rerouting, keeping us free from Big Brother."

Some 10 minutes later me, GPJ and 2 others sat in a tight circle, with a pile of fones, messengers, and pushers in front of us. Basically any time anyone called in with a live report, the 2 girls took the call/ read the text/ message/ mail, then passed them on to Gwen who cut them into small lines and passed them on to me to write up as live feed. It was intense.

14:10 > Marchers all now in rally area outside Gatwick airport. Crowd estimated at between 2000 and 5000. Police presence growing but as yet no cause for alarm
14:20 > Workers Walk arrives Rugby. 4th day of march. Mass walk out from print factory swells numbers. Crowd now esti- mated at 20,000. Report of photographer being arrested for refusal to give name and details after photographing police .
14:30 > Update on the 13:20 arrest in Ealing indicates that t detainee was filming a Fit Officer and was arrested under Sec.56428 of new counter-terrorism laws.
14:35 > 500 marchers leave A23 and enter Gatwick complex. Despite heavy security mood is positiv
14:48 > Update from Ealing: 2 police vans arrive at scene. Vocal protesters. 3 metre banner visible. 'Energy for all, not just the rich.' Energy minister expected in next few minutes. Now over 800 people present and approx 100 police.
14:50 > Gatwick, another action commences. Protesters gathered outside Focus 5 headquarters. (key home office contractors for forced deportations of 'undesirables.') Banners saying 'No more forced deportations' are hung on gate. No police presence so far, bul situation likely to change
 14:52 > Workers Walk protest in central Rugby. Now clashes between protestors and local shop owners. Row of shops has windows and doors broken, some looting.
15:20 > People still protesting outside Focus 5. Headquarters. Police presence growing, but protesters distribute leaflets. Banners visible. "No One Is Illegal" and "No Borders No Nations". Some of protesters leaving the perimeter of police station get penned in. Negotiations ongoing with police.
15:22 >Energy minister arrives in Ealing. Violent surge from crowd, police react with shields. Minister makes no attempt t talk to protestors, despite promises last week in Parliament.
15:56 > Asylum seeker leaving Focus 5 headquarters becomes angry. The police, now present in large numbers, surround him and violently push him to the ground. The asylum seeker clearly extremely upset. The police handcuff his hands behind his back and push his face to the ground, causing injury. He i:
                    ·····rs challenge the police abo·
                         ·f the brutal arre
                            ·lice v

GPJ sighed. "It's like this everywhere now. That's why we've got to be out there, so the gov can't just lie and cover up stories like they used to."

On my way home I sneaked into Canning Town Mickey D's and blew a whole day's money on a Happy Meal, just to balance out the universe. Man, that woman is serious.

## Tues., Feb. 21

Oh, God, I flicked on the news this evening to see a massive spurt of water smashing thru the Abingdon reservoir wall. I called home in panic.

Mum picked up. "Aha! So you do care about us after all," she drawled.

"Are you OK? How bad's the flooding?"

"Oh, we're perched on the top of a hill and they've managed to get the water pretty much under control now, although some of us on very low ground were hit worse than others, of course." She sounded like she was laughing.

"Mum, what's going on?"

"I tell you what, I'll mail you a photo. It'll be so much clearer then." And before I could reply she hung up.

I flipped on my station and logged on with shaky hands, picturing her paddling a phantom boat in a mental ward somewhere. After a minute her message flashed up. I clicked the attachment . . .

I laughed so much I practically ruptured a vessel in my eye. Go, Mum!

**Wed., Feb. 22**

I woke up at dawn to radio static and random bursts of words filtering into my dreams. I jumped up and padded over to the window. Outside it was barely light, but I could just make out 3 squad cars and maybe 10 feds, all slinking around the entrance to the Excel Centre, checking eviction notices, taking fotos, and recording. Then somebody shouted from the building opposite and they all jumped back in their cars and shot off.

My life is just so extreme right now, but I'm starting to get into it. I'm like a girl in a movie. Yesterday the flood, today the cops, and all on €6.33 a day. After I watched the taillights of the last police car disappear, I just shrugged and slithered back to my cold and hungry bed, like a Nile crocodile waiting for its next juicy antelope.

## Fri., Feb. 24

Sam came over this afternoon and we worked on the first mock-ups of the joke kits. It's looking good. My favorite so far is the joke tire slasher knife. I love it when I get properly into a project.

We'd just finished gluing the knife handle together when Sam's fone began to vibrate. He glanced at the screen and frowned. "Oh, Jeez, it's my mum."

I glanced over. "What, you don't get along?"

"Nah, it's just I'm doing this mini gig tomorrow night and she always wants to come and see me play." He narrowed his eyes. "She's a *rock* parent."

"Ooh, badness. Does she lurk in the shadows with a HD camera?"

"Worse. She dances."

"What happened to parental disapproval? What have we got to do to make them hate us?"

Sam laughed. "Actually I've got a theory on this. See, the thing is my mum's generation is harder than us, we're all soft and Nikey and Big Brothery. But they're BCCTV."

"Huh?"

"Before CCTV—you know, security cameras 'n stuff. More freedom back then. I reckon she did like years of vomit, pills, and skanky toilets before kids and a mortgage dragged her down."

"So you're saying we've got to get ourselves more hard core?"

"Definitely. We need a tough-love plan for the wannabee rock stars of today . . . like bringing in random drug tests for band members. No illegal substances, no gig . . ."

I flipped my fingers. "Or what about doing gigs in the day, so kids'll have to skip school and the rock parents'll have to pull a sick day to get there. That'll weed out the straights."

Sam narrowed his eyes. "I like your thinking, Miss B."

## Sat., Feb. 25

I flicked on the bedroom light this morning and nothing. My heart sank; I hate, hate blackouts. I threw on Adi's old sweatshirt before jogging along the walkway to check out the other flats. Alky Bob was leaning against his front door, puffing on a fat rollie. It smelled like burned cabbage leaves.

He shook his head. "Nah, we ain't got none neever."

"Uh?" I stopped in a cloud of smoke.

"Electric, like. We been cut off. There's a meetin' at 10 down at the Dox meetin' room."

By the time I got there, the hall was packed, with GPJ standing at the front, shouting to get herself heard.

"Yes, it's true we've been cut off for nonpayment, we owe €2,450 for the whole site."

"So, what we gonna do?"

"Er, fight to pay it like we always do. It's not that we don't want to, it's that they don't want us to have a supply at all, so they keep closing our account. So everybody give something and let's not turn this into a big thing. It's not forever; Tano and the team are working on the second turbine now. With the first one and the panels on the Excel roof we're at 60% self-sufficient. We *will* be independent of the grid, but it's going to take a bit more time."

Emanuel stood up, red-faced. "I . . . uh . . . don't want to pay those . . . uh . . . bastards like nothing. That's why I . . . uh . . . basically . . . came . . . uh . . . uh . . . here."

It's weird hearing someone so angry speak so slow, like a kind of militant sloth.

GPJ shrugged. "Then prepare to be very cold. You can handle that?"

"Yeah, cold? So, like what? If we keep on . . . uh . . . giving in, paying ev'ry time they er . . . basically . . . uh threaten us . . . then . . . We've gotta . . . uh . . . fight back."

Gwen kept her voice calm. "We need to pick our battles. Work for changes in law, not street battles with police."

"And even if they do . . . uh . . . change a few laws? Nothing ever . . . happens. A few uh . . . smiles, a few . . . uh basically totally . . . uh . . . *oily* promises . . . and emissions keep . . . uh . . . climbing."

"It takes time."

"We . . . like . . . uh . . . got *no* time."

GPJ sighed. "All right, let's vote. All those in favor of not paying, raise your hand."

One, two, five, ten hands were raised. The rest, at least a hundred, stayed down.

Emanuel threw his hands up in the air. "Bunch of pussies. We got to totally . . . uh stand an' . . . . fight now!"

GPJ turned on her heel. "Fight. That's all you people ever talk about. Has even one of you been under fire, seen a dead body, felt a bomb blast?"

The room was silent, just the thud of the door as GPJ slammed it shut behind her.

How did she get this radical?

## Sun., Feb. 26

Very, very fine band meeting tonight. Claire ran into the room screaming: "This promoter's just called me asking do we want the chance to hook up with a bunch of bands for a European tour? There's gonna be a trial gig for it in the middle of April."

Stace whooped. "We want we want we like!"

Claire threw her head back and laughed. "And the best part is the headliner. It's *Tiny Chainsaws in the Distance*. They rock!"

Stace clapped her hand over her mouth. "Don't lie. I'm like in love with them!"

Claire screamed, "I know, me too, me too."

I glanced over at Adi. He was rubbing the neck of his guitar with a cloth.

"Don't kill yourself with thrill."

He gave a half smile. "Nah, I'm happy . . . it's just I want us to get the sound right."

Claire held her hand up. "Yeah, actually there's something I want to say to you all. About the sound . . . you've been telling me it's shit for ages and I've been a total bitch about it. But after that Suzi gig review I've got it . . . I was wrong . . . and as my way of saying sorry . . . I've found us a sound engineer." She turned toward the door. "Come in, mate!"

I swiveled around, and there, in freshly washed dreads, stood Emanuel.

He raised his paw in slow greeting. "Uh . . . uh, like . . . hi."

**Tues., Feb. 28**

I've just finished another design for the project. It's a kit for how to get out of those fines for having fewer than 3 people in your car in central London. Basically the kit comes with 3 dummies and a range of wigs, mustaches, and glasses to dress 'em up. Never be busted for driving alone again.

# March

## Wed., March 1

This evening I put the key in the lock, pushed my front door open, and heard voices. Weird. I went thru to the kitchen and found Claire sitting at the table, deep in talk with this slim, dark girl, about our age, maybe a bit older. She glanced up at me.

"I used my key. I lived here before. Monica."

"Oh, right."

She glanced around the room, like the walls were coated in vomit. "I see you've done some *Trading Spaces* shit in here."

I let that one go. "So, are you moving back in?"

"Yeah, just for a few months. Good with you?"

I smiled. "Course, I mean this was your place after all. . . ."

She gave me a small nod before turning back to Claire. "Anyway, so the first priority is to keep on-line. I tell you they are trying to shut down the whole grid . . ." My ears closed off as she ranted on and I took the chance to look her over. She's one of those beautiful-ugly girls; y'know the ones you see them and go urggh, no—*ugly*, then they smile and you're like actually, no—*gorgeous*. Tricksy, very tricksy. I zoned back in on their conversation. Claire was going, "But not here, in Europe?"

"They do it all the time, in Burma, China, Russia, Iran, Saudi . . ."

"Yeah, but they're not like . . . democracies."

A sound like the creak of a rusty hinge came out of Monica's nose. I think it was laughter. "You've got a lot of faith in the system.

Personally I'd avoid using major corporate search engines; they pass on sensitive information to the CIA and MI5."

"Really?" Claire breathed deep, loving it.

"Tano Adile went to prison for 2 months. I got 6 for previous. The prosecution had evidence that could only have come from mails we'd sent."

I glanced over, surprised. I didn't know that Tano had been inside.

Monica chewed at a nail. "I don't use my fone for important stuff anymore."

"Isn't that a bit paranoid?" I asked. She was pissing me off big time.

Monica spat out a sliver of nail. "Laura, right?"

I nodded.

"It's not a game. I've been inside before, yes? But this last time they put me in the Box. You know what that is? It's a room, 2 meters wide and 3 meters long. No bed, no bunk, no toilet—just a hole in the floor. Five years ago the House of Lords declared it illegal—but it still exists. And you know who goes in there? Green Activists, people who are prepared to use force to get emissions down faster."

I came upstairs. I'm lying on my bed but I can still hear her droning voice thru the door. Brilliant. Now I've got Che bloody Guevara living in my flat. I'm sick of politics.

6 A.M. Woke up starving. How long, oh lord, before my loan?

## Sat., March 4

We've only got 2 days till our uni project deadline, so me and Sam hooked up at Tano's warehouse to work on the final bits. It was a clear sunny day and I took the long way around the Docks, climbing the footbridge to get up high over the city. London sparkled and shimmered in the light, almost like nothing bad had ever happened. I took in a deep lungful of fresh air and had a moment of happiness.

Straight-up happiness. I flicked on *The Stranglers, No More Heroes*, and I *ran*—I wasn't cold, I wasn't hungry, I wasn't mental—I was good! And when I got to the bit about Leon Trotsky getting an ice pick in his head, I launched into a monster karate kick, aiming it square in the chest of all the bullshit. Nearly snapped my spine in two. Excellent. I didn't stop till I got all the way to Tano's in the old Spillers Building and arrived totally out of breath, but clean and fresh. Sam was already there, leaning against the doors. He looked me up and down.

"You need to knock off the burgers, girl. You're out of shape."

"Jus . . . buzz . . . in . . . you . . . pig . . ." I wheezed.

Tano's warehouse turned out to be a whole office suite on the 5th floor. In the receptionist's area there was still a buzzer with a *Ring for Attention* sign above it, as if the office workers had just nipped out for lunch, instead of the reality, that the Thames had come thundering in up to the second floor and wiped out the whole building.

I eyed the buzzer. "You think it works?"

Sam shrugged. "Try it, I guess."

I leaned forward and pressed down. From along the corridor came a whoop like a New York cop car and after a moment, Tano himself appeared, wiping his oily hands on a rag. His face lit up when he saw us. "Eh, the revolutionary *disegniatori!*"

He waved us inside and we followed him along a corridor, with offices off to each side. Quite a few had meetings going on inside.

I peered through the nearest glass door. "Who're all these people?"

He waved a hand. "Different all the time . . . Anti-United Front, recycling, *regenerazione*, action groups . . . many people come here."

We carried on thru a final set of doors and then suddenly Sam stopped and spread his arms. "Jeezus!"

I peered over his shoulder. We were now in the main central open-plan section and laid out in front of us were hundreds of meters of panels, tiles, wires, cables, tires, leads, motors, plastic,

boxes. Anything I'd ever wanted was in that room. I stood moment.

"Oh, Tano . . . It's paradise!"

He laughed and led us to a cleared area to the right where tl was a half-built shallow boat with a long propeller hanging off back. He ran his hands down the wooden side. "A long-tail bo like from Thailand . . . so we can travel on the river using only motor running entire from water and solar power."

Sam looked at him. "Do you think you can really get independent of the electric grid?"

"*Si*, why not? Human can do anything once they decide. We are the supreme *adaptori* . . . Anyway, let me see your work."

It felt a bit embarrassing taking out our joke kit project with all the serious work going on around, but Tano really liked our idea, and we soon got to work. Actually, I'm dead proud of it. Every new bit we do is my favorite. Today it's the Fake Car Scratch. It comes with loads of letters so you can put together any message you want. Like this one . . .

STICK IT TO 'EM
FAKE SCRATCHES

CONTENTS:
5 FAKE CAR SCRATCHES
THEY'LL BOIL WITH RAGE!

BREAK
MY
WINDOWS

We finished up at about 8 when Tano rocked up with beers. Sam popped his and leaned back against a pile of tires with a sigh. He nodded at a kid editing footage of a riot on a monitor to our left.

"He's been working on that all afternoon. Isn't that the United Front march down thru Forest Gate? I heard they were like taunting all the Asians, the black community, the Eastern Europeans . . . screaming at them to go home, that they're taking all the jobs. I can't believe the feds allowed it."

Tano took a swig. "Believe it."

Sometimes he seems like a different person, super serious. Fighting broke out on screen and the camera zoomed in on a group of 20 UF skinheads.

"And that is Leader Guard; not ordinary fighter . . . No, these are *paramilitare*."

The camera now swerved on to a bunch of protestors, who were hurling bottles at the UF. A whole section of them were dressed all in black with covered faces.

"Who are those people in the black masks?" I asked.

Tano tapped his mouth with his thumb. "Hard to know for sure."

Sam narrowed his eyes. "Aren't they 2 supporters?"

I turned to him. "Who the hell's the 2?"

"It's this global underground green army."

"Why's it called that?"

"You know, the idea that if temperatures rise by 2 more degrees then we'll be at the tipping point cos all the permafrost will melt, releasing a zillion tons of methane, and basically then climate change will be irreversible. End of the World stuff. Anyway, I think the 2 came out of the old anarchist Black Block, but they're even more radical. People say it was them that bombed the G30 energy conference last year in Venezuela."

"Why haven't I heard of them?"

"Dunno, probably cos they're super secretive and they operate in little cells. That's as much as I know."

"What . . . like green terrorists?" I jerked my thumb at the screen. "But then how come we're seeing them out in the open, on the streets?"

"I guess there are different levels of involvement . . ." Sam began.

Tano made a cutting motion with his hand. "Eh, talk, talk . . . There is not really proof . . ." He sighed. "But for me, I don't like to see . . . whoever it is . . . on the street like this, in the mask. It's too dangerous, too easy for the *racisti* or *polizie* to infiltrate us."

"Why?"

"Because we *also* don't know who is inside the mask. It can be bad people. It's too late when the fighting's begun."

On the screen red smoke bombs filled the air.

I suddenly got this moment of real sadness. Tano reminds me of Arthur so much, my old ex-next-door neighbor who died last year. The same humor, courage, and . . . I dunno . . . zest for life.

Later on at home I was curled up tight in bed, waiting for Adi to finish burning some tracks.

"I saw some footage from that anti-UF fight with Sam today. Extreme."

Adi turned, flipping the station into sleep mode. "And what's up with that? Somebody's got to take on the UF for real. I mean, for the last 6 months I've been going to all these protests, yeah? And it's always the same. Bored police watching skinny do-gooders from the left, waving their arms around and singing sloppy slogans. *Again and again and again.*" He sighed, before suddenly breaking into a sly grin. "Anyway, what's going on with you an' that boy? He's a bit pretty for you, ain't he?"

"Who? Sam? We're just mates is all. You know that."

He bounced onto the bed and slid under the covers. "He'd be mad not to try something."

I slid my arms around him for extra warmth. "You're joking, right?"

Adi turned. "Ha ha."

I kissed his nose. "Are you excited about the tour?"

Adi nodded, but didn't answer.

"Don't you care anymore, about the band? It's OK to tell me, you know?"

"I don't know what I feel about anything anymore." He kissed me. "'Cept you. You're the one clear thing in my life."

Student loan tomorrow!

## Sun., March 5

Dirty Sexy Money! I jumped up dead early and caught a bus to the nearest cash machine in Canning Town. I couldn't believe it when I saw the numbers on the screen. €2,800. I strutted into Somerfield like a supermodel and stacked up bacon, eggs, sausages, mushrooms, coffee, before catching the bus home to make me and my boy the biggest fry-up the world has ever seen. Ah, the smell of bacon grease in my hair! I might keep some in a jar to rub on my bangs for if I ever starve again.

## Mon., March 6

Oh yeah. Back in the land of the living! Points a-go-go. Thank God for the Docks.

| Brown, L | | Feb 01/2017 - Mar 01/2017 |
|---|---|---|
| | C0 Acc No: 4547 9410 0982 5954 | |
| C0 POINTS AVAILABLE: | 200 | |
| POINTS USED: | 40 | |
| Congratulations. You are within your allocation for the period. | | |

## Wed., March 8

My flat has turned bad. There's a political meeting going on 24/7 in the kitchen. Adi's always down there now when he comes over. Maybe I should move out . . . but I kind of like it now. I'm staying undercover in my room, sweating it out till The Monica moves on. On my way upstairs last night, I overheard her saying she was going to picket a Climate Conference at Easter and I immediately checked my calendar. Another 6 weeks. I don't know if I can last that long.

## Thurs., March 9

My fone buzzed this evening. I glanced at it. Dad. Strange. I picked it up, cautious.

"Hey, what's wrong?"

"Nothing, I—was just thinking about you."

"*Right . . .*"

I think I've spoken to my dad a total of 3 times on the fone my entire life. Mum was clearly using him as bait to get to me. I waited, like a shy trout on the riverbed.

He cleared his throat. "Well actually there was something . . . I was thinking of doing a day course in Epping Forest, y'know . . . it's ah . . . close to you. On moth trapping."

I blinked. This was weird, even for him. Couldn't he come up with something better? Why's he got to drag moths into it?

"Er, I'm not sure, Dad—" I began and then suddenly there was a harsh whisper in the background and a scrunching noise as Mum wrestled the fone off him. The hunter revealed.

"Laura, darling!" Mum's Super Voice bounced off all available molecules. "What on earth's going on down there? It's all over the news—the marches, the graffiti, the gang fights . . . I have to say I'm not at all happy about you—" She stopped abruptly as if remembering the original idea again. "I mean—oh, look, I'm going on and on, well, here's your father again. . . . Go with him on the course, I think it'll mean a lot to him. He's been a bit down lately. Byee!"

Dad's voice. "So, are you free on the 23rd of this month? It's a Thursday, I think."

I sighed. "Sure."

I am a moth trapped in my parents' net.

### Sat., March 11

We played a blinder at UEL tonight. When we walked into the union, there were all these cool posters plastered all over.

"Where did this lot come from?" asked Stace.

Claire smiled. "They're good, no? I got Laura's mate Sam to do them for me."

Adi glanced at me but said nothing.

Anyway, the gig was awesome. We sound like a totally different band with Eman on sound. After the gig I climbed up to see him in the sound booth; he was coated in wires and chips and pins. I tapped him on the shoulder. "Thanks, Eman. That was brilliant. We are so getting on that Europe tour sounding like this."

He pinged an earplug out of the nearside lobe for a moment and bobbed his head. "Uh . . . yeah, like uh . . . *yeah*, y'know." A pause, then he reinserted the plug and turned back to his real friends, the wire people. He is one strange lifeform.

## Mon., March 13

When will it stop? I went into uni today to hand my project in and the place was buzzing with the news that the gov is going to slash student loans by 50% and take away our free travel. If it goes on like this education will only be for the rich.

**5 P.M.** 5,000 Oxford University students walked out this afternoon and in Bristol, Bath, Exeter, and Oxford, kids are refusing to leave school. They say they're gonna camp out over the weekend in protest. Like that'll bring Parliament down.

## Tues., March 14

Hmm. 140 schools and 60 university demos happened today.

## Wed., March 15

Day 3. My uni, LCC, came out today, so I'm officially on strike. I had no food in the flat, so I took the chance to sneak off and shop at a dirty old supermarket. You've got to do stuff like that undercover on the Docks—people around here'd crucify me if they knew.

Anyway, when I got off the bus at Beckton, there were kids swarming about everywhere, all blocking the subway station exit and the bus stops. It was dead funny watching people trying to push their way through a bunch of schoolkids in little blazers. But the best thing was when I got inside. I heard some shouting and peered over the crackers to see a standoff at the entrance. 3 black girls were leading a posse thru the sliding doors. A lady manager was trying to stop them, but they just pushed her corporate ass over before rushing inside, all with raised fists, chanting: **"Every Little Lie Helps! Every Little Lie Helps!"**

After that they zoomed all over the store. The nearest group to me had just started stomping on a crate of Israeli avocados when the whine of police sirens filtered inside and they all scampered to the exit. I watched thru the window as a bunch of police vans screeched up and the feds jumped out. They ran all over with outstretched arms, trying to trap the kids, but there were like 10 nippers to every officer, squirming all over, like escaped eels. It was excellent.

When I was leaving, I saw the kids had sprayed all down the long glass windows

**THE CUSTOMER IS ALWAYS RIGHTEOUS**

Who says schools are dumbing down? That's some serious wordplay for the junior brain.

### Thurs., March 16
Day 4. The Minister for Education has ordered students to go back to study. He said *the government could not and would not be terrorized into changing its policy.*

The students have now called for a complete blackout strike and loads of teachers have come out in support. (Anything for a day off.)

This evening I slinked around to Stace's to watch a movie. I pulled my hood down low to avoid the protestors. I asked Stace how she gets away with it.

"I'm a drummer, Laur. I'm s'posed to be stoopid. No one bothers *me*," she grunted, stuffing a fistful of popcorn in her jaws.

I reached for the bowl. "We're never gonna be ready in time for the Europe gig unless Claire and Adi quit spending their whole time picketing the campus."

"Ah, chill, it's not for weeks yet. Now shut up, my mate told me this is the bit where she sticks an ice pick thru the dingo's head."

I shut my eyes, but too late. A mournful howl filled the room.

## Fri., March 17

Day 5. The gov and the students met, but all that happened was the minister repeated they would not back down, that the student demands were impossible, that *we all have to make sacrifices* in this difficult period. It's all right for him, he's got an education. Anyway, the whole thing's gone massive. 6,000 schools, colleges, and unis are shut down. The media are calling it the Tellytubby Riots.

## Sat., March 18

Claire's just called me to go to an overnight demo at UEL. I know I should go, it's not that I don't care, it's just I really hate demos; I hate all the people on them; I hate all the slogans; I hate all the herbal tea; I hate all their eyes. But obviously I can't tell Claire that so I said I had bad period pain.

I locked off and there was a knock on the door. Sam.

He smiled. "Wanna play pool?" And when I nodded, he handed me something. "OK then, but put this cap on and wear it low. We've got to bust you out of here."

I laughed. "Hang on, I'll get my jacket."

Huh, I was on fire tonight. I got myself in the zone (2 double rum&Cokes) and I just couldn't miss. It was like I was controlling the balls with my mind. After I'd whipped his arse for the 3rd time, Sam threw his cue down on the table.

"You're too good. This is embarrassing."

"Why, just cos I'm a girl?"

"No-o, I don't mind getting beat by a girl if she's ugly. But when a cute girl beats you, it's not right. It's like the cosmos is out of balance."

"Oh." I suddenly worked out what he said. The thing is I can never tell when he's joking and when he's not. He keeps flipping between flirty and dead straight. I blushed.

Sam reached into his back pocket. "Another one?" As he pulled out his wallet, a piece of paper fluttered to the floor.

I reached for it. "What's this?"

He blushed. "Ah, s'nothing . . . it's this anti-UF graffiti thing I'm working on . . . but it's kind of lame. I've done one hand but I can't get the other one right. Keeps coming out backward."

2X
RUM+Cokes

I frowned. "Yeah, and why's the UF on the grenade? It's kind of confusing . . . almost like the bunny's the Nazi."

He tried to snatch it off me. "All right."

I lifted the paper high. "But it's cool!"

His face lit up. "Sure?"

"Sure I'm sure, but what are you going to do with him?"

"Well, if I can get him sorted out, I wanna spray him down inUnited Front territory. Maybe down in Romford. Just to piss people off."

"That's kind of dangerous."

Sam shrugged. "So? Wanna help?"

I thought about it for a moment and grinned. "Definitely."

He slammed a euro coin down on the table.

"OK, rack 'em up. I'm gonna crucify you next game. Winner takes all."

Winding up white, right-wing Romford? Now that's my kind of protest.

## Mon., March 20

Every single U.K. school, college, and university is on strike. Nearly 5 million students and teachers.

I haven't seen Adi for like 10,000 years. Every time I call him it goes thru to voice mail cos he's stuck in a meeting or wrestling with some police dog on campus.

Ooh, one piece of goodness today though; Dad called to cancel the moths.

Something to do with pig pressures. Every pig has a silver lining.

## Tues., March 21

Unbelievable! I am amazed. The government's *backed down*. We're keeping our student loan and free travel. This is the first time I've ever seen something real happen from protesting; makes me feel a bit guilty for not getting stuck in.

Anyway, I've pinned Adi down and am finally seeing him tomorrow evening. I've saved up €30 and I'm gonna take him out for Mexican to try and get him to lighten up. Oh, God, I'm like those nagging wives with disappointed mouths trying to get the sparkle back in their love lives.

## Wed., March 22

I got my project grades today. 82%. Yahooo! I'm dead proud. I legged it all the way home to find Adi already there—I heard his voice coming thru from the living room as I ran in. I wanted to surprise him, so I softly closed the door behind me and crept up the hallway. I stopped dead when I realized he was deep in talk on the sofa with Monica, with a nearly empty bottle of vodka between them. A flash of jealousy shot thru me. I leaned up against the door frame and listened in, like a child.

Monica was kind of half lying with her legs propped up against the wall. In her dark military jacket and boots, she looked like a revolutionary out of a movie. She took a swig from the vodka bottle. "A radical group's got to make an impact before it's driven into secrecy. Like in Cuba, when Fidel Castro started, he was out there on the Havana campus . . . so by the time the military were on to him and he was forced to hide in the hills, he was already famous and the Cuban people went and found him themselves."

Adi waved an arm toward the window. "Yeah, not so many hills to hide out in around here."

"There's plenty of places to get undercover in the city if you use technology as camouflage." Monica tapped the bottle with nervous fingers. "There's no turning back. The UF want to march down the heart of Asian Brick Lane in ten days—that is a declaration of war. We've got to say no, enough. You are not allowed to use people when you need them and turn on them when times get hard. We've got to fight—but when *we* fight we won't just be some random mob—we'll be a smart mob. It'll be so hard for them or the feds to stop us—cos we've got no leader, no center. No place to raid and close down. Just a thousand fones, pushers, portals."

Adi reached for the bottle, eyes narrowed. "So how comes you're not at uni now?"

She shrugged. "Flunked my A-Level exams 18 months ago, after I got arrested for the 5th time." She gave a short bark of laughter. "All the other kids in an exam and me in a cell."

It's official. I hate her.

I didn't bother with the Mexican after that, just didn't feel like it.

## Thurs., March 23

This morning I was fishing around in my bass bag for some strings and in the inside pocket I found this half-ripped zine article from back in the day.

rock !! 4get the female bass players
that big-selling bands recruit as a token
gesture.
We got our token black boy o    uritten,
That's how cool we are T'        !
female-performed, fe  at'
For now we are 100%  i
independent, bu
We're releasin'
download we
ecorded our
elves and
designed
the cover
art for.
We don't
want any
ip off

"Hey, look at this." I slid it over the bed toward Adi.

Adi scanned it and laughed. "Token black boy?"

"Damn right, we only let you in cos you was cute."

He rolled on top of me. "Is dat right?"

Suddenly there was a knock at the door. Monica.

"Adi? I'm going down to the Fashion Street Centre in 10, wanna come?"

Adi sat up. "Ah, shit, babe . . . I promised Nate I'd meet him down there . . ."

I sighed. "Yeah, yeah."

"C'mon, it's only till this anti-UF march."

I folded the article. "But you're still coming to rehearsals and doing the Europe tour gig in April, right? I mean you're not bailing on us—"

"Chill, course I'm still doing the band stuff, it's just gonna be a bit intense for a couple of weeks, then I'll be your boy again."

"My token black boy?"

"100%." He kissed me and jumped up off the bed.

He's gone and the flat is empty and dark, that kind of shocking dark when a fuse has blown.

## Fri., March 24

Oh God, oh God, oh God. I don't know what to do! It all started with a fonecall this morning.

"Sweetie, it's me! I'm back in London."

"Kier?"

"Yes, yes, oh, you've got to come and help me, pleeaaase." He groaned. "I'm suffocating in velvet. It's for this new gorgeous Slo-Date Night for Carbon Dating . . . I've been setting it up for weeks and now everyone's let me down at the last minute! I'm not going to make it. Aargh, slipping!"

"What?"

"Goddamn midnight-blue velvet curtains. All over the floor. Ruined. Oh, God. Please?"

I giggled. "Of course I'll help you, you big gayer. Tell me what you need."

"Can you meet me at the usual place in Soho?"

"Sure, I'll get down there as soon as I can."

An hour later I was standing outside the Leopard, just off Brewer Street. From behind me came a scream: "Laura Brown, there you are!" and suddenly I was in the middle of a giant Hugo Boss hug. We stayed like that for ages. Damn, it felt good to see him.

"All right!" said Kieran, pulling away and dabbing his eyes. "Come on, come on! No time for dramatics. Follow me." We went inside and just before we got to the top of the stairs he jumped ahead. "Wait there a mo, I just want to drape this and *then* you can come in." After a few minutes he reappeared. "OK . . . shut your eyes," he breathed, propelling me thru the doors. "And now . . . *open!*"

I flicked my eyelids open and gasped. "Oh, Kier, it's . . . amazing."

"Really, truly?"

I gazed around the room. He'd totally gone for it; a raised stage was draped in heavy velvet, a beautiful ornate mirror covered fully half the length of the room, and in the center there was a long banqueting table, glistening with candles, tableware and glasses, finished off with a colossal bouquet of roses and lilies. I took a deep breath. It feels like ages since I've seen luxury.

"I'm going for a touch of old-world opulence . . . a sort of antithesis, sweetie, of modern times. This is *slow* dating. There are to be five courses and between each one, the gentlemen have to move up two places—ooh and there'll be dancing, lots of it. Fox-trot and waltz."

"Er, does anyone under 90 know the fox-trot?"

"We *all* will, once Eduardo's put us through our paces. He's this fantastic camp old band leader from Venezuela or somewhere." Kieran's face suddenly crumpled. "Oh, God, I'm just so nervous!" He suddenly stamped his foot. "NO! For the final time, the sorbet doesn't come out till the last minute."

For a second I thought he'd gone mad but then I turned to see a fat kid with a pierced head standing next to the stage, scowling over a tray of mini sorbets. He turned away, sulkily. "F'got."

"Have you opened the red wine yet? It needs to *breathe*."

The kid picked his nose. "Dunno."

Kieran slapped his head like a bad guy in a pantomime. "You see? I. Need. Help. Fast."

I flipped my fone open. "I'll call around."

And so at 8 P.M., I stood at one end of the long table and watched Sam light the last of the candles. He was the only person I dared call for such a shallow mission. (Stace is out of town.)

"You are such a star," I whispered.

He looked up and grinned. "S'cool. I'd come to this if I was—"

"What? Desperate? Over 30?"

"I was gonna say looking for looove, actually. Maybe I am."

Hmm. There he went again. Mr. Ambiguity.

"People!" cried Kieran, suddenly appearing in a Paul Smith suit, a pink handkerchief angled in the breast pocket. "It's time to get started." He nodded at Eduardo. "You boys all ready? All right, let's do it!" He took a deep breath, walked to the entrance, and pulled the doors back with a magnificent sweep. There was no one there. Not a single person. The band members looked down at their shoes. We all stood in complete silence for 1 minute, 2, 3, 4 . . . ticktock . . . ticktock . . . ticktock . . .

"Oh, man," Sam muttered. "Super intense."

Kieran still stood at the top of the stairs like an action toy, completely still and stiff . . . and then from far, far away came the sound of footsteps.

"S'gotta be, man," said Sam, through clenched teeth. Kieran took a step forward—and then, miracle of miracles, three women and four men stepped into the room, all looking nervous as hell.

"Strike up, cats!" hissed Kieran. Honestly I don't know what century that boy thinks he's from, but, anyway, it's OK, cos Eduardo's from the same one. The old boy clicked his fingers—and by the time his band got to the 3rd song, the room was full of middle-aged Carbon Daters, all clutching glasses of wine and doing those white-people body sways as they checked each other out. What happens to people when they get older? At what point *exactly* do they go weird around the hips? Nobody my age would ever move like that. I've got 15 years, tops, to work it out.

After half an hour Kieran leaped on to the stage. "Ladies and gentlemen, I'd like to welcome you back in time to the very first Slow Dating night. It's love in a new era. May it be the first of many!" All the oldies clapped and cheered and looked so full of raw hope I had to fight back tears. And 3 hours later, after I'd finished serving 5 slow courses plus coffee, I went outside onto the fire escape with Sam. I was leaning back against the railings, looking up at the stars, and it just happened. He kissed me. I pulled away, shocked . . . and then the next second I was leaning forward, kissing him right back. There was just too much love in the air. It's my only defense and I'm sticking to it.

Oh, God, I feel so GUILTY. And I've got to see Adi tomorrow at band practice.

### Sat., March 25

Adi came in dead late.

"Where's your guitar, mate?" asked Claire.

He just stood there with a weird expression on his face and shook his head. "I can't do it."

"What?"

"The Euro gig next Saturday. The UF have just changed their Brick Lane march time to the same day. They did it last minute to try and catch us off guard. I—I can't back out now. People are relying on me, big time. I know it's bad, but there it is. I'm sorry."

Claire slammed her mic down on the table. "Oh, you have got to be joking, Adi. This is the big selection. For the *tour*. You can't not do it."

"I got no choice."

"Of course you've got a choice. You just don't care anymore, do you? Why don't you have the guts to leave so we can get someone new in?"

She stomped out of the room, leaving the rest of us staring at each other. Stace ran her fingers thru her hair. "Jeez, Ad, you've gone well radical. Next thing we know you'll be joining the **2**."

"Shut up!" Adi glanced at me. "Laur?"

I stood there, stunned. How could he do this to us, to me? But what could I say after what I did yesterday? Anger and guilt battled inside me. Adi's eyes were drilling into me. I dug my hands in my pockets. "I . . . understand, babe. This means a lot to you."

"Oh, what?" cried Stace.

Adi grabbed me. "Really?"

I nodded. "I guess sometimes the band has to come second."

Stace threw her hands up. "Unbelievable. This is a tour we're throwing away. What's wrong with you guys?"

Guilt. Massive guilt. That's what's wrong.

## Mon., March 27

Adi's gone down to the Fashion Street Centre.

Aarrghh! Shall I tell him? Yes, no. I don't know.

Aarrghh! The bastard. How could he let us down like this?

## Tues., March 28

Mental, mental, mental. Messaged Kieran.

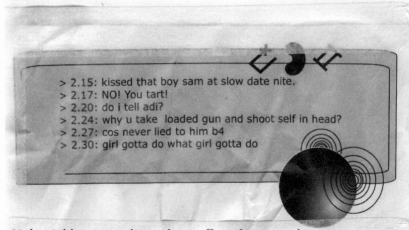

> 2.15: kissed that boy sam at slow date nite.
> 2.17: NO! You tart!
> 2.20: do i tell adi?
> 2.24: why u take loaded gun and shoot self in head?
> 2.27: cos never lied to him b4
> 2.30: girl gotta do what girl gotta do

Huh, it's like getting love advice off an electronic drag queen.

I can't get hold of Adi. I've called him loads, but he's not picking up. I just want to hear the sound of his voice, make sure I'm safe.

I slept for about 6 minutes last night, just kept going over everything in my head. I've got to get control of this thing. Jesus, all I did was kiss the guy, it's not like I killed anyone. I'm gonna to leave a message for Sam tomorrow first thing. I worked on it from 3–5 this morning. Got it down. I know what I'm gonna say. Feel cool and calm. In control.

## Wed., March 29

I forced myself to wait till 10 to call Sam so as not to appear to be insane girl psycho early caller. First time I called, it went thru to voice mail and I hit *disconnect*. I paced the room and scrunched up my fists and then called again. . . . This time I got thru to the beeps, took a breath, waiting for his message—and then another tone clicked in—incoming from my mum. I panicked and locked them both off. Oh, God, oh, God. Not the cool style I was going for. I ran to the balcony, yanked the door open, and screamed. Then my fone buzzed again. I picked it up.

"Hello."

"Yeah, Laura? It's me, Sam. Did you just call me?"

"Er, yeah. Hi."

"Er, hi. Look." He paused. "I wanted to call you to say that was a big mistake the other night . . . and I'm sorry. I mean we can't . . ."

I stared down at the shimmering water of the Docks. "I agree."

His voice filled with relief. "Really? You're cool with that?"

"What, d'you think I'm in love with you or something?"

"No, but—"

"But what? Get over yourself."

"Fine."

"Fine right back at you."

We both locked off simultaneously.

I feel sick. How could I do that to Adi?

**11 P.M.** Pissed off with Sam for stealing my lines. It was supposed to be me saying no to him.

## Thurs., March 30

Claire banged on the door tonight. I opened it and she rolled inside like Hurricane Katrina. "I just don't get it. You of all people. Something's up, or you'd never back Adi like this. What's going on?"

"Nothing."

She shook her head. "You're a shit liar. We've got to *make* him do this gig."

"We can't. He's not my slave."

"You could make him if you wanted to. You know that."

I spread my hands. "I *can't*."

She rubbed her head. "Unbelievable. I thought the *angels* was everything to you."

"There's still a chance we can make it, can't you call the promoter and—"

"What? Say we can't go cos we're on a march?" She glared at me. "Grow up, Laura."

She's right. I don't know if I can ever forgive him for letting us down like this. Or myself. If I wasn't feeling so guilty I would have forced him at AK47 point.

## Fri., March 31

Adi called this afternoon asking if I was coming tomorrow. "Normally I wun't ask, but this one means a lot to me. It's kind of personal."

I forced myself to sound normal. "I'm coming for sure, but what's the plan?"

"We know the feds will try to split us up with roadblocks, so what we're gonna do is send small groups to different places to pretend they've divided us. The UF march starts at Victoria Park and so we'll be there, but in small numbers, while really we're secretly massing here. Brick Lane is the heart of it."

"Adi . . ." I forced myself to say it. "You're not going to get yourself . . . hurt or anything."

A pause. "I ain't planning on it, but, Laura, we can't just let this happen anymore." He sighed. "Look don't stress, it's all gonna be cool. Come down early, though, to miss the crowds, yeah?"

"Sure, maybe 7."

"OK. Call me when you get close. Laur, I feel so bad about the gig, but this is too big."

"I know. I'll see you tomorrow."

I shut my eyes, trying to block out the band, the tour. I've just got to get thru tomorrow. After that I'm gonna get the promoter's number and stalk him till he gives us another chance. I've got to make amends.

# April

**Sat., April 1**

I left the flat at 7 and walked thru the dark, silent Docks. The subway was dead slow and it took me a whole hour to get to Mile End before they kicked us all off cos they'd closed down the Central Line westbound. When I got up to street level, the road was jammed with parked coaches, cars, bikes, and thousands of people. Adi called straightaway, asking where I was.

"Up near Mile End. Had to get off the Central."

"How many people?"

"Hard to tell, 5,000 of us maybe. And a hell of a lot of them. It's not just skins, there's loads of ordinary-looking people." I glanced at my watch. "And it's only 8. What's it like down there?"

"Tense. The feds raided our center at 3 A.M., but we'd been tipped off so we cleared everything out last night. All the shops are shut; the owners are boarding the windows up and there's roadblocks and thousands of police everywhere—I heard that coachloads of them've been bussed from all over the southeast. You better get down here fast if you want to get thru the cordon, Laur, so don't go into Victoria Park, will you?"

"No way." I could hear a speech drifting over from the tennis courts. Not the words, just the tone and rhythm. It sounded ugly.

In the end I had to walk in a slow shuffle towards Brick Lane. The mood was good, though; people were laughing and singing, but by the time I got near Liverpool Street it was nearly 10. I called Adi, but my signal had gone, the fone just showed a network busy signal. It was hectic and I was getting nowhere; every side road was blocked off and it was clear there was no way I was making it to the Fashion Street Centre. For a minute I stood at the side of Commercial Street, trying to work out what to do, when I heard my name called. I looked over to see Claire, standing by the entrance to Spitalfields Market. I quickly crossed over to her, but a policeman moved over to block my way.

"She's a steward," she shouted, holding out a red armband.

He paused, then quickly motioned for me to climb under the tape.

We stood there on the side of the road for a moment in silence.

I tried a smile. "Didn't think I'd see you here."

"You neither, you ain't exactly the activist of the year, mate." She turned toward the market.

I put out my hand. "Claire, I don't think he would've listened to me . . . I'm as gutted about this as you are. I'm gonna do everything I can to get us back on the tour, I promise."

Claire nodded. "Finally, you're starting to sound like you give a shit—what the hell's up with you and Adi, though? You used to wrap him around your little finger."

"If I knew I'd tell you."

She sighed. "Well, whatever, come on, then. We've got to focus on today now."

I followed her through the market gates to where a group of people from the Docks were setting up a first-aid center, pulling out stretchers, opening packs of bandages, splints, needles. Claire handed me a pair of gloves. "Look, Gwen's there . . . can you help her with unpacking those boxes?"

I had my first thrill of fear. "Do you think it's going to get bad?"

"I don't know, but I saw Nate earlier and he said the UF crowd had all kinds of shit: chains, knives, iron bars." She looked down. "It's good that we're here. I understand that, but . . ."

I spread my hands. "Claire, I know."

It was after 1 when we got thru all our work. I tried Adi again, but the network was totally dead—I think it was overridden by security signal or something. So much for Monica and her smart mob plan. Someone said they'd seen Adi and Nate down at the center only an hour before. My heart gave a twist, but there was no way I could get down there.

"Come," said GPJ, handing me a bottle of water. "The police are asking for more stewards, so let's get ourselves up to the march route."

We pushed through the crowd till we got to the crossroads of Commercial and Shoreditch High Street. I've never seen so many feds—it was a solid tight row of blue stretching all the way down the road, and all to protect that bunch of United Front bastards. And then, in the distance, we caught a marching drumbeat. They were coming!

We stood there packed, hot, tense. Then, finally the head of the march appeared—2 skinheads straining to hold up a huge UF banner that billowed out in the wind.

A rush of fear and hatred ran up through my spine and the bodies around me surged forward, pressing tight up against the linked arms of the police.

There were roadworks about 200 meters away where Shoreditch High Street joined Commercial, and as the front of the demo reached it, you could see the UF marchers getting squeezed and shoved by our crowd. Out of nowhere the feds suddenly decided to widen the route, but instead of asking, they just pushed us back off our feet. Our lines broke and fell back about 5 meters, but after a few moments, the police withdrew and we surged forward again.

GPJ nudged me. "Look."

I followed her gaze. The side street closest to us was filled with Asian kids with a few older people, mums, dads, grandparents, mixed in. For now they were silent, just watching and waiting. My throat tightened.

By this point the march was nearly level; their chants and drumbeats filled the air. For a moment I stared at them, wondering how people could have such hatred in their minds. I mean, there were whole families there, even kids—and they looked so weird, all young and sweet, next to the shaved heads and tattoos. Just beyond us the march reached the first obviously Indian shop, a Bangladeshi newsagent. The UF leaders stopped, turned, and faced the store, shouting and spitting—and then a group of skins forced their way right thru the feds and hurled themselves at the shop window. In a second the street was full of fighting bodies with stuff flying thru the air. I bent down, twisted around to see gangs of Asian kids lobbing half bricks over our heads into the UF lines. And then it really kicked off.

The police were caught between our demonstrators and the UF marchers. They tried to charge us to get to the Asian kids but by time they got thru, the boys had all melted away into the backstreets. When I watched the news reports later, I could see the feds had a plan of how to separate and control us, but they just couldn't execute it.

Meanwhile me and GPJ found ourselves as part of a big group driven toward a wide-open square behind the Truman Brewery.

"I don't like this," she muttered, as we were squeezed into an ever smaller space. On 3 sides we were faced with a solid line of blue. The fourth side was a line of blocked-off warehouses. Everyone started to look scared, but it was still under control. Nobody had any weapons, any armor, just T-shirts and jeans.

Claire suddenly appeared beside us. She grabbed my hand. "Jeez, this is like a battle, not a demo. What they got there?"

GPJ scanned the ranks. "Everything. Short shields, long shields, crash helmets, truncheons, dogs, tazers."

A piece of brick crashed down at Claire's feet. "What the . . . ?"

Another lump of concrete slammed into the ground. We crouched down, covering our faces.

"What's going on?"

GPJ shouted: "It's coming from our side. They're throwing stuff at the feds over the top of us."

Claire cupped her hands around her mouth. "Quit it. You're hitting—"

A wooden plank, bristling with nails spiraled down toward us.

"Shit!"

I looked around. We were packed in so tight now that the protesters at the sides were nearly crushed into the surrounding fed lines—and the bricks and rocks being thrown over the top were bouncing off the police shields and ricocheting right back into our people's faces. Our front line was yelling at the stone throwers to stop, but then a push started and suddenly I was in the middle of a giant surge. I saw Emanuel a few meters in front of me get rammed right up against a long shield. And then after a few seconds, the push broke up again and we were all just facing each other like before. Eman hobbled back, rubbing his thigh, face drawn with pain.

"You all right?" asked Claire.

He nodded. "Yeah . . . uh . . . colossal, like . . . uh dead . . . uh leg . . ."

And then, directly in front, the center of the police line opened and about 50 officers on horseback galloped right at us. Everyone started screaming, running backward, to the sides, anywhere to get out of the way. I kept tight hold of GPJ and Claire as we legged it toward the Truman Brewery. I tell you, those horses look like monsters when they're charging right at you. And then, without any warning, the feds retreated again.

We had nowhere to go. We were trapped on all sides by warehouses and the law. I couldn't understand what the plan was, I mean they had us pinned in one place, but they still went on attacking us for no reason. We surged forward once more, this time angry; pushing and straining to get at them. They charged again on horseback, but this time we met them with a storm of stones and bricks, which forced them backward. The air was full of panic, screams, and threats, adrenaline surging thru us all. Everyone understood it was a battle now. And then a bullhorn order rang out along the police lines. "No heads, bodies only."

The crowd went weirdly quiet. The feds lined up in front of us, grasping shields and truncheons.

GPJ whispered, "Oh, God, short shields. They're going to beat us."

And then they ran straight at us. Pure panic spread across the square. People were trampling over each other to get away, but there was nowhere to go. And so they started to beat us up. One by one. No heads? Don't make me laugh.

Some of us stood and fought, or at least tried to save others from being mashed up. There was this Rasta on the ground next to me with a pair of officers sitting on his chest and a third one kicking him in the stomach. I tried to help him, but I was just grabbed and thrown back like a doll. After what felt like hours, finally a bunch of us broke into this mad clothes shop called Junky Styling and ran thru into the warehouse offices above. Once we got up there, we started throwing everything we could find down onto the street—chairs, boxes, filing cabinets, desks, fire extinguishers—someone even set a strip of carpet on fire and rolled it out below.

I ran to the top floor with a couple of others to search for more stuff to chuck out. We'd just run into an office when the window-pane shattered and a canister rolled across the wooden floor toward the far wall. And then it exploded. I watched fascinated as white gas poured outward. Suddenly I couldn't breathe, couldn't see, and I fell to my knees, clutching my face. Around me I could hear more explosions and coughing and gasping.

Someone screamed, "Tear gas!"

For a moment I blacked out, then I was picked up and dragged along the floor to the window. A hand pushed my face out the window. "Breathe!"

I tried to take in some air, but my throat felt like it was full of razor blades cutting into the flesh. All I could do was lie there, slumped against the windowsill and watch the madness below. The police had just gone crazy after being tormented by the UF and pro-testers—and now they were running down anyone they could catch. There were kickings and beatings going on in every alleyway, fone box, street corner. Truncheons rising and falling again and again. Everywhere people were wandering around with blood streaming from their heads. I must have blacked out because the next thing I knew it was dark and the square below was empty. A hand gripped my shoulder.

"There you . . . are, I've uh . . . been like, uh . . . searching for friends . . . ah . . . uh . . . all over." Eman was bending over me. "Are . . . uh . . . you OK?"

I shrugged.

He scanned my face. "Come on, we've got . . . like . . . ah . . . get . . . uh movin'."

I swallowed hard, throat dry and aching. "Where's the others?"

"Arrested . . . I . . . guess." He drew his hand across his face. "I don't . . . er . . . uh like . . . uh . . . *believe* what just . . . totally . . . happened."

I checked the square. "D'you reckon it's safe to leave?"

"We've got . . . uh . . . to try . . ." He nodded at my fone. "You got any . . . uh . . . signal?"

I glanced down and shook my head. "Nope. Still dead. OK, help me up, please, I've messed up my ankle."

"Yeah, look at my . . . uh . . . leg." Eman opened a rip in his combats and showed a long gash all the way down the shin.

I winced. "Can you walk?"

"Have to. Come on."

He hauled me up and together we limped downstairs.

"I reckon uh . . . keep to the edges of . . . uh . . . like . . . the buildings an' . . . uh go . . . south, to the . . . uh . . . ah . . . back of Old Street."

We set off, flitting from shadow to shadow. 4 or 5 times we came across roadblocks and groups of officers. At one point Eman froze. "Dogs. Don't uh move." We stood in the dark, behind Bank station, for minutes until the officers moved on.

At last we got on the subway. I kept checking my fone cos by this time I was desperate to know that Adi and the others were OK. I was amazed at how much I wanted to get back to the Docks; it totally feels like home now.

Eman sat slumped on the train. "I . . . uh . . . don't want . . . uh . . . like nuthin' to do with . . . uh . . . people no more. Too . . . ugly."

But when we finally dragged ourselves into The Dox Centre, the place was full of protestors—in total chaos with blood everywhere and people moaning and crying. I was desperate to get news on the others so I set off, searching for Tano. I finally found him in the first-aid area.

"Have you heard from Adi?"

He nodded quickly and dropped his voice. "Look, there is trouble—"

"What d'you mean?"

"Fighting . . ."

My heart thudded, deep. "Is he hurt?"

"Not sure, a rep just call me from Newham General Hospital saying there is maybe 20 serious injuries . . . and he may be one."

"A rep?"

"*Representativo* . . . from the **2**."

I stood there for a moment, stunned. "I've got to go to him right now."

Tano grabbed my arm. "No, Laura, you cannot. The *polizie* are . . . everywhere. If you go to hospital, they arrest you right away."

"So what?"

"What use you are to him, then?"

"But I can't just do nothing . . . What if he's hurt bad?"

Tano ran the back of his hand across his forehead. "I know, but for this night we can do nothing. The rep promised me to call with any news."

I turned away, sick to my stomach.

## Sun., April 2

I went back to the flat, but I couldn't sleep—just way too much adrenaline running thru me—so at 6 I gave up and went back down to the Dox. The latest figures are 930 arrests, with 82 police and 840 protesters hurt. The injury figures are way too low, it's just no one's going to the hospital cos they know it means getting arrested. The word's got around that the Dox Centre is a safe place and so all last night and this morning people have been streaming in. The police are crawling all over the city, arresting anyone who looks like they might have been at the demo. Claire's mate, Johnny, just called from Whipps Cross Hospital. He said he'd got as far as Leyton last night before he was picked up by a police van and thrown in the back, but not before they'd jumped on his foot and broken his ankle in a bunch of places.

Claire herself walked in at 9, looking shattered.

I ran over to her. "You all right?"

"Yeah, but spent the night in the cells. They released me this morning, but I've been summoned. Got to appear at Bow Magistrates at 10 on Tuesday . . . me and the other 200 who were arrested at the same time."

I dropped into a whisper. "Look, Claire . . . they think Adi was mixed up with the 2 and he's been hurt—"

She grabbed my arm. "How bad?"

"Don't know. Tano got a call from a contact."

"Hard core. Jeez, I can't believe, *Adi* . . . People were talking about them last night in the cells. They reckon it was them that kicked off the big fights. They kept rocking up in gangs of 10 or 20 in hoods and ski masks so no one could see their faces. I definitely saw a bunch with the Asian kids, throwing Molotovs and bricks at the police."

My fone buzzed. Adi!

"Babe, you OK? Where are you?"

"I ain't hurt, I've just been in the cells overnight so I couldn't call before."

"You're not in hospital? They said you were injured."

"Nah . . . I'm fine . . . cuts and bruises is all. It's not me . . ." His voice distorted for a second. "It's Nate."

I felt so guilty for the rush of relief pushing thru my veins. "Where are you?"

"Outside the fed station. They've just released me, but I'm going straight down to the hospital."

"Is he bad?"

A long pause. "Can you meet me down there?"

"Tano said not to go, that it was probably crawling with police."

"I don't care. Please?"

I walked over to the hospital, stomach churning, but when I walked into the A&E there were no police there. They must've been redeployed somewhere else. I saw Adi right away, this lonely figure on an orange plastic chair. I went over, put my arms around him. He was trembling.

"They kicked him so much he lost consciousness." His face cracked. "They were beating us like animals."

"Adi . . . who's us?"

He shifted in his seat.

I scanned his face. "Tano said a contact called from that group, the **2**, and reported you were in trouble. Were you with them?"

Nothing.

"Adi?"

Finally he shrugged. "It's not that simple . . ."

"What does that mean? I'm scared to death and you can't even be straight with me."

"I can't deal with this right now. I'll talk to you, but later. OK?"

What could I do? I took his hand in mine. He was such a mess.

I've just spent an hour trying to make up a text message that won't make my parents go ballistic. In the end I went for a classic straight-up lie.

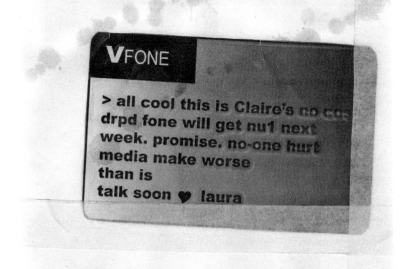

**V**FONE

> all cool this is Claire's no co:
drpd fone will get nu1 next
week. promise. no-one hurt
media make worse
than is
talk soon ♥ laura

## Tues., April 4

We spent all of yesterday at the hospital. I saw Nate for a moment thru the glass door of the ward. I caught a glimpse of his face. Dead gray, blue veins, white lips. Apparently he keeps drifting in and out of consciousness. Adi won't leave, just sits there, hour after hour with Nate's family.

I had to drop something into uni on my way home and bumped into Sam in the corridor. We just gave each other a massive hug. I scanned his face; a huge black eye and cut spread out over his cheek. "What happened to you?"

"UF chain. Lovely, ain't it?"

"Did you get it checked out?"

He raised an eyebrow. "What d'you reckon? I don't need to get into any more trouble. Anyway, I'm seeing it more as a battle scar."

I gave a half smile.

He put his arm around my shoulder. "I heard about Nate. Is he gonna be all right?"

I felt my chin start to go and before I knew it I was sobbing on his shoulder.

"I—I'm scared, Sam."

He held me tight. "I know, but it's gonna be OK."

"Everyone keeps telling me that, but it's a big fat lie. Nate's unconscious."

He hugged me tight till the tears stopped.

"C'mon, let's get you home."

Well, at least there's one good thing to come out of this mess . . . there's just too much going on for us to waste time being pissy with each other.

## Wed., April 5

I made myself go to a lecture this afternoon, I've missed so much uni time it's unreal, but somehow my 2,500 essay on the History of Oil in Design don't seem super important right now.

## Thurs., April 6

There was a meeting between the Home Office and the London Met police chief today. He's demanding emergency powers to "clean the streets." I'm so angry. The feds are crawling all over us, the media's making out we're demons. The public hate us. And why? We're not the ones spitting and smashing and shooting and beating innocent people till their ears bleed. Saw this headline in *The Times* today and it made me so mad I pulled my own hair.

I don't want to be like those Dox anarcho kids full of stupid conspiracy theories and hating the pigs. It's just too obvious. I know the feds are ordinary guys, just doing their job blah blah, but why do they always come down on the side of the gov? Aren't we worth protecting, too?

My hair hurts now. I didn't know it could do that.

## Fri., April 7

Adi's just texted me. Nate is sitting up and talking BS. Definitely on the road to recovery.

## Sat., April 8

Kieran called me this evening, going, "It's me, but not really me . . ."

"Eh?"

"I am officially an envoy of your mother."

"Oh, Jeez, Kier, why can't she just chill out?"

"Cos she's out of her mind with worry. Look, I did a deal with her . . . told her I'd check you were OK in return for her not coming down here with a bunch of Abingdon lollipop ladies on a kidnap mission."

"I told her everything was cool."

"One lousy text? Come on, Laura. And, anyway, is it? I'm not crazy about you being down there, either."

I sighed. "I know, but I've got friends hurt and I don't want to just leave them."

He was silent for a moment. "Listen, here's the thing. I'll tell your mum that I've seen you and you're safe . . ."

"Oh, thanks, you're—"

"Wait! I haven't finished. I'll tell her that if, and only if, you promise to call me the second it gets too dangerous. If that happens I'm getting you out of there."

"But—"

"Official envoys don't deal in buts. This is not a negotiation."

I chewed my lip. "OK."

"I've got your word?"

"Yes."

"Bye, then."

"Bye, Kier. Thanks."

He locked off.


I gazed around the silent flat, then realized I hadn't seen crazy Monica for days. Maybe she's been locked up again. It's getting really heavy. I don't want to go home, but the thing is, I might not have any choice.

## Tues., April 11

65 people from the Dox appeared in court today. There were 2 main charges: *Threatening Behavior* and *Possession of Offensive Weapons*. I don't know what the hell the 2nd one is about, what weapons? All we had were planks of wood and broken bits of box as shields against the beatings. I went to the library to write my oil essay. I got halfway down the page and stared into space. It's much easier to study revolutions than it is to be in them.

## Thurs., April 13

I woke in the night with a start. Adi's body slumped next to mine. My poor boy.

## Fri., April 14

We went together to see Nate this morning. He was sitting up in bed, looking pretty dazed, but otherwise all himself. His face is a mess, though; it's one big bunch of cuts and bruises. He can't remember anything much from the day.

He shook his head. "I remember a gang of skins charging us from one way and the pigs from the other, and the next thing I know is I'm tucked up in bed here. I don't even know what day it is. I ask the nurse and the other patients. Has there been a riot? I don't remember nothing."

## Sat., April 15

Oh, what?

My dear little sister

And even as you are moving within the timeless land of the soul, you know you never have been away, and deeper inside you, you know this true, no matter how fast the world spins. Time is but energy ... and so you have all the time of the world, and yet you have none at all.

All you need is already here ... it is in your hands, it is in your mind and your vision, and it is sealed deep inside your heart. Everything in your life is a Door to Becoming Whole.

Listen to the soft song of the inner voice. Wholeness is KNOWING we are all connected, not only with all other living beings - included mice, ferns, tigers, star systems and all kinds others - but with your own fabulous, unending, whole and complete Self ever growing, ever changing and ever dancing to the beat of all that is.

Hari Om!

Kim xxx

But it really made me laugh. A lot. For the first time in weeks.

## Sun., April 16

The band met tonight at my place. Everyone was sitting around silent, so I took a breath and started. "So, what are we gonna do? We missed the tour gig, but I reckon we shouldn't give up on it yet. What if we tried to speak to the promoter?"

Stace shook her head. "Yeah, but it's not so simple now, who knows how long we can even stay here?"

I frowned. "What d'you mean?"

"Where've you been, mate? They're starting to arrest students identified from CCTV along the march route and in Brick Lane. And how long d'you reckon the Docks'll be safe for? Everyone knows it's a refuge for the protestors. What'll you do if you're evicted?"

Claire crossed her arms.

"We keep going, fighting, of course. This is total oppression, we can't just—"

"Oh, leave it out, Claire!" spat Adi. "You din't even want to cancel the *angels* gig for the march and now you're a friggin' guerrilla."

She looked across at him, speaking so quietly I could hardly hear her. "I don't want to be in a band with you anymore."

Adi nodded. "That's OK, cos I quit." Without looking around, he picked up his guitar bag and walked out. And then Claire stuffed her mic in her pocket and stomped out, too, leaving me and Stace sitting there like total dummies.

I slumped down on my bass amp. "Shit. Now what?"

Stace stuck a drumstick in her ear. "Get drunk. They always fight and make up so there's no point getting dragged into it. Our role is to remain neutral via the medium of beer."

"What if it's for real this time?"

"Our bodies will be in a relaxed state to deal with the shock."

I glanced at her. "Stace, I'm serious . . ."

Suddenly Sam's voice came from below. "Oi, Laura, you in? Wanna go to the pub?"

Stace burst out laughing. "A sign. Thank Ye, oh Lord." She pulled me up by the wrist. "C'mon. Course I care, but you guys are just so melodramatic all the time; it's my role to balance out the universe."

15 minutes later we stood at the bar in The Swan. Stace turned, chinked her bottle against mine, and then suddenly froze, whis-

pered. "Don't look now, but you'll never guess who that is behind you."

I twisted in my seat. "Who?"

"Chill, Brown. That boy there, with the tattoos. Oi, don't stare!"

I casually turned my head. A supercute boy in blackspot sneakers was leaning on the side of a pool table, talking to his mates. I frowned, trying to zone in on what he was saying.

"Yeah, jus' make sure u don't tag a wall in ur white Nike hat, tracksuit, and Air Max 90s/BWs coz then you just look like a writer and cops know that shit."

I jammed Stace in the ribs. "I still don't know who it is."

Suddenly he looked up at us. "Oi, Sammy boy! Iz dat u?"

Stace whirled around to face Sam, hissed, "You know Mikey from *Tiny Chainsaws in the Distance*?"

Sam smiled and pulled us forward. "Yeah, it's me, Mikey. And this is Laura and Stace from the *angels*."

Mikey narrowed his eyes. "No shit. I heard good things bout u but the tour rep says u wuz a no-sho for the gig. How cumz?"

Stace muttered. "Cos we were all at the anti-UF march."

Mikey whistled. "Politicos. Huh." He rubbed his nose. "Tuff. Hope it wuz worth missin' a tour 4."

Suddenly she was right there in his face. "Yeah, it was. We sing about revolution and we do revolution and we ain't just one of those wimpy shallow pissy fake punky piece of shit groups that look pretty and do jack shit."

Another long silence. Then Mikey smiled. A long, lazy smile. "Well, Miss . . . ?"

"Dooney. Stacey."

"Stacey, a'ight. I like ur style an I see wot I cn do K? No promises but I'll put in some words." He nodded at Sam. "Come by my yard and do sum drawing, yeh?" And then he turned back to his mates. "Personally, when i go out to tag at nite, i put on a black bandana. But . . ." he held up a warning finger, "even so, I don't want to b 2

94

predictable so I change up my route an' my walls on a reg'lar basis . . . so's I cn pop up like a little ol' rat and do my ting any times I please."

I marched Stace over to the bogs. "What just happened to you?"

She shook her head in wonder. "Dunno. Think I was just chanveled by the Spirit of the Revolution. I feel super weak now."

"You wanna get some fresh air or something?"

"No, I wanna drink." She pushed me. "Fresh air? What's wrong with you?"

Called Adi, but no reply. Idiot.

## Wed., April 19

Today the Home Secretary gave the police *sweeping emergency powers* to deal with all protestors. He's even talking about freezing the carbon cards of any student proven to have been on the march. It's no good, I've got to get out of the Docks for a while. It's basically red hot here. I've left another message for Adi asking if I can go to his for a week or so till things chill out. Where the hell is he when I need him? Man, I really don't want to have to go home. The only good thing is it's Easter break next week so if I do have to go back, at least I can cover it up with a surprise holiday visit. Ha! My mind is always working.

## Sat., April 22

I don't believe today. Adi showed up at my place first thing. He banged on my door, shouting that there was going to be a raid, but before we had chance to get moving, the scream of sirens and alarms cut thru the air. We both ran to the window; armored riot vans were bombing into the Docks with feds already pouring inside the building opposite and the Excel Centre. There was a thudding noise from the 3rd floor walkway opposite. I looked over to see a group of police in padded vests bunched around a door.

"Shit, that's GPJ's place!"

5 officers with guns stood outside while a couple of others started to cut thru the metal with saws.

The walkway echoed with the sound of screaming metal. Adi scrambled toward the door.

"Where are you going?" I shouted.

"Got to do something. Can't just stay here."

I grabbed him. "And do what, Adi? They're kicking people's heads in." He pulled away, but I held tight. "What you wanna do, get beat like Nate? What's that going to prove?"

"I ain't no coward."

"Is that what all this is about?"

Strain, then I knew I'd won. He slumped down by the window.

By this time they'd hacked GPJ's door off its hinges. Screaming and shouting came from inside and then she was dragged out and slammed up against the wall, arms pulled back and wrists cuffed, her feet bare on the freezing concrete. Meanwhile, along the walkway, officers were throwing furniture, pictures, clothes—anything they could find—out of the doors and windows of the other flats. In a few minutes they'd lined up a big bunch of Docks residents, who they then kicked and pushed into the backs of vans. We could hear stuff happening at the Excel, but couldn't see what was going on. I sat there, waiting for the thud of boots on our walkway.

Then Claire called. "God, Laur—they've trashed The Dox Centre . . ."

"Are you safe? I thought you were sleeping there."

"No, I'm in Tano's place, by pure chance. Jesus . . ." Her voice cracked. "There was still hundreds hiding inside. Are you in danger?"

"For sure. I don't know why our block's not been hit, but it can't be long. Adi's here with me. We've got to get out of here."

"Tano says to just stay low . . . there's a news chopper circling overhead so the feds'll quit soon."

"Honest?"

"Yeah. Unless they wanna star live on YouTube. Wait till it's clear before you move. But where will you go?"

I sighed. "Abingdon."

"Shit."

"Yeah. What about you?"

"Dunno yet. Not my parents' that's for sure. They've pretty much disowned me. Nah, I'll find somewhere to hide down here."

"You sure? You can come up with me, you know?"

"I can't just run away . . . there's shit going down."

I counted to 3. Even in a life and death situation, Claire can still annoy the crap out of me.

"Got to go. Call me and let me know where you're at, OK?" I disconnected and turned to Adi. "Wait up while I get a bag together and then once it's clear we can go over to Kier's."

Adi looked at me. "Laura, I . . . ain't . . . I . . . don't know if I'm coming with you."

"What d'you mean?"

He tried to take my hand. "Can't live like this anymore, feels like I'm playing around at uni, in the band . . . when there's this reality going on."

"Jesus, Ad, is this **2** crap? I've totally backed off and given you space after Nate, but now you've got to be honest with me. Are you with them?"

He balled a fist. "I told you before, it's complicated."

"I feel like I don't know you anymore."

"It's still me, Adi. I'm not *with* any group. I just know I can't be like this any more. I need to go away . . . get my mind clear."

"Away where? And what about me?"

He jumped up. "I . . . don't have any answers, Laur. I know this sounds harsh, but you got to believe me that I love you."

"No shit, but you're still gonna leave? I've been here before, Adi. Remember?"

He grabbed my shoulders. "No way. You can't compare me to your ex, Ravi. I just need some space, some time. Please?"

I stared at him. Tears streaked his cheeks. And then, all of a sudden I couldn't feel anything anymore. I just went numb. I reached out and took his hands in mine.

"That's good. I understand. You take all the time you need."

"Really?" He dragged his fist across his eyes. "I mean, I ain't decided . . . I'm still thinking it thru."

"It's cool, honest. Look, I'm going up to my parents'. You work your stuff out then come up and see me and we'll talk then."

## Sun., April 23

It's midnight and here I am, sitting on my single bed in Abingdon, thanks to St. Kieran and his scooter of doom. I can't shake this numbness. I don't care about politics or action or fighting or anything. I'm going to sleep.

## Wed., April 26

3 straight days of sleep. I finally woke up this afternoon and found Kier perched on the end of my bed reading the paper.

I focused on him, slowly. "Mate, you still here?"

He glanced over. "Ooh. It stirs in its sickly broth."

"What time issit . . . ? I can't seem to wake up."

"4 in the afternoon." He held up the front sheet of the paper. "But check this out . . . Back in London students are locked up, beaten, terrorized, but don't think things aren't kicking off here."

# THE ABINGL

RESERVOIR HOLDS
*'BUSINESS AS USUAL'*
**- SPECIAL REPORT -**

Local swan dies    'Killer' Digger rams toddler    2-0 Shock Cup Defeat

## 'Get smart!'

By **Karen Mitchison**

Local schools have launched a crackdown on 'unnaceptable and lax dress code' in the area. In a press conference on Monday they announced: 'That as of today uniform rules will be followed to the letter. There will be no untucked shirts, no low slung trousers, no jewellery or make up.' Head teacher, Martin

Stewart added, 'we are increasingly concerned that students have no boundaries any more. Following the recent school riots in March, we feel we have no option but to crack down on wild and undisciplined behaviour before it spirals out of control.'

So far the student response has been muted, but all that is set to change if Ernest

Broomfield and Amina Lyons have their way. In only three days they have already set up a new defence campaign, **Smart Enuf** in defiance of the schools' plan. 'It's pathetic. Obviously they are trying to control us because they are frightened of what is going on in London,' said Amina, 'but dressing us like clones isn't going to help one bit.'

I squinted at the page. "Smart Enuf? I'm liking that."

Kier stabbed at the caravan ad. "And I'm *not* liking the Hot Caravan Offer. Is that where we're at now? We're rocketing back in time. Soon we'll be in the 60s, 50s, 40s . . . It'll be animal skins before you know it."

"The 40s to the Flintstones? You're jumping a bit ain't you?"

Kieran sighed. "The 40s was the War. What if we—"

"Don't." I dragged the duvet up around my neck. "It was always gonna be mad going into rationing."

"But like this? I've never seen anything like that UF march. I don't know if I want to be in London right now. It's too dark."

"But where else would you go?"

"I've had an offer to go to New York, to set up a Carbon-Dating thing. I mean, not exactly the same cos obviously they don't have rationing, but . . ."

I struggled up in bed. "New York? Really? How d'you even get there?"

"On a container ship."

"A *tanker*? You?"

Kieran folded the paper up. "I resent your tone, young lady. I'm not just some limp-wristed laydee traveler. I can slum it. Anyway, your mum believes in me, it's her that's been researching it all."

"I bet she has. Watch out or you'll find her in your luggage, mid-Atlantic."

Adi mailed me to say he's coming up next weekend. My heart went all hot when I saw his name in my inbox. Bastard.

## Thurs., April 27

This evening I made it downstairs and had a pretty woozy dinner with the parental units. They're kind of treating me like a sick person and not lecturing me, which is fine by me. The radio news was on, it was all about blocking loans for students who went on strike. Mum raised her eyebrows and Dad leaned back and flicked the station over to Classic FM. Got a message from Claire at midnight.

**Fri., April 28**

Dead emotional day. Kier left first thing—first to London, then on to New York as soon as he rents his flat out. I started to cry when he put his jacket on. "What, you've actually gone and bought the ticket?"

"I've booked the *passage*, darling. It's going to be so glamorous."

Mum began blubbing, too. "You'll be an emigrant! You'll get on that boat and never come back to us. I can't bear it. First Kim and now you."

"God, let the man go. It's only 8-days' travel," huffed Dad, before blowing the macho with a really high and quavery, "Good luck, my boy," and turning away, red-faced.

I went out to Larkin's pen and told him. He spat out half a spud in disgust; like he says, after all we've been thru together, Kieran's like family now.

## Sat., April 29

Today I caught Dad staring into space with glazed eyes in the middle of the yard. He looked like a man on the edge.

I squelched over. "What's up?"

He did a weird smile. "Hmm? Oh, nothing."

"Dad, c'mon—"

"Yoo-hoo!" Mum flung open her bedroom window. "What d'you think of this? It's for the reservoir picket." She waved a banner at us with: **HANDS OFF OUR WATER** printed across it.

He sighed. "Hold on to your hat. Your mum's gone radical again."

"You sure you're fine?"

He stretched his arms wide. "Yes, yes. Never better. Right, got to muck out the far pen."

I looked around and suddenly realized what was different. No pigs, except for Larkin and a small posse in a pen at the end. "Where've all the animals gone?"

"O-oh, sold mostly."

"Didn't the pig oil plan work?"

He shook his head. "No, not quite. Ah, well." He set off, before stopping mid-stride and reaching into his pocket for an envelope. "Oh, I forgot. This came for you this morning."

He watched as I ripped it open. "It's nothing serious, is it?"

I scanned it and folded it quickly. "No, Dad . . . s'just a library fine."

He smiled. "Well, keep that away from your mum. She's death on late books."

"Will do."

I watched him stride off thru the muck before opening the letter again. Oh shit.

# SUMMONS:

IN THE MATTER OF CAUSING PUBLIC DISTURBANCE 1/4/2017
Shoreditch High Street, Hackney, London E1
CCTV Footage Review

Dept of CO2 Rationing

rebuilding london

**London Metropolitan Police**

                                   Plaintiff    )

               v                                   )

**L Brown**
AshGrove Farm
Steventon
OX13 6RS                Defendant   )

## TO THE CHIEF OF LONDON METROPOLITAN POLICE

YOU ARE COMMANDED
To summon the above named defendant so that, within 20 days after service hereof upon defendant, excusive of the day of service, defendant shall serve upon Dunn & Mackenzie Esquire, plaintiff's attorney, whose address is 14th Floor, 1 Canada Square, Canary Wharf, London an answer to the complaint.

To serve upon defendant a copy hereof and of the complaint

Dated   29|3|17                Name

## TO THE ABOVE NAMED DEFENDANT

In the case of your failure, within 20 days after service hereof upon you, to serve on named plaintiff's attorney named above an answer to the complaint, judgement by default will be rendered against you in your absence.

## Sun., April 30

I called Claire and Stace to find out what the hell's going on down there, but neither of them are picking up. I'm not letting myself panic. I reckon the gov's just trying to frighten us; where's the proof I was on the march, or living in the Docks squat? All they'll have is some dodgy footage of the back of my head.

I forced myself to look at the worst-case scenario. Even if they freeze my loan and my credits, I can always ask my parents to cover me for the summer term. It's only a few months.

# May

## Mon., May 1

Bizarre and manic day with Mum.

I flicked open my lids this morning to see her pegging a line of dried fish to the wall above my head.

I blinked. "What's going on?"

"Hish shokery fudda illage."

"Eh?"

She took the last peg out of her mouth. "Fish smokery, for the village." Like this made any more sense than before. She straightened a withered head on the line. "Anyway, chop chop, you've lazed around long enough. Today we get to work."

"I don't think so."

She whisked the comforter off the bed. "It's either that or we join the May Pole Dancing Group as they welcome in the spring."

"Urggh."

Mum grinned. "So I'll see you downstairs in five minutes!"

She swept out of the room and I swung my legs onto the floor, willing myself to stay positive, but when I got downstairs it was like the set of a cable cookery show. Mum looked up from a book. "Smoking fish can be easy if you follow some basic steps! All you need is a smoker, fuel, and some fish." She bent over a diagram. "I've been doing hot smoking for months, but today we're going to try something new and set up a *cold smoker* with our old fridge. It says here: Time Required: 4 to 6 hours, Difficulty Level: Average. Hmm, no problemo."

I poked the fridge with my foot. "Didn't you only just get this thing?"

"Yes, but your dad went and replaced it with a bloody talking one."

"Eh?"

Mum waved her hands. "Well, it doesn't speak *English*, but it orders on-line for us when it gets empty."

"Honest?"

"Yes. *Driving* to the supermarket is so *passé* now, the fridge does most of the ordering on-line. It's very energy efficient, but really it's just another way for your father to sideline me. Anyway, let's get going, shall we?"

There were rows of scaly bodies on the kitchen counter, with blood oozing all over the place. Mum picked up some scissors and started clipping off their fins. "Can you make some brine, sweetie?" She turned to a chart on the wall. "Er, that's one tablespoon plain salt to one cup of water . . . One quart of brine for every pound of fish."

I stared at her. "Mum, it's me, Laura. Not know brine, not know quart."

"Salt water . . . twenty minutes per half inch of fish. Very simple." She nodded at a bowl and smiled. I know that smile, it's dangerous. I reached for the salt.

Some 10 minutes later I looked up from my miniature salt mine to see flames flickering from the old fridge. "Are you serious? You're going to set fire to it in here?"

She pursed her lips. "Well, the book says it's very safe, and I've made double sure I got rid of all the plastic parts. Now, I just connect up this tube . . . and yes, see? Smoke!"

I watched as, weirdly, smoke curled up into where the lettuce should be.

And so there we were, in a conveyor belt of happiness. Me, salting and racking up fish bodies on wire trays, and Mum slotting them into the burning fridge.

My eye traveled over the trays. "Where d'you get all these from, anyway?"

She glanced sideways. "Well, I *am* the regional coordinator of the Reservoir Defence campaign . . ."

I burst out laughing. "You're a total gangsta."

"Well someone's got to fight for keeping local water here and owned by us. Thames Water has already built one colossal reservoir and are now planning a second; like we're just a big glass of water for London any time it gets thirsty." She raised an eyebrow. "Anyway, I see myself more in the Robin Hood mode. Taking from the rich to give to the poor . . ." She checked a dial. "All right then, that's steady at 150, so we can leave it for a while."

"Does that mean I can go back to bed now?"

She sighed. "As you please, you awful teenage cliché."

I sank back down on the bed, started to drift away . . . but then weird noises filled my dreams . . . wailing . . . sirens . . . someone shaking me, hard. "Laura, get out, get up now!"

For a second I couldn't work out where I was; home, the Docks, the march . . . and then I leaped from the bed and ran down the stairs thru a haze of wicked oily smoke. Only when I got to the garden and saw the kitchen, all crowded with firemen, did I fully get it. How could I have gone to sleep with a lit fridge downstairs?

They left pretty soon. It wasn't much of a fire, but the house now smells like it's made of burned fish guts. I went over to Mum. She was sitting on the wall, head in hands. "Oh, God, your poor father. I was just trying to save us some money. This'll kill him."

I put my arm around her shoulder. "Oh, come on, don't be such a drama queen. You've been pulling stunts like this for years."

She dropped her head into her cupped hands. "No, it's different . . ."

"What is?"

"I'm . . . not supposed to tell you."

"What?

"No-o."

"Mum, if you don't, I'll fire up that fridge again and cold smoke you into hell."

She lifted her head. "OK, then. He's . . . we're . . . bankrupt!"

I stared at her. No more college, no more London, no more band.

She smiled faintly. "It was the pigs. Those bloody pigs did for us in the end. Swine fever and 50 dead in a week. Thank God Larkin survived, otherwise I think Nick really would've topped himself. Didn't you notice there's hardly any pigs around?"

"Well, yeah. Kind of," I mumbled. "But what are you going to do?"

"Don't know, we'll fight the bankruptcy and Dad'll have to get a proper job."

"Doing what? There *are* no jobs. Mum, why didn't you tell me?"

"We didn't want to worry you and . . . we'll get through, he's got his name down for a wind engineer retraining scheme up in Inverness."

"Scotland? That's forever away."

She shrugged. "But that's where the work is, with all those wind and wave stations going up along the west coast. I don't know if we have a choice . . . and . . . it won't be forever." She hitched up her trousers and put on a positive voice. "Come on, Laura, we'll be fine, our bank is nationalized for Christ's sake. By law they have to give us 6 months before they foreclose—we'll come up with something by then."

I'm up in my bedroom now and I feel so guilty. I am the ultimate selfish teenage stereotype. When she told me all I thought about was myself. If I was in the past now, I'd be going up chimneys to keep the wolf from the door.

There's no way I'm telling my parents about the summons now. Not that I know what's going on, anyway.

## Tues., May 2

I caught Mum and Dad at breakfast this morning and offered to quit uni and get a job to help them out. Dad fiddled with his cornflake spoon for a second, then jumped up, muttering: "Over my dead body, young lady. I . . . we . . . never . . . love . . . Laura!" then burst into tears and shot out the door. Mum just sat there, clutching a toast triangle. It's the first time I've ever shut her up.

I did mean it, but it's not like I'm Lady Di or something. There's a good chance I'm going be kicked out of uni, anyway, so I might as well stay here. Wait, what am I saying? Shit, shit, I can't move back here and smoke fish. But kids used to do it all the time. NO! Aaargh! I've left like a million messages for everyone and no one's getting back. Maybe they're all locked up. What am I gonna do?

## Wed., May 3

I was pacing around the garden when I heard Mum give a squawk of surprise from inside the kitchen—and then the back door opened and out stepped Claire Connor.

She flung her arms open. "Laur, I just had to get out of town, it's gone ultra hard core."

I froze. "Did you get the summons, too?"

"Mate, practically every student in London's gotten the summons."

"But how do they know who's done what?"

"They don't—but they're hauling everyone in and checking them off against ID cards and CCTV and fed footage from the march. You've got no idea how many hidden cams there are in town. Anyway, The Dox Centre is locked down, all the squats are raided . . . and my parents won't even answer the fone to me . . . I—I hate them." Suddenly her face collapsed. "I couldn't think of anywhere else to go but you . . . Can I stay here?"

"Course. Jesus."

I looked at her sobbing on the lawn. How did things get so messy?

Claire and me stayed up till dawn talking everything thru and we've made a definite plan. We've decided that there's no way we're going to the court summons—we were dead visible on the march and there's a good chance we'd be identified and have our carbon credits frozen. But if we don't attend then we can kiss good-bye to uni this year. It's a high price to pay, but it's the only way to keep out of trouble for sure. We're just going to have to wait for next September to re-enroll and pray they don't chase us down. *Everyone's* got the summons, but they can't go after every single kid in town.

I sighed. "Don't know how I'm going to sell this to my parents, tho."

Claire smiled. "Yeah, well I ain't told you everything—there is one good thing going on in our lives. Stace chased up Mikey from the Tinys and he called her yesterday to say the tour's been delayed and if we want it there's another trial gig in June."

"No way. Why din't you say? But what about Adi? He quit. In fact you quit, too."

Claire scuffed up her bangs. "We'll work it out. We always do. When's he coming again?"

"Keeps changing all the time. Was supposed to be this weekend, but he's put it off for a couple more days cos he's at some demo."

"What's going on with you guys?"

I shrugged. "If I knew I'd tell you. Adi's going thru some stuff and I . . . can't." I blew out my cheeks. "I dunno. I guess we've got some talking to do when he comes up."

"But you'll be OK, yeah?"

"Yeah. It's a bit like you and him. It always works out in the end."

I am such an excellent liar these days.

## Thurs., May 4

This morning I told Mum I didn't want to go back to uni, skillfully building up a beautiful image of the band in France and playing on the fear factor of London.

She frowned. "But what's gone wrong for you? You've never been scared before."

I shook my head "I just don't feel safe down there right now. Y'know with the riots, the feds . . ."

"But you're not in any trouble, though, are you?"

I fought to keep my voice non-squeaky. "Course not. I'd tell you, Mum." I forced myself to keep my mouth shut, knew silence was better than the BS that was likely to spill forth.

Mum tapped her fingers on the kitchen counter. "So, if you don't go back you've got a definite thing with this European tour?"

"As long as we can pass the trial gig."

"Well, can you?"

Fear whooshed up inside me, but this was no time for showing it. I had to make like a gazelle on the plains. Outface my opponent. "Yes, Mum. It's a great chance and if we're ever going to make it with the *angels* we've got to take things like this. The trial's in June, and we'll rehearse and get some part-time work to pay our way here."

"OK."

I jumped up. "Really?"

She held out a hand. "On two conditions. One, you promise to go back to uni in September. And two—you've got to really do it, not play around at it."

"Honest?" I took a deep breath. "But Mum, I meant it when I said I'd stay. If you and Dad really need me, then I'll do the band later."

She patted my hand. "Both you and Kim are adults now and I'm happy for you. Go and be radical, Laura Emmeline Brown."

I closed my eyes in pain. Why'd she have to bring that up? Anyway, our first priority is getting a job. We can start rehearsing next week when Stace and Adi come up.

## Fri., May 5

Hmm. Tough. Day 1 of job hunt and nothing. People are even fighting over those potato picker jobs farmworkers do. In desperation I scrolled down the au pair jobs. "OK, what about this one?"

**family assistant**

_date posted :_ _05/05/17_

Keen tennis player and cook to join us in our beautiful house with swimming pool and tennis court in Tuscany this summer. Must also hold full international driving license.
Duties would involve shopping some cooking and clearing up and playing tennis with the children.
We are all very relaxed and just keen on someone to muck in. Kids are 17 years 15 and 13 so not babies!
€300 per week

Mum came in and peered over my shoulder.

"What d'you reckon, Mrs. Brown?" asked Claire.

"Julia, please." Mum scanned the screen. "God, I'd forgotten people still lived like this. Well, if you want a summer of slavery and middle-class condescension, _respondez vous._"

Claire grinned. "You're well cool, Julia. I wish my mum'd chill out like you."

Huh.

### Sat., May 6

We've had no reply to any of our office job applications, not even an auto response, so today we went for catering stuff.

Claire made a call for an ad and got a trial for this place in the afternoon.

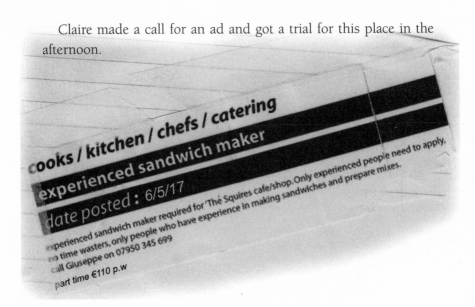

cooks / kitchen / chefs / catering

experienced sandwich maker

date posted : 6/5/17

experienced sandwich maker required for 'The Squires cafe/shop. Only experienced people need to apply. no time wasters, only people who have experience in making sandwiches and prepare mixes. call Giuseppe on 07950 345 699

part time €110 p.w

She's got some nerve, that girl. I overheard her describing herself as the *Queen of the Prawn Sandwich* just before she hung up. I frowned. "Really? I've never seen you make a sandwich in your life."

She snorted. "C'mon, how hard can it be?"

An image of her Docks kitchen flipped into my mind.

I didn't get any callbacks from my applications, so late afternoon I went down to the bus stop to meet Claire. The bus rumbled up, the doors slid back with a pssst, and she stomped out with a face like thunder.

"Oh," I said.

"Oh, is right," she growled as the bus rumbled away. "That Giuseppe was a total octopus, he kept touching me and taking my hands in his . . . *no signorina, we donta cutta lika dat we cutta lika dis.*"

"So you turned him down?"

Claire kicked a stone. "No, not exactly." Her face flushed red. "Laura, there were 2 other people there and . . ."

"What?"

"I dropped a sausage roll and when I tried to sneak it back on the shelf, Giuseppe told me to take off my apron and leave. I had to do this total walk of shame thru the café. I'm the lowest of the low . . . I'm a sandwich maker reject."

I blew out my cheeks. "You are such a loser."

She whirled around to face me, caught my eye, and we both started laughing.

"Yeah, but what are we gonna *do*?" Claire flapped her arms. "We've got to *live* while we get ready for the gig, can't just sponge off your parents."

"Keep trying, I s'pose."

Claire glared around at the surrounding fields. "What about farmwork? Somebody's got to pick all this . . . *green stuff*."

Someone named Amanda from Manhattan Style called me this evening. She said, "Here at Manhattan Style we are looking for fun, positive, outgoing young people who are raring to go the extra distance. Laura, does that sound like you?" I stared out at the pig yard, mind reeling. After about 20 seconds of silence, Amanda said, "I'll take that as a no then, shall I?"

Adi's texted me to say he's definitely coming up next Saturday. What if he wants to leave the band for real? Nah, that's just mad. What if he wants to leave me? Ooh, interesting case of brain shutdown.

## Sun., May 7

Dad says don't even bother thinking about farm jobs. He's just got work for 6 weeks driving a tractor, but that's cos it's his mate's place. "It's an old man's job really," he sighed, flexing his weedy biceps. "Forty-five and over the hill. Look at these old pipe cleaners. Rotten."

Mum glanced over. "It's time we stopped being so passive. Otherwise they'll keep on offering less and less money for the same jobs."

Dad sighed. "I know that, Ju, but . . . we've got to eat, haven't we? And if it gets out that—"

"What?"

"You know . . ."

"That I'm part of the Reservoir Defence? Oh, c'mon, Nick, you frighten way too easy."

Dad swished a piece of bread around his plate, swallowed it, and then licked his lips like a dingo.

I looked around us all at the table. We're poor.

## Tues., May 9

This came up today.

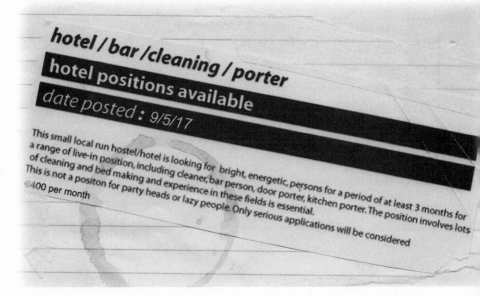

**hotel / bar /cleaning / porter**

**hotel positions available**

date posted : 9/5/17

This small local run hostel/hotel is looking for bright, energetic, persons for a period of at least 3 months for a range of live-in position, including cleaner, bar person, door porter, kitchen porter. The position involves lots of cleaning and bed making and experience in these fields is essential. This is not a positon for party heads or lazy people. Only serious applications will be considered €400 per month

Claire sucked her teeth. "*Party heads?*"

"I know, but they'll see us this afternoon. No one else has even got back to us."

"Where is it?"

I scanned the rest of the ad. "Er, The Ashes, about a mile outside Steventon. We can go on bikes."

* * *

We put the brakes on when we caught sight of The Ashes thru the trees. It was a huge old Victorian hotel, all gray stone and pointy roofs.

"Creepy." Claire nudged me. "Why do they need more workers? What happened to the last ones, huh?"

I did my best death-movie voice. "Murdered, cut up, and served as pork chops. *The Ashes*, a *Family Hotel*, coming to a theater near you."

We rode up to the main reception and went inside. It was kind of gloomy in there with a woman at the desk in her 50s with a ramrod back and no lips. Claire cleared her throat and the woman took her sweet old time looking up from her station.

"Can I help?"

"We're here about the job . . ."

The woman opened her eyes wide. "Aha, well I'm Mrs. Huckstable and you are . . ." she traced her finger down a sheet of paper, "Claire and Laura, I presume?"

We nodded, like peasants.

She turned, swished behind a curtain, and hissed, "Glenys!" before reappearing at the desk. "You have done this sort of work before, hmm? We are awfully busy. British hospitality is booming, of course, now that flying's off the menu." She smiled, showing a set of teeth like an old Welsh sheep. I willed myself to keep it together. I could feel Claire starting to giggle.

After a few moments the curtain flicked back and this . . . hag appeared, like from one of Kieran's soap opera shows. She was about half my height with a gargantuan mole on her chin and one solid overarching eyebrow. The mole was so big it was like it had its own ego, that *it* belonged on her neck and her face was just having a bit of a laugh on the side.

Mrs. Huckstable gushed, "I shall leave you in the capable hands of Glenys. She's been here *forever*, haven't you, cherie? Ha ha! So, girls, one-week trial, commencing tomorrow at eight thirty, ante meridian. We'll see what you're made of then, hmm?" She turned away,

117

leaving us with Glenys, leering at us out of her tiny squishy bluebot-tle compound eyes.

"Foller me, girrls."

We set off after her. First she led us outside and around the build-ing before ducking back inside thru a grimy doorway.

"Servants' entrance," whispered Claire.

We scampered together down miles of old rambly, dark corridors that got hotter and hotter until finally Glenys pulled out a set of keys and we filed into a dusty office that stank of hot-food air.

"Pooh." Claire fanned her nose.

Glenys whipped around and glared at us for a minute. She nod-ded at Claire: "Beds." At me: "Kitchun."

"We're not working together?"

A classic *evil laughter* look filled Glenys's eyes. "No, Princess, you're not. Any questions?"

We stared at our sneakers.

"Then jus' sign here an' you can go. Back 'ere at eight thirty sharp tomorrer."

Once we got outside, Claire grabbed me. "I'm scared."

"Yeah, pork chops are too big. Our DNA'd be written all over 'em. It'll be *mincemeat* for us."

She looked at me with proper fear in her eyes. "Let's go. Now."

"We can't," I hissed. "400 euros. 1 month. We can do it."

Job! We've got a job! Now on to phase 2: Get Stace and Adi up here and fix this band up good and proper.

## Wed., May 10

I got to The Ashes at 8:15 and the kitchen was like a total scene out of hell. It was a massive room, sweltering in the shade cos of a huge row of ovens blasting out, with a gang of chefs chopping, stirring, whisk-ing, pouring, and all the time screaming at a group of sloppy waiters, balancing trays, pots, jugs, wine bottles all over their bodies.

I was put on this conveyor belt of steaming pots that rolled out of a giant cleaning machine. As soon as I'd grabbed all the clean plates and bowls and cups from one end and stacked them up, I had to run around the other side and load the dirty ones in. At first I was dead slow and once I dropped a pile of saucers, and they had to press the red panic button, forcing the machine to a grinding stop. The head chef charged up and loomed over me. Everyone stopped working to enjoy the show.

"Look at this *idiot!*" he shouted. "This is type of girl they sendin' me. Why you no in college?"

"I'm on a gap year," I mumbled.

"Hah! You hear that? The girl is on gap year." He threw his hands up in the air. "Well, that's for sure. You jus' keep a big gap from me is all and don' let me catch you messin' up this goddamn machine again. Got it?"

I nodded. Forcing myself not to cry, I plunged back into the steam. At lunchtime this other chef told me to stop working and eat, but after all the adrenaline and screaming I couldn't even swallow one mouthful.

It chilled out a bit for a couple of hours after that, but then came dinner. I've never known madness like that before. Hieronymus Bosch could've just put down an easel and sketched us, straight off. Running, dropping, colliding, shouting—drenched in sweat—slipping, sliding, never catching up. And the bitching—the second chef was totally at war with the head waiter, and the waitresses were all out to kill the sous chef cos he slept with a waitress and never called her, but that was nothing to how much they hated us, the *washing-up and trash crew*. We're the total bottom of the feeding chain—there is no lower life-form. They stomped us into tiny pieces of dirt under their heels and then made us sweep ourselves up. I never knew people could be that bad to each other. And then at 8, suddenly everything stopped and all of us just collapsed on the floor and lay in the brown disinfectant swill, not caring. The head chef dragged a crate of beer into the middle of the washup room. He pulled a bottle out, grinned, and passed it to me.

"Good job, mouse . . . now take a beer and chill out!"

And everyone popped a cold one like best buddies.

Bizarre.

## Thurs., May 11

All is dark. My arms and legs are lifeless stumps. I can't remember any good times, the feel of sunshine on my skin, the sound of children's laughter. When I close my eyes I see steam and white plates, bowls, cups, and saucers mashing down on me.

## Fri., May 12

Heard nothing on the court summons. I reckon as long as we keep low they won't chase us. Got to keep positive!

Adi tomorrow. Good thing is I'm too wiped out and scared about other things to be scared about him.

## Sat., May 13

I cycled over and met him at the train station. He looked just the same. Don't know why I was expecting him to be different. He waved from the end of the platform and came running down to me. My heart lifted. It was all going to be all right. Then I looked at his face and I knew. For a second I thought I was going to black out.

"Laura! Hey!" Adi grabbed my hand and led me over to a station bench. He kneeled down in front of me, took a deep breath. "I've made my mind up. I'm going away . . . I'm no good for you right now. And we both know it."

"But, Adi, you can't do this—it's not just *me*—it's the band. We're finished without you."

"C'mon, I was shit for ages. Claire's right. You're better off with someone who cares. Loads of kids'd kill for the chance."

He started to blur in front of me. "But you can't go, you're, we're *us*."

Adi flung his arms around me. "I know . . . I . . . don't know why I'm hurting you . . . but I can't live like this no more!"

And then for a while we clung to each other, sobbing, on a bench on Didcot Parkway Platform 1, with commuters getting on and off their trains around us.

I pulled away. "But where will you go?"

"With the Red Cross to Sudan. This senior guy from the anti-UF campaign has hooked me up with them, says I'm the best organizer he's ever seen. Tano's going with me as far as Sicily. There's a colossal refugee crisis there cos of the drought in Africa—thousands every week are smuggling themselves into Europe thru Italy, Spain, Greece—and he's going over to help."

"But when are you coming back?"

He sighed. "I ain't sure. Few months?"

"But we can't go on like this. Are we together or split up?"

He took my hand. Long pause. "I don't suppose you wanna come with me?"

"O-oh, Adi. I'm just not ready for that shit."

"You sure?"

I nodded, slowly.

The platform P.A. burst into life as the London train pulled into the platform.

I took a breath. "Come on, I don't want to cry in front of any more strangers. We can talk about this later at the house."

He ran his hand over his face. "No, I—I'm not coming back with you. I can't handle it."

I whirled around. "You're going to get back to London, now? That's it? An hour on a platform is all I'm worth?"

"Laura, we've said everything. My feelings for you ain't changed, but it's not fair what I'm doing, so it's up to you if we're over now."

And then he sprinted down the platform, across the bridge, leaped on the train and left.

Everything's black.

## Sun., May 14

I cried all day. At one point at work I was crying so much my tears and the steam joined together and formed soap clouds over me. Claire's been really cool and just backed off, but I just couldn't deal with my family, so this evening I sort of dragged myself down to the end of the garden and slumped down by the hedge. I'd only been there a few minutes, though, when I heard footsteps: Dad trudging back from his job. He looked up in surprise.

"Laura, why are you weeping by the compost heap? I thought you had more style."

I laughed and stuff came out my nose. "Don't."

He clambered over the fence in his old wellie boots and came and sat beside me. "Adi?"

I nodded. "He's gone away . . . doesn't want to be with me . . ."

"Really? Did he say that?"

"No-o. He *says* he still loves me . . . but he's gone . . . away to Sudan, says he can't just stay here doing nothing. So it's just words, Dad."

Dad kicked at the mud on his left boot. "Well, no it's not."

"How isn't it? He's leaving me just like Ravi did. They just get tired of me . . . why can't they be . . . honest and say it, 'stead of . . . making up some—"

Dad laughed. "Exotic holiday plan? You must frighten them half to death if they have to leave the country to get away from you! C'mon, Laura. Look outside yourself a bit. There are big pressures. In fact if I was your age I might be tempted to do what Adi's doing."

"So you think I'm shallow cos I wanna be in a band and . . . anyway . . . it's all a big fat ego trip, this *helping people* anyway."

He sighed. "Not always. Forgive me for saying this, but maybe you need to stop judging people who do things differently from you. There isn't only one way."

"I can't see *any* way that works."

He put his big woolly sweater arm around me and drew me close. "All right, then, creature of doom, just give it time. If you really love him, give it time. And in the meantime get on with your own life and stop feeling so sorry for yourself."

I pulled away a bit. "Dad, are you doing tough love on me?"

He threw his head back and laughed. "Aaargh! I'm channeling your mother."

I couldn't sleep last night, and so finally I went downstairs and pulled a Coke from the fridge and went outside into the cool garden. There was a big moon hanging over the roof and it was dead peaceful. I thought about Adi, where he was *right now*. It's all just so confusing. He's right, we were stuck and everything's changed so fast. I know he loves me and . . . it's just I can't lose him. He's Adi, he's on the inside.

Suddenly I heard the back gate creak and footsteps crunch up the gravel. I pulled back behind a bush. A figure, in a sweatshirt with the hood pulled down low, moved carefully toward the door . . . and then stopped and turned to face the moon. Mum! What the hell's she been up to?

When I went back upstairs, I found Claire crying.

"Mate, you OK?"

"No-o. Adi's gone and I'm scared and we can't do it without him, but I don't wanna—"

"What? Hassle me cos of what I'm going thru?"

She smeared her sleeve over her face. "Well, yeah."

"He asked me to go with him, y'know."

"No way. I thought you two were finished."

Suddenly things went all clear. I smiled. "Claire, I don't know what we are, but me and Adi ain't done with each other. Not by a long shot."

She flopped back down. "Well, one thing's for definite, the tour's finished."

"I know."

I sank back down on to the bed and we both lay there in the dark. Silent.

## Mon., May 15

We are zombies. This morning at 10 the kitchen doors were flung open and Claire was marched in by Glenys and put on *slops* cos she was busted sleeping on a bed in the "Gladstone" wing. I could hardly stand to see her. They'd dressed her in a trash bag and she looked tiny, her hands a blur as she scraped plates and dumped Tupperware full of gloop into an incinerator, like in a Karl Marx nightmare. I kept expecting to see her throw herself into the grinder.

Laur
im gone! 5 am &
 on boat 2 france.
its bare cold & 3 kids next me pukin
up sogoin up top in aminute. plan is
cross from sicily then on 2 africa.
. Laur, it feelsgood 2 b movng, going
somewre.. i don kno what else to say i kno u
hate me rite now an im missin u like crazy
get on tour wi Angels im so proud of u

A x

**Tues., May 16**

And how the hell am I gonna do that since he's bailed on me? After my Zen moment the other night, I now find I keep flipping into anger. Deep anger. And then I'm happy for him again. Don't know if I'm going to mail back or not. What do I say?

**Wed., May 17**

Another bad day at work. Claire's eyes look like a pony's that's reached the end of the line. Like Ginger in *Black Beauty*.

## Thurs., May 18

We had dinner with Mum and Dad tonight. The news was on, some really depressing story about how Colorado is refusing to let its winter river water run out of the state cos its farms and cities are all drying up. The governor came on screen, surrounded by state police, saying he refuses to release any more precious water while the Arizona Central Project just blows it all on swimming pools and golf clubs and fake lakes in gated communities. The screen then cut to some aerial footage of endless flat American fields, covered in a white shimmering layer.

Claire frowned. "What's that?"

Dad glanced up. "Salt. Caused by irrigation. Basically each time water leaves the river, flows around a field and then returns, it picks up salt from local rocks. So the riverwater just keeps on getting saltier and saltier, and in the end the land dies." He reached for the pepper. "That's what happened to the Mesopotamians in the end."

Mum snapped. "Never mind that. Look at the drought in Africa now, one year and counting. Not to mention Israel, Chile, Brazil, Spain, China, Australia, Pakistan . . . And don't get me started on the Midwest—the amount wasted on farming back home is horrific."

I glanced at her; sometimes I forget she's from the States.

Mum drummed her fingers on the table. "I've been doing research for this Thames Water court case we've got coming up." She turned to Claire. "Did you know the U.S. government sells farmers water at ten cents per thousand gallons?"

Claire mumbled. "Is that cheap?"

"You bet it is . . . and so all those Midwest farmers do is waste it, basically pour it straight into the soil to grow stupid crops that don't belong there—it's been going on for 20, 30, 40 years. And they wonder where all the water's gone. It makes me so mad!"

Silence. Mum glared around the table. None of us was looking good; all stooped around the table, gray-faced, communicating in grunts. She suddenly scraped her chair back and jumped up. "Stop it, all of you! I can't stand it anymore."

We looked up with stupid faces.

"I . . . we . . . are not going to let ourselves go under." She pointed at me and Claire. "Look at you two, what happened to the band? Just cos Adi's gone! You're not just going to quit, are you? The deal was that you did something with your lives, not take a year off. Otherwise you can go back down to London right now and finish the summer term." Claire pushed a spud around her plate, said nothing.

A flicker of a smile crossed Dad's face. I think he likes having someone else around to share being shouted at.

## Fri., May 19

When we finished work tonight, Mum was waiting for us by the iron gates of The Ashes.

"Come on."

"Mum, just leave it, all right?"

She snorted. "On your bike, missy."

We were too tired to fight so we set off behind her. We wheeled down the hill . . . and at the bottom Mum braked . . . and there, slouching against the bus stop was Stace . . . and behind her, Sam.

Claire gazed at them. "What's going on?"

Mum turned to her. "This is your band. This is your dream. Get on that European tour and LIVE IT." Then she pedaled off into the dusk.

Stace jerked her thumb at Sam. "Found this one in a Hare Krishna free food line. He plays pretty good."

"But—" I began.

Sam spread his hands. "I know, I ain't Adi. If you want me to go, then just say the word and I'm on the next bus back." He was so thin and pale, couldn't control a tremble in his chin.

Later on we sat in the garden and stared at each other.

Stace drummed her fingers. "The gig's on June 4. That's just over 2 weeks, which is tight, anyway, but now we've lost Adi . . . Can we do this? Seriously?"

Claire shrugged. "Basically it's down to Sam."

Sam gave a bark of laugher. "No pressure, huh?"

"But can you do it?" I asked.

He looked at me straight. "Either that or I'll die trying. Uni's totally messed up for me, too."

We all looked at each other, hardly daring to hope.

Stace growled, "Oh, pass me my sticks, please, before someone starts crying."

And so we did our first practice, right there in the garden. Stace drumming on an old snare she left here years ago and the rest of us unplugged, like a tragic folk band.

I finally mailed Adi. Just a couple of lines, nothing big. I ain't getting into any emotional stuff till I know what I really feel. It was weird, but I felt kind of guilty in practice, like I was cheating on him, even though there's totally nothing going on with me and Sam.

## Sat., May 20

The court summons date is today, but still we've not been contacted. No chase, no calls. It's clear the gov can't handle the sheer number of prosecutions. Maybe we should've just gone back, faced them down. Anyway, too late now. It's the tour or nothing.

When we got back from work we found that Dad had helped Sam and Stace set up a tent in the back garden to sleep and a practice space inside one of his dead pig pens.

Stace caught our look. "Yeah, I know, if you'd told me a month ago I'd be grateful to be rehearsing in an ex-pig's bathroom I'd've laughed my head off, but Laura, your parents are total lifesavers. At least they've given us a chance to pull this *angels* shit off. There's no way we could've done this in London. People are losing it big time, hiding out, staying away from uni."

Sam nodded. "S'true."

"My flatmate, Petra, was weird to begin with and now she's gone proper medicine mad. I came home the other day and she was sticking scotch tape all over her head and pulling it off. I tried not to ask her why for all of *EastEnders* before I finally got the courage. I went, "'What are you doing? You're gonna pull all your hair out, mate.'"

"What she say?"

"She threatened to kill me if I asked her any more questions."

"She probably watches you sleep," I said.

Stace flipped a stick up in the air. "It's no joke. Yesterday someone called me twice, unknown number, right? The second time they left a voice mail of music from *The Nutcracker*. I'm gonna be murdered, guys. A victim of mental breakdown caused by state-sponsored police oppression."

It's so spooky playing without Adi, kind of like we've lost an arm or something. We keep turning to Sam and going *no, the other thing* or *like how we did it on mp3?* and he just stares at us. In no time we turned him into a nervous wreck.

I shucked my bass strap off my shoulder. "Look, this isn't fair. We'll teach him the parts bit by bit on his own, then pull it all together after."

Sam dropped to his knees. "Aaargh! I suck!"

Stace stared at him. "Nah, mate. S'just too much pressure. But do me a favor and get off the pig floor. I've got to sleep next to you in a tiny tent."

## Mon., May 22

Yesterday at work, 2 trash cleaners, the people who basically climb inside the million ton industrial bins and wallow around with the kitchen waste, walked out (surprise) and Glenys asked me if I knew anyone who could cover at short notice. So now Sam and Stace are the new wallowers. They're even lower down the order than us—we can't be seen talking to them on our shift.

I went out with Claire on her cig break at lunchtime.

She took a sharp drag and gasped, "Look!"

I turned. Sam was perched on the side of a trash can, practicing his parts on the metal edge with his fingers.

"Mate, we'd better get this tour, otherwise he'll be traumatized for life."

## Tues., May 23

When I got home, Mum was hooked up in the kitchen talking to her sister in the States. She waved me over. "Hey, Carol, Laura's just walked in. Wanna say hi?"

I reached for the mic. "What's going on over there? Are you guys at war or something?"

Carol sighed. "I was just telling your mom, it's not exactly a war, but it's a battle, all right. They've mobilized the state police on both sides and the National Guard are out patrolling the irrigation blocks."

"Over a river?"

"Tell me about it. I mean, this is the USA, the *homeland*. We aren't poor, we're not meant to pick up sticks in the thousands and cross state lines, like immigrants. But . . . this drought's changed everything."

Mum shook her head. "I just don't understand how they let it get so bad."

"Julia, it's like everything else; it din't start out bad. Back in the 20s they shared the Colorado River. Upstream you had Colorado, Utah, Wyoming, and New Mexico, and downstream there was California,

Arizona, and uh . . . a bunch of others. And all of them ever since pouring water into the dirt and building sprawls where people had no right living. Sure, in the past we had our dry spells, even bad droughts sometimes, but then a wet year and a cold year would come along, and between the ice melting and the rain, the lakes and rivers would fill up again. But now the wet years are gone, just gone."

## Wed., May 24

I practiced with Sam tonight; he's nailed 4 songs. At one point, he dropped his pick and when I bent down to get it, our hands touched and I felt a bit tingly. What am I thinking? It's way too complex. Plus, super obvious—like I just upgraded my old guitar boyfriend for the new version. Plus plus I don't know if it's just me with the tingles. Plus plus plus I'm still going out with Adi, aren't I? Get hold of your-self, Brown.

## Thurs., May 25

Mad life. As if I'm 16 again and living at home. It's a bit like those dreams where you're at college and everything's normal, but then suddenly you're in the canteen and you look down and you've got no underwear on.

## Fri., May 26

Stace's been upgraded to the kitchen so we can fraternize again. It's so hot in there that we're meeting in the walk-in fridge on breaks to practice. When I went down this morning, I found her hugging a hanging piece of beef to cool down faster.

Adi sent me a really long, lovely mail about Sicily and missing me, and he was all full of hope for the future, *our* future. It made me feel really bad reading it—I'm so shallow compared to him. Anyway, it's made me sort my head out re Sam. I ain't going to let it go any-where. It's just too disrespectful to Adi.

## Sat., May 27

We had our first proper whole group practice tonight . . . and we sound . . . weird. Sam's got a totally different style from Adi, more wild. In *Manifesto* we'd blasted into the chorus:

```
The men in gray
Stole the truth today
It's in their manifesto
To return it some day . . .
```

when Sam suddenly shoved in this big chonk of feedback.

Claire turned, shouted. "What the—"

Sam cut the sound. "Huh?"

"Why you do that for?"

"Dunno." He grinned suddenly. "Just felt good."

And then all of us cracked up. I hate to say it but its only since he's gone I've realized what a downer Adi was in the band.

At the end we went thru plans for next week. Basically the gig is next Sunday—but the thing is, even if we get the tour, we won't leave till the 15th, so we want to come back up and get another week's cash. Me and Claire won't even get paid for our month from The Ashes till after the gig, cos we get paid by the month. We'll get something on the tour, of course, but Stace says it'll be peanuts, more like beer and cig money. *So* . . . we've basically got to get all 4 of us away from work for 2 days and not get busted.

Claire shook her head. "It'll have to be a military operation to get this past Glenys. She can *smell* slacking."

Stace narrowed her eyes. "It'll have to be Mass Food Poisoning, then."

"Oh, c'mon. So obvious."

Stace started playing a military drumbeat. "In the hands of a lesser person maybe. But you got Private Stacerooni behind you now and I've run this kind of outfit before. PBS. We *Prepare* the ground, we *Build* the symptoms, and we *Stagger* the casualties."

"You really know how to do this?"

"Sir, Yessir!"

Claire picked up her mic. "Then you're in charge. Now let's get back to it. If we ain't ready then it don't matter how much salmonella chicken biryani we fake puke."

## Sun., May 28

Practiced all day. We are def getting there.

## Mon., May 29

Work. Practice. Watched the news. Why is it always so depressing? Today was all about the drought in Africa. How it's getting out of control, millions on the move.

## Tues., May 30

Same, same.

## Wed., May 31

Final rehearsal before Operation PBS and we smacked it! We stormed thru the set and nailed each track. Tight as a drum. Sam chopped off the last chord and looked up at us.

"So?"

We looked around at each other. We're ready.

Aaaaarrrgggggh! I can't let myself hope.

# June

**Thurs., June 1**

Stace lined us up in my room this morning for Phase 1. *Prepare.*

She squeezed a chunk of Mum's Shiseido under-eye bag concealer into her palm. "OK, so let's get pale lookin'. No big drama today, this is preparation for *Build*. All we want is to look a bit dodgy and it'll pay off beautiful tomorrow afternoon when, after an excruciating day of cramps, Claire and Sam will go home sick. People, why only Claire and Sam?"

"Because of *Stagger.*" I replied, straight off.

She curled the corner of a lip. "Ha! Glad you got all your pistons firing, Brown."

Everything went according to plan, and we all got back from work in good form, but just as we jumped off our bikes, the air suddenly erupted with screams—Mum!

I froze. "What the—"

But Sam and Stace had already legged it around the side of the house. I got all tangled up in my bike and by the time I got around there, Sam was wrestling with one fat dude while Stace was climbing on the back of another, punching him like mad. The garden was covered piles of our stuff—TV, dishwasher, solar charger, Smart Meter—and in the middle, Mum and Claire were racing around trying to drag everything into one big mound. Mum turned and waved an iron in Sam's wrestler's face. "You get off my property, you bastard!"

The guy shook Sam off and backed away down the path, shouting at his partner. "C'mon, mate, let's get out of here. We'll come back later with the team!"

"I dare you! I'll bring the village down on you!" shrieked Mum.

He turned to her, chest heaving. "Mrs. Brown. I have a court order. The only way we're not coming back is if you pay what you owe."

And then they were gone. We all sat there in silence.

Finally Claire cleared her throat. "Mrs. Brown . . . I get paid soon, if you'd . . ."

Mum burst into tears. "Oh, God. How did it all go so wrong?"

How can I leave them like this?

## Fri., June 2

I got up dead early so I could talk to Dad alone. I found him pulling on his boots at the back door.

"Dad?"

He glanced at me. "Second time in two weeks? Are you mistaking me for one of those modern caring dads with parenting skills?"

"I'm serious."

"Then come on, there's something I need to check up on the high back pasture."

We set off across the damp fields.

"Where are we going?"

"To look at my new dew pond. This old boy from the village helped me set it up, it's some ancient secret process, not quite sure how it works except that it's a way of harvesting water in the air. It kind of captures tiny water droplets in passing clouds and fog, and in the morning—bingo—the pond's full of water."

I sighed. "But what's going on, really?"

"Er, I told you I'm not sure of the ins and outs, but the key to it is the hilltop location, because as the air rises it cools and cold air holds less moisture. Forget Africa being in drought—there's been precious little rain in Europe this year, and I want to make sure we've got a viable source of water."

I turned to face him. "Quit stalling. I mean with . . . the bankruptcy. Are we going to lose the house?"

He shook his head. "I hope not. I'm hoping to get an eco-building apprenticeship in Oxford. If all goes to plan, in six months I can be earning again."

"But Mum said you might have to go to Scotland."

"I really hope not. 50% of all houses in the county need to be rebuilt from the ground up to get them fully green by 2020, so there should be work for me here."

"Yeah, but, Dad, will the bank wait for 6 months? Those guys yesterday didn't look very patient."

He sighed. "I don't know. After the bank crash of '09, it's been almost impossible to predict what they'll do, but I've got to try and negotiate something. Businesses are going down and homes being repossessed all around us, that's for sure, but I'm not going to give up."

"I can't go away with you in this mess. I'm gonna tell the others today—"

"No!" His shout carried weirdly across the field, bounced off some rocks. "That's not how it's going to be. I want, I *need* for you to be living your own life. It can't just be about survival." He looked at me. "Things can't have become so desperate . . . And Arthur, he wouldn't want you to give up like that."

"Don't," I said, biting back a choke.

We reached for each other; hugged dead tight.

"I think about him all the time."

"Arthur?"

Dad nodded. "Me too. It's strange, I keep finding myself thinking, don't panic, Nick, what would *he* do now?"

"I know . . ."

"Go, Laura. He'd want you to. Otherwise what's it all for? But be careful, France is all over the place now."

"Politically, you mean?"

"Yep, the right wing, the *Front National* are gaining power."

I sighed. "Great. Isn't there anywhere normal anymore?"

"No. Extremism is on the rise. Germany and the Scandinavians are swinging toward a kind of green collectivism and meanwhile the neo-Nazis are making huge gains in France and Italy. Plus Spain's almost ready to go to war with France over the Ebro River. It's either share out all we've got or it's protect your own at all costs." He grinned. "It makes a change from all the parties being the same, at least."

"I hate politics."

"That's because you think it's got nothing to do with you."

"It doesn't. Bunch of gray men."

Dad gazed at me, thoughtful. "Hmm, we'll see. Now get on with your plans. Aren't you on *Stagger* today?"

"How d'you know about that?"

He rubbed his nose. "I know a lot of things. Watch out for us quiet ones, Laura, we're the most dangerous kind."

Claire and Sam came home sick this afternoon and picked up the train tickets to London on the way back. God, the world has shrunk so much, it's like we're going to the moon. Our turn for the shakes tomorrow!

## Sat., June 3

I don't believe what's just happened. It was about 4 this afternoon and Stace and me were practically winning an Oscar for our stomach cramp simulation, when Glenys marched into the kitchen and tapped me on the shoulder.

"Office. Both of yer. Now."

We followed her into the room. Mrs. Huckstable was sitting at the desk, toying with a pepper grinder like a James Bond villain. "It's come to my attention that that all of you are miraculously experiencing stomach pains. Hmm?"

I gazed at my washing-up gloves.

"But we're genuinely sick—there's a bug going around—" began Stace.

"Stop lying, girl. It has also reached my ears that four return train tickets for London have been purchased for tomorrow morning. Unfortunately for you, Glenys's sister, Carys, is the lady who sold your friends the tickets. As she has seen you working here, she mentioned it to her Glenys, who brought it to *my* attention."

I kept my focus on my pink marigolds. Bloody village people.

And then the H bomb cleared her throat. "May I make it perfectly clear that if by any chance all of you are *off sick* tomorrow, then you can consider your position here terminated. *Without pay.*"

Stace gasped. "You can't—"

Mrs. Huckstable gave a tinkly laugh. "I think you'll find that fraudulent absenteeism is a sackable offense. And as such the terms and conditions of employment and payment are dissolved."

"But we've slaved here for weeks . . ."

"You have worked here of your own free will and next Wednesday is your first scheduled monthly payday. Unless, as I say, you are all mysteriously absent tomorrow."

I thought Claire was gonna have a brain implosion when we got back with the news. She clutched her head and screamed. The rest of us stared around at each other, grim.

Sam kicked the ground. "What the hell are we going to do? Those train tickets cleaned us out."

Stace growled. "Torch the place."

"Yeah, but it won't get us any funds. They've screwed us over big time."

I balled my fist. "I don't care. We're going even if we've got to beg on the streets. Nothing can get in the way of this gig. Right?"

We all started to pack in gloomy silence.

## Sun., June 4
*Jour du* Gig!

London. We stepped out of Paddington Station in the rain at 8 this morning, and the first thing we saw was a massive **2** sign, sprayed on the wall.

I whistled. "Hard core."

Stace grinned. "Told you, the place has gone well radical."

In just 5 weeks all the people I know have gone. The Docks are locked down, Kier's gone to New York, Tano to Sicily, GPJ's arrested, Eman's vanished, Claire's parents won't see her, even Stace's aunt has told her she can only come back if she goes back to uni. I don't know if Nate's still around, I've messaged him to come to the gig but haven't heard anything back.

We pooled our funds on the train, € 22, nothing basically. The day stretched out in front of us like a damp nightmare. We made our way over to Camden and hung around the market, then when it got too wet we sat in a café, but they chucked us out after a couple of hours of nursing a cup of tea, so we went and sheltered under some shop awnings before being moved on again by one of those plastic police, a fat woman in a park uniform who looked at us like we were criminals. "Don't you have places to be?" she asked, flecks of mayonnaise around her soft lips. We din't get into it, just shuffled on like tramps.

At 5 we were finally allowed inside the club. There were 2 rooms, one of them for electro sets and the other for guitar bands. The producers' monster beats were booming out from the other side of the wall, but on our side it was total chaos, cos the sound guy had just been arrested that afternoon in a sweep on an estate in Brixton. Everyone was now forced to use the same amps and stuff, and once we got onstage and plugged in, it was a nightmare. My bass sound was out of control; I flicked the E string and a great slab of low-end throb pulsed out thru the flabby speaker. Meanwhile Sam's guitar sounded like cats clawing a pile of tin cans. I couldn't even hear Claire. She was going 1, 2 . . . 1, 2 . . . but no sound was coming thru. We stood there, helpless . . . trapped in a cage of swirling bad noise. I saw her eyes start to fill up, then suddenly from behind the stage appeared Emanuel, rising up like Jesus on the concrete steps.

"Uh . . . uhm . . . yeah! I like . . . could check . . . er . . . you guys . . . yeah?"

Claire practically jumped into his arms. "Eman! How come you're here? Thought everyone had left town?"

He shrugged. "Nah . . . uh I'm like the, totally . . . uh original . . . ah . . . underground . . . uh sound man. Can't . . . like uh . . . make me . . . uh . . . leave town."

Claire clutched him like a drowning soul. And so Emanuel climbed up into the mixing booth, his fingers flicking and twirling like crazy mosquitoes over the dials, and a few minutes later we smashed our way thru *WKD* and it sounded like us.

Stace blew out her cheeks. "Cool. Now all we gotta do is do it." She winked at Sam. "You're gonna be good. Don't stress."

Sam didn't say anything; his face super pale.

After the check we went outside. By this time there was a pretty decent crowd, all crushed behind barriers and stomping and falling on cans and water bottles. This bouncer guy reached across Stace and tapped an electro skater kid on the arm.

"Oi, oi, you feller. I told yer drop the beer can or I drop you."

The kid let go of the can straight onto Stace's foot. She poked him. "What you do that for?"

He shrugged, eyes slitted like a dead shark. Those electro kids are plugged into the mainframe or something.

I scanned the crowd. "Is Mikey's promoter guy here yet?"

Stace shook her head. "No. He's coming, tho. I can feel it."

Claire grabbed my hand. "He's gotta come or else."

"Don't even say it."

She nodded. "Let's go and jack a beer."


We sat and watched the first couple of bands from the back, getting more and more wound up with each song.

Claire groaned. "Too much strain. Where is this guy?"

A girl weaved thru the crowd, saw us, and stopped. Then she leaned forward, right into Claire's face. "I jus wanna say girl power in a male-infested world." She looked from me to Claire, went, "Right?" and disappeared into the crowd again.

I smiled. "Infested? I like that," but Stace suddenly grabbed me. "He's here!" she hissed, flicking her head in the direction of the bar. Me and Claire both turned.

"Oh, my God!" cried Claire.

"Is that—"

Claire nodded.

Stace turned to look again. "Wha, wha? That's the promoter, right?"

"Yeah, but that woman with him . . . with the massive pearl earring is . . . Suzi K."

"But she destroyed us in her last review! Shit, shit." Stace stomped the ground.

Claire looked at me. "We're finished."

I looked back direct into her eyes. "Hey, I just wanna say girl power in a male-infested world. Suzi's going to come good for us tonight!"

Claire burst out laughing. "You got style, LB. Where's Sam? It's time we got backstage."

I can't hardly remember the set. It's just a smear of adrenaline and fast chords. Sam, fingers blurring between changes. Claire stage diving in *twist n doubt*. Stace smashing her stick thru the snare skin. My fingers, gripping the neck of my bass like a psycho killer, hitting every note perfect as Claire screamed:

```
I see no freedom
I see only exploitation
Leaders growing fat
On the cheating of a nation.
```

After it was over I felt sick. I found my way to the toilets, went in a cubicle, and locked the door. The electro bass set was so loud it was shaking the whole line of stalls. I put my head in my hands and breathed, deep. Suddenly the bathroom door opened. Someone was crying. Then screaming my name. I said nothing. Didn't want to know.

Claire kicked my door. "Laura, I know that's you, I see your sneakers. You got to come out and face it."

"I don't wanna."

Another kick at the door, then the lock sprang back and the plywood door swung inward. Claire was standing there, her face red like she'd been slapped. I fought down the urge to puke. And then she started to count off on her fingers. "Lille, Reims, Rennes, Bordeaux, Toulouse, Nimes, Montpelier, Marseille . . . we friggin' smacked it, Laura!"

We both ran, screaming all the way down the corridor and found the others. Sam grabbed me, picked me up, and twirled me around.

"Stop, stop I feel sick!" I gasped and so he let me down slowly and as my face came level with his, he paused and held me there for a moment. No, no, no, Laura Brown.

Oh, what a feeling! After all the crap and disappointments and struggle we've finally made it. Eman got paid with a crate of beer and we ended up going back to his place, a tiny room in a squat in Vauxhall, where we partied before falling asleep as the sun came up, all super close, breathing into each other's faces and waking up all the time cos our legs and arms kept touching. Gruesome.

## Mon., June 5

Got woken by a message from Adi. His e-mail quality is breaking up big time, like he's on another world. There's a deep metaphor in there if I could be arsed to dig it out.

LB
on way to refugee camp, got tckets to
Khartoun on semi-OK lookin bus wiv Yes Sir
Air Con! down the side. All bags on roof an we
set of wiv bout 300 pple crammed insde. prtty
sn realis wasn't gonna be no Air Con. i15 mins
an we wuz rollin in sweat. evry kni is getin
hotter an hotter. Nthing to do cept slp an stare
out window. Is basically planet Mars with
goats.
but guess what? Ii jus seen 1st mrage! I hu
my eyes were foolin me but no mtter how hard
I looked I still saw huge areas of l lu floating
bove the earth

I lay back and smiled. Yeah, yeah, Adi, I'm on my way, too, now. It's not just you who can leave, you know?

Anyway, we've spent today camped out here at Eman's trying to work out what to do next. It turns out he's coming on the tour, too, as the Tinys' sound engineer. He's basically the only one left in London. He grinned. "That's uh . . . the beauty of . . . uh . . . being radical and . . . uhm . . . ah sticking around in . . . a . . . like crazy London. All the . . . uh pussy . . . like uh . . . engineers . . . are long gone . . ."

Claire was on the fone all afternoon sorting out the tour deal with the promoter.

She locked off and sighed. "Like Stace says, not much pay, but enough to live on. *Just.* The other bands'll make money from selling T-shirts and downs, but we haven't got any of that stuff, so we get a cut of the door and that's it. At least we can use their PA and drums."

VFONE img name:QE2 >sender:kieran mac >5/6/17
La la la la la la l'America... 42 sailors and me, can you possibly imagine! K x

No show from Nate, tho I was dead disappointed. I've messaged him again, telling him we're here. Ooh, and this just came from Kier. I must've just missed him, the big old fruit.

### Tues., June 6

We sat all day in the park cos it's the only place that's free and you don't get hassled. Today we were too hungry to do anything but think about food, and we spent the longest time coming up with our best meal. Mine was a starter of tempura prawns and spicy chicken wings, then Pad Thai with extra chili sauce and a side of crispy seaweed, followed by double-cream strawberry ice cream with almond flakes with a bottle of super-chilled Cobra to chase it down. My stomach's become like this separate animal, with a scavenger life of its own.

## Wed., June 7

London's kind of edgy. Today there was a big all-day demonstration against a new Citizen Tax. I glanced at Eman's monitor screen, at the crowds gathering on the South Bank.

"Another tax? My parents and all their friends are right on the edge already."

Claire nodded. "They say it's to kick-start the new economy, but all the gov does is take the money and do nothing with it. And it's massive—every adult will have to pay about €2000 a year."

"Even us?"

"Yep. Once we leave uni and get a job. Immediately."

"But how do they expect us to live?"

Claire shrugged. "The gov's so used to bullying us, they can't imagine that anyone'll stand up to them."

## Thurs., June 8

When are we going to get a break? Super-shitty day. We were in the Hare Krishna homeless food line in Soho Square when Claire got a call from Mikey's promoter to say he's in a cash crisis and is downscaling to a smaller tour bus, and he's very sorry but there's no room for us anymore. So, unless we can get our own bus, we ain't going. Stace crunched a wafer in her fist. "Well that's it, then. There's no way we can do this. After all we been thru!"

And then my fone buzzed. Nate. He went, "Hey, Laura, what's going on?" and all the tears I'd stored up sputtered and fizzed out of me like a burst water pipe. Poor guy, he doesn't speak to me for a month, then he gets that. He's promised to come and see me, but I think he was just trying to get me off the fone.

## Fri., June 9

Packed up my stuff at Eman's. I'm going back to Abingdon in the morning. The tour's over. Too depressed to write more.

## Sat., June 10

I came out of a deep sleep to a heavy *boom boom boom*—someone kicking Eman's front door. Eman backed up against the wall. "Shit . . . the feds . . . oh, man . . ." He nodded to me. "Can you . . . uh like . . . uhm . . . check it?"

A voice came up from below. "Yo! Eman! Laura! Are you alive or what?"

"That's not the police." I crawled past the others, yanked the window open, and stuck my head out. Nate was standing on the doorstep, gazing upward. When he saw me he grinned and stretched his arms out wide. "Ta-da!"

"Oi, Nate, bit early, mate!"

"I wuz overexcited and I couldn't wait to bring down my little beauty."

I glanced behind him—just a row of parked cars and a beat-up, rusted old orange van.

"What?"

He jerked his thumb over his shoulder. "Remember dis bella?"

My eyes flipped back to the van and I started to laugh. "You're joking, right?"

He crossed his arms. "Do I look like I'm jokin'? Sure she's got a few days' work to do on her, but she's sweet . . ."

Claire dragged herself over to the window. "What's he saying?"

Nate cupped his hands over his mouth. "I'm sayin' we are takin' a ride to France in my Chevy ride. I am the driver and you guys are gonna cover the gas credits. But this Laura girl is laughin' in my face."

Claire leaned out. "Don't take no notice of her! You got yourself a de-al!"

I tugged her T-shirt. "But, Claire, you haven't seen it close up—"

She swung back inside. "You got any other plan?"

"Well, no . . ."

"Then let's go."

## Mon., June 12

God, it's like I'm living in that hideous back in the day *Summer Holiday* Cliff Richard musical that my nan loves where they dance around fixing up a London double-decker bus and drive it to Greece. Except in reality our first gig is on Friday night in Lille and if we can't fix up this pile of oxidizing metal we'll have to forget about our whole future, so we've spent the day crawling around trash cans and junkyards for spare parts. Stace nearly got bit by a rat this afternoon. I don't remember *Summer Holiday* being so dark.

## Tues., June 13

Picked up a mail from Mum this morning.

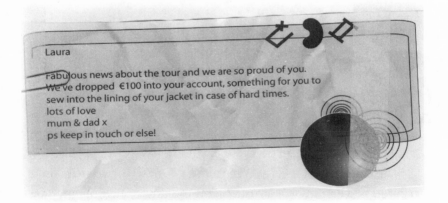

Laura

Fabulous news about the tour and we are so proud of you.
We've dropped €100 into your account, something for you to
sew into the lining of your jacket in case of hard times.
lots of love
mum & dad x
ps keep in touch or else!

I had to press my fingers into my eyes to not cry, but by lunchtime I'd blown the lot at Kwik Fit on new brake-pad linings. Claire can smell parental money, even if the source is bankrupt.

## Thurs., June 15

It was dark when Nate finally got the motor running. We circled the Chevy, now with added bright green splotches where he'd slapped on a bit of paint to cover up the rust.

Sam kicked a tire. "Jesus. Is this thing really gonna get us 'cross France?"

Nate sucked his teeth. "Have sum faith. She don't look like much but she got hidden depths. Now we've got the hydro-converter running, she's gonna run like a dream."

Stace peered inside. "How are 6 of us gonna live in there?"

"We'll go it in pairs, I guess," said Claire. "2 in the front, driving, 2 in the middle on the seats, and 2 at the back sleeping. And then change every few hours."

"Who's sleeping with who?"

Nate grinned. "I'm happy to sleep with *all* the ladies as long as you don' go fightin' 'bout who goes first."

We leave first thing tomorrow morning.

## Fri., June 16

France!

It's late afternoon and we've just driven off the ferry. I didn't think we were going to make it. The roof solar circuits overheated on the M23 and Nate and Sam spent hours lying under the body, with us girls sitting on the grass and letting them rescue us like feminism had never been invented. But they got her going again, and then at Dover we had to beg the ferry company to let us on a later boat. These officials were going *"no, no, it's not procedure,"* and then Claire basically flashed them her tits, and they just laughed and waved us on.

"I can't believe you just did that!" muttered Stace.

Claire sniffed. "It's a postfeminist age. We got to take our power where we find it, Stacey."

God, it feels good to be moving on our way, for real. There's a hot wind blowing thru the front cab and I'm sitting up front. My partner is Nate; the girls flat out refused to go anywhere near him. Anyway, aargh, got to go now, I think we're lost already.

1 A.M. We found the venue in Lille after a lot of driver drama. By the time we drove into the car park, it was already dark and someone was cooking up a vegan chili on the main tour bus. I was nearly fainting with hunger pangs and scarfed a giant plate down. Hunger has no shame.

And so at 9:30 the *angels* did our first-ever foreign tour date. There's 3 bands—us, *Tiny Chainsaws in the Distance*, some radical group called *SIM* who are big in France (*SIM* is short for something dead political)—and Eman who's basically the sound engineer for the tour, but Mikey lets him get up and torment people with distortion and bleeps between sets. I can't believe we're on tour in France . . . it's just so weird, like everything's the same, but in French. I wish I'd concentrated a bit more in school. Stace is the only one who's got a clue what anyone's saying.

After it was over, we threw everything into the van and now people are just sprawled asleep in their seats in the van. We look like a suicide pact. Glamour rock 'n' roll, here we come!

## Sun., June 18

We played tonight in Reims surrounded by champagne factories. The kids here are much more aggressive than at home. Loads of pushing, moshing, bleeding, and a couple of fights. Dad was right, there's a national election in a couple of weeks and there's a big chance of this really extreme rightwing party, the *Front National*, getting into power, so everyone's going nuts. Leave it to us to walk into another disaster zone. Sylvie, the lead singer from *SIM*, the French band, was standing outside the club on a pile of crates, shouting at everyone in English. "You look at me like I'm talking out of a history book. Like that Hitler was a cartoon. You think he invented fascism? You think we can't go back to there?"

And then Eman kicked off his set and all sound folded in on itself. I watched as he flipped the low-frequency dial and a giant pulse of deep energy surged thru every molecule in a 5-K radius.

Sam clutched his chest. "Ah, this is what it's like the moment 'fore you die."

I spoke to Mum after on a super-bad line. Her voice was all warbly.

"Oh, everythingulluble foiione . . . Dad's startluiooodlue . . . wind—y I—aa!"

After five minutes we gave up. I think basically they're fine.

## Mon., June 19

We've got 3 days till the next gig in Rennes in Brittany, which is away west. So today we drove for 6 hours, then pulled into a dirty campsite to break the journey. All of *SIM* are vegan and super serious, but I don't want to piss them off cos they do all the cooking, so I went over and helped Sylvie wash up while the others were hanging around the fire. She speaks dead-good English; I feel like a bastard for not knowing more than *bonjour* and *je m'appelle*.

I picked up a cloth. "So what's going on here? Y'know, with all the fighting?"

She looked up. "In France, you mean?"

"Yeah."

"I don't know. If you say one year ago that the *Front National* can win an election *regionale* I—I will laugh at you."

"But what's happened? It can't just be cos you're on carbon rations now."

"No. It is more complex. It is for protecting what is ours . . . and with this . . . *sécheresse* . . . in Africa . . ."

"Drought?"

"*Oui.* It is very bad. It is already in Europe, in Spain. All those stupid *tourisme* golf course dry up the Ebro River. But Afrique, that is the real disaster."

I frowned. "But there's been loads of droughts in Africa before. Why's it different now?"

"Because it's worst it's ever been. There is practically no rain for over a year now for everywhere . . ." She ticked off her fingers. "Zimbabwe, Mozambique, Malawi, Zambia, Namibia, Ghana, Nigeria, la Corne d'Afrique, the Sahel, and now also in North. And so the people they come here, or *en réalité*, they *die* coming here in the thousands. And now we say we have nothing to spare. No rain in France for 6 weeks. Go home."

"I ain't seen this on the news much."

She shrugged. "Fences, walls, detention center, private security, REFLEX agents. Europe spends much money hiding all this. And there is a water war, for real, building between Palestine and Israel. Right now."

Suddenly Mikey's nasal voice drifted over from the fire. "S'weird, man. 2 Sundays back we wuz taggin' like 4 ever down on the South Bank an' my right . . ." He tapped his nose. "Wha' you call dis?"

"Nose?" said Sam.

Mikey glared at him. "You think I don't know nose? I mean da *hole*—"

Sam paused. "Nostril?"

"Assit! Ever since den my right *nostril's* totally blocked, numb. I can't feel it." He looked around at the others. "That ever 'appen to u?"

A long pause. Then Nate looked up. "No, never. I think you got cancer."

A burst of laughter came from around the fire.

Beside me, Sylvie sighed, like they were idiots—and I felt dead awkward. Grrr, why does everything have to be so complicated? Why can't you care about shit and still have a laugh?

.

Ha! Me and Stace so busted Claire kissing the French vegan drummer behind the tour bus. She climbed into our van later, acting all cool. "Nothing's going on. We're just friends is all."

Stace smirked. "What were you doing, then? Digging for chickpeas?"

## Tues., June 20

I stumbled out of the boiling-hot Chevy late this morning to find everyone'd disappeared. And then I caught sight of Sam, hunched up over his laptop in the shade of the big tour bus.

"Where's everyone?"

"Gone to the river to cool off. Hey, what d'you think of this? It's a new bit of graffiti I'm working on." He turned the screen toward me, showing an image of Robert De Niro.

"Where's that from?"

"Stock site. It's not him, it's like one of those impersonator guys."

I watched as he put a blur filter on Bobby's face. "Just got to soften him up a bit before we grayscale him."

"You're getting better. What happened to that bunny?"

"I can't draw for shit . . . so Mikey and the guys've been teaching me how to build up layers in Photoshop to make stencils . . . I'm nearly done now."

He pointed at some letters. "I've left this *O* to the end cos it's evil. Basically when you cut the letter *O*, the middle bit falls out, so you don't cut it all the way, instead you've got to attach the middle bit to the outside by making a thing called a bridge. One at the top and bottom, to make a shape like. You wanna try?"

Half an hour later. Mikey appeared from inside the bus as I scrunched up another messed-up *O*.

He laughed. "Yo, *patienza*."

I rolled my eyes and snatched up my knife again.

Mikey took my hand in his. "Take it easy. Don't go in so hard. If u don't cut good the first time, then go again, but press harder." He tapped my hand. "But, careful, 2 *much* pressure an' fssst! You gotta blade in da eye."

I blushed big time when Mikey took my hand. He's dead sexy. I looked over at Sam, tried to keep it cool. "So what you going to do with Bobby when he's done?"

He glanced at me and Mikey, shrugged. "Get spraying, next chance I get."

"Can I come?"

He turned away. "Maybe. Whatever."

Definite symptoms of jealousy! They call me heartbreaker Brown! I'm not going to do anything but, man, it feels good to get some attention. I'm sick of being second best to a protest meeting.

## Thurs., June 22

Dad sent me this bullet point list today.

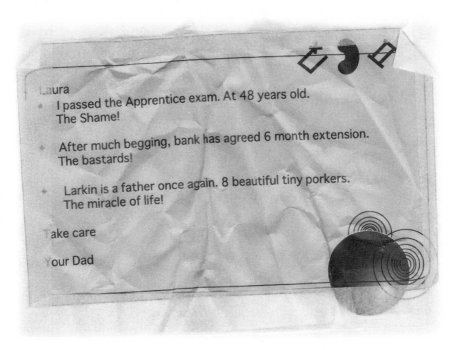

Laura

- I passed the Apprentice exam. At 48 years old. The Shame!

- After much begging, bank has agreed 6 month extension. The bastards!

- Larkin is a father once again. 8 beautiful tiny porkers. The miracle of life!

Take care

Your Dad

He is a strange, strange man. Anyway, it's all good, this takes the pressure off me big time.

## Sat., June 24

It's so hot; I've got no energy to write. Between gigs all we do is lie around in the shade, panting like dogs. And forget about traveling around and checking out the area; the Chevy van sucks up all our carbon points like a black hole. An orange and green black hole.

Other than that the only news is that Nate has kissed a different girl every single gig. Sam shook his head. "How you do it, mate?"

Nate put his arms behind his head. "Natural charm, beauty . . . and I rub a bit of engine oil on my biceps, it gives me mo' definition."

## Sun., June 25

We're on our way south thru Bordeaux toward Nantes and we've totally got a routine going. Everyone moves slow inside the Chevy now; you only need to rip a strip of leg flesh off one time on the melting leather seats to chill all your moves. The tour's become a blur of hot dusty roads, fields full of foreign stuff: figs, grapes, sunflowers, and tiny battery-powered Proto-Citroëns weaving in and out of lanes, couples gesturing, fighting, flinging their arms around with only one thing on their minds. Overtaking. All time is now cut into 3-hour sections—up front and driving, legs up on the dash, wind thundering in thru the open triangle windows. Middle section—still awake but more private—practicing guitar, reading, writing. And then the back—the full chill-out section, where you stretch out half asleep, rocked by the engine and punk and hot air, staring at the clouds and tops of trees flashing by.

## Mon., June 26

No! Kim taught me never to listen in on other people's conversations and I didn't mean to, but I was too hot to move. All I heard was a tiny thing, but enough to make me question everything. It was just after lunch and Sam was scrubbing the giant vegan chili pot with Eman.

"So how long were you hiding out in the Docks after I left?"

"Oh . . . uh yeah . . . maybe like . . . uh . . . couple weeks . . ."

"On your own?"

"Nah . . . er . . . uh . . . with . . . Adi and . . . uh . . . Monica."

"That hot politico girl staying at Laur's?"

"Uh-huh . . . uh . . . hard core."

"Were they like *together* together, though?"

"Like you . . . uh . . . said . . . she's uh . . . uh . . . hot."

They both started laughing.

My brain went cold. Monica? But now, when I think about it, I think I already knew. When I heard Eman say the words it wasn't so much shock I felt, more a dull thud of recognition. What else am I hiding from myself? Oh, God, I just want it not to be true.

## Tues., June 27
Rennes, Brittany.

But it is true and I woke up in the middle of the night with this huge space inside me. It was a place just for him. And now he's gone. I'm such an idiot; I wrote and deleted and wrote a mail to him about a hundred times, but I just can't get that level of betrayal into words. I'm not saying anything to anyone. I don't want any sympathy.

I sat in the front of the van, my head pounding, as we drove to the gig. It took hours cos there was a blockade of trucks and tractors protesting about fuel prices. People are dead angry, which suits me just fine. We got to the club at about 5 and after we'd finished the sound check, there was still a bit of time before the show started, so we stepped outside into the packed town square. On the far side there was a stage, draped with banners, surrounded by a row of speakers, booming out some bizarre military-style music.

"What's this?"

Claire shrugged. "Election stuff I guess. It's sometime next week."

The military music suddenly turned into something like the *Rocky* theme, but with a choir singing over the top. I poked Stace.

"What are the words?"

She shrugged. "Dunno."

"You didn't even try," said Claire.

Stace curled her lip. "Curse my schoolgirl French . . ." She scrunched up her face in concentration. ". . . Er,

```
La freedom to work together
This flame will lead to la freedom
To ask for a better tomorrow."
```

A howl of feedback shot across the square and bounced off the old buildings.

Nate covered his ears. "Woo-ooh!"

In front of us a group of little girls did some horrid dance moves.

"Now you see how the Nazis got started," muttered Claire.

Stace grimaced. "Forget Brownshirts, this *is* my Girl Guide camp, Epping Forest, 2008. No difference. No irony."

We sat on the cobbled stones in the shade and watched. The crowd was mostly silver-haired men with big bellies and their crinkly, leather-faced wives in gold jewelery. And then suddenly a big group of men in dark suits marched thru the square and climbed up on the stage. A tiny man stepped to the front and started screaming like that footage you see of Nazi rallies from the '30s. He was a blur of flashing hands and cutting arm gestures, veins bulging in his neck.

"Slow down, daddyo . . . there's a heart attack comin' your way," grunted Nate.

After a few minutes Stace turned to us. "Y'know it's kind of clever. All he talks about is church and family and togetherness. Nothing about scummy immigrants or water or oil."

Sylvie nodded. "Yes, that is how they do . . . keep it all simple, about old France, our tradition . . ."

"But what about the left, where are they?"

"Pff. They are *pathétique* . . . they do nothing."

"George Orwell calls them the 'boiled rabbits of the left.' All white and limp and full of good intentions."

Sylvie smiled. "*Exactement*. You see why we maybe go to the **2**. At least they fight for another way."

"You into that shit?" asked Stace.

Sylvie chewed her lip. "I don't know. They are *dangereux*, yes? But this is a bad time. Maybe we need something *strong*."

I looked around the square with a strange feeling: half dread, half excitement. My heart's in agony, but at the same time it's like there's something bigger going on, like I'm really part of something. That boy can go to hell. I ain't putting my life on hold for him anymore.

The gig was manic. *Tiny* Mikey's like a monkey on acid onstage and the crowd was going wild for him. I've never seen moshing and diving like it. There's a weird energy building, like people know something's gonna crack soon.

## Wed., June 28
This came today. I deleted it immediately. I'm not wasting any more tears on that loser. St. Adi, my arse.

laura
2nd week r u gettin mail? wy u not rite bak? Jus fnshed nite shift. Wve started at 7 with 30 patients. Most evry1 on IV fluids + vomiting/suffer fro sevre diarrhoea or both. All nite ran intra fluid into them as fast as cud take it. Had to B sure the containers fluid dint run dry + veins dint break down

from 3 i c0llected + emptd bckets for catchin vomit and dia stool from the nite. woman workin wiv me vomited x4 times herself cos so gross. . At 1 point she had to stop, sit down + cry B4 she cud go on

## Thurs., June 29

This evening we pulled into a site outside Bordeaux. We're not playing till Sunday, so Sam and me are gonna try out Bobby De Niro tomorrow evening in the town.

"You got any ideas where you wanna do it?" I asked.

"Nope. I guess we'll just take a look around. As soon as we see somewhere we like, we'll go for it."

## Fri., June 30

We took the bus into Bordeaux, 20 peasants and us with a supersize me pizza box full of stencils. After an hour of searching, we found a cool place under an old bridge. Sam bent down and opened up the box.

"OK, you ready? I'll hold the stencil in place and you tape it?"

I nodded and quickly tore off the first strip of tape, and as Sam placed the first dark-tone stencil on the tunnel wall, I ran the tape along the top edge, cut it, then tore off another strip and stuck it with my thumb along the bottom.

"All clear?" he hissed.

I looked back toward the street and then turned and checked the dark interior of the tunnel. Nothing. I nodded and Sam started to spray. As soon as he finished the first layer, I ripped it off the wall and picked up the second shade stencil, and this time Sam taped it up. He nodded at the gray spray can.

"Go for it."

I reached for the can, shook it and started to spray, but I was so nervous I blasted the nozzle too hard.

"Whoah! Too close. Take it easy."

I pulled back. Gray paint was spattered across my hands and T-shirt. I took a breath and started to spray again, this time much steadier.

Then the next layer. We were working well together now. Wordlessly, I picked up the highlight stencil and Sam taped it against the wall in one easy motion. It's weird when you're actually tagging cos you don't get time to look at what you're doing. You just have to trust to the stencils. White-and-black layers followed in quick succession and suddenly there he was. Bobby, pulling a gun on all the assholes in a tunnel in Bordeaux.

"He's a handsome bastard, ain't he?" Sam twisted his wrist and a rapid series of flashes from his fone lit up the concrete in front of us.

Then came the sound of voices . . . from the road. I started to throw the stencils back in the box, but Sam just pocketed the 2 closest cans, threw another at me, and turned. "Leave the stencils. Run!"

"But—"

"Run!"

We legged it thru the dark of the tunnel, but a few meters from the exit, I put my hand on Sam's shoulder. "Wait up." I shucked off my T-shirt, turned it inside out, and dragged it on again. "Are the cans hidden? Check hands."

He stuck his hands out. "I'm good. It's you who's messed up. Keep 'em tucked in your jeans."

I took a breath. "Let's go, then. Casual."

"OK, Brown." He grinned. "Nice tits, by the way."

And then, in the dirty tunnel we lunged at each other, kissing. Mad, crazy, brain-melting moment. The sound of footsteps getting closer. And then we broke apart and walked out into the sunshine and didn't say a word till we were well out of the area, but as we were waiting for the bus, Sam turned, eyes blazing. "Again. We've got to do that again."

I nodded, my heart beating *boom, boom, boom.*

# July

## Sun., July 2

For the first time tonight I was scared. Our van got rocked by this gang of skinheads outside the club, and onstage, when Claire sang:

```
Is there any mercy
Is compassion gone?
Is there no account
When bullet enters bone?
```

There was a wicked bang, like a gunshot in the hall.

Later on a fight broke out between kids from the left and right, and this skinhead jumped onstage, grabbed the mic, and started screaming in French.

I looked at Stace. She shook her head. "It's disgusting . . . basically, *We, the Front stand up for French, for European people. Immigrants are flooding in looking for water, if the gov won't stop them then we will, we're gonna kick the shit out of the* bougnol!"

The skinhead boy went down under a pile of bodies. Then suddenly Sylvie emerged, clutching the mic. "*C'est de la merde*, this left and right. There is no hope for the future for any of us divided . . ."

Nate grabbed my arm. "What you doin' standin" here? Get in the van, I'm gonna try an' get that crazy French girl outta here!"

163

"What about our stuff?"

He pushed me, hard. "Van! Now! We'll get our shit later."

It's 5 A.M. and we're on the road. We had to wait till the police cleared the area before we could get our gear. We were super lucky—a couple of amps got smashed up, but we rescued everything else. Nate's driving in silence, but his hands are tight on the wheel. God knows what's gonna happen at this festival in Nimes. We play the day of the election.

## Mon., July 3

Me and Sam keep getting caught in these long, long, breathless stares. I can't believe the others aren't picking up on it.

## Tues., July 4

*Nimes. Election Day.*

We left Nate's Chevy a few Ks outside the festival site and all piled into the big tour bus cos it was cheaper to just use one vehicle. As we drove into the site, Sylvie pointed at a group of feds.

"This is CRS. In English?"

"Riot squad." Nate caught my eye, looked down.

We play tomorrow night in the newcomer tent. Puke. But still, it's our first festival. After we'd set up a place to sleep for the night, I just wanted to be alone for a bit, so I slipped away into a side field and lay down on the burned-out grass, staring up at the blue stretching out above me; clouds, blurring and tumbling, forming and separating—and swifts, darting, cutout black flecks, sweeping and swirling like cinders flying up from the fire. I stayed there for ages; people looming up over me as they passed, caught in my own strange angled slice of earth and sky as night fell. It was one of those moments when you remember how beautiful everything is.

Later on we drank cider and watched a bunch of bands, but we were all in a strange kind of mood, maybe because the festival seemed so familiar, like we'd gone back a few years to when everything was normal and for one night we were living our old lives again.

It was cool at the end, though. The headliners finished up with a final powerhouse chord and a blaze of white lights before plunging us back into the night. The whole crowd wheeled away from the stage and surged forward, us with it, torches flaring all around.

"This is primal, man," growled Stace. "T-shirts, shorts, and sneakers instead of furs and loincloths. That's all the difference."

Claire nodded. "It's like in Australia in the '50s with the Aborigines. Their gov had this whole plan of how to wipe them out by separating the teaching from the learning generation. They worked out it only takes one generation to do it and all the previous culture is lost. 40,000 years, gone, in 30 years."

Eman watched as 2 girls fell into a pile of plastic bottles. "Yeah. The oldies . . . are uh . . . our only ah . . . hope, man. Find uh . . . yourself like . . . uh . . . piece of silver and . . . uh totally, uhmm . . . keep uh close. Them . . . uh . . . silvers, they . . . ah . . . uh been thru . . . uh . . . war and like uh . . . total . . . depression an that. We . . . uh . . . jus . . . ain't got the . . . uh . . . skills no more."

I couldn't sleep cos the jazz tent was churning out revolting acid jazz at 2 million decibels, and at about 3, Sam crept into our girls' tent and tapped me on the leg.

"Aaaargh!" he hissed. "Just pour hydrochloric acid on me and kill me now. Better that way."

I sat up. "What you up to?"

He pointed toward a garbage bag outside, bulging with massive stencils. "I've got another image ready to spray. Want to come?"

I nodded and started to creep out of my sleeping bag, but then Claire stirred in her sleeping bag. "What's going on?"

I squirmed backward. "Nothing."

Sam glanced at me in surprise.

I ran my fingers thru my hair. "Y'know what, mate, I think I'm too tired, maybe 'nother time?"

I don't want anyone else to know what's going on before I know myself. Is this how old people get so old and wrinkly? Trying to keep track of all the screw ups?

## Wed., July 5

"Laura. Got to go. Now!"

I sat up. Still dark. Claire was already stuffing her things into a backpack.

"What's going on?"

"Riot police. The *Front National* have won the election and someone in power's sent the feds down here, I guess cos this place is swarming with activists. Sam and Mickey just saw them by chance when they were spraying. Looks like they're gonna move in on us before dawn."

"But what about the van and all our stuff?"

"Take your bass and leave the rest. C'mon! This is serious."

I jumped up, quickly rolled up my sleeping bag, and ran to the van.

Sylvie stood, head down. "*Nique la police* . . . I'm not running . . . and we have to warn these people."

We stared at her in silence. We've all been thru too much in London to go looking for a fight with the feds.

She bit her lip. "I don't believe this is happening . . ."

Nate put his arm around her. "But it is."

She nodded. "OK, but if we leave we must go straight from France. There is a protest camp where we can go to, on the Italy border . . . yes? There we will be safe."

After some 10 minutes of crouching and running low, we reached the fence. Mikey held up his hand. "Here, stop, dis is where we cut a gap b4." He crouched down and pulled back a piece of plastic sheeting and peered thru. "Oi, dere's like hundreds of 'em. We got 2 chill here till dey start comin' in, or we'll jus' get busted."

And so we sat there, clutching our backpacks as the riot police silently poured into the festival gates and surrounded the lines of tents.

Sam tapped me on the shoulder and pointed to a section of wall farther down. "What you reckon?"

I smiled. "It's good, mate."

He sighed. "But now no one'll see it. I'm an artist doomed to failure."

Stace curled a lip. "Oh, I dunno, could be seen by millions world-wide . . . as a backdrop to a bloodfest beating. This could be your big break, buddy."

A piercing siren filled the air and simultaneous loudspeaker orders. The lines of feds began to move toward the gates, beating time with batons on their shields.

After 5 minutes, Mikey waved his hand. "S'all clear. Let's go."

As we crawled across the outer field, we could hear the sound of screaming behind us. We didn't look back, just kept going till it was full light, and then we found an old barn and hid. And here we are now, waiting for dark so we can get to the Chevy, about 10 Ks down the road.

## Thurs., July 6

After a long, hungry day of waiting we set off just as night fell. We'd been walking for a couple of hours, when suddenly up ahead we saw a light . . . flickering . . . like something on fire.

Claire nudged me. "What's that?

And then Nate began to run. "No! Shit, no!"

But there it was, our beautiful orange Chevy blazing in the night sky.

There was nothing to do, we just stood there and watched. After, we walked on for a few more hours to get out of the area, then threw ourselves down into a cornfield and slept.

We are tramps, basically. No band, no van, no money. Again.

## Fri., July 7

The sun rose. We sat there on the edge of nowhere, with miles of reeds and mud stretching out around us, trying to figure out what to do. Not that we've got much choice. We've got to get out of France, and fast. So we're about to set off to the Italian border, to the place Sylvie knows.

I sighed. "But then what? Are we going back home?"

Stace jammed her hands on her hips. "Let's deal with that later, mate. There's 14 of us and it's too obvious being in such a big group to hitch. I reckon we should split into pairs—and leave a few hours between us."

"Who gets to go first?"

She shrugged. "Draw straws, unless anyone's got a better plan."

I've just pulled my straw. Typical. Me and Nate got the short one. We leave last. Tomorrow.

## Sat., July 8

I said good-bye to Stace and Claire at first light.

Claire stared around at the reeds. "All that pissing work for this."

Stace rubbed her nose. "Yeah, yeah, but at least it gives us depth to write songs about. We'll get to this place, chill out a bit, and get the *angels* going again." She grinned and punched my arm. "It's not like we've split or anything."

I watched them trudge off down the road. Stace turned, cupped her hands around her mouth. "See you on the other side!"

And then they were gone, leaving only me, Nate, Sam, and Mikey. We started to pack up our stuff when my fone buzzed. I flipped up the screen, read the message, and sat down, hard, on the ground.

Nate glanced at me. "What's up?"

Laura
I hope for this to reach you, for I have bad news. Red Cross have contact me riguardo Adi. He is diagnosed with malaria. It start maybe 1 week ago with headache and then to nausea. The doctor got to him as soon as they can, but it's a massivo camp, and so many people sick and dying. For few days they have give him antibiotici, and he was stabile but high fever,, but suddenly 2 days ago, he collapsed. Red Cross are now to fly him to centro medicale in Sicilia for emergency treatment. I will be there with him. I have not his family contact and I hope this will to reach you for thheir informazi-one.

I will update you for as soon as I know more, please contact me on mail or cell: +0039 435 3475
Tano Sciortino

I flicked the screen toward him. Frowning, he bent down. I grabbed his arm. "Have you got his parents' info?"

"No-o. They've gone outside London somewheres. Watford maybe, but dat's all I know."

"I don't know, either. Nate, what am I going to do?"

He gave me a long look. "You mean, what are *we* gonna do? An' the answer is go to him. Call Tano now."

I sucked in a breath and stood up. Sam put his arm around me. "Do you want me to come as well?"

We stared at each other. He cleared his throat. "But—it's not like a **2** thing is it?"

"I don't know."

Nate spun around. "So what if it is?"

"Nothing, but I don't wanna, I mean I can't get involved with—"

Nate held up his hand. "Don't worry, bruv, he's our friend, we'll deal with this." He turned away, muttering, "Jus' go to your hippy camp an' fry your head wid weed is all."

"What you say?"

I glared at Nate. "Hey, c'mon, that's not fair. He don't even know Adi."

Nate spat. "Yeah, but it's at times like this you see who's for real, not just college buddy buddies."

Sam sprang toward him, but I pulled him away before it got ugly and walked him to the edge of the road. "Sam, it's fine . . . honest. But can you tell the others what's happened?"

He grabbed my hand. "I *will* come with you . . . y'know . . ."

"It's cool. Just get Claire to call me." I looked at him straight. "But I need to ask you a favor."

"Anything."

"Look after my bass?"

Sam pulled me close. "Course. I'll guard it with my life . . . and . . . he's gonna be fine."

I let him hug me, feel good about himself. After I saw the look of relief on his face when all I asked him to do was to take my bass.

After Sam and Mikey left, I sat there for an hour trying to get thru to Tano, but all I kept getting was those foreign long beeps. In the end I threw the fone down and kicked the dirt up in a big spray. On the run out of France, all our stuff up in smoke—and now I'd got to get myself down to that lying, cheating little ex-boyfriend of mine.

Nate sighed. "Let's just get goin', then, an' we'll talk to him laters."

"You got any idea how to get there?"

He squinted at his fone GPS. "Accordin' to dis, we cross the border into Italy then down along the coast. Genova to Livorno, then Napoli, then Reggio something, then a boat to Palermo in Sicily. South basically, nearly all the way to Africa."

"How long you think it'll take?"

"Dunno. You got any money?"

"'Bout 10 euros on me. The rest was all hidden in the van."

"Card?"

"Only 40 points left for the month. Def not enough to get us on a train. You?"

He groaned. "Same. That last hydro stop cleaned me out. Parents?"

I shook my head. "One, they're bankrupt, and two—yeah sure, '*Hi, Mum and Dad, I'm on the run from the Nazi French police and I'm on my way to a Sicilian refugee commune. Don't suppose you'd give me a hundred chillers for the trip?*'"

Nate grinned. "Truesay. All right, then. Let's go."

We shouldered our backpacks. Thank God he's with me. I'm so scared.

It took us all afternoon, but eventually we picked up a ride, crossing the border near San Remo. There was a checkpoint, but it seemed pretty random and we got thru fine. Our driver pulled off at this little town called Sayona, just as the sun was setting. We got out and I tried Tano again. This time, finally, he answered.

"Tano, what's going on? Is Adi there yet?"

"*Si*, he just arrive in Palermo. They have him with heavy sedation."

I fought to keep my voice calm. "But people don't . . . die from malaria . . . there's like drugs and that . . ."

"I know but some types are more dangerous. *Apparantamente* forAdi now there is danger for the red blood cells breaking down."

173

Freezing cold fear rushed into my heart and it took me a few seconds to realize he was still speaking. ". . . Laura, he's a strong boy and they do everything they can. But for safety we now must contact the parents."

"But that's the thing, Tano, I don't know where they are . . . but *I'm* coming. I'm in north Italy and I'll get there as soon as I can."

His voice changed. "You are comin here? Alone?"

"Nate is with me."

"*Va bene.* That is good. Come quick, but be safe . . ."

"As soon as I can."

It was dark by this time and there was zero traffic. Nate scanned the length of the road. "No point now. Let's go again first thing tomorrow." He picked up my backpack, put his arm around me, and we walked till we found a small barn set back in a field. There was no moon and the night was very dark, so we felt our way around in the straw, wrapping up as best we could. I lay for a few minutes in silence, listening to Nate's already sleepy breathing.

"Nate—did you know about him and Monica?"

He shifted. "Uh?"

"You heard."

Pause. Then, "I ain't gonna lie to you. I knew. And partly I think that wuz why he went away, he felt so bad, couldn't face you."

"Was it serious? I mean, are they still together?"

"Don't know." He reached for my hand. "I understand if you don't wanna do this trip. I can go alone."

"No way. Girl or no girl, he's still—"

"What?"

"Dunno."

He groaned. "Just don't say *like a brother*. That means he's got no chance to get back with you ever."

## Sun., July 9

We got nowhere today. Nobody would pick us up.

"Racists!" screamed Nate, after the thousandth car shot past us on the melting hot tarmac. "Laur, we ain't getting anywheres. Let's get down to dis Genova place an' jump the train."

"Where to?"

"Rome? Napoli? Anywhere south."

It took us till evening to get to Genova, and by the time we found the station, the last train to Napoli had just left. It turns out only half the trains are running cos of all the fuel cuts, so we'll have to wait for tomorrow morning for the next one to Rome.

Nate blew out his cheeks. "Nothing for it. We'll have to cotch here down by the tracks."

I trudged after him. I'm so starving I feel like I'm gonna faint the whole time.

We broke into a warehouse by the station and flattened some boxes, lay down, and fell asleep in minutes, like a pair of old bums. I woke up in the middle of the night to the message tone from my fone. I squinted at the screen from the light cast by the moon.

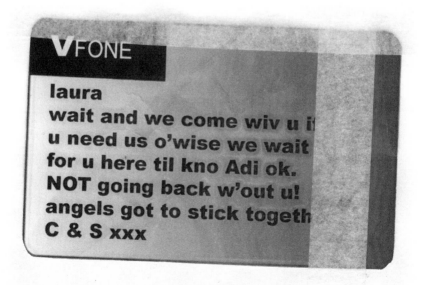

**V**FONE

**laura**
**wait and we come wiv u if**
**u need us o'wise we wait**
**for u here til kno Adi ok.**
**NOT going back w'out u!**
**angels got to stick togeth**
**C & S xxx**

My heart went all hot. There's a whole bunch of people I didn't choose, but they're *family*, somehow. I sighed and flipped the screen off to save battery. Then I lay there for a bit, gazing up at the moon thru a broken warehouse window and thinking about all the people I cared about, wondering where they were *right now*.

## Mon., July 10

We jumped the Rome train early this morning and split up, each doing the 3-hour journey in separate boiling-hot toilets. I spent the first bit trying to write a message to Mum that wouldn't freak her out, i.e. not *I'm sending you this in total dehydration from a train toilet floor as I travel into the mafia/drought/immigrant war heartland*, before I just gave up and told a total lie about going with the others to the French border. And then I fell into a kind of daze; only woke up cos Nate was banging on the door.

"Hey, c'mon! They're doing a ticket check down the train. I jus' dodged mine, but they're in the next carriage down. We've stopped at dis little station so let's jump."

I leaned my cheek against the filthy door. "But we're not there yet, are we?"

"No, but I reckon we jus' outside Rome." He banged again. "It's no jokes, the ticket guys've got guns. Let's get outta here."

We stumbled off the train, just as it started to move, and for a moment I stood there on the platform, blinking in the searing bright light. Beside me, Nate peered up at an electronic screen. "No worries, just gotta check out when's the next train . . ." Big pause, then: "Ah, shit. There is no next train. This ain't a proper station . . ." He threw his backpack on to the ground and flumped down on it. "Dis is some kind of joke."

I put my hand on his shoulder. "C'mon, let's go and get some water, then we'll go hitch again."

The rest of the afternoon we spent walking along a roasting highway to where it joined the motorway at a service station. When we finally got there, there was a tiny wood and a picnic table at the back of the gas pumps, and we were so hot, we just stumbled under the shade of the trees—and straight into a group of young African guys. We all froze, staring at each other for what felt like minutes. And then the nearest boy to me leaned forward, picked up a loaf of bread, ripped off a chunk and held it out. I didn't even stop to thank him, just seized the bread and sunk my teeth in it. It was the best, best thing I've ever tasted. The men all started to laugh, then patted the ground and invited us to sit down. Later one of them handed me a plastic bottle of wine, and as I drank it, it went straight into my veins like pure honey.

We ended up spending the night there with them. They were basically the best people we've met since being away. They shared everything they had with us and kept laughing at Nate, at his hair, the way he spoke. Night started to fall and after we'd eaten we drew closer together. A white dog with a skinny tail appeared out of the woods and came close. Nate threw a stick at him, and the dog cowered and backed away to the edge of the woods.

I nudged him. "Leave him alone. He's not doing any harm." I turned to Abe, the guy who'd first given us the bread, and finally got up the courage to ask the question that'd been on my mind since I joined them. "So why are you here?"

Abe shrugged. "It's a long story."

"We got time," said Nate, wrapping his jacket around his shoulders. Out of the corner of my eye I saw the dog creep forward again.

Abe sighed. "Well, as you can see, we are mostly young men, like me. Our families have given everything to get us out of the danger. If they can see us now, hiding here like animals!"

"But how did you even get this far?" I asked.

He glanced at me. "You really want to know these things?"

I nodded.

"Well, I and my brother here . . . are from Monrovia, in Liberia, yes? We start the trip with 8 others . . . and we are taken to a warehouse in a port and told to stay hidden."

Nate leaned forward. "By who?"

"The *scafisti* . . . the traffickers . . . After two days we have no food or water, but the next night they come and we leave in a small boat from the harbor. The following night we move to a bigger ship and after five days on the sea they set us loose on a beach, we don't know even which country . . ."

His brother poked him. "He thought it was France!"

All the group burst out laughing.

Abe waved his hand. "Very funny. You were too busy being sick to care, if I remember." He turned back to us. "So, again, we hide on the beach and then new *scafisti* come. We pay them another $400 for another boat. This is the money we have for our future. All gone."

The men around him now sat silent. Abe sighed. "On this boat there is maybe a hundred men from Nigeria, Ghana, Liberia. Again, young men. After three days on this new ship, the engine blows black smoke and the water, the sea, y'know . . . she starts to pour in. We are sinking, fast. A fishing boat is in the distance and so the *scafisti* force us with guns to jump so they can get away. The boat picks up about 12 men. The rest they leave to drown." He shrugged. "And so we come to Italy. We are *free*, as long as we don't try to work." Abraham gazed out over the highway. "Free! I can't go back, there is no home anymore, it is just a desert, but I want my family. I would like to die surrounded by the people I love."

I glanced up. The dog had made it, and was now sitting close. Watching me. Smiling.

Later on, my fone buzzed.

**VFONE**

Missy B
I feel bad, really BAD for leaving you
there in France. I keep thinking how I'm
gonna jump on a train down to sicily
so's I can be with you but then do you
need another complication in your life?
So maybe it's better like this.. Anyway
I'm thinking about you ... a lot. Promise
you'll call me if you need anything?
Sam XX

I lay back on the grass with a sigh. I've only got myself to blame. I mean, I picked him cos he was the total opposite of Adi. Boyfriend Lite.

### Tues., July 11

Unbelievable, astonishing, vivid change of fortune. My fone woke me early this morning.

I reached for it, groggy. "Hello?"

"Laura, hi, it's me, Gwen."

"Ey?" I struggled to sit up.

"I'm at the protest camp near Genova, I just bumped into Sam and he tells me you're on the way to Sicily. Well so am I, going to join Tano. Any good for you?"

"This isn't happening." I blinked hard, looked around to check I wasn't dreaming. But no, Nate and the white dog were curled up next to me, good and solid.

GPJ burst out laughing. "It is, though. Tano invited me to come as soon as I was released from custody. Stuff like this makes me think there might be a God . . ." Another long pause. "Well, as I say, do you want a lift?"

I sat there in silence. It was just too weird to get into, like blood might start pouring from my eyeballs or a chasm might open up in the tarmac if I even said one word. Finally I croaked out. "Yeah . . . that'd be cool . . . we're on our way down to Adi . . . he's sick . . . with malaria . . ."

"I know. Look, we can talk later. For now tell me where you are and I'll get there as soon as I can."

A few hours later a beat-up car pulled into the car park, horn tooting. Nate whooped and ran over, yanked the back door open and then I slithered in behind him, laughing.

Gwen glanced over my shoulder. "Is he coming, too? Tight squeeze if he is."

The white dog had jumped in behind me and was now staring straight at the horizon, like a poet, his body tight and tense, willing us not to send him away. I gave a minuscule nod and he gave one back.

"Yeah, he's coming."

Nate groaned. "Great, all we need. A flea bag." He leaned forward as Gwen pulled out. "Hey, miss . . . what's Italian for flea?"

Gwen frowned. "Er . . . *pulche*, I think."

He leaned forward. "Wha?"

"*Pul—che*."

"Che? As in Guevara?"

"Hmm?"

"Pulche Guevara. I like it."

Nate pounded the white dog's flank and Pulche grinned back like a fool.

Gwen swung into the fast lane. "I'm planning to take the small coast road all the way down to Reggio Calabria, you know, the toe of Italy? It'll take about 8 to 10 hours, I guess. Then we'll catch the ferry across to Messina."

"Where?"

She twisted in her seat. "Sicily."

"Adi's in Palermo. Is that far from there?"

"No . . . don't worry, I'll get you to him as fast as I can. You guys got many swipe points, by the way? I'm getting dangerously low."

We shook our heads.

I tried to call Tano for news on Adi, but again just got long beeps. In the end I just had to send a message to say I'm on my way. I slumped back in my seat. There's no way we're seeing him today. I fell into a half sleep, kept dreaming horrible dreams about Adi, then Sam, and then waking up to endless dusty brown fields rolling by and the same messy flat block towns—Aquino, Marzano, Capua, Sarno, Battipaglia, Padula, Mormanno, Cosenza, Sant'Onofrio, Seminara . . . all mixed up with Pulche's manic hot dog panting. At one point, Nate sat up and poked him. "Oh, man, he's too hot. He's gone all wrong."

Pulche swallowed, and for a second his diabolical tongue disappeared, then out it came again.

Nate wrinkled his nose. "Lizard boy."

And then the night rolled on and I slept again.

## Wed., July 12

Like the trains, the ferry crossings are cut down cos of the oil shortages, so our boat was packed out to fainting point and we spent the crossing squished against the deck railings. One false move and we'd've been swimming with da fishes. I turned to Gwen. "So what are you going to do here? It's kind of a change from the Dox commune, isn't it?"

She shrugged. "I know, but after I got arrested, they kept me in custody for 50 days under those insane counterterrorism laws . . . and when I came out, the whole place had been locked down. I've worked in refugee crisis centers before, so I'm here to do whatever

Tano needs for me to do. Work with the Red Cross, some Italian volunteer groups . . . basically help the refugees get food, water, shelter, medical help."

"But don't they get that stuff by right?"

"There are no rights any more. In the holding centers they treat them like dogs and there are 4 secret floating prison ships crammed full off the coast. The Sicilian police and Frontex are trying to clear the island and the coastline in the south, but there's no chance. Hundreds of boats are coming every day from Africa . . . tiny little dinghies, rafts . . . it's unbelievable. They say the beaches are like a battlefront."

I glanced across at her, wind whipping her hair back. "Why do you do all this stuff? No one else bothers."

"I ask myself the same question all the time. I—I just *can't* ignore things. Wish I could, sometimes."

"But don't you have like a—"

Gwen smiled. "Family? Partner?"

"Well, yeah."

She ran her hand along the rail. "Not really, no. I mean, I used to, but . . ." Suddenly she glanced up at the shore, growing closer by the second. "Hey, is that Tano?"

I was her student for long enough to know this meant End of Subject. "Where?"

Nate leaned forward. "Yeah, there's our man. At the end of the dock . . . See him, waving a red scarf?"

An hour later we stood in a tiny hospital room in the Red Cross Hospital in San Lorenzo—we'd finally made it to Adi. He was so thin, out of it, strapped up to a monitor with tubes sticking out of him. I stood there, swaying with exhaustion. And then I started to sob. Couldn't control myself. For the first time I realized he could die. Actually die.

Tano put his arms around me. "Eh, it is a big shock to first see him, but the *dottore* they think they are getting the *infezione* in control."

Nate tapped his chest. "Like they did wid me—an' look at me now. Strong like a ox."

Tano glanced at Nate. "It is good that you are here."

## Thurs., July 13

We've spent 24 hours straight at the hospital. The doctors are still keeping Adi completely under sedation and pumping him full of drugs to keep his temperature down to safe levels.

It's mid-morning, already steaming hot, and I'm here on my own. Nate's gone back to Tano's flat to sleep. I feel a long, long way from home. It's just me, Adi, and the steady beep of the heart monitor. It feels like when I was waiting on the steps of the old Co-op Building waiting to see if my parents were alive. Very simple. Very clear. I just want him to live. And I want to talk to my parents so badly, but I don't want to freak them out.

## Fri., July 14

It's like living under a grill. I spent today in a heat haze trying to contact Adi's family thru the Home Office and the police, but it seems like the U.K.'s just gone nuts with Citizen Tax riots. Gwen says that loads of local councils are backing the people and refusing to collect the tax.

I went outside at dusk, just to get some air, and found Pulche sitting beside the sliding doors, waiting. He's such a noble hound.

## Sat., July 15

I left Nate on the ward and went to Tano's for a couple of hours to take a shower, but when I turned the tap, all that came out was a pile of brown sputtering gunk. Pulche backed out of the room, ears flat.

Tano glanced up. "No water? Then the drought is *officiale*, they have cut the supply and now we are in trouble. Everybody have blue water container on the roof for *emergenzie*, but they can only last for a few days, maybe a week."

I slumped down on a chair by the window. And then my fone buzzed. Dad! I stared at it a moment before pressing *connect*.

For a second I couldn't believe it was him, the sound of his familiar voice was too weird in this place. "Laura . . . it's me . . . look . . . I don't want to come on too strong, but I don't feel France is a safe place right now."

I forced myself to act innocent. "Why, what's happening?"

"Oh, come on! The French election, this Israeli water war looming . . . I don't want you out there . . ."

"It's not so bad, the media—"

"Stop feeding me that nonsense line . . . Your mum and I want the family together."

I closed my eyes. "The thing is, I'm not in France."

"Where the hell are you, then?"

"Sicily. It's Adi. He's got malaria and there was no one—"

"Else in the whole wide world to help so you had to go down there on your own without telling us?" Pause. "I . . . want you to come home to me."

This coming from my dad, who'd rather die than ask me for anything.

I squeezed my eyes shut. "Dad. I can't."

"Laura!"

"I can't just leave him."

He exploded. "Unbelievable! You listen to me, now. You're getting yourself a ticket out of there. I'll transfer the money and—"

"It's not that simple!"

"I won't take no for an answer. Call me when it's done." And then he hung up. Mr. Macho.

I went onto the balcony and stood there for a while, gazing down over the town. Palermo's like nowhere I've ever been; it's like Europe in collision with Africa. The streets are lined with balconies where the women lean over the railings, shouting and laughing, or when they see me, shooting long, cold, hard stares in my direction.

On the corner directly below there's a shrine with soft candles glowing under a tacky framed painting of Mary. A family is out there right now, sitting on a swing seat in the street, with a lantern blazing and spicy sausages spitting on a little fire. It makes Abingdon feel like night of the living dead. I don't want to go home.

And then, weirdly, Radiohead drifted up from a passing car stereo and I had the most massive wave of homesickness. I came indoors, started writing.

```
I need to know
Who I am
I need to know
Where I belong
I need to know
My destination
This is my quest
For liberation.
```

I so want to get back to the band; to tell people about all the things I'm seeing here.

## Sun., July 16

I sat with Adi all day. Right now, I've got no feelings; they've all wizened up like sun-dried strips of beef jerky in the blazing sun. Gwen came and joined me in the evening. She shook her head. "Can you imagine we were all sitting in a classroom not long ago?"

"No."

"Me neither. Even I didn't expect change like this. It takes a long time, but once the ice cracks . . ."

I reached out to smooth Adi's sheet and she touched my hand, lightly. "I'm dead proud of you, y'know. None of my other students are out here."

"Yeah, well I'm here cos of Adi, it's not like I'm really helping out. Not like you."

She smiled. "He's got lots of other friends, but you and Nate are the ones who came through for him. That shows something. And, anyway, how d'you think I got started?"

Oh, God, is that my future? Is this my first step toward being super radical with unshaved armpits, whomping up industrial-sized pans of mung dal in an anarchist squat? Aaaaaargh!

## Mon., July 17

I was kind of daydreaming in the hospital ward, thinking about what to say to Dad, when I realized Adi was watching me.

"Laur, is that you?" He tried to stretch out his arm, but he was too weak.

I jumped up and ran down the corridor, calling for the nurse. A bunch of doctors ran into his room and did some tests. They only let me in for a couple of minutes after they'd finished—but they say it's looking really positive . . . and they're hopeful, blah blah blah . . .

I ran back from the hospital like a crazy chicken. When I got back to the flat, me and Nate totally danced around the room and then we went onto the balcony, stared up at the stars, and breathed deep. A moment of pure, pure *happiness*. That's the great thing about when you're living one day at a time, everything goes dead alive and *now*.

## Wed., July 19

GPJ strode into the flat this morning and sat down heavily. "Well, looks like we've got ourselves a proper little water war. The Palestinians, backed by Egyptian and Jordanian troops, have taken over a whole section of Israeli land that lies over an aquifer, and the first thing they've done is take control of the water supply. They're point blank refusing the Israelis water."

Nate shrugged. "Can't someone else give it to them?"

"Well, somewhere like Turkey's got the water, but how the hell are they going to move it? That's a lot of pipe to get though hostile Arab countries. It's never going to happen."

"But why cut off the Israelis' water? Ain't they got any tanks or nothin' to fight with?"

GPJ gazed at him, curious. "Don't follow the news much, do you, Nate? No, the Palestinians don't have much in the way of tanks, or any other weapons. Maybe they've just discovered a deadly new one. Thirst."

I stretched out. "But those guys are always fighting. It's not gonna affect us that much, is it?"

Gwen shook her head. "You're joking, right? There's never been international conflict like this over water before. Little battles, but not outright war. The USA is Israel's biggest friend and they are threatening to get involved. If that happens, the first thing Europe will do is close down its borders. Sicily is a key place."

"What about the UN? Won't they stop war?"

Gwen glanced at me. "Like they did before in Iraq, Iran? I don't think so."

I gazed out over the sea. Israel's only on the other side.

Just got this from Mum. Looks like she's chilled Dad out for me.

Dearest L

Why are you upsetting your father? That's my job, darling.
I don't know why he thinks you'll be any safer at home when the whole
of Oxfordshire's gone wild with the Reservoir Defence
campaign. All the locals are getting involved, even the hideous Mrs
Huckstable was dragged away from the Village Green Sit In by the police
last Tuesday. Can you imagine?! And it's spreading across the country.
The people are taking back their power and finally saying sod off to this
stupid bunch in power. They can't just keep draining local water away
anytime a big city gets in crisis. Country people have got rights too,
y'know?
As for me, I'm proud of you...out there, battling for the immigrants, and I
trust you to take care of yourself and to come home to us safe and
sound... and in time for uni in September (hint hint)
PS Your sister'll be home soon so that'll cheer your dad right up. I think
he secretly believes women belong in the home. He's such a Neander-
thal!
Love from your mother xxx

Battling for the immigrants? That woman's totally living in some action movie. If she saw what was really going on down here, she'd . . . what? Actually I don't know what she'd do.

## Sat., July 22

For the past few days, Nate's been walking Adi up and down the corridors, trying to build up his strength. I watched them joking around, kind of mock wrestling, and for the first time, it almost looked like Adi again.

On our way back to Palermo, Tano stopped the van. "Come, I want to show you something."

Nate and me jumped out and followed him down a series of tiny cobbled streets, past rows of boarded-up doors and windows and under sheets hanging across the streets in great loops—and all around us, scrawny cats, dogs, and kids, playing and fighting around dry fountains—with cars and scooters gunning along the narrow streets, scattering the pigeons.

Tano came to a stop at a ruined crossroads. "This is Vucciria, a very old French district from hundreds of years." He pointed down a dirty alleyway lined with ruined buildings. "From the Second World War, the bombing."

I laughed. "But that was over 80 years ago."

"*Si*. And this is Palermo. More as Beirut than Italy, no? In the day there is no one, but in the night, many hundred of *clandestini*—illegal *immigranti*—they come here to sleep and eat a little. Like a secret town."

"Where do they live? It's just ruins."

He pointed at a shattered flat, with bits of walls remaining. "Here, for one."

We stared in silence. "But—" began Nate.

"No but. They have no choice." Tano turned on his heel. "In *gen-erale*, the *polizie* just don't come here no more. Sometimes they do a

189

big thing, you know—*raid*—and arrest everyone, but the next day it just come full again. So many people here. And all the time more."

The water war is still going on. I miss Sam. No one makes me laugh around here. Even Nate's going dark.

## Mon., July 24

I was alone with Adi this afternoon. He put his arms behind his head, sighed. "Din't think my big adventure'd end like this, with you sitting on the end of my hospital bed. I was gonna be such a big man . . . and in the end . . ." He reached for my hand. "So good to see you."

I moved my hand away, pretended I was reaching for a grape. He's too sick to fight with yet. I'm waiting for his body temp to reduce. 2 more degrees and *you're* at the tipping point, Mr. Adisa.

Stace has just called me, asking when I'm coming back. "I ain't got no place to hide, Laur," she groaned. "This camp is crawling with activists, and they're working me like a dog!"

"Doing what?"

"This week? Digging a well for a local village. My hands are one big blister, but they don't care, all they do is feed me macaroni, do a bit of Reiki on me, and next day throw me back out again. You know what I really want, more than anything?"

"What?"

"A chicken & mushroom cup of noodles."

## Tues., July 25

This morning I woke up to the sound of shouting from across the road. I peered outside. A line of stumpy women in aprons were dragging great piles of rubbish, fruit, fish, boxes, crates, old fridges, and furniture up the street to block the far end, while a super-fat woman stood on top of the pile, screaming.

I turned to Tano. "What's she saying?"

He listened for a moment. "Basically . . . my children are dying of thirst . . . but over there those bastard African *immigranti* are washing their clothes!"

"What, in the Immigrant Aid Centre?"

"*Si.*"

"Is that what people are saying now? Can't they see how desperate they are?"

He waved his hand. "Ah *si*, but soon it will not be European against African. It will be us against each other. Town against town, family against family."

A tiny Fiat pulled up and some policemen jumped out in those stupid Italian cream hats and pansy white sashes. Like anyone's gonna take them seriously in that.

I can't believe I'm here. Can't take it in somehow.

```
A people left abandoned lost dismissed
Cut dead from the memory
Like the cutting of a wrist.
```

## Wed., July 26

Today the UN Security Council gave a warning to the Arab forces to withdraw from Israeli territory. They've given them till noon on Friday to respond.

GPJ smirked. "Or else *what*? They're gonna throw paper clips at them?"

Adi is to be let out from the hospital on Friday. It's so time to be going home—this place is getting dangerous for real. Boyfriend Lite thinks the same, too.

Hmm. London feels like another life right now. And so does Sam.

### Thurs., July 27

When we got to the hospital this afternoon, we found Adi outside, leaning against the glass windows.

"What's going on?" asked Nate.

"I can't spend another second inside that room. I've been out of London for like the whole summer and I ain't even made it to one stupid beach."

So, with him between us, we hobbled slowly down to a little bay near the hospital and sat under some palm trees. The light was so clear; the mountains looked like they were drawn with a fine pen. I tried to keep focus on the distance cos all around us on the beach there were Italian girls astride boys, slapping, pinching, rolling, knotted up together. It made me feel like a chunk of driftwood. After a while, Adi tried to put his arm around me, but I jumped up, quick.

He frowned. "Why you always brushing me off?"

"I—I'm not, it's just—"

Nate caught my look of panic. He opened his arms wide, grinned. "Luvverly, luvverly girls. I've missed you all so much!"

Adi had another go. "Babe, I can't believe you came all this way for me."

Pulche suddenly sat on his arse in front of us, stuck his leg out and got into some serious action.

Nate sucked his teeth. "That dog ain't got no class. My boy here is having a moment and all he can do is chew his arse."

I've made up my mind, I'm going to talk to Adi the first chance I get to be alone with him. I can't carry on like this.

## Fri., July 28

**12:00**. There's been no Arab response to the UN deadline.

Nate nodded like a war journalist. "Ah, they're still gonna back down. I can feel it."

It's getting panicky down at the Immigration Centre, though. I've spent the whole day down there with GPJ sorting out food packages, and all anyone talks about is leaving.

## Sat., July 29

Shit. Overnight the U.S. has acted independently from the UN and moved 5,000 troops onto the Gaza Strip and fighting's broken out all along Israel's borders.

We sat in Adi's room and tried to work out what to do. Nate reckons we should call the others and all get straight back to the U.K. He went, "I mean, what we doing here? This ain't our home."

Adi frowned. "That's just ducking the issue again. These people need us."

Nate jumped up. "That's it, I'm sick of you lecturing me. I know what's happening . . . an' it kills me to see what's goin' on, but honest, what are we gonna do? Look at what happened to you in Sudan . . . you wound up costing the Red Cross a fat load of money in chopper rides and medical bills. Some help."

"Thanks a lot."

"I'm sorry, bud, but it's the truth. I mean, ain't you sick of this action hero shit yet?"

Adi took a sharp breath. "War is coming. We face it now or we face it later. What you wanna be? One of those people who always keep themselves safe, all cozy an' hidden away?"

"Those people are called survivors, Adi," Nate spat. "And I ain't gonna feel guilty for wanting to be one just cos of your college boy guilt."

I sat there feeling so bad. It's all gotten so heavy so quick. It's like

I'm being dragged in against my will. I don't even believe in politics, all that left and right . . . it's all crap . . . But then I look across the road at the detention center and what's happening there is so wrong. Maybe Adi's right, there is no choice now.

Suddenly Adi burst out laughing. "I don't know why we think we're so special. This is what every normal person has felt for thousands of years when they're on the edge of being dragged into war. I'm amazed there ain't a reality TV show on it yet."

I glanced over at him. For a second he seemed like the old Adi, the funny outsider, the one that used to take the piss out of everything. The one I fell in love with.

### Sun., July 30
The U.S. is demanding that Europe gets involved after some battle yesterday at the Sea of Galilee over an irrigation pipe.

I frowned. "Isn't that where Jesus walked on water?"

Nate grinned. "Yeah, but don't remember no irrigation pipe in my Bible class."

I was with GPJ all afternoon, so Nate went down to the port to book ferry tickets, but came back with nothing. He shook his head. "You should see the line. It goes halfway up into the town center."

We're going to go back tomorrow and stay all day if we need to.

### Mon., July 31
We all went down to the port and waited in line from first light until dark—and only moved forward about 500 meters. It's going to take a long time to get off this island. I knew they'd be freaking out at home so I called Mum 3 times today, but no response. Strange.

# August

## Tues., Aug. 1

U.S. warships have rocked up on the far side of the Mediterranean overnight. Shit. Tano reckons it's better to stay until the crisis calms down, but GPJ says we should get moving.

Nate frowned. "But is Europe gonna get dragged in?"

"I don't know, but for sure we'll send troops to borders like Sicily and target immigration aid places like this, too. Your mum must be going nuts!"

"Well, that's the thing, I've been trying to get thru to her for days but she's not picking up."

Gwen frowned. "Maybe because it's all kicking off at home—the drought's spreading and great swathes of the countryside have gone up in protest with the Citizen Tax. If I know your mum she'll be up to her neck in it."

I shook my head. "Great *swathes*? Why do you teachers always talk like that?"

Maybe she's right about Mum, though. I've decided to stop stressing about home and just focus on getting there. We're going to camp out tonight so we don't lose our place in the ferry ticket line. This afternoon I sent a mail to Dad saying I'm already on my way home. I got the idea from some pathetic self-help book of Kier's called *The Positive You*, which says that if you act positive, like something's going to be real, soon it will be real!!!!

## Wed., Aug. 2

More bad news today. Adi's relapsed. After I took Nate's place in the ferry line, he went back to the flat and found Adi shivering, curled up in a sweat ball on the bed. He had to take him back to the hospital. So much for my positive thinking—or maybe my hidden anger at Adi is so powerful it's jamming all my fakey positive wavelengths.

## Thurs., Aug. 3

Got this from Claire today. Blimey, it's like the whole of Europe's exploding. Anyway, we've had to quit the ferry line, can't go anywhere till Adi's better.

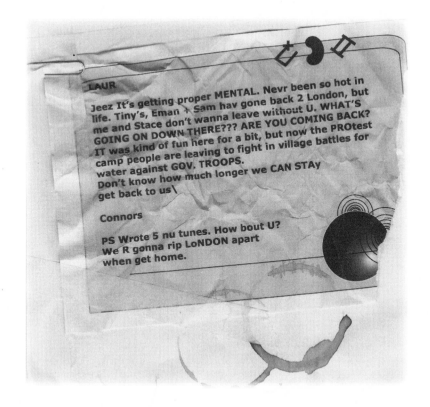

> LAUR
>
> Jeez It's getting proper MENTAL. Nevr been so hot in life. Tiny's, Eman + Sam hav gone back 2 London, but me and Stace don't wanna leave without U. WHAT'S GOING ON DOWN THERE??? ARE YOU COMING BACK? IT was kind of fun here for a bit, but now the PROtest camp people are leaving to fight in village battles for water against GOV. TROOPS.
> Don't know how much longer we CAN STAy get back to us\
>
> Connors
>
> PS Wrote 5 nu tunes. How bout U?
> We R gonna rip LoNDON apart when get home.

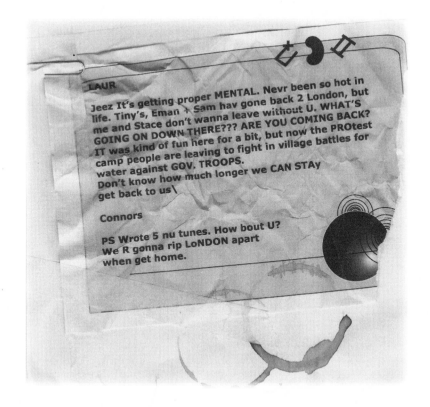

Huh. So Sam's gone home without even texting me? My bass better be safe.

## Sat., Aug. 5

"Laura, Nate, wake up!"

GPJ shaking my arm. "The EU has invoked emergency border control powers . . . We've been tipped off that they're locking down the ports and raiding all immigrant aid worker buildings. We've got to get under cover. Now!"

"But Adi's too sick to move."

"We've got him in the van. He'll have to make it." She smiled. "The dog's with us, too. Wouldn't take no for an answer."

Within minutes we threw whatever we could find into our backpacks, ran down downstairs, and clambered inside Tano's van. Adi was hunched up in a corner, face blurred with sweat.

Gwen threw me a blanket. "Cover him with this."

I put it around his shoulders and took his hand in mine as Tano set off, crisscrossing the city via a maze of back streets. After about 40 minutes he twisted in his seat. "OK, we have cleared Palermo . . . so you can come out, but if I tell you, you go straight down."

I slid into a pile of medical supply boxes as we swerved on to the SS 624.

Gwen frowned. "Hey, slow down. We don't want to draw attention."

Tano laughed. "*Vero*, so I drive like a Siciliano. We *live* for the smell of burning rubber."

Nate peered out of the window. "Where we goin'?"

"To the south of the island. They will not expect this—they will try to catch most people at the ports, at Palermo and Messina. I have friends, they will hide us."

After an hour we hit the coast and Tano pulled off down a dirt track, coming to a stop on the edge of a wood. After a few moments a dark-haired man in uniform appeared at the driver's window.

"Shit!" Nate hit the floor.

"*Tranquilo!*" hissed Tano. "This is Salvatore, he is from the *guardia forestiera*, but he is one of us." He rolled his window down and the two of them spoke in rapid Italian. The man glanced at us, touched his cap. "So we go to a place by the beach. It is safe for this night."

"We sleeping outside?" asked Nate, glancing at Adi.

Salvatore flicked him a look. "Better than in a cell." He turned and set off down a path. "Keep close."

We followed in single file thru the scrub grass and tiny, bent olive trees until suddenly there was the sound of waves and we came to the edge of a wide bay, with an ugly village of concrete flats perched on the left side.

"That is Marinella. Not there." Salvatore motioned ahead. "Up here."

I followed his gaze and gasped. Up ahead loomed a great pile of ruins, overshadowed by huge stone pillars.

"What the—?"

GPJ laughed. "Incredible! The Acropoli. Are we sure it's safe?"

Salvatore nodded. "We use this place for to hide people . . . there are 8 of us helping . . . *locali*, me, a priest . . . my brother in *polizie*."

"But what about the other locals?" I asked.

"Some are good, some no. In Sicily, we are used to strangers. We have had Arab, Spanish, Greeks, American . . . and now these people. But the villages are poor and it is too much now. There are 20, 30 boats coming to the island a day . . . there is not enough to share."

Tano shook his head. "Sicily can do more, much more. Some of these *locali* are bastards. Like in Nazi Germany, I never know before how ordinary people can live close to concentration camps and say they know nothing. But now I see how—you jus' pretend not to see, focus on something else. Make *them non umano*."

Nate scowled. "Tano, mate, was you always this cheerful?"

Salvatore left us some food and blankets and then disappeared, so we found a grass hollow in the ruins and laid the blankets down.

Nate and me put Adi between us. He was burning up, but at the same time shivering with cold. We just couldn't get him warm, and then Nate snapped his fingers.

"I got it! Oi, Pulche, mate! Get over here, we need some monster heat."

The dog trotted over and curled up next to Adi. It was amazing—after a few minutes, Adi's shivering started to stop. Adi opened his eyes a crack. "I got to tell you, dis hot dog breath in my face is a high . . . high price."

Nate nodded. "Yeah, he's the original Stink Lord."

Adi groaned. "This ain't a proper south London boy death. I shud be stabbed up or shot, not slowly crushed under a fleabag belly."

Nate sucked his teeth. "You got to take what you can get these days, bro."

10 P.M. Tano has just taken a call from Salvatore. The plan is that we sneak along the coast to a nature reserve place called Lo Zingaro, where we can catch a local fishing boat off the island. The bad news is we'll have to start out on foot cos there's roadblocks everywhere and we can't risk getting stopped. After he hung up, Tano peered at his fone. "*Catso*, only half bar left. Anyone else got more solar cells?"

I shook my head, visualizing the solar charger sitting on the kitchen counter of Tano's flat. I pulled out my own fone. Dead. Great.

## Sun., Aug. 5

I woke up in the early morning with a great big rock in my back. Tano and Nate were poking about on the edge of the ruins, so I checked Adi was sleeping fine, and crawled out of my blanket and joined them.

Nate stretched. "So what's this place?"

Tano smiled. "It's Acropoli . . . Y'know, a Greek *tempio*."

"It's old, man."

"7th century B.C. People have been traveling, going to new places for a long time. Modern Europe has forgotten this."

Nate pointed across the bay to the little town. "Check it out—Acropoli versus Marinella—basically 3,000 years versus the 1960s and a pile of shitty concrete. Modern life sucks."

Then I glanced out over the ocean and saw the boat. It was tiny, like a little sailing dinghy, and crammed full of people. Suddenly a marine flare shot up from the town, followed a minute later by a boat, speeding toward the immigrants.

Tano sighed. "*Guardia costiera.* End of another journey."

I watched as they closed in on the yacht. I could just make out people throwing themselves into the sea trying desperately to escape, but then a second coast guard ship appeared, heading toward them. They had no chance. Everything they had gone thru for nothing. I turned away, sick. But what can I do?

## Mon., Aug. 7

Last night was intense. We set out at dusk in a great orange burn of a sunset toward a place called Marsala. The coast was wild, spray splashing over us; as night fell we tramped inland and the journey turned into a blur of olive trees, sharp hill ridges, barbed wire, grape vines, and creaking wind turbines. When it got too dark, Salvatore led us on to the train tracks and we stumbled forward, hour after hour, alongside the rusted track. Adi looked like a corpse; we all took turns in helping him keep going. And then, finally, birds singing and faint light. GPJ pointed to a wooden shed at the end of a lane.

"Let's rest up in here."

Tano caught sight of the road name and spread his arms wide in welcome. "*Amici!* Welcome to the Via delle Stelle."

"What's that mean?"

His teeth flashed in a wide grin. "Road of the Stars!"

We ate some bits of bread and cheese, with Pulche doing heater duty again for Adi. I bent down over him. "Can you do this?"

"Have to." He looked down, "I feel so bad, slowing everyone up."

GPJ took his hand. "Adi, it's not your fault. That's your problem, you take everything on your shoulders."

He smiled slowly. "Huh, take a look at yourself. Talk about God complexes all around."

I went outside with Tano.

"He can't take another night like this. We can't walk all the way there."

He sighed. "I know." And went over to talk to Salvatore.

I went inside and tried to sleep, but kept thinking about the war. Fighting over water, I still can't believe it. Salvatore says Europe is still refusing to get involved. I wish I could get a message thru to my family.

## Tues., Aug. 8

There was a football match on tonight—Palermo against Napoli—so Salvatore took the chance to get us on the road. He smiled. "War or no war; the roads will be clear, everyone inside this night watching the *calcio*."

And so at 6 this evening we got in the back of a stinky fish truck belonging to a mate of Savatore's. We lay down, sort of covering ourselves in boxes and bits of disgusting old seafood. About an hour into the journey, the coast changed to these weird squares on the sand and we shot past a line of soldiers guarding a wire fence.

"What's that?" asked Nate, peering thru the truck's wooden slats.

GPJ glanced out. "Salt-processing place."

"Why's the army care 'bout that?"

She shifted a foam tray under her arse. "Are you kidding? People used to get paid in salt, it was so valuable."

"Yeah, yeah, back in the day. But why now?"

"Cos we're traveling backward in time. When the fuel goes, so does the refrigeration . . . and back comes salting, drying, pickling. Otherwise your food rots and you don't eat."

My mind suddenly flashed back to my mum and the smoking fridge at home. I had to hide my head behind a lobster pot to cover my tears.

At around 10 we pulled up in a small town and Salvatore jumped out.

Adi stretched his arms. "Man, I'm good again . . . when the shakes come on I feel like I'm gonna die, then a few hours later it's all over. Can't we get out and eat something?"

Tano shook his head. "I don't think so."

"Where we at?"

"San Vito. It's a little town on the sea. A place for *touristi*."

Nate frowned. "But why bring us here? Why ain't we goin straight to this Zingaro place?"

GPJ gave him a look. "Nate, you need to chill out. We have to go by foot from here."

We were parked on a back street that overlooked the main square. It was lined with bars and little tables and umbrellas, but there was hardly anyone about. Tano glanced around. "*Strano*. Normally this place is full, full with Italian *famiglie* . . ."

I gazed at the outside of a bar where a big guy, like a troll in golf pants, was shouting at a little guy. I can't ever tell with Italians if they're fighting or just talking. Everything's super intense with them. Suddenly the big boy did a series of fast slaps with his hands, like he was gonna make pizza dough out of the other one, but then burst out laughing before slamming his hand down on a table, *hard*—bowls of peanuts and olives bounced off the table onto the ground. Pulche's eyes bulged. He loves Italians.

Anyway, no bar for us. Salvatore's just come back and told us tonight we sleep on the beach.

## Wed., Aug. 9

I woke at first light, chilled, with the cold, damp smell of wet sand and seagulls screaming overhead and I looked along the shore and felt so . . . alive. I'm like a girl in a movie . . . the sky, the sea, the chase . . . and over there, Africa! And the person I really wanted to call was Dad, tell him what I was seeing, feeling, how it's all so real. How the people helping us here, it's not a game to them and it isn't about ego and politics . . .

Before it got too light, Tano got us moving and as we trudged along the sand, we could make out other groups of people slinking off the beach for the cover of the forest. A mountain ridge loomed up in front of us.

Tano pointed. "This way."

Adi rolled his eyes. "What is this, *Sound of Music*?"

For hours we stumbled along, all of us with T-shirts wrapped round our heads to cover up from the sun. Thank God Salvatore had plenty of water for us. I kept stopping and looking around. I'm not joking, I don't think I've ever seen a place so beautiful. Blue, blue, sea stretching out—and far down below us, shimmering golden beaches dotted with people.

Nate caught my eye. "S'like one of them holiday brochures, innit?"

Tano clicked his tongue. "*Si*, if you minus the *immigranti*, drought, *polizie*, malaria, war—"

Nate flung his arms up. "There he goes again! You was definitely at the back of the line when they wuz handing out positive thinking, mate."

Everyone started laughing. Thank God for Nate, really—between Tano, GPJ, shivering Adi, and me, ready to kill him once he's better—there's not a lot of laughs around here.

I walked alongside Salvatore. "Are we nearly there?"

"*Si*, this is Lo Zingaro. Now is a nature reserve, full of *cavi* and little beaches, but before was famous for . . . how you say when people use the boats to bring things in secret?"

"Smugglers?"

He nodded. "This is a wild place for these men. After the war here was Bandito Juliano, and before many pirates." He stopped and asked everyone to gather around. "Now, what do you think is the best to do? We must wait for our boat. It may be one or two days, I cannot tell, so we have two choice. We can stay high here on these paths—"

GPJ glanced down at the beach below us. "But what's the point? People can see us from here, anyway."

"*Si, essato*, so the other choice is to just pretend to be *turisti* and go to the beach. Also the paths down there are much easier."

We looked at each other and smiled. The beach! On the way down, Nate found a baseball cap and put it on backward. "I am so blending in. Look at me. I'z an American fool."

And then for one afternoon, we were normal. We lay in the shade, swam, played football, ate a weird picnic of sardines and olives . . . Pulche found a shoal of tiny fish near some rocks and spent the whole day bullying them. Salvatore even went and got us ice creams, before he left to check on the boat situation. But it was over all too fast and when the sun set and the few other tourists went back to their hotels or whatever, we sank back down into undercover mode, wrapping ourselves up in blankets and settling down in the mouth of a cave a few meters from the sea.

Adi came and sat close to me, just as the sun was dipping below the horizon. He sighed, "It's unbelievable, but beautiful somehow, y'know? How close you can be to—"

I stood up, fast. I don't want any sunset moments with the boy. I can't face dealing with this right now. I just want to get off this island and get back to some kind of normality first.

## Thurs., Aug. 10

No Salvatore, no boat. We're all just trying to keep chilled. In the evening, Nate found a plastic radio on the beach and we jammed it in a rock and all gathered around, leaning in to hear the super-faint and crackly World Service news, like a WW2 family. Anyway, the reports are basically good. As of today there's a cease-fire in Israel and the UN is going to send in peacekeeping soldiers next week.

GPJ sucked her teeth. "Hmm, but will it work? There's no more water to go around today than there was yesterday."

Tano shook his head. "Who know? Let us pray so. Otherwise this war must come to Europe also."

I snuggled deeper into my blanket. Home feels like a long, long way away.

## Fri., Aug. 11
Really hard day. All of us kept to separate bits of the beach. Waiting.

## Sat., Aug. 12
Finally, this afternoon Salvatore returned. "Pack up your things, it will be tonight, after dark. The boat will take you to Palermo, where friends will take you undercover on the ferry to Genova."

Tano reached over and gave him a massive hug and the others stood around grinning, but I couldn't keep still, kept pacing around and later I went and sat on my own at the far end of the beach. After a while I heard footsteps crunching over the pebbles. Adi.

"Want some company?"

I shrugged, turned away.

He grabbed my arm. "Right, that's it. Tell me what I've done wrong."

"Don't know, you tell me."

"What?"

I felt the anger start to build. "Er, apart from leave the band, abandon me, and drag me into . . . this?"

He grinned. "Well, yeah. But it's kinda cool—"

"It's not a game."

"Beats being bored."

And then I slapped him. "Is that why you cheated on me?"

He stared at me, shocked. "But—"

"Don't. I was such a fool . . . oh, Adi needs his space . . . oh, Adi's trying to find his way . . . and all the time you were just with that girl."

"No!"

"Yes. Don't lie to me. You were with Monica when I left London. For all I know you're still with her now." I pushed him in the chest. "How could you've done that to me? After all we've been thru?"

"Because I'm an idiot. And every day since all I do is think about you."

I shook my head. "Words."

"But you . . . you *must* still feel for me. Otherwise why you came all this way?"

"Because . . . me and you—"

His face lit up. "Exactly—*me and you* . . ."

Suddenly the *putt putt putt* of an engine came drifting on to shore. We stared at each other . . . the boat! There was no time and without another word we ran back to the others and gathered up our stuff. Together we all plunged into the sea and swam out toward the light of a little fishing boat, rocking at the entrance to the bay. When we reached the side, Tano had to drag Adi onboard cos he had no strength. I glanced at him, gasping on the deck and my heart went all tight. But that's pity, not love.

The boat engine sputtered into life and Tano turned to us. "So now I say good-bye . . . I . . . my work is here."

We stared at him, light falling across his face from the boat lantern. He tried to smile, but suddenly his face crumpled and he grabbed Adi. "You are with good people now . . . so take care and go straight to the border, eh?" And then he slipped down into the sea, disappearing in seconds. One of the men shouted something and we started to move away from the shore, all of us straining our eyes to catch one last glimpse of him. But the boat moved on into the darkness, and the only sound was Pulche barking madly from the beach. I've never seen GPJ cry before.

## Wed., Aug. 16

We've finally made it! After 3 days of bribes, hiding, and puking on boats, we got to Genova, caught a ride to the protest camp—and today we pulled up in a tiny abandoned village up in the hills, basically just a row of broken down houses lining a dusty road. I climbed out of the van and immediately heard The Clash, *London Calling*, drifting down from the upstairs window of the nearest ruin.

I started to laugh. "Stace, Claire? Is that you?"

A moment, then Stace's shaggy head popped out of a first-floor window. "Laura Brown?"

I squinted up at her. "Jeez, Stace, your hair's gone well radical."

She grinned. "Piss off."

And then Claire came running out of the door. "Where the hell have you been? We've been calling and calling . . . din't know how long we could hold out here for."

I glanced behind her at the ruined house. A spiral of herby smoke wafted gently through a gap in the roof. "Yeah, must've been tough for you."

## Thurs., Aug. 17

I can't stay awake; I don't think I slept more than 2–3 hours a night in Sicily. As soon as I got here yesterday, all I did was set my fone to charge before falling onto a blanket in a kind of coma. Today I forced myself to wake up long enough to call home. Long beeps of the fone. No reply from Mum, so I tried Dad, but nothing again. Then I tried the home number. I could see the fone there on the kitchen sideboard in Abingdon. Click, someone picked up. My heart lifted.

"Julia and Nick are not in right now, please leave a message and we'll get back to you as soon as we can. . . ."

All I want to do is talk to them.

## Sat., Aug. 19

Finally. Fone rang. Abingdon home number.

"Laura?"

I sat up, woozy.

"It's me. Kim."

"Kim? What the hell are you doing there?"

"Yeah, I missed you, too, sweetie."

"Sorry, sorry . . . just wasn't expecting you . . ."

"To be home? Well I am and it's all good."

"Really? I couldn't talk for days cos I didn't have a charger and I knew you'd be freaking out and—"

"No, no one's freaking. All busy, getting the harvest in . . . and basically as I say, all good."

"Er, OK. You already said that. Is Mum or Dad around? Neither of them is picking up."

"No-o, they're . . . out in the fields."

"Mum's in the fields?"

"Yes. In the fields. Look, I really wanna talk properly, but it's just a bit of a busy time and there's this guy at the door . . . so can I call you back soon?"

"Well, yeah . . . Look, Kim, you sure everything's cool?"

"Totally. It's all . . ."

"Good. Yeah. You said."

I slumped back on my sheet. I'm too exhausted to deal with this right now.


## Mon., Aug. 20

Aha! I woke up this morning all fresh and normal again, like a young spring leaf. I bounced down the stairs and found the others sitting outside under the shade of a fig tree.

As I stepped out, a smell of burning hit me. "What's that?"

GPJ waved her hand in front of her face. "Forest fires."

Claire looked up. "Ooh, it's alive!"

I gazed around the deserted village. "Where's everyone else, anyway?"

Stace ticked off her fingers. "Well, French Sylvie left for Chiapas . . ."

"Where?"

"Mexico. To join that revolutionary group, the Zapatistas. It's totally mental over there. You know, they've practically set up their own country, declared war on the World Bank, and chucked all the U.S. corporations out. Brazil is about to do the same and half of South America is behind them."

"God." I paused. "What about Sam, Mikey, and all those?"

"Went back to London 'bout 2 weeks ago. Sam wanted to wait for you, but in the end Mikey just said he was going . . . so he had to make a choice."

"Yeah, bet he did," muttered Nate.

I ran my fingers thru my hair. "But my bass is safe, right?"

"Yep. He left it here for you, good as new. He looked after it dead well. This kid tried to jack it the other week and Sam ran after him and beat him up to get it back."

"Really? Sam?"

Claire nodded. "Well, it was the least he could do, after—"

Long pause. Adi glanced at me for a moment, before turning to Claire. "But I thought this place wuz like a protest camp or something? Where's everyone?"

"All over the place. Spain, Greece, France . . . there's water battles going on everywhere. And some people have set up a new camp near here to help the villagers. Since the end of July, a load of private and Italian gov tankers have been coming from Genova and the big towns to take water away from local wells."

"So why you still hanging around here, then?" asked Adi.

"We have been helping out, Saint Adi, but we didn't want to be gone too long in case you came back. Nobody could get hold of you . . ."

I looked around at the others. "So, what? You guys ready to go home?"

Stace nodded. "Totally. It's getting too manic. And I want to see what the deal is with uni."

Adi shook his head. Stace turned to him. "What?"

"Nothing."

"No, mate, if you got something to say then say it."

"All right, then. I can't believe you just want to go back to uni. This is the front line—people *need* us here."

Stace rolled her eyes. "Be real. And my aunt is well freaking out; she wants me back home where it's safe."

GPJ muttered. "Safe, right."

Stace jumped up. "You know what, I'm sick of you guys preaching. You want to go and save the world? Then go for it! But me, I've been here just over a month, dug about 50 piles of dirt and got a bunch of blisters to show for it. Big deal. We can have so much more impact with the band in London, not playing around at being heroes here. Mikey's got gigs lined up for us and they're even gonna release a download of our Bordeaux gig."

Adi spat. "You're just scared."

Stace glared at him. "Maybe, but why are *you* still here, anyway? I hear the **2** just blew up a dam on the Swiss border. It's only a few Ks away. You too chicken to join them?"

## Tues., Aug. 21

Some of the camp people came thru today and told us the army's raiding the area and has set up roadblocks all over the place. There's even proper fighting on the Italian border with the Swiss over reservoir water. Even worse, there's a rumor of a refugee internment camp up in the hills. There's no way we can get up to France for a couple of days. And there's fighting again in Palestine. An *Israeli* suicide bomber protesting that his village on the West Bank is dying of thirst. Unbelievable role reversal.

I can't believe I'm writing about *politics* in my diary. It used to be all about Ravi and Thanzila and shit at school. I'm so getting old before my time.

## Wed., Aug. 22

Uh-oh. Big fight with Adi today, but I guess it was only fair he knew the truth.

He caught me after breakfast. "So what's this I hear about Sam?"

I tried to shrug it off. "What is it to you? You'd upped and left."

"3 weeks before, and we weren't even split. Took you a long time to get over me, huh?"

"You've got no right—"

"To be angry? Cos of Monica? Yeah, well, I messed up, but at least I admit it. But you—innocent little Laura, all confused and abandoned . . . you make me sick."

I took a sharp breath. "I make *you* sick? You've changed so much I don't even know who you are. I never thought you'd cheat on me . . . and then to cover it up with some bullshit volunteer holiday."

"You call cleaning toilets in the Sudan a holiday? Cholera, malaria?"

"You know what? I can't stand you right now. You never laugh, you're never fun like you used to be. All you do is judge. At least Sam's—"

He slammed his hand down. "Don't say no more! I don't wanna know. And you've changed, too. You never used to be frightened of things . . . and now you're like all the rest. Run home to Mummy and Daddy."

We stood there, glaring at each other in deep, deep silence. We'll have to travel home together, but there's no way I'm talking to him ever again.

## Thurs., Aug. 24

Too hot and depressed to move today. Me and Stace lay upstairs on the cool stone floor, hardly breathing.

She flopped her hand out. "What do you think about what's happening at home?"

"How you mean?"

"You know, the place's gone mad. All the local councils and towns and villages are at war with the gov over like, water, electricity, recycling, roads, everything. It started off with the Citizen Tax and now it's gone mental. My mate John says it's well cool, all these posh old battle-axes and suburban housewives and anarchist lefties joining forces with a ring of Labradors and rescue dogs all around 'em. Thought you'd know all about it cos of your mum and that."

I sighed. "I haven't spoken to her in weeks. Don't know why she's being so chilled, normally by now she'd be freaking out and calling the Red Arrows in to rescue me." I banged the mattress. "Oh, God, these flies are driving me nuts, all I want to do is sleep. I can't even stand this sheet on me, but if I leave any bit of my body out it turns into a total helipad for flies."

Stace looked up. "Try this sol-fan." She turned it toward me and the stream of air blasted the flies off—but it wasn't powerful enough to reach my head and feet, so after a few seconds the flies changed tactics and started to party on my face and toes.

"Urggh!"

"Use mind power to block 'em out. They're not so bad. They ain't heavy, they don't sting . . ."

I took a breath. "You're right. They haven't got claws or teeth . . . they're fine, all fine . . ." I focused my will like a laser beam on loving the fly. And then one walked right across my eyelid. I shot up. "You know what, Stace? I ain't so sleepy no more."

She burst out laughing. "Fly one, humans zero. They'll rule us in the end."

Later on, when Stace'd gone to get lunch, GPJ came in and started stuffing things into her backpack.

I glanced over. "What's up?"

"Nothing. Getting ready to leave."

"But there's roadblocks everywhere."

"So?" She started to zip up the side pockets. "I've got to *do* something. . . . All this hiding is driving me crazy."

I sat up. "I know, with us it's a bit like kids messing around . . . But you'll find your next project, maybe join the protest camp?"

She suddenly stopped, turned to face me. "You know what, Laura? I don't care anymore, about talking, meetings, peaceful protests . . . So you listen to me now. Once you asked me about my family, my life, who I am. Well, I'll tell you. I'm done with it all. All I care about is putting an end to this disgusting, messed-up, futile, hypocritical system that is screwing the planet. And right now that only means *one thing*. Do you understand? There is no going back for me now."

We stared at each other a long time. I nodded.

## Fri., Aug. 25

She's gone. Just left in the night.

Nate frowned. "But what's up with dat? Why she leave without saying nuthin?"

I dug my hands in my pockets. "Don't know."

Adi glanced at me. "Oh, cut it out, you know she's gone to join the **2**—an' I know what you're thinking."

"What?"

"That I don't have the guts."

"Yeah, well, do you?"

"I ain't justifying myself to you—I go my own way. There's ways other than terrorism and running home to hide. So when we get to the protest camp up in the hills, I'm staying there to help."

I stuck my hands on my hips. "You do that, mate. But you aren't going to make me feel guilty no more."

"Yeah, count me in on dat, too," growled Nate. "I love you, man, but you are one big pain in the butt right now."

I looked around at the others. "Are we all the same on this? We keep low, no getting involved with the protests . . . I mean, I want to get home, I'm worried about my family."

Stace nodded. "Low, low, low. No more shit. It's uni in September."

"But we could stay and help out for a week or two. Enrollment and the gigs aren't till the start of October," Claire began.

Adi whirled around. "You? Wid me on something?"

Claire rolled her eyes. "You're not the only one who's not sure about going back to study."

I threw my hands up. "Do what you want, but I'm going straight home."

"We *all* are, the *angels*'ve got to get gigging. Got that, Connor?" growled Stace.

Later on, Nate came and found me. "You two ain't never getting back together while we're in this mess."

I put my hand out. "I don't think we're—"

"Don't say the words. Don't make it final!"

"Why are you on his side all of a sudden?"

"I ain't . . . It's just he's been sitting by himself all evening down by the pump. He looks so lost, Laur."

## Sat., Aug. 26

My fone buzzed me up in the dark. I jerked awake and grabbed it.

"Laura E. Brown? It's me and you'll never guess what's going on—"

I shook my head to de-fug it. "Kier? It's the middle of the night."

"Yeah, but I got to tell you this thing, it's just so *freaky*. There's been a massive underground explosion in New York and all these manhole covers are shooting into the sky . . ."

"You woke me up to tell me about manhole covers?"

He cackled dead loud into the fone. "Too right. They rocketed up 20 meters . . . and that's just the start." He dropped into a campy broadcaster's voice. "As we speak, Miss Brown, thousands of gallons of toxic gunk are spreading across the city. Like a giant amoeba. The first anyone knew about it was about midday in a park in Williamsburg. These lezzies were having a picnic or something and suddenly they saw this stinky slime oozing over the grass toward them."

I struggled up in bed. "Are you on drugs?"

"No-o. One of them acted all butch and went over and fired up a zippo lighter to test it. Nearly blew her spikes off. Can you *imagine*? One minute you're eating your tofu wrap or whatever, gazing up at the clouds, and the next you're starring in your own personal horror film."

"Are there giant mutant rats? That's when you know the shit's hit the fan."

His voice went all prissy. "Huh, make fun if you want. Turn on the net and check it out.

"OK, I will." I clicked the connect button on my fone and the screen sprang to life.

He was still gabbling. "You're the first person I called cos I thought you'd appreciate the total weirdness, but . . ."

I scrolled to the breaking news page. The screen filled with one of those aerial chopper shots of New York with some reporter going: *"We're looking at the overflow of a vast underground lake—more than 55 acres wide and 40 feet deep—over a hundred years of waste, poison, and dumped oil and chemicals—and because it's oil, it can't sink—and now it's on the move."*

I flipped back to voice. "Oh, my God."

"Told you."

"Are you safe?"

"Think so, I'm in a different district, but they're clearing the whole Greenpoint area. Newtown Creek and Queens to the north, Flushing Avenue to the south, and the East River to the west. They've totally stopped the train. You can't go farther on the G than Nassau and the L train is out of action."

"You sound kind of happy . . . You sure you're OK?"

"Yeah, yeah. They reckon they'll get it under control in a couple of days, weeks tops. Apparently it's happened before and Exxon is clearing it up, but super slowly cos it ain't exactly a big money spinner for them." He sighed. "There are still those water battles out in the Midwest, but New York's kind of been dull so far. I miss the excitement of London."

Suddenly there was the sound of shouting and the fone went all crackly.

"Kier?"

"Ooh, you'll never guess what! My flatmate just went to the bathroom and there's oily gunk trickling into the toilet. *Our* toilet! Bring on the killer roaches! If I die I want someone young and hot to play me in the movie. Promise?

"Mate . . ."

"Oh, stop being so dull. It's an adventure . . . so, promise? Hunk or no one. I don't want some hack."

I nodded.

"Huh?"

"I'm nodding."

"Got to go . . . but I'm sending you a foto!"

I waited in the dark till the image flashed up in my inbox.

**VFONE**

img name:NY >sender:kieran_mac >26/8/17
check out the sludge n' slime in the Big A.
I feel like 20 greasy big macs rolled into a ball
of skin... oooh er... K x

## Sun., Aug. 27

Woke up to another disaster. The shit's really hit the fan in Milan. The **2** bombed and destroyed a hotel at an international oil company meeting and the city is in total chaos and lockdown. But there is a cease-fire between Palestine and Israel. Weather definitely cooling down. What am I . . . a broadcaster now?

## Mon., Aug. 28

This came today.

VFONE img:name:Milan central >sender:GPJ > 27/8/17
don't like goodbyes. Milan ... then who knows?
It feels like the only sane place to be. take care GP

One thing you can say for my friends. They ain't dull.

I tried to message her, but it bounced back. I guess she's gone undercover with . . . *them*. I can't believe what I'm writing. It's so weird being inside history. I keep waiting for someone to press the stop button. All I want to do is get moving. Kim still hasn't called me back.

## Tues., Aug. 29

We were upstairs, packing to leave this morning when a line of military jeeps shot thru our village. They slowed right down, but didn't stop. Thank God we were all inside; we'd definitely be in trouble if they saw us with all the **2** stuff going on.

And then, finally, this afternoon Kim called.

I punched *connect*. "Hey! Why's it taken you so long to get back to me? What the hell's going on? Where is everyone?"

"Well, that's what I'm calling about . . . they didn't want me to say anything—Dad still doesn't, he'd kill me if he knew."

"Kim?"

"Mum was arrested about three weeks ago."

I gripped the fone. "What for?"

"Leading the reservoir protest. She was sleeping overnight out at the lake camp and . . . they were raided and the whole place smashed up . . ."

"Is she hurt?"

"Few cuts and bruises, y'know, nothing bad. But she's really lost it in there . . . keeps crying and that."

I shut my eyes. "But, Kim, come on, how long can they hold her for?"

"That's the thing. The police can hold her for 50 days without charge. And it looks like they're going to prosecute—to set an example. Her voice broke. "Dad's there every day . . . and I'm here all alone. I'm so scared for her."

I've just *got* to get home. Typical Mum, though. The woman's always got to out-radicalize me.

## Wed., Aug. 30

Now there's fighting on the border between French and Italian soldiers over access to reservoir water. The area's exactly on our route out. It's like Tano said, now it's European versus European. Anyway, we've made a decision together. Tomorrow we leave. Whatever happens, we leave. Walk, hitch, whatever—we're out of here.

## Thurs., Aug. 31

We're resting now so we can set out tonight. Claire knows the first part of the way to the protesters' camp. She reckons it'll take a couple of nights. We don't really want to go that way, but it's the most direct route north.

The only good piece of news right now is it's definitely cooling down. I even put a pair of socks on last night, but then I had to take 'em off after a couple of minutes. Wool is weird.

# September

**Fri., Sept. 1**

The walk last night was way worse than the night walk in Sicily. We had Tano and the others then and it was kind of an adventure—but this just feels dead real. I mailed Tano last week, but no reply yet, I hope he's OK.

At one point we were climbing along a path through a wood and it was so dark I couldn't even see my hand in front of my face. The only way we could move forward was to hold hands and walk in a chain.

**Sat., Sept. 2**

We rested up in a smelly old caravan in the woods during the day and then set off at late afternoon. The water situation's pretty scary; we're down to a bottle each. About 4 hours into the walk I was so thirsty and tired, all I wanted to do was sit down and cry. I started to fall further and further behind until, stumbling around a bend in the path I found Adi, waiting.

He sighed. "C'mon, you've got to keep up."

I sagged against a tree stump. "I've seen it a hundred times on those survival shows—y'know when people are begging to give up and just be left to lie down in the desert—and you're watching it going, *no, don't stop, keep walking, what are you begging to stop for? You'll die if you do that!* And now here I am *begging*."

He held out his hand. "Up you get."

I shook my head. "I'm fine . . . and, anyway, . . . I ain't even talking to you."

I am so thirsty it's untrue.

## Sun., Sept. 3

Disaster Day. We hardly bothered sleeping after last night's walk cos Claire reckoned we were really close to the camp. So in the early morning, we set off along a lane, but we'd only been going a few minutes before the lane joined a main road closed off by a flying checkpoint. We just managed to get ourselves into the bushes before being seen.

"What's going on?" whispered Stace.

I peered out; there was a bunch of soldiers surrounding an old couple. "Not sure. It's something to do with them not having the right papers."

"Papers? What they need them for?"

"Dunno."

Claire tapped me on the shoulder, hissed, "I know where we are now, I was here a few weeks back. There's a village and then the camp is just over that hill. Let's sneak up this way thru the woods."

Keeping low, we followed her under the trees until we reached the top and there, spread beneath us was a little village, with the camp just beyond.

"That's it!" cried Claire. "Look, you can see the protesters' tents down by the river."

Nate turned, frowning. "But just for tonight, yeah? We ain't stopping."

"I know that, but they've got food and water and we can find out what's going on up on the border."

Nate sucked his teeth. "I got a bad feeling 'bout this. Don't wanna get into any trouble."

Claire shook her head. "No one's gonna do anything stupid, Nate. Have some trust."

We speeded up, excited, and 20 minutes later we climbed over a field gate and finally stepped onto the main road. We followed a long curve into the village, past the first group of houses, and then the road bent sharply and . . . oh . . . I'll never forget the scene before us. The main square. Like a painting, a moment frozen in time.

In the center of the square there was a tanker, with a giant hose attached, sucking up water from a shattered well—and guarding it, a row of armored troops. Facing them was a line of locals and pro-testors, moving silently across the ground, toward the well. And then, suddenly, a farmer, an old man, just lost it. He broke from the protestors, pushed his way thru the troops before falling down on his knees in front of the tanker—and starting to beg and plead with the driver.

*"Aqua. Per vivere!"*

A young man, I guess his son, ran forward to drag him away, but the old man had lost it. He kept repeating, "Water. *Per vivere*! To live! *Non capisci?"*

The driver and the soldiers just stared back at him, impassive. This drove him even crazier. He pitched forward and grabbed hand-fuls of dry dirt, then staggered to his knees in front of the com-mander. Thrusting his hands forward, the farmer slowly released the dirt through his fingers. It was so silent, you could hear it thud down on the commander's boots.

The church bell began to chime. Nobody had seen us. We had a moment, a tiny gap in time in which to pull back off the road, sneak away. We looked at each other, nobody spoke—and then—without a word or a sign—we all walked forward and fell in line with the people. *There just wasn't anything else to do.* Among the protesters, nobody even acknowledged us, they were all so intent on moving forward, foot by foot. It was like a game of chess with neither side wanting to make the first move. But when we'd gone forward maybe another hundred meters, almost level with the church, the soldiers suddenly turned aggressive and pressed forward, trying to push us back across the square. Some fighting broke out and suddenly there was a searing, battering barrage of noise. People covered their ears and threw themselves to the ground.

Adi clutched his head, screaming: "Sound bombs!"

After a couple of minutes the smoke cleared. And then the soldiers came at us again. Someone shouted: "Go limp, link arms!" I hooked my arms into Stace and Nate's and together we dropped to the floor. The troops started to pull people from the end of the line, straining to drag the heavy bodies along the ground. When it came to my turn, an officer grabbed my wrist. I tried not to react, not to fight, just let myself be as heavy as I could. He twisted my arm back, hard, and yanked me up into a standing position. Tears flooded into my eyes.

He laughed. "*Non pianga*, don't cry, *bella!*"

And then I just lost it, screamed: "It's not your water! You're thieves! You're leaving them nothing!" Next to me some protestors started struggling and fighting, pulling soldiers to the ground. I heard popping noises and suddenly my eyes were stinging, weeping, with tear gas. Fighting to breathe, I stumbled over to the side of the square before falling in the grass and vomiting. Slowly I came to, regained focus: found myself watching a lady bird *right there*, clambering up a poppy stalk. I gradually became aware someone was moaning. Stace, she'd been hit by a gas canister, a red blister was bubbling up the length of her right arm.

The soldiers rounded up a bunch of protesters and led us along the road thru an open field gate where they forced us to sit on the burned brown wheat stubble. At least we were still together.

Nate hissed: "Er, was dis the plan?"

A soldier looked over and motioned him to be quiet. I looked at the man. He was clutching a gas bomb, seemed only a couple of years older than me. He caught my eye and then straight off looked away. I kept on staring at him, just to let him know that he hadn't beaten me. Even though he didn't meet my eye, he knew I was watching him. He tightened his grip on the canister and swallowed uneasily. Minute after minute passed. Me and Claire peered thru the branches toward the village. By now more protestors had rocked up and were marching again on the tanker, but even as we watched, another military van arrived and another set of troops jumped out, clubs raised, and started to beat the villagers again.

Adi whispered, "We've got to make a run for it."

Stace hissed, "Which way?"

Adi nodded toward a bunch of trees. "There. If, *when*, we get a chance."

All of our group were on their feet now, watching the action in the village, and then, suddenly to my left a group of locals made a break for the village and ran straight at the gate, scattering the guards, who immediately ran after them.

"Now!" shouted Claire.

Together we grabbed Stace and ran, ran, ran. The trees coming closer—and then a strange sound—like a metallic clicking, flashing, hot, near my face. Nate shouting, "Down! Down! Bullets!"

I flung myself down. Dust, stones, earth flying up, choking me. A long moment, silent, gasping for breath. And then the soldiers, standing over us.

Caught again.


And so here we are. There's a group of about 40 of us under military arrest inside the town hall. They've taken all our fones and comm devices off us. I don't know exactly what happened to us back there at the protest, but it happened to all of us the same. We're in the shit for sure, but in a way I'm glad, I mean what kind of person turns away from something happening right in front of their eyes?

Jesus! A soldier has just burst in, waving his gun. We all threw ourselves to the floor, but he was shouting something: "*Piogga, piogga!*"

The Italians around me jumped up and ran to the windows. A man turned to me, laughing. "Look! Rain!"

I'm writing this as fast as I can. They're almost definitely gonna take all our stuff away. My bass, my diary . . . everything.

## Tues., Sept. 12

I can't believe it. This morning we were driven to a train station called Modane on the French border. As we stepped off the bus, they gave us our stuff back—minus cards, money, and fones, which were *lost in transit*. When the soldier shouted, "Brown, Laura!" I went up, hardly daring to hope. He turned to a pile of stuff and pulled out my battered backpack. But no bass. I pleaded with him, repeating *bass, bass, please*, but he just laughed at me, till another guard came over and threatened to take my backpack away if I didn't shut up. There was nothing I could do. I picked up my bag and returned to the line. As soon I got back, I bent down and unzipped it, pawing thru the stuff till I found it—underneath my old Slam City Skates sweatshirt—my diary! I'm amazed they didn't use it against me. I didn't want to show too much emotion, in case the guards noticed and took it off me, so I just zipped it back up and sat down like nothing had happened. But inside I was buzzing. At least I hadn't lost everything.

Now we are rammed in a platform waiting room, sheltering from the driving rain. There's about 300 of us being deported, mostly protesters from the camps, students—even holiday people caught in the madness. We're all going to be under police guard until London. I'm sitting here, just staring at this diary. I don't even know how to begin, don't even know if I want to write about the last 10 days, but Stace says I have to do it, so I've got the facts down for if we need them later. A guard has just come in and told us the train is going to be delayed because of flooding, so I guess I should start now.

The day after we were arrested at the village, they moved us to a police station in a nearby town. We weren't allowed to see or talk to each other for the first couple of days. It was just this endless thing of being marched into an "identification office," which was basically a basement room with a table, an officer, and a monitor. Each time it was identical, with him asking me the same stuff over and over thru an interpreter. Where are you from? Why are you here? If you're just a backpacker, what were you doing in the village protest? Have you heard of the organization called the 2? What proof do you have that you are really a student?

Before we were separated in the village hall, we worked out our story—*we're English university students, in a band, we're backpacking in Italy, on our way home*—and vowed to each other to stick to it, with no word of Sicily, the immigration center. GPJ, the Dox, the protest camp. Claire made us go over it again and again. And thank God she did. It was so hard in that room; the officer kept telling me that the others had told a different story, that I was going to be charged on terrorism charges unless I told the truth. So many times I nearly cracked, and I don't know how I got thru the nights alone in my cell, but I just tried to keep focused on their faces, Claire, Stace, Adi, Nate. Knew they were doing the same.

After my first interrogation, they searched me, confiscated all my stuff, and took my ID. Then they did a retina scan and added me to the database like a criminal. Number 0032395.

On the 3rd morning I was led outside to a van with a bunch of other women and girls and driven to a "deportation center." My heart lifted, I thought they were going to just boot me out of the country. But when we pulled up to the gates, it was clear this was a proper camp—at least 5 acres in size and surrounded by high-wire fences. Inside, there were rows and rows of tents and low plastic sheds, all set up in lines. There were hundreds of people there, standing, sitting, talking, pacing around in the mud. I stood there, dumb, scanning the crowd for my mates. It was the first time I felt terror, real fear. And then I saw Stace and Claire, standing on the other side of the wire. Oh, the feeling. It's making me cry remembering it.

After I'd been processed I ran across the compound toward the girls, but before we got a chance to talk, the guards started shouting at everyone, ordering us to sit on the wet ground in rows of 20. I glanced around, most inmates looked like immigrants, but others seemed to be ordinary Italians, with like little T-shirts and Gucci shades. (Even in jail Italians keep it together.) A guard shouted at us to join the farthest row, but when we got there, there was like this brown, stinky sludge seeping from a plastic tank across the ground.

Claire hesitated. "I don't want to sit there, it's disgusting."

A female guard walked over and slapped her across the cheek with her glove; not hard, but it was still super scary. Then she forced us to all sit on our arses in the filth. The other officers started laughing, like it was a game. Some people looked terrified, others stared at the guards like they wanted to kill them. After this they made us sit there in silence for an hour, while they "counted" the rows, until, finally we were allowed to get up for lunch. As we walked to the line, I linked my fingers with Claire's for a moment. "Mate, are you OK?"

She squeezed my hand. Just. "Been here since yesterday."

"Did you stick to the story?"

"Yeah. You?"

I nodded. "You think they believe us?"

Stace glanced over at the guards. "Don't know. How much is intimidation and how much is for real? I mean, we've got rights, ain't we?"

I glanced around the camp. And then I realized where we were. "Shit, this is—"

"An airport?" Stace grinned. "Yep. Talk about irony. There's even some old Ryan Air planes over on the far side, near the men's section."

"Adi and Nate?"

"Yeah, they're here, too. Arrived yesterday, same as us. We've seen them by the fence, but there's no way to talk to them."

"Who's running this? Army, police?"

Claire shrugged. "God knows. I think it's something to do with Frontex, or like a cross-European force. But they got power, for sure.

Basically they can hold us here without charge or communication with the outside world for up to 80 days if they want."

A guard yelled at us to stop talking and so we took our place in the food line in silence.

The next day passed in a blur, but the following night there was a huge thunderstorm and it rained so heavy that our row of tents partially collapsed. Claire dragged herself up out of her sodden blankets. "Why the hell didn't we run from that village while we had the chance?"

Stace wiped her wet fringe out of her eyes. "C'mon, mate. We did it for good reasons."

Claire started to cry. I put my arm around her, but I didn't join in, couldn't allow myself to feel anything.

For the next few days, the camp basically turned into a lake of liquid mud, like Glastonbury, but minus the burgers and lasers. 600 women and girls were allowed access to only one of the airport bathrooms, basically 6 toilets and 6 sinks. We had to roll up our trousers to go in there cos the floor was a river of brown gloop, full of hair and filth. But it was even worse inside. There were no doors, no electricity, no privacy. We basically had to piss in front of each other. With no toilet paper, only hands.

"Well, it's one way to get to know each other better," muttered Stace.

On about the 5th day in, Claire got to see a camp lawyer for a few minutes. He said we were going to be deported soon, provided our stories checked out and no further evidence came to light. Then he threw her out of his office for demanding to make a call. A big soldier guy escorted her from the hut, with her yelling, "We've got rights. We are allowed to contact our families!"

The officer nodded, but mimed there were no working fones, and then another stopped her and offered to sell her a fone card. Both laughing. But Claire told us the news and was smiling as she walked back. At least we'd been given a little piece of hope, something to hold on to.

We were never allowed back in our tents after breakfast, so all we could do for the rest of the day was roam around the compound. All of us were the same, we'd be OK for a bit then we'd get these moments of rage, pure rage at our helplessness. I spent a lot of time thinking about Mum and hoping she'd been released. Stace got obsessed with contacting Adi and Nate and spent her whole time scratching weird unreadable notes on bits of metal and rubber. 3 times a day, every day, we were lined up in rows of 20 for the weird counting ritual. And the food, always the same. In the morning ginger tea and a stale muffin. In the evening, spaghetti with onions. If it was a good shift of officers, they'd leave us alone, let us talk, squished under the edges of plastic roofs, sheltering from the rain. But some of them were vile. One really brutal squad of bitches lined us up out in the rain for hours and made us clean the toilets with bits of old rags and broken brushes. Again laughing, videoing, taking fotos. What for I don't know. They could hardly show 'em on flickr.

Every day there was constant movement as people were brought in or taken away. About a week in, a really big group of women and girls arrived from Ghana. Over the next few days, we hung out with them a lot; they were lovely, dead funny, and kind—I've got no idea *how* after all they'd been thru. Anyway, there was one girl about my age who was kind of separate from the main group. I noticed her right from the start and soon I started to watch her all the time, couldn't help myself. She had these dark rings around her eyes like she never slept—and I never saw her rest or eat; she just kept moving, wandering, pacing along the fence.

After about 2 days of this, I saved my hot tea from breakfast and went over to her by the fence. She stared at me for a second, nodded, and took the cup in her tiny hands. Then she began to talk as if we were in the middle of a conversation. "Just a small open wooden boat, out there in the big waves. Me, my brother, and sister . . . we were packed . . ." she bent double, "like this for almost 5 days. And then the storm came . . . we clung to the boat sides, praying for the shore." She paused.

I glanced at her arms, covered in cuts. Some of them healing, others fresh red blood streaks.

". . . And then the boat hit something. All of us flung like little dolls to one side . . . my friends disappearing into the dark. I grabbed on to the side of the boat, but it was sinking, the wood slipping beneath me, the water dragging me down . . . I cannot swim, but I kept tight hold, swallowing seawater, oil . . . watching the people slip underneath. I screamed out for my family, but they did not answer. Suddenly, there were sharp rocks there. I grabbed, held on, stayed like that until the rescue boats came."

I just stood there. How can you say anything back to that?

She tossed the cup aside and the tea spattered up the fence. "Dead. My brother and sister both drowned that night." Her eyes bore into mine. "Is that what you wanted to know?"

I've never felt so divided from someone in one moment. The difference between us hit me like a black wave. My choice, my home, my future—and this girl, nothing. The unfairness. It nearly made me choke with shame.

The next day there was a rumor of a cholera outbreak in the men's camp. Nobody could believe it was true, but they woke us up at dawn the following day and ordered us to move all our tents over to the far side of the field to make room for an emergency hospital. At one point, there was nearly a riot on the men's side. The soldiers only got it under control by shooting bullets over their heads. Claire gazed at the temporary shelters as the medical staff and soldiers began dragging piles of bedding and buckets in. "Oh, shit."

Stace dropped her head in her hands. "You got that right."

I put my arm around her. "C'mon, stay positive. We've been here for over a week and loads of people have come in later and got out earlier. It's got to be us next."

"Yeah? You think they're gonna let us go if there's a cholera out-break? Remember London? Kim? This means quarantine."

That night was the worst for me; for the first time I started to lose my faith that we'd get out of there. I'd been clinging to the same hope for days, that we were being processed, that we would be deported, that they had nothing on us. But after day after day of no rules, no rights, no contact with the outside world, I didn't know how much longer I could carry on. But the next morning we were called into an interrogation office and told to be at the gate the following morning.

"Where are we going?" asked Stace.

"Deported. Home. Train."

"Are our friends being released . . . the boys?"

The officer waved us away. "No more questions." Then she gave us each a package containing a white T-shirt and new sneakers, like a goody bag from a festival.

None of us slept that night. We were too scared it wasn't going to happen or that Adi and Nate wouldn't be released at the same time. The next morning we were out in the yard at first light, pacing up and down. And then at 7:45 the transport crew arrived and this fat woman officer shouted out a list of names. It seemed like forever till we got thru the perimeter fences and were stamped out. I kept look-ing around for the boys, so stressed I felt like I was gonna puke the whole time.

"Maybe they're already on board," muttered Stace.

We walked to the bus and climbed inside, peering forward into the dark interior. They weren't there. We stood there, wild, looking all around, willing them to appear. And then Claire screamed, "Nate! Nate!" and banged on the window. I whirled around and saw him, being marched between some guards. He was thrown on board, but the troops kept him away from us, right down the front.

"Where's Adi?" I screamed.

Nate shouted. "Got into a fight with the guards, he's in solitary confine—"

I ran forward, but a woman shouted for me to sit down. I refused. Two more guards stepped forward and Stace had to drag me back. Then, waiting, waiting, waiting. Each minute an agony. So ecstatic to be leaving, but ruined by leaving Adi. Stupid, stupid boy . . . And then, finally, the doors closing, the engine growling into life, and the bus starting to churn its way thru the potholes and mud. I turned and took one last look at the camp, watching as the wire fence receded into the distance. Even now I can't believe it. I can't write any more today.

## Wed., Sept. 13

I feel like I'm going to faint the whole time. After nearly a day of waiting we are now moving slowly thru Switzerland. The train is so jammed it's impossible to move, with us guys squished together just by the toilet. The train stopped in the middle of the night, and when dawn broke, we were just outside a town with a river bursting its banks. It's impossible to believe after the summer. What was all the fighting for? After a long stop the train eased out of the station. I curled up next to Nate. He took my hand. "I couldn't do nothing, Laur. He wun't back down . . . he wuz standin up for this Algerian kid . . . the guards were beating him . . ."

"When we get back to London, we'll get help." I squeezed his hand, tight. Didn't have any more words.

And from then I fell into a dark, dreamless sleep as the train jolted its way across France.

## Thurs., Sept. 14

London! Free!

A bunch of U.K. transport police climbed on to the train as we pulled into King's Cross, but there was no way anyone was going to be busted again, and the whole lot of us rushed them and scattered across the station, darting, racing, jumping over the barriers like a herd of gazelles. After we were sure it was safe, we started to hunt for a free fone hub point. The nearest we could find was at Centre Point. When it was my turn, I went all breathless. I dialed. Tone, click. Dad's voice. "Hello?"

A huge choke jumped thru my chest. "Dad, it's me."

Big intake of breath. "Laura! Oh, God! Where are you?"

"London, Centre Point!"

His voice broke. "Right, right . . . don't move. Oh, God . . . Julia! Come here now . . . right, OK . . . I'm coming to get you. Don't move. I'll be there as soon as I can."

I leaned against the booth. Suddenly felt really weird.

Nate bent over me. "Hey, are you a'ight? You're dead pale."

## Fri., Sept. 15

Don't remember journey home yesterday. Can't stand up. Dizzy.

## Tues., Sept. 19

Shivering, puking, and dreams, such bad, dark, endless dreams.

## Fri., Sept. 22

Woke up this morning with someone sitting by my bed.

I tried to focus, couldn't. "Mum? Is that you?"

She lurched forward, grabbed me in her arms. "Oh, Laura!" Rocked me in her arms, me crying like a little child. I can't believe I'm home.

## Sun., Sept. 24

I've never felt this down before in my whole life.

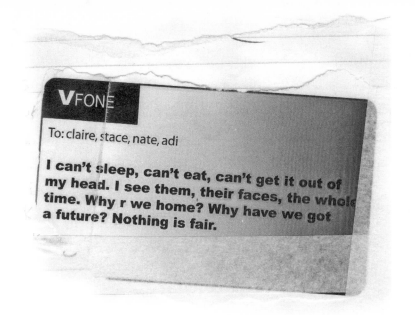

To: claire, stace, nate, adi

**I can't sleep, can't eat, can't get it out of my head. I see them, their faces, the whole time. Why r we home? Why have we got a future? Nothing is fair.**

I sent it to Adi as well, even if he can't read it right now. His parents are out in Italy now, trying to get him free. I can't exactly imagine Che Guevara's mum and dad waiting for him outside a camp, like a naughty schoolboy.

### Tues., Sept. 26

I know she's only trying to be positive, but honestly I just felt sick when I think about getting back to normal.

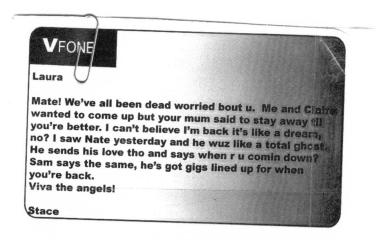

Laura

**Mate! We've all been dead worried bout u. Me and Claire wanted to come up but your mum said to stay away till you're better. I can't believe I'm back it's like a dream, no? I saw Nate yesterday and he wuz like a total ghost. He sends his love tho and says when r u comin down? Sam says the same, he's got gigs lined up for when you're back.**
**Viva the angels!**

Stace

235

## Wed., Sept. 27

I've switched my fone off. I don't want to talk to anyone. Don't want to be made to feel better, don't wanna think about the band. Don't the others care? I'm sick to my stomach. Are the **2** right? Do you get to a point where words are useless?

## Sat., Sept. 30

Kim came into my room and tossed the Abingdon paper on the bed and I laughed for the first time in weeks. I couldn't help it. That paper is genius.

# THE ABINGDON HERALD

'Reservoir 4'
## Released on Bail
'Vow to keep up the fight!'

020 checkpoints    sewerage system 'out of control'    Pig swill crisis

# When the chips are down..

**..bring back the spud!**
They may not be sexy, but the humble potato is storming back up the 'carb charts.' After the drastic failure of many crops over the summer, food prices are at an all time high and the government is waging a campaign to convince millions of us to Think potato, Grow potato, Eat potato!

**By Karen Mitchison**

According to the national Potato Council spokesman, Harry Dowd, 'The board is seriously urging people to turn to the home-grown potato to keep them going, just as our great grandparents did in the 'Dig For Victory' campaign in the second world war. They're a fabulous source of iron and potassium and they certainly offer more for your money than exotic rice

and pasta, both of which have nearly quadrupled in price due to the world water shortage crisis.'

But there's more to this unassuming tuber than you might think. It was once an exotic and expensive food with a reputation as an aphrodisiac! And maybe they weren't so wrong. Recent studies show that vitamin B sharpens up your verbal skills... great for chat up lines!

Local celebrity, Frankie Aggers, who plays simple Billy Johnson in EastEnders has come out and backed the potato. 'They're naturally fat free, low in calories and are an all round meal solution. Why not give 'em a try.'

**HOTLINE**

If you're interested and want to find out how to get in on the **Abingdon 'Potato Ring'** call the *Allotment Hotline* on 07798 448 9000 or visit their new portal at www.spudweallike.org.uk Thanks for all the readers who've mailed in their fave spud dishes

*I love to fry them slowly in olive oil with gaarlic cloves and a hom-grown hot chillies –* **bam8forth**

*Jacket potato. Nuff said.*
**Thomas, Stuttgart.**

236

Kim threw the curtains open. "C'mon, mate. You've been locked in this room for a week in the dark, not said a word to anyone. Mum and Dad are going out of their tiny minds."

"So?"

"You know."

"What? *Start again* and all that shit?"

"Yep."

"Kim, you've got no idea . . ."

She turned to me. "Don't I? Oh yeah, that's right, I didn't dick around Europe for the summer . . . I was only here with Mum in prison. Cut out the drama queen, Laura—cos at least you've got a choice."

I slapped the paper. "And that's what's killing me. I'm just another spoiled, stupid, white girl."

Kim nodded. "Exactly! That's why you've got no choice but to carry on. Out of bloody respect."

I hate, hate, hate it when Kim's right.

# October

## Sun., Oct. 1

I forced myself out of bed today and went for a walk around the village with Kim. The whole place has gone mad with live updates everywhere on the village's carbon points, water usage, waste purifying targets, allotment rotation, blah blah. We even saw a couple of beefy blokes in caps patrolling the trash cans.

"Who are they?"

Kim sighed. "Trash and Waste Patrol. It's death to flush a turd down the wrong pan. I couldn't believe it when I first got back."

"When did this all start, though? It was still pretty chilled when I left."

"June 25th, when the Citizen Tax became law. Everyone's just totally lost faith in the gov . . . specially that Carbon Dept., it's so useless. So instead of paying, people just turned around and did their own thing. Y'know, villages setting up their own generators, getting independent of the national grid, whole suburbs refusing to pay council tax and using the money to set up water purifiers, housing estates digging up parkland to grow stuff. From what I've heard, London's *covered* in cabbages."

"How's all this happened so quick?"

"Dunno. Strange times all right. It's a weird mix, part . . . what's the word? *Euphoric*—like people getting off on the thrill of doing things themselves and not waiting like stupid kids for the authorities to fix things for us. But there's anger, too, real rage. This Citizen Tax is just taking the piss."

I studied her. "So what are you gonna do next?"

She shook her head. "I don't know. I mean, there's nowhere *to* go anymore."

"Kier's in New York, you could join him."

"And slosh around in oil? He says it's under control, but it ain't exactly *Sex and the City* no more. Anyway, he's coming back, didn't he tell you?

"To London?"

"Far as I know."

I stopped. "On the level, are you really planning to stay here with Mum and Dad?"

"Thinking about it. You didn't see her when she got out of the cells. And Dad nearly collapsed with the strain. The good thing, though, was they started talking to me like a human being, instead of playing the Nick and Julia show . . . I kind of like them now." She suddenly turned and hissed. "Never repeat that. I will deny all knowledge."

"But, Kim, this can't be it. Both of us stuck here in Abingdon forever."

"No. You're going to uni—and you've got the band. Me? I'm not sure yet. I mean, they've only just held on to the farm and someone's got to make sure Mum keeps her head down. One more bit of trouble and she's in serious shit. There's been some confiscations of entire property for protestors."

"You're gonna stay here and keep Mum under control? You?"

She raised an eyebrow. "What's the matter, missy? Ain't only you can be the saint around here. Anyway, I've got plans. A couple of my mates from London College of Fashion have come back to live here and they want to set up a design studio that only uses 100% natural fabrics, wool, and leather from the area. We're going natural."

Blimey, all that Buddha's totally gone to her head.

3 A.M. Just woken from such a bad 'mare. The boat tossing on the waves, darkness all around, screams.

## Mon., Oct. 2

When I went down for breakfast this morning, my parents were bent over a letter at the kitchen table, but as soon I walked in, Dad covered it with the Sunday supplement and Mum did a kind of squawk, which she tried to cover by pretending she'd burned her hand on the toaster.

"Owk! Toast, sweetie?"

I slid over to the table. Dad flicked a tiny glance at me over the top of his paper and started whistling, while Mum spread marmalade on a slice, like I was a mentally ill person they had to work around.

"What's in the letter?"

Dad's eyebrows shot up. "Uhm?"

"The one you hid when I came in." I nodded. "I can see the corner right there, under Britain's Top 10 Sexiest Veg."

He blushed. "Oh, it's nothing . . ."

"Mum, tell him to quit lying. He's rubbish."

She smirked. "You're right, dear. He *is* a dreadful liar . . . look at all his telltale signs. The flushed cheek, the sweaty palms, the high and girly voice . . ."

"All right, all right!" Dad pushed the letter over to me. "It's about your mum's trial. We just didn't know if you were ready."

"I was like a POW, Dad. I can handle a letter."

Dad smiled. "Oooh, you've come back all dramatic. Kind of reminds me of your mother at your age."

Mum tutted. "As if you knew me at Laura's age. Honestly, Nick, you're hanging on by a thread . . . and, anyway, I was far more politically active at eighteen."

He took a big crunch of toast. "Na-ah, well not anymore. Your crown has been stolen by our POW here. Unless, that is, they make you stand trial. That's your only way back to the top." He tapped the letter. "But, unfortunately, it looks like they're going to drop the charges, the same as with Laura at uni. I mean, it's just counterproductive to prosecute everybody, half the bloody country'd be in jail otherwise."

"Well, I'm not going to sit around, waiting in fear. We've got to get on with our lives. I'm going back to the library and Laura's got her second year coming."

I shook my head. "Do I? I don't remember making my mind up."

"They'll take you . . . there's an amnesty for all students."

"You know about my summons, then?"

"We guessed, made some inquiries." Mum's face suddenly creased. "For me, sweetie? I—I just want to know you're safe. I can't take any more . . ." She put her head down, shoulders shaking.

Dad put his arm around her. "Hey, come on, love . . . Laura's back and everything's going to be fine."

The thing is, right now it all feels like I'm in a dream. I can't believe I've come back and people are just still living their normal lives. Don't they care about what's going on in the rest of the world? Thank God the drought is over at least. But Mum—it's horrible, she seems kind of broken—not like her at all. Maybe I've got to go back, be *normal*, for her. Jesus, what's happened to us all over this summer?

I've been calling and texting Adi every day, just on the chance he's free. His parents have promised to call me the minute they get news. So much for my Complete Break with Adi Plan. In the day he makes me mad with all this heroic shit, but it's in the night, when I have nightmares about him, that I get really freaked out. Next time I see him I'm gonna slap his face, big time.

**Tues., Oct. 3**

I was driven out of bed this morning by a blast of high-pitched squealing. I threw on some clothes and went to investigate and found Dad in one of the pens, covered in piglets. He waved and grinned when he saw me, like those 1950s birthday card dads with pipes and vintage sports cars. Poor bastard; he works an 8-hour shift for the building company, then comes home and milks the cows and mucks out the pigs. And then goes indoors to Mum and crazy me.

"Well, you're a sight for sore eyes, young lady!" he began.

I stamped my foot. "Enough of the mental patient cheerfulness, Dad. It's freaking me out."

"Fine with me." He grabbed a tiny body and reached for a saucer of milk.

"What's going on?"

"Their mum died. It's 50-50 whether they'll survive or not."

I watched as he squeezed a tiny eyedropper of milk into the piglet's mouth. He glanced at me. "Want to help?"

I nodded.

"OK, but do it slow, otherwise the milk'll go into the lungs."

For a bit we sat side by side in silence, squirting milk into tiny pink mouths. And then Dad sighed. "If you want to know the truth, I feel terrible. When your mum was arrested, I just couldn't focus on anything . . . and there you were in that detention place. And I . . . didn't call you . . . or try to find out . . . I mean, what kind of father—"

"Dad. Shut up, please. Like it's anyone's fault."

He wiped his nose. "The thing is, Kim kept telling me she was in contact and you were fine, so really, truly I didn't know . . ."

There was the sound of a rattling bucket and suddenly Kim's voice drifted up from the other side of Larkin's pen. "Thank God one of us still remembers the value of lying. It kept you calm while Mum was inside. It's worked for us for 17 years; this family is getting way too into the truth if you ask me."

Larkin let out an approving squeal.

I looked up at Dad. "Do you want me to go back to uni?"

He shook his head. "That's not my style, Laura; it's your choice alone. But you need to be doing something." He grinned suddenly. "At least one good thing has come from all this. The useless teenage layabout is officially a thing of the past, my child. The Age of Wii is over."

I spent the rest of the morning with Larkin and Dad, and together we came up with a flyer to find new homes for the young 'uns, cos Dad's not got time to look after them properly.

# Orphan Piglets for Good Homes, now!

**Play with your pig.** Pigs love to play; they will run in circles and chase each other, grunting with delight! Make sure you've got plenty of toys for them - anything from a cardboard box, bucket, plastic bottle etc.

**Spend time with your pig.** Pigs love people, but beware, they need to know who's the boss – otherwise you'll end up with a spoiled, stroppy 2 tonne teenage pig who pushes everyone around. A complete nightmare, basically.

**Don't underestimate your pig.** Pigs are very clever. They'll learn how to open doors and gates, pull up carpets, open feed sacks before you know it. You need to keep one step ahead of them at all times.

**Don't be fooled by your pig.** Pigs are master manipulators and will do anything to get their own way. Always keep them on their toes with new stuff to do. Let a pig get bored at your peril!

**Love your pig.** Pigs like to scratch and be scratched. It's a wonderful feeling when a porker squeals with delight on seeing you before he flops down for a tummy tickle.

Interested? You'd be crazy not to be ... Call round the farm or bell Nick Brown on: 077783 455 328. Anytime.

Larkin insisted that we put in all the dark stuff. He says people need to know what they're getting into, otherwise they'll just be total putty in pigs' trotters.

"Do you think you'll get any takers?"

Dad grinned. "Of course, a piglet's like gold dust."

"So d'you know everyone around here now?"

"S'pose I do. It's kind of nice. I can't believe we all used to be so cut off from each other, sitting around like zombies in front of *X Factor*."

## Wed., Oct. 4

Tano sent me a long mail from Sicily saying things are getting better there, now that the drought is finally over in Africa. Also his aid agency has managed to get a story in the Italian papers about the illegal prison ships and there's a big scandal about it. But nothing from GPJ. She's another one in my dreams. A lot.

Claire and Stace are coming up on Friday. I don't know if I'm ready to see anyone yet, even the *angels*.

## Thurs., Oct. 5

It's so cold. I'd forgotten about cold. Why couldn't we be from a hot country? It's much more crazy than it was last year in London. Then it was a few people digging up gardens, keeping a couple of chickens, now it's like a total sin to have even one ornamental shrub or flower in your garden. Women have all got arms like tree trunks now . . . All that size 0 shit has totally vanished.

A branch of the Allotment Committee met at our place today. I glanced in at them from the hallway. Their faces, all glowing, like the spud is the new Messiah. I tell you, Christians believe in Jesus but our village believes in . . . THE . . .

Is there no plan B?

## Fri., Oct. 6

I met Stace and Claire off the bus this afternoon. When I first saw them the whole camp thing hit me, hard, and I could smell the toilets and feel the cold damp mud all over again. I still can't believe it happened; every time I try to remember, my mind kind of closes down. Claire ran off the bus, shouting, "The Tinys' manager released our gig in Bordeaux last week. 2,000 downloads for it so far!"

I grabbed her. "What?"

Claire laughed. "Unbelievable! Forget uni, let's get gigging."

Stace came up behind her. "C'mon, mate, how we gonna stay in London with no loan? We'll make about €50 max with the downloads and there's no jobs and the Docks are locked down. Uni's the easy option . . . we can gig like last year, I mean, it's not like a big deal. Two semesters and a bunch of puny modules."

Claire spat. "And they've got us under control."

Stace blew out her cheeks. "Man, after our summer I'd sign away my own brain. I wanna get back to some kind of normality."

"Normality? After what we've been thru? That shit's gone for good."

"I hate you when you go political, like you're the only person who ever felt anything. You and Adi both," growled Stace. She glanced up at me. "What d'you think?"

I stared from one to the other. "No idea. Can't we just chill a bit?"

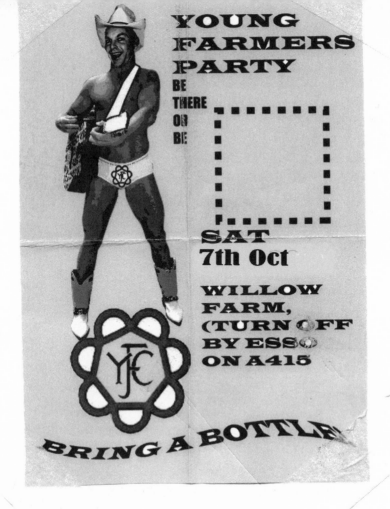

**YOUNG FARMERS PARTY**

BE THERE OR BE ☐

**SAT 7th Oct**

**WILLOW FARM, (TURN OFF BY ESSO ON A415**

**BRING A BOTTLE**

Stace dug into her back pocket, pulled out a flyer. "You want chill? Some kid gave me this on the bus and we are so going."

I wrinkled my nose. "Er, why?"

Stace snatched the flyer back. "Cos, one, we got to have a laugh. And, two, it's your birthday on Sunday, and we need to celebrate your continued existence on earth. Deal?"

"Deal."

We started to walk back to the house.

"So what about the others? Who've you seen?"

"Most people are around . . . There's a real vibe in town—there's a total standoff between the mayor and the gov. City Hall's on the side of the local councils and all the little independent projects. The gov is suing them cos they won't collect the Citizen Tax."

Claire nudged me. "Saw Sam as well. He's got a whole bunch of stuff sorted for us . . . if he's still in the band, that is."

I ignored her. "Is it definite about the uni armistice thing? It's not just a trick to get us to enroll and then bust us?"

Stace shook her head. "No, it's for real. A couple of mates who were on the Brick Lane march have got back into Brunel Uni."

"Yeah, after a biometric scan and signing a contract of good behavior. Don't forget that, Stace."

"What? That's heavy." I shook my head. "I don't want to do that, that's like massive control."

Claire flipped her bangs back. "That's what I'm saying."

Stace threw up her hands. "But what's the choice? Right, Laur?"

I shook my head. Seems to me like there's less and less choice all the time.

## Sat., Oct. 7

I was dead excited about the Young Farmers Party all day.

I'm so broken. We had to get a ride there in a minibus from the village, and when we finally rocked up, it was in an old barn in the middle of a plowed-up field.

Stace clutched me. "It's the Wicker Man."

Claire hissed, "They're all looking at us. The *outsiders*."

"It's going to be cool. We just need to get drinking." I glanced around. "Where's the bar?"

Claire pointed. "We just walked past it, and, Laura, tonight we will mostly be drinking . . . homemade cider in 5-liter plastic jugs."

Stace whistled. "Hard core."

A couple of hours and 2 full jugs of cat piss later, we were flying. The whole barn was going for it, it was like a rat's nest of kissing and groping in the hay. Even old Stace was fooling around with some giant orc against a wooden beam. I got myself sort of jammed behind a rusty plow and watched the action with woozy eyes. It was a bit like when you see those old documentaries about the war, and people are always going to dances and getting pissed in their best frocks—and you think *how can you be doing that? . . . There's bombs dropping on your head . . . Go home!* Now I see why. We've all gone kind of wild, like we've got to go for it when we can. All that gap year, internship, pension, mortgage, middle-manager aspiration crap has basically exploded.

Claire weaved over to me, smirked. "You'vegon wrong."

"Don' care. Wan' mo' cider! Mine's finis."

I flung my arm back and my fingers clinked against something hard and cold. I reached back and pulled out a bottle of cider. "No way! Secret stash."

Claire pursed her lips. "Dangerdanger, local spittle."

"Foof! I'ms tuffs oldboots." I tipped the bottle up and let the cider roll down . . . then, no!

Something in my mouth. I started to spit, gag, clawing at the hay to get up.

"Whatsup?"

I rolled over and spat out . . . a cigarette butt. Glistening on the ground.

Claire grimaced. "Oh, man. Even for us, that's low."

"Urghh."

She looked at me for a moment. "So, yougoin back uni? Doin' safe way?"

I ptuued out a bit of loose tobacco. "Jeez, Claire. I looksafe to you?"

She sighed. "Can't get it out my mind."

"The camp?"

"Yeah and ev'thing else we saw. Feelso weird. Can't see point in nothing."

"'Cept the band, right?"

"It's the only way I c'n make sense . . ."

I nodded. "Me too. At leas' do something to get people . . . to tell what's goin on."

Claire frowned. "But why we got togo London an' uni? I mean we cud do the *angels* from here . . ."

"You've gottobe kiddinme."

She rolled her eyes. "Youso jujmental."

Suddenly 2 girls threw themselves on a hay bale right next to us. I turned my eyes their way, but I couldn't see their faces, just a nest of back-combed hair. A wave of nausea shot over me and I shut my lids, let their words roll by.

"omygod rite so Tony mod says to Lorraine he dint like her hair that way, feathered, yeah? so Lorraine runs in the bogs and starts hackin off all her hair with nail scissors. her mate Wendy tries to stop her but Lorraine pushes her off cos shes like gone mad an shes had that carrot wine off of her uncle."

The other girl gasped. "so what's Tony do?"

"he comes into the bogs after her cos Wendy told his mate Carl that she wuz sobbin in there an he told Tony . . . so he pushes his way into the lavs, looks one look at her an says *no way you crazy cow u an me is thru.*"

"no!"

"yeh. so he jumps in his car and Lorraine starts runnin after him, rite, but he aint seen her. so he starts reversin, rite?"

"wot can't he see her?"

"that's wot he's saying, that he din't see her—so he puts his foot down . . . an . . . he basically like *runs her down.*"

"omygod. like a rabbit, like roadkill!"

"yeah."

"well wot now, hav they called the hospital?"

"well thats the thing cos its dead spensive an they make you pay by the km for the ambulance so Tony put her in the backseat and drove her there by himself."

"ah he treats her all rite innit?"

*   *   *

I flicked my eyes open, glanced over at Claire. She giggled. "OK, OK, you're right. It's London or nothing."

## Sun., Oct. 8

Happy birthday to me. I will never see, hear, smell, speak of cider as long as I live. This is my solemn vow.

Mum made me a birthday cake and at 5 this evening. I forked a mouthful in before running to the bathroom and puking up. She passed me in the hallway later, gave me a *how did I ever give birth to such a monster* look.

Anyway, got some good news late this evening. Adi's gonna be out later this week. His mum was crying on the fone when she told me.

## Mon., Oct. 9

Stace and Claire left for London this afternoon. My uni registration is on Friday, so I guess I'll see them there. Being miserable here ain't going to fix anything. We've just got to get playing and make what happened over the summer count. At supper I told my family, and Mum flung her arms around me. "Oh, that is such good news. I just want us all, y'know, to be . . . *on track*."

Dad frowned. "But is this what you want, or are you just doing it to please us?"

Mum waved her hand. "Don't complicate things, Nick. She needs to get an education, do the same things we took for granted."

I nodded at Kim. "But you're not pressuring *her* to go back."

"Your sister's going to go into business with her friends here. Out of harm's way." Mum clanged a saucepan lid back on a pan of mashed potatoes.

Dad raised his eyebrows but said nothing. Seems to me they are going thru a mad role-reversal phase right now.

"Adi's parents left me a message saying they've got a release date for him."

He shook his head. "I'd tan that boy's hide if I was his father. Putting them through all that."

A wave of guilt wafted over me. "Dad, cut it out. Making me feel bad isn't helping right now.

He smiled. "Yes, but it's my job. Of course, you won't find it in any stupid *parenting* book, but it's the basis of all dad maneuvers. Guilt. Pressure. You pile enough of it on and eventually you'll turn your little lumps of child carbon into diamonds."

**Tues., Oct. 10**
I swiped my card thru the Smart Meter and nearly fell over.

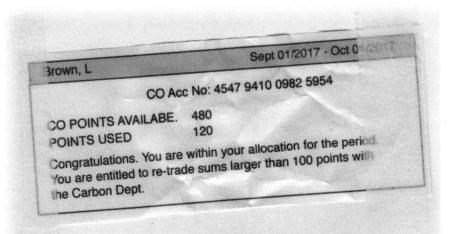

Sept 01/2017 - Oct 0  /2017

Brown, L

CO Acc No: 4547 9410 0982 5954

CO POINTS AVAILABE.    480
POINTS USED              120

Congratulations. You are within your allocation for the period.
You are entitled to re-trade sums larger than 100 points with
the Carbon Dept.

August and September on the run/in detention camp/too depressed to move has done wonders for my carbon emissions. Carbon Dept? No way, José. I'm so trading those puppies in for a bass as soon as I hit town. Ooh, I almost felt normal when I wrote that. Just a flicker.

## Wed., Oct. 11

A woman in a green cap and body warmer with an acorn logo on it knocked on the door and forced Dad to show her our Smart Meter reading to "ensure the East Wing of the village is on track."

East Wing?

On her way out, she glanced at the front vegetable patch. "Raspberries? Bit frivolous, eh?"

Dad smiled. "Well, I do like a raspberry tart."

Her eyes glinted back at him. "Yes, but it can't be about personal likes and dislikes if we come to food rationing."

Dad watched her walk off down the lane. "Sometimes I would kill, and I mean *kill* for my old life back."

Kim punched the air with her fist. "*Finally*! It's only taken you 2 years to say what everyone else's been thinking since day 1."

He winked at me. "I'm a slow developer."

## Thurs., Oct. 12

Kim dropped into my room after supper. "There's a lot of agro in London. Not just the gov and the council stuff, but the United Front have taken control of some areas . . . and there's rumors that the 2 are gonna start a campaign."

"So?"

"So stay out of trouble."

"You're telling me to behave myself?"

She groaned. "Don't say it. I'm turning into Julia, right? I've got to get a life."

I nodded. "Yes, you do. Before it's too late."

Later, I was walking upstairs when I caught sight of Mum in her room. She was sitting on her bed, just kind of staring into space. I leaned up against the door. "Mum, you all right?"

She reached for her moisturizer, tried a smile. "Course, sweetie."

I went over and sat next to her. "What happened to you, y'know, over the summer?"

"Oh, look, I'm fine. Everyone's blowing it out of proportion, really."

"No, they're not. You're—different."

She glanced up, anxious. "I haven't really told your dad and Kim this, but at first I liked it in jail. I mean, it was all angry and me versus them, kind of like a game, you know?"

I nodded, remembering Sicily.

"But after a few days it really started to get to me. They were talking about holding us for 5 weeks before prosecution on counterterrorism charges, Laura. All I could think about was your dad and all of you . . . and I was so frightened!" She covered her eyes with her hands. "Me, frightened! And now I can't seem to shake it. I—I hardly know myself." Suddenly she grabbed my arm. "So ridiculous! Over a group of local people standing up to Thames Water. But this government's on a knife edge and they'll do *anything*, and I mean, *anything* to stay in power. Promise me you'll stay out of trouble."

I blew out my cheeks. "Mum, trouble's the last thing on my mind."

Heard nothing from Adi. What's going on over there?

## Fri., Oct. 13

London. Very strange. This morning I caught the super-packed early bus and chugged into town. It was like those buses in India with passengers hanging off the roof; the driver had to make loads of people get off before he left the depot. Once I got into town, I made my way over to Elephant and Castle (the elephant has now got a bullet hole thru the eye from some riot in the summer), where I met Stace on the uni steps and we went inside to register. First a biometric scan, then signing a behavioral contract before being stamped, dated, and filed on the database. I almost walked out when it came to my turn on the retina scan. But like Stace says, what choice have we got? Apart from those weeks of the French tour I've never earned a cent with the *angels*. Downloads are cool and gigs bring in a few euros, but they don't pay the rent. She's right, if we want to carry on, uni's the only way.

## Sat., Oct. 14

It's getting worse. After another day of processing, they've housed us both (compulsory) in a weird sanitized university dorm in Vauxhall called Cornbrook House. They're putting all of us *At Risk* students in places like this, among the "normal" kids. Ours is full of goody-goody 1st-year students full of fake rebellion and bad hair. Me and Stace are like grizzled wolves next to them.

## Sun., Oct. 15

The Cornbrook House intercom buzzed this morning and a 17-year-old girl with black gelled wisps picked it up, went, "It's for you. A *boy*," and rolled her eyes at the others, like a boy was a bad, bad thing.

I scanned the screen, but could only see the back of someone's head. "Hi?"

"Er . . . Laura? It's me."

"Who?"

He suddenly turned to face the screen. "Sam! You forgotten me already?"

I tossed the receiver back in its case, snatched up my jacket and ran downstairs.

Just for a second we stared at each other like strangers, then Sam went, "Looking a bit porky, Brown!" And we both burst out laughing. My arms are like sticks and I've got the boniest arse in the universe. Maybe I should write a diet book—*Get the Pigs to Chase You Thin in 30 Days!*

And then we went for a long walk down to the river. I tell you, London is so different. It's gone like Palermo with pigs and chickens grunting and clucking all over the place. All the houses and buildings have those orange plastic water catchers on them, and every single bit of garden and scrap land has got vegetables growing in it. Even the roofs of bus shelters are either grassed up or turned into solar catchers. Plus cos of the price of fuel there's hardly any normal private cars now; no one can afford them. The only things running are tiny Thai-style tuk-tuks that run off solar panels and mini chargeable batteries. God knows where they've all come from.

We walked as close as we could to the flooded Thames, down by the old London Eye. We went past the National Theatre and then suddenly there was a great bank of waving reeds in front of us, stretching to the water's edge. I stopped dead.

BACK IN LONDON

"What the hell?"

"Reed beds . . . for sewage treatment. It's always flooded here now, so I guess it's a good place for them." Sam shook his head. "My parents pressured me to come back to study, but I ain't so sure 'bout it no more. My mate's just got a job installing roadside top-ups for cars. He's passed his trial and the company's taken him on full-time. What's this degree in Design Communication gonna do for me?" He stretched his arms out. "Anyways, been doin' some wicked tagging since I been back with Mikey. And he's lined us up a stack of gigs if we're interested." He paused, glanced down. "Guess all this sounds lame compared to what you've been thru."

"Different for sure."

"When's Adi back?"

"Any day now. At least I think so."

His cheek flushed. "How come? Aren't you talking?"

I turned to him. "It's complicated, Sam. You know that."

Big silence. Then Sam went, "So you wanna go tagging again? It's not like, too babyish?"

I shook my head. "I don't know if I can. I can't afford to get into any trouble, mate."

"Don't worry. I go places no one'll ever catch us. We'll be like the most invisible taggers of all time."

"You sure?"

"Definite. And I'll stand by—not like—"

"What?"

"Ah, nothing." He grinned and put his arm around me. "Jeez, it's good to see you again, LB. We're gonna kick some arse this term!"

"Well as long as we don't get caught, it sounds be-yu-ti-ful."

I watched him as he stood gazing out over the flooding river. I'd forgotten how he makes me feel. Light.

I know I promised Mum to stay out of trouble, but there's limits to how straight a punk girl can go and still be herself.

### Tues., Oct. 17

Stace stomped into my room this morning and threw a scrap of paper at me.

I bend to the floor,
Tears spiraling from my eyes.
I have learned to despise you,
Along with all your lies.

So how come I still love you?
Why am I still here?
When you have destroyed me,
and still not cried one tear.

"The 1st years were doing *mood poetry* around a synth in the kitchen last night. We've got to get gigging, otherwise what are we doing here?"

I sighed. "I haven't even got a new bass yet. What about your drums?"

"Just need a couple of pedals and I'm good to go." Stace flumped down on my bed. "Remember when all this was simple?"

"I dream about the camp all the time."

She drummed a nervous rhythm on her leg. "I don't dream about it, but I'll be doing something normal, like buying a coffee and then it'll just hit me. Where are they now? All those people."

## Wed., Oct. 18

First day back at uni. Unbelievable. The other students looked like they'd had their brains sucked out. We were marched into the lecture hall to do an icebreaker activity. Ha, ha!

10 minutes later, me and Sam still sat there, our cards untouched.

The icebreaker "facilitator," a strange woman in a blazer and split-endsy red hair, came over and glanced at our blank postcards.

"Come on, you two. I'm sure there's lots of things you'd like to get done by December!"

I dropped my head into my hands. "Make this *thing* go away!"

Red leaned right over me, glanced at her clipboard. "Laura Brown, right? I think you're in enough trouble without making a start like this. Hmm?"

Sam reached for his postcard, started to write. "Yeah, look, we're doing it, it's all cool . . ."

He swerved a paper under my elbow. "Here you go, Laur."

I reached for a pen while she stood over us till we squeezed a couple of lines out.

She took our cards. "There. See, wasn't so bad after all! Things'll be just fine if we all work together."

I nudged Sam on the way out. "I wrote I wanted to achieve the highest grade possible on my next piece of course work. Beat that."

He shrugged. "Can't."

"Why you so serious? What did you put?"

"Ah, you'll have to wait till December."

"Fine. Be like that."

What's up with him?

## Fri., Oct. 20

Black Friday.

Our first proper band meeting. We've been offered a good gig next Saturday, but we had to turn it down—there's no way we can play till we've got all our instruments back, so we've set ourselves a deadline of 2 weeks to tool up again. "Let's get on it!" shouted Claire. "5,000 downloads and counting on the *port* for "Not Dead in Bordeaux"—and Mikey's manager is trying to sort us out a 3-track release, in a professional recording studio. We've got to strike while we're hot."

I felt a flush of excitement and on the spot I made a vow to myself to keep hold of the feeling, to keep things super simple, one stage at a time. First job: new bass. And then my fone buzzed. Nate.

"Have you seen him?"

I went cold inside. "Adi? No! Is he back? Why din't he call me?"

"I dunno. He's been in town for a few days. I just met him now . . . an' man, it don't look good."

"What d'you mean?"

"He was pretty weird, talking 'bout the **2** . . . and you."

"Me?"

"Yeah. A lot. Look, I know it ain't my place, but can't you . . . y'know, try?"

"Nate, you don't know what you're asking."

"I know, Laur. It's just I think you may be his last chance, his like, last bit of normal. My mate says he saw him with this guy Ian Phillips, who's deep in the **2**, last night."

My hand clenched around my fone. "Then how the hell am I supposed to help him?"

I locked off and pulled on my jacket to leave.

"Where you going?" asked Stace.

"Dunno. Just need some space."

"Na-ah. I know that face. We've finished here, so let's all go and shoot some pool."

"I'm not in the mood."

"Don't care. Right, Connor?"

Claire nodded. "There's no way you're being on your own right now. Let's go."

Sam peeled off, but the rest of us went to the Union bar and an hour later I started to chill. I was playing Stace and she'd just lined up a long pot, when suddenly her gaze shifted from the table to the far side of the room. She gasped. I turned. Adi, standing by the door. I couldn't help myself, I just ran across the room into his arms and we fell into a deep, long, crazy kiss. My stupid, messed-up, idiot of a boy!

He laughed. "Are you happy to see me, then?"

"Course I am, you fool. When did you get back?"

"Just now. You're the first person I came to see."

I pulled back. "Oh, Adi. Don't."

"What?"

"Start with a lie."

His face darkened. "Oh, I see you bin talking to little man Nate."

"He's your best mate."

"Used to be."

I put my hand on his shoulder. "Please, let's be . . . us again?"

"That's what I want, too," he whispered. "More than *anything* I want you back."

"I—I . . . can't we be friends for a while?"

"Friends? You and me?"

"You know what I'm saying, I don't know if I *can*."

He frowned. "Jesus. One thing. One time. I know it was bad, but how many times do I have to say I'm sorry? Can't we get over it? And if you wanna be friends, why you just kiss me like dat?" He pulled me close. "Please, Laura? You're the only girl . . ."

We stood there, real close, with the noise of the bar swirling around us, my heart beating slow and heavy. I wanted to say yes so much, but how could I? So I made myself say the cold, hard words. "But it's not just one thing—I know about you and the 2. You're not telling the full truth, even now."

Adi clutched me, gave a kind of choked sob. "Don't do this to us, we're—"

"What? Really, what are we? We've moved so far apart."

"Only because you can't deal with reality. You can call it what you want, but in the end, you're just scared."

Anger flashed thru me. "Why are you here, anyway? Aren't there some dying people somewhere hot for you to hang out with?"

Adi spat: "You're such a baby. War is coming *here*. In the end even you might have to fight."

"Maybe I will. Until then I choose to have a life."

He tried to pull me to him again. "Please, babe, don't . . ."

But I dragged myself away. "I've got to go now. See you around, OK?"

And then I walked away, forcing my legs to take step after step till I was out of sight, then I sort of hurled myself at a wall and wept as if my heart was broken. It finally hit me. We're over. I feel like I've taken a knife and stabbed myself in the heart. But I just can't go where he's going. I have to protect myself.

And now there's only one solution. Get numb.

## Mon., Oct. 23

Colossal lost weekend. I woke up in some serious stink clothes this morning with a mouth like I've been sucking on the blood of a dead badger. My only memory is Claire going, "More, more tequila, more." I also found this stuck to the back of my head.

> **1) Chill out**
> **2) Stay away from terrorist ex-boyfriend.**
> **3) Anaesthetise self with alcohol til pain dies back.**

My drunk alter-night-ego self makes a lot of sense. Let's face it, she can't mess things up any worse than the day version.

### Tues., Oct. 24

I'm back on my keep-it-simple plan. I'm not allowing myself any feelings till I've found a bass. So, no tears till then. Followed up a load of ads, went to see 3. No good. The last bass was in Clapton. It was shaped like an ax, like those ones that old death metallers play. I was tempted. Sorely tempted. Nobody'd mess with me, then.

### Wed., Oct. 25

There was an explosion at the desalination plant in Beckton early this morning. Thames Water is saying it was a "technical malfunction." Nobody believes them. It's got the **2** written all over it, even though they've totally denied it. Is this the start of bombing in London now? Oh, God, I'm crying again. How can he be with them? Come on, Laura, keep it together. No bass, no tears.

### Thurs., Oct. 26

Followed up a ton more ads, but all rubbish. Rumors are spreading about the Beckton plant. Claire says a guy no one knew just appeared at her mate John's squat last night and then in the morning he was gone.

"What was he like?"

"That's the thing. John said he was like a nerd, nobody you'd notice in the street. Certainly not someone who'd, y'know, blow stuff up."

I forced myself to sit in my dorm room tonight and work on a rechargeable solar jacket design for uni. My brain feels like it's melting. I had to run out and buy a bottle of rum to keep sedated.

## Fri., Oct. 27

Finally! I saw it for sale in *most wanted*, called up, went straight over to the guy's flat in Bromley—and there it was, the most beautiful bass in the world. A black stingray, with a pearl scratchboard. I tried to act like I didn't care, although I was trembling inside. I offered the guy a few chillers like I was doing him a favor and he shrugged and went, "Whatever, I never touch it anyhow."

It's like I've rescued a princess from a dark tower. Why can't people see beauty in front of them? Anyway, I've spent the whole day in my room, playing. Oh, I'd forgotten about this feeling. Happiness, concentration, pure simplicity. And then, suddenly, I knew what I wanted more than anything. I wanted to see him.

He opened the door, grinned when he saw me. "Yes! Art and Revolution are happening in this house . . . and now we got Beauty, too."

I frowned. "I'm not coming in if you're just gonna mess with me."

Sam threw his head back and laughed. "You ain't like other girls and that's for sure, Brown."

I tossed my head. "Thank God."

Suddenly, the door was flung open behind him and Eman grabbed me by the wrist.

"Yeah, oh . . . hi, Laura . . . come . . . uh . . . totally . . . uh in. We . . . uh . . . *creating* . . . uh like genuine . . . uh *guerrilla* art." He dragged me inside like we were in the middle of a chat, not that we hadn't seen each other since our van was on fire in France. He led me over to a monitor screen filled with images of shattered glass.

"We . . . uh are . . . uh going to . . . uh . . . project all these like . . . uh cracks and smashes over City Hall, so, right . . . Uh . . . it'll look like . . . uh . . . every single . . . ah . . . uh . . . window's been . . . uh . . . busted up."

I frowned. "I don't get it. Aren't we on the side of City Hall?"

Sam shook his head. "I ain't on anyone's side. The mayor promised to insulate all the council estates by the end of the year, but he's done nothing. If you're rich you're fine, but all the poor people are basically freezing to death and spending all their carbon points on keeping warm."

Eman punched a key. "Yeh . . . Laur . . . you gotta be like . . . on . . . *no one's* . . . side, right?"

But neither me nor Sam was listening, we were locked in one of our long, long stares.

## Sat., Oct. 28

It's official. Claire just called—we've been offered a 3-track deal in a high-end studio. Oh yeah! After all we've been thru. Claire checked out the studio prices. €2,000 a day. This is the real deal!

I'm going with Sam and Eman to do the City Hall guerrilla projection tomorrow. Keep busy, LB, don't think.

## Sun., Oct. 29

Just after dark we set out, riding along the river, until we found an abandoned flat building opposite City Hall. We broke in and quickly started to unpack the camera, projector, and laptop.

Sam bent down, passed a lens over to Eman. "Your eyes are nasty, mate. You get any sleep last night?"

Eman glanced up. "Er . . . uh no . . . up till 6 A.M. . . . uh . . . retooling this . . . uh . . . mini . . . ah . . . projector . . ."

Sam handed me a tripod. "Can you set that up? At exactly 35 degrees. We need the projector to overshoot the building by a meter on all sides."

I started to unscrew the tripod arm. "Why are you putting the projector horizontal?"

"Gives us wider coverage . . . and that way we'll hit the whole building. Got to make it look like every single windowpane's been smashed up."

After a couple of minutes, Eman slotted the last cable in place and glanced at Sam. "OK . . . uh camera on manual . . . uh . . . ah . . . screen at 1024 × 768 . . .?"

"Yep, yep."

"Laur . . . a uh . . . you cool?"

"Yeah."

Sam tightened a final projector lever and stepped back. "Nobody come near this now. Even a move of 1 mm will mess up the whole show."

Eman grinned and waved a grubby finger in the air. "Good to . . . uh . . . totally . . . uh . . . *go!*"

He leaned forward and flicked a toggle switch, and the projector hummed into life before suddenly shooting a beam of light across the water and onto City Hall, transforming it instantly. Super dramatic. Like every single window had been smashed to pieces.

Sam punched his fist. "How you gonna stay warm now, Mr. Mayor?"

We stood for a second in silence. Very, very, very cool.

Sam started to stuff cables in his backpack. "Right, let's get out of here, hopefully it'll take them at least 24 hours to find the source."

I glanced around at the equipment. "You're just going to leave all this stuff here?"

Eman glanced down. "I . . . uh . . . built it like . . . uh before an . . . I can . . . uh . . . build it again."

As we were running down the stairs, I slipped and Sam grabbed my hand and we ran madly toward the river together, total electricity shooting thru my veins. I feel like somebody just handed me my life back. Adi can go to hell.

## Mon., Oct. 30

This afternoon I came out of class, kind of giggling with Sam, and nearly walked straight into Nate.

I gasped. "What're you doing here?"

"Came to see you." He looked from me to Sam. "That's deep. Movin' on nicely, huh?"

Sam threw his hands up. "Ah, not this shit again."

Nate squared up to him. "What's your problem, bruv?"

I put out my hand. "Stop it! Sam, go on, I'll see you in the bar in 10."

He glared at me. "You can't just order me around. If Nate's got stuff to say to me, I'm ready to hear it."

Nate whistled. "Ooh, the boy's got attitude."

Sam whirled around.

I shook my head. "Just let it go. This isn't your thing."

He stared at me for a moment. "Yeah, well I'm going, but don't look for me in the bar cos I won't be there."

I watched him stride off down the corridor before turning to Nate. "You're well out of line. You don't get to control me like this."

"Yeah—but him, *Sam*—?"

"It's not your business. And . . . at least he's here, solid. Not messing me around."

"What is he? A pet?"

"Why am I suddenly the bad person?"

"Adi's messed up, he ain't got everything squared away, he's confused . . . sorry if he don't fit into your new beautiful little world."

"Nate, I'm just trying to get by."

"You've changed," Nate snapped. "You're not the girl dat went all the way 'cross Italy to be with your boy."

"So? What's it to you?"

His eyes blurred. "What's it to me? You my family, man."

And then he pushed past me, breaking into a run as he went.

For a second I saw myself dead clear. He's right. I'm not that girl anymore.

## Tues., Oct. 31

I called Sam, but he's not picking up. I'm gonna let him chill out, I've had a bellyful of moody boyfriends. Instead I spent the evening practicing all my bass parts with Stace. Jeez, my fingers are slow like tiny slugs sliming on the fret board.

Just got a message thru from Kim to say Kier's coming back this Thursday. And Dad just called to say the piglets are the total stars of the village, people are practically fighting over which one is the most beautiful. Strange times.

# November

**Thurs., Nov. 2**

I met Kier at Waterloo Station this afternoon. When he saw me, he hurled his backpack down, flung his arms out wide, threw his head back, and warbled an opera tune.

I ran over and hugged his skinny bones. "You're back!"

He rolled his eyes. "Thank God, ghastly trip. I kept trying to pretend I was an American multimillionaire, y'know on a glamorous 1920s cruise—and then I'd get a waft of industrial fertilizer. Plus we got delayed in New York cos of some customs mix-up, so we spent three nights next to a Colombian tanker in a loading bay thingy. Have you ever listened to 10 zillion tons of scrap metal being poured into a ship?"

I shook my head. "No. Is it cool?"

He glanced at me. "It's like the end of the world. In tin cans."

**Fri., Nov. 3**

4 A.M. I came back to Kier's place yesterday and we sat up most of the night talking. Now I can't sleep. It's so strange being back here, next door to our old house . . . and Arthur's place. It's still empty.

This morning I had to run across town to make the dorm before midday cos I can't be out for more than 36 hours without permission.

Kier frowned. "I'm hearing a lot of that CAN'T word since I've come back."

## Sat., Nov. 4

Kim came down last night to see the boy wonder and we all went out with a bunch of his mates, ending up in a club near the New Astoria. Gay people have gone even madder than the straights. They were playing this new music called DRILL; it runs at 200 bpm and it's like having a dentist grind out your own teeth without an injection. Kier's mate, Big Phil, says it's down to this new drug that's sweeping all over town that's speedier than speed. He jerked his thumb at all the dancers. "Check it out, it's called Speedy G. Short for Gonzalez."

I looked around the club; it was totally manic with everyone jerking around in dead fast little hops with their elbows all angled out.

Kim squinted. "It's making me sick."

Kier grinned. "Yep. It's like the madness before the end of the world. We're the gays, we're more sensitive, y'know, *attuned* to apocalyptic vibrations."

Next to us a boy slid into the darkness, pulled out a pack, and hoovered up a line of G off the back of his hand.

Kim nodded. "I see that."

Why hasn't Sam called me yet? I'm done chilling, now I want action. Ooh, I suddenly got a glimpse of what I must be like to go out with. Impossible. Aargh, too much clarity. Turn it off, turn it off! Fog be mine!

## Sun., Nov. 5

I woke so sad, remembering how Arthur did indoor fireworks to cheer me up when my parents nearly split up, years ago. I made my way back to the dorm and was just at the gates when I heard someone calling me. I turned—saw Sam, waving from the other side of the road. He crossed, dodging a tuk-tuk. "Been looking for you . . . got . . . rockets!"

"Really?"

He glanced up, put his arm around my shoulder. "Yeah, but no need to cry 'bout it."

And so we walked down to the river and fired off 3 beauties. The last one nearly made it all the way to the other side, sent a wicked trail of reflected red sparks across the dark water.

Sam suddenly turned to face me. "Do you hate me for leaving you in Italy?"

"No-o."

"Yeah, you do. I don't blame you, it was lame."

"What were you supposed to do? Sit on the side of a mountain till I came back?"

"You went all the way to Sicily for Adi."

"But that's different . . . it was—"

His shoulders slumped. "Adi, Adi. I ain't ever going to match up, am I?"

"Don't do that to yourself."

"I—I need to know what's going on, Laur. With you and him."

I shook my head. "You and me both."

"See? You never give me a straight answer."

"Cos there isn't one. But there's no way me and him can go back to what we were before."

"Do you want to?"

I stood there a moment; all the dark past with Adi bearing down on me and this boy, standing here, nervously flicking a lighter, *wanting* me. So simple, so lovely. "You ask too many questions."

Then I leaned in and kissed him.

5 A.M. Woke up in a bad sweat. But. I. Refuse. To. Feel. Guilty. Anymore.

## Mon., Nov. 6

Claire called this afternoon with the dates for the recording. "5 days in a studio in Camden from December 1st."

I gasped. "That's in 3 weeks. Major pressure, we're only just getting it together again."

She laughed. "I know, but I guess that's the way it always is with us. We've got to do it, though, right now it's the only thing that's keeping me sane."

We've got to make it work. Last time we were meant to record, all of London flooded. Can't be so unlucky a second time.

**Tues., Nov. 7**
Message. Tra la la.

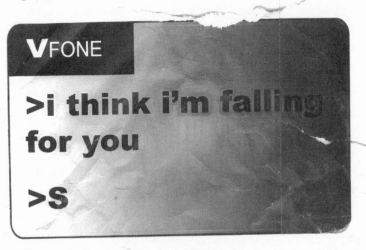

**Wed., Nov. 8**
Tonight we had our first practice with a fully tooled-up band. I totally blushed when Sam arrived, but fortunately Stace covered me by bursting in, seconds later, screaming she'd heard someone playing our track, "world on fire," on the bus. She grinned. "It was so weird. I heard it, right, but for a second I couldn't work out what it was . . . and then I looked over and this girl was singing along to the words and I realized it was us." She glanced around. "Us! We have so got to smack this demo."

Sam cleared his throat. "Well, we've also been offered a bunch of gigs. The first is on the 18th at an anti-Citizen Tax demo at the Hackney Empire. The crowd'll be huge, at least 5,000. What do you reckon?"

I frowned. "But that means there's bound to be feds there."

Claire laughed. "Yeah, but think of the size."

"But if we get blacklisted we're finished."

Claire coiled up her mic lead. "I don't know how much longer I can do this. If there was a job, just one job I could get, I'd leave that stupid uni in a second and be free."

Stace cut in. "But there aren't any jobs. And even if you've got one, you're on strike. The student loan is the only thing that's keeping us going. For now, it's the only way."

Sam sighed. "It's going to get better, right?"

Claire clenched her fist. "It's got to. Otherwise it's gonna be murder on the dance floor."

After, me and Sam slipped away and kissed for hours outside my no-boys-allowed dorm. He's so my dirty little secret.

### Thurs., Nov. 9

My fingertips are killing me today. Soft as butter. And my lips, too. I'm totally out of practice on all fronts.

### Fri., Nov. 10

All the transport workers came out on strike this morning cos of the price of fuel. Subway, bus, train, taxi, courier drivers, all out. Nothing. Absolutely no mechanical thing moving except private tuks. Kieran buzzed me at lunch break. "Can you hear it?"

"What?"

"Go to the window and stick your head out."

I slid the window back, straining my ears. "Nope. Nothing. No wait . . . a chicken."

"Exactly. How long do you think it's been since all you could hear in London was a chicken?"

I listened to the wind rustling the leaves. "Er, dunno. The Iron Age?"

"How fabulous is that?"

I frowned. "Yeah, but, Kier. There's a place like this already. It's called the *country*. People come here cos they want their chicken fried at 3 A.M."

He sighed. "I don't know why I bother with you. You're such a philistine."

Got a text from Adi. Felt sick when I saw his name come up. Deleted it without even reading it. A complete cutoff is the only way.

## Sat., Nov. 11

2 bomb. Blew out all the Xmas lights on Oxford Street. About 20 shoppers injured in the blast. Everywhere I go, all people talk about is the Citizen Tax, the strikes, the price of fuel, the price of food. But at the same time, there's a real sense of excitement, adventure, like we're all waking up after years of poison shopping malls and shitty 9 to 5 grind.

## Sun., Nov. 12

*Another* bomb, this time in a Polish community center in west London. The United Front have claimed it. There's bits of east London like Ilford and Beckton totally under their control—3 estates in Silvertown have hooked themselves up to a generator and declared a "state of independence," with white thickos in Burberry guarding the roads in. Not that anyone in his right mind wants to get in. I always used to think the UF were nasty, all that *send 'em home* shit, but after the refugee crisis in Italy, I really, truly hate them.

Anyway, I just got to keep my head down, keep focused on where I can make a difference with the band. That's all I've got to do. I get scared I'm on the other side now, that I just want it easy—but it's all just getting so extreme so fast. Today I read this thing in the news with some spokesman from the **2** saying they are prepared to kill the prime minister to bring the gov down. I mean, the guy's an idiot, but where are they gonna get by killing him? At least those Zapatistas in Mexico have got a plan; they're not just threatening to kill people like a bunch of thugs.

## Mon., Nov. 13

I had such a heavy dream about Adi. I can't even remember the details, just a feeling of heaviness, longing, dread.

## Tues., Nov. 14

Band practice and we took a final vote on whether to play the Hackney Empire this Saturday.

Sam went, "It's like the beginning of the year all over again with the UF and the **2**. But now it's spread out everywhere. The unions are calling for a blackout strike, there hasn't been one of those for 80 years. If it kicks off this time, there'll be millions involved. Heavy."

Eman nodded. "It's uh . . . intense . . . all right . . . I was . . . ah . . . close by that . . . uh . . . first Beckton bomb."

"The Thames Water one?"

"Oh . . . uh . . . yeah. I uh . . . wuz . . . down . . . by the . . . old Excel building . . . uh . . . an' uh . . . there . . . uh wuz . . . like a deep BOOM! Uh . . . uh . . . glass an shit . . . uh everywhere . . . I . . . uh used to . . . er . . . support . . . the **2** . . . but I . . . er don't, like uh . . . know what . . . uh . . . blowing nails into human flesh . . . is gonna . . . do. Jus' . . . ah . . . make the gov . . . uh get . . . more militant."

Claire turned to me. "So, Laur, what's the deal? Is Adi really with them now?"

I shrugged. "Don't know. It's nearly a month since I saw him."

"Oh, come on, you'd know . . ."

"No, I wouldn't. I don't talk to him now, I . . . I don't *want* to know. Anyway, thought you were the radical one. Why ain't you in touch with him?"

Her lip curled. "I've never been into that stuff and you know it. But I thought you'd at least stay in contact. Why not, Laur? Too afraid of what you might find out?"

A wave of anger shot thru me. "Back off! You don't dare talk to me about that stuff."

Stace held out her hand. "Enough. All of us are the same, scared. So let's keep it simple. Do we do the Hackney gig? Forget about all the other stuff. Just think about us. Sure it's dangerous, we've got to be careful not to get busted, but it's our gig, our fans, and we'll go and do *our* thing. But I say we've got to do it, otherwise we're going thru all this uni control for nothing. Right?" After a moment's silence we all nodded.

## Wed., Nov. 15

After the rehearsal, I just wanted to get drunk and have a laugh. Sam took me down to this mad underground club in Soho and we spent the night dancing and drinking with all the misfits. Wild. I can't even remember getting home . . . but this morning I woke up and just lay there in a half dream, watching him sleep. And then he murmured something, reached out and drew me close to him, and I shut my eyes and drifted back to sleep. A normal boy, a normal girl. So good.

## Thurs., Nov. 16

The intercom buzzed this morning, and the next thing I knew Mum was standing in front of me, thrusting a piece of paper in my face. "What the hell is this?"

2 spokesman Ian Phillips, marching at Climate Camp back in 2008

Are you saying you were misquoted when you said, 'we should kill the prime minister?'
**It was taken out of context. So what's new?'**
But you did say it?
**Yes, but within a much wider context.**
So...
**That's to say that a lot of things have to change and fast, but I did not specifically say we should assassinate the prime minister.**
Did you or did you not say at the World Trade Protests: 'If we have to we will kill the prime minister, we will kill anyone who blocks our freedom.
**My words were taken out of context. They were not aimed at any one individual. I was talking about our right to fight for our freedom.**
But would you kill him?
**Anyone who raids us, exploits us, imprisons us is in the way of freedom.**
Are you talking about the prime minister?
**A: He is the elected leader of the people and if he is not responsible for the police and MI5 then he should tell us he's not**

I struggled to sit up. "Unghh, what's going on?"

Mum sat down on the bed. "I just can't deal with it all. What the hell is happening to this town?"

"Mum, chill out. It's just a stupid interview."

"You'd never get involved with them, would you?"

"Course not."

"And Adi? We spoke to his parents last week, and they're out of their minds with worry."

"No. Look, honestly I *don't* know what's going on with him. I wish everyone would stop hassling me. Breathe, Mum. Breathe."

She took in a slow, juddering breath. "I think about you all the time—I—I just had to come see for myself how bad it is."

I put on my best-daughter smile. "It's all cool. I'm always telling you the news makes things out to be worse than they are. Where d'you get that article from, anyway? *The Daily Mail*?"

"Don't be fresh." She shot me a fierce glance. "Anyway, what are you doing just sitting there?"

"Eh?"

"We've got to get going."

I went cold. "Back home? You can't just drag—"

She tutted. "I'm not planning on any *dragging*. I want to take a look around with you."

"Where?"

"Oh, nowhere in particular. The West End maybe, I want to see it for myself."

"But—

She smiled. "You see, the media is forever making things out to be worse than they are, I want to look with my own little Middle England eyes."

Half an hour later we were on the subway into town, but we only got as far as Holborn cos of a bomb alert. As we made our way out of the exit, I paused. "You sure you want to go on?"

She curled her lip. "You think I've not lived through bombing before in London? I was here in the 80s when the IRA were active." She sniffed. "The whole city turned into a sty overnight when they took all the trash cans off the streets."

We started to walk toward Covent Garden. The main Kingsway road was closed, so we cut a left down Keeley Street and weaved our way along the backstreets. There were a few police around, but mostly it seemed pretty calm, but wary. We'd got as far as Long Acre, when we ran into a crowd gathered down by the old City Lit building. They formed a tight circle around a girl in a bandana who was standing on the edge of a yellow trash can. Even though her face was half covered, I was pretty sure it was Monica. My heart squeezed tight. I looked around, trying to see if Adi was there. The girl held up her hand. "We are in the second decade of the 21st century. We maybe have 10 more years before we reach the tipping point, when there is no return. The methane released from the melting permafrost in the North will send us over the edge. We are a million strong, and we are armed and we are not afraid, and we demand change, now! No more lies and corruption!"

The crowd cheered, shouts of "Yes!"

Mum moved a little closer. "Is this the 2?"

"I guess so. I've never seen them in public like this before."

The girl climbed higher, leaped onto the wall. "There can be no liberation, no hope for the future of the earth while capitalism still exists. It is an endless raping of the world . . ."

A police siren cut across the square and the crowd immediately started to break up, melting away down the side roads.

Mum put her hand on my shoulder. "Come on, let's head down to Neal Street. But don't run."

We set off at a fast walk, but then suddenly a police car screeched up in front of us.

Mum nodded to the left. "Quick, inside here!"

And so we ducked thru a set of wooden doors and into the interior of an old Victorian pub. It was like stepping back 200 years—a total fantasy of mirrors, horse brasses, and copper pans. Mum gazed around. "God, I used to come drinking here after work." Suddenly she caught sight of herself in a mirror and a strange expression came into her face. "I tell you, Laura. If I was your age . . ."

"What?"

"It's just they seem so sure, so clear . . ."

I stared at her. "Mum, you need to get your message under control. One minute you want me to keep my head down and get thru college and the next you want me to join the revolution."

"I never said that. Of course I don't want you to get involved with a group like that, but . . . I mean, just . . . keeping yourself safe so you can get an education . . . it's got to be . . . *hard*."

"Welcome to my world."

She sighed. "This blackout strike is due to start Monday. Even in Abingdon, everyone's preparing to join in. It's make or break time, but this government has got to go. I'm supposed to know what to tell you, but . . . well . . . I haven't got a clue."

I burst out laughing. "Mum, that's the most straight-up thing you've ever said to me."

"Is it?" She nodded at the bar. "Well, then, let's have a drink to celebrate."

"Are you going to strike, too?"

"Your dad and I have been over this a million times. I guess in the end we just have to."

"But what about the house?"

She sighed. "Some things are more important than *stuff*."

As I moved forward, she suddenly squeezed my hand.

"What now?"

She sniffed. "I'm just so proud of you. I don't know if I could've done this at your age."

"It's just another month till the end of term. I've got to handle it."

And then we got drunk. Me and my mum. Hilarious. There's a lot about that woman I don't know. For a start she can flick 12 peanuts off the back of her wrist and catch em in her mouth. That's a total misspent youth, Julia.

## Fri., Nov. 17

The deal tomorrow for the gig is we leave our ID cards at home and go masked-up. Apparently everyone is doing it—the bands, the crowd, the organizers. I'm not sure about this, not sure at all.

## Sat., Nov. 18

Me and Stace bused it down to Matalan this morning to buy a bunch of ski masks for the band. Stace paused at the sliding doors. "Is this how the revolution begins? Going down to a mall on a bus to buy a woolly mask? We're more like seniors."

I winked. "Aye. First decision of the guerrilla—to knit or not to knit."

When we got back to the dorm, we dragged them on over our heads. Stace is gonna wear hers with a pair of retro shades she stole from her aunt. After a few seconds of tryout, she yanked it all off. "That is some hot wool action, Laura. Prepare to sweat for your beliefs."

### Sun., Nov. 19

Best Gig of All Time.

Nate drove me and my gear down to Hackney Empire in his cousin's tuk to make up for being such an asshole the other day. He pulled up just off Mare Street and together we scanned the outside of the theater. The police were patrolling outside the doors, openly taking fotos, and searching kids. No one fought back—the only thing people wouldn't let the feds do was take off their masks. Every time they tried it, kids would knot up in a big circle around the victim and record the officers with their fones until they backed off.

Nate tapped his nose. "You sure 'bout this?"

"No. But I'm doing it, anyway."

He nodded, sighed. "A'ight."

I looked down. "You heard . . . anything?"

He shook his head. "Nah . . . an' I dunno what's worse, knowing or not knowing what's going on wid him."

"I know." I sighed, nodded toward the theater. "So, you coming in?"

"Nah man, not my thing."

I pulled out my mask. "OK then, I'll see you soon, yeah?"

"You seriously gonna wear dat bit of wool?"

"Yep."

His face split into an old-skool Nate grin. "You got balls, girl. More'n Adi, I reckon."

The night was pure fire. There were 6 bands in total, each one more venomous than the last. And I've never seen English kids so angry, so insane.

Claire stared around, open-eyed. "Nobody's playing around anymore. This is the real thing."

Stace growled. "Uh-huh. Like France."

We went on at 10. As soon as I climbed up onstage I was hit by this wave of emotion and mania, sweeping in off the crowd. And when we started I could hardly stand up to play cos of all the diving and moshing. We'd got to a new track, "liberation," that I wrote in Sicily—and it was going good—but then, suddenly, this mad kid leaped onto the stage, picked up Stace's snare drum and tried to hurl it into the crowd. Everyone froze for a second, then Stace just threw herself at him like the total kamikaze drummer girl she is, grabbed the snare, and kicked him off the stage. Then she seized the mic and screamed:

```
Innocence is a myth
Soaked up in blood
Have you had your fill?
Pull the trigger feel the pain
As killer becomes killed.
```

The hall went totally silent, just the back echo of her voice. She stomped back to the drums, dragged her snare into place, clicked her stix, we flew into the chorus, with the crowd flaming into a spontaneous, colossal roar. When I got off stage I was crying. All the others the same, tears, trembling, puking. Pure, pure adrenaline. All the stuff we've been keeping inside for months.

After a while I needed some air, so I pushed thru the crowd and slipped out a side door into a back street full of smokers. Eman was there, so I went and sat next to him on the curb. I'd only been there a minute when this boy and girl started kissing right next to us, but then, suddenly, the girl's knees went and she toppled over sideways. I *actually* felt her lips slithering across my face and something slimy coat my cheek. I yanked my body back, but too late. A strand of vomit drool from her mouth hung across my neck, like some ghastly Camden craft necklace.

I smeared my jacket sleeve across my neck. "Oh, gross."

The girl pawed her way upright before grabbing her boyfriend's arm and pulling him into another massive grope.

"Stylish."

Eman grinned. "Ah . . . I . . . uh . . . dunno. As . . . uh long . . . as we're . . . like . . . uh . . . kissing we're . . . uh . . . like still . . . young . . . an' havin' *fun* . . . *an' uh* . . . *ah the bastards* . . . *like* . . . *uh* . . . *ain't won.*"

I raised an eyebrow. "You making rhymes now, mate?"

But soon I went inside, looking for Sam and some kissing action of my own.

## Mon., Nov. 20

The blackout anti-Citizen Tax strike began today. The trade union leaders say this is the big one and they won't quit till the tax is abolished and this corrupt gov is brought to its knees. I don't reckon they'll get anywhere, but I'm going down to Somerfield later to stock up on cans, just in case.

## Tues., Nov. 21

There was a march in the city this morning. Sam cycled thru the edges on his way back from the Aldgate campus. "I tell you, Laura, it was just ordinary people, families, Lidl shoppers. No crusties, no dreads, no dogs. If I was the gov I'd be seriously thinking about backing down on this one."

I picked up my bass. "Jesus, Sam, enough politics. We've got to keep focused on this recording session. In the studio's where we belong."

"Yeah, all right . . . just thought you'd want to know what's going on."

"Well I don't, all right? I had enough of that with . . . before."

His face tightened. "Fine. Let's practice."

Is he going to start getting serious, too? Maybe it's me. I turn normal boys into Trotsky wannabees.

## Wed., Nov. 22

Ben Nichols, this really quiet boy in my course, didn't make it into class for the 4th time in 2 weeks; there are whispers he's been withdrawn. And then later on in the canteen, I saw a student getting dragged away by security for refusing to show his ID card. One thing's for sure, though. I'm going to pass this semester—out of respect to my mum if anything. I've only got 10 days to hand my project in, so I forced myself to spend the whole day in the plastics workshop, head down. On my way home, I dropped into the corner shop to get some gum and the shelves were already half empty. I'm now sitting on my bed surrounded by 12 maxi tubes of barbecue beef Pringles.

## Thurs., Nov. 23

Claire came to mine tonight to go thru the studio track list. But when she got in my room, she sat down on the bed and took a deep breath. "Laura, I've got something to tell you . . . They're looking for volunteers to help with the strike meetings in the Docks. After the gig and everything—I can't just stay on the sides. This isn't Italy or France or someone else's deal now. This is us."

I dropped my head in my hands. "Then why did you even bring the track list around? You're gonna be jailed for sure."

"Don't be so dramatic. We'll make it to the studio."

"Like we did last time? Are you gonna risk losing this chance again?"

She nodded, pale. "Got to. But I promise to be careful."

I suddenly exploded. "That don't mean anything. So all this shit we've been thru this term is for nothing? You can't just throw it all away!"

"I want the band more than anything, but I can't go on being apart like this anymore . . ."

"You! It's always you! What about the rest of us?"

She glared at me. "Yeah, well what about *you*? How long can you carry on being like—"

"Like what?"

"Oh, come on. We were there in Italy, too, y'know . . . but we can't be scared forever. And this playing around with Sam . . ."

I whirled around. "What are you saying?"

"Come on, Laura. Get real . . . Adi goes and a week later you're with him. Everyone can see he's in love with you and you're just . . ."

"What?"

She dropped her gaze. "Using him."

I took a sharp breath. "Is that what you really think?"

Claire crossed the room, reached for the door handle. "It don't matter what I think, it's what you think that counts."

Shit, shit, shit.

## Fri., Nov. 24

Found an A3 sheet of paper slipped under my door when I got back from uni.

I stared at it for a moment, laughing. Then I burst into tears. She's totally right.

## Sun., Nov. 26

Blimey, my dad's gone on strike and Mum says Abingdon's like a ghost town. No change there, heh, heh. But right now I don't want to know. I turned my fone off all weekend and all I did was play bass. Saw no one, went nowhere. Only 4 days till recording. Keep low, low, low. Sam's coming over for practice tomorrow. I'm dreading seeing him.

## Tues., Nov. 28

I didn't know what I was going to say to Sam, but when he got to my flat, it all went dead clear. He came running up the stairs, super excited, waving a 'zine. "Read it and weep, baby! Suzi K review!"

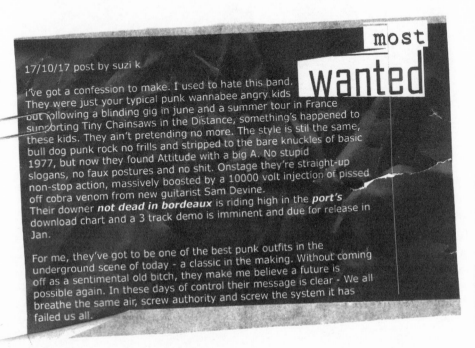

**most wanted**

17/10/17 post by suzi k

i've got a confession to make. I used to hate this band. They were just your typical punk wannabee angry kids but following a blinding gig in june and a summer tour in France supporting Tiny Chainsaws in the Distance, something's happened to these kids. They ain't pretending no more. The style is stil the same, bull dog punk rock no frills and stripped to the bare knuckles of basic 1977, but now they found Attitude with a big A. No stupid slogans, no faux postures and no shit. Onstage they're straight-up non-stop action, massively boosted by a 10000 volt injection of pissed off cobra venom from new guitarist Sam Devine.
Their downer **not dead in bordeaux** is riding high in the **port's** download chart and a 3 track demo is imminent and due for release in Jan.

For me, they've got to be one of the best punk outfits in the underground scene of today - a classic in the making. Without coming off as a sentimental old bitch, they make me believe a future is possible again. In these days of control their message is clear - We all breathe the same air, screw authority and screw the system it has failed us all.

I took the paper, scanned it, and it was like a rocket went off in my head. Such a blinding flash of realization. I just laughed out loud.

Sam grinned. "Amazing, ain't it?"

"Yeah, and you wanna know why? Cos I am such a little hypocrite and I'm getting away with it, big time. I strap on my bass, scream some angry words, spray some clever shapes—and everyone just sucks it up."

Sam frowned. "What are you talking about?"

I looked at him straight. "You see, the thing is, I've cracked it, cos I *look* the part, without ever, ever meaning to *live* it. Brilliant, Laura Brown. Just bloody brilliant."

He was staring at me like I'd lost my mind. "You're way too hard on yourself."

I shook my head. "No, I'm way too soft . . . and the thing is, you're the same. Just like me . . . and I—it's enough now."

"Are you breaking up with me?"

"It's not you, it's me. I'm not being straight with myself."

His voice cracked. "You think I'm stupid? I've always known I didn't stand much chance, but I thought . . . with time. I ain't Adi, I know, but I'm trying—"

"Spraying a few walls isn't ever going to make you him. Is that why you're doing it?"

He snatched the paper out of my hands. "You know why I do it."

Silence. I reached out my hand. "I'm sorry. I didn't mean to hurt you . . ." But he pushed my hand away, turned and ran, taking the stairs in great blind leaps.


There was only one thing to do. I slipped out of the dorm into the dark, took the subway and 3 stops later, joined a steady flow of people, keeping to the shadows, speaking in whispers. I followed them to a huge, unfinished office block down by the river, all bare and gloomy, half lit by a few bare bulbs hanging from exposed wires. As my eyes got used to the light, I realized the place was packed out, with people even perching high up on piles of brick and metal girders, listening intently to a man standing in the center. He was pacing the floor, his face pale in the swinging light. "The government taxes us more and more. The Green Economy! they cry. But now, 2 years later, where are the new jobs for ordinary people? And who is looking after the old, the poor, the weak? And who is protecting the immigrants? The Eastern Europeans, the Muslims who've been here for generations? And what is the future for the young? The right is rising and this government is corrupt through and through. We will not pay the Citizen Tax. We are finding we are strong again. Some of us have taken back the water and the energy into our own hands, but we cannot rest until each and every person has an equal share in this country and each and every country in the world. Not just the rich. Not just those who support the government. Not just those who live in the cities!"

The hall rose, thundering, and then suddenly I saw her, leaning against a pile of frames over on the left. I pushed my way thru and slipped my hand into hers.

Claire turned, trembling. "You know I've got some nerve calling you chicken. It's not you, it's me who's terrified. These people haven't seen what the army can do. Do they think the gov is gonna just let them walk in and take power?"

I squeezed her hand tight. "I saw the Suzi K review . . . and it made me so ashamed, cos I know what's really going on with me."

"Oh yeah? And what's that? That you're shit scared like everyone else? Big deal. At least you admit it."

"But, mate, you're right, we've got to get stuck in, otherwise we're just a bunch of fakers onstage."

"Nah we ain't. At least there we're real . . . we can handle ourselves. But out here, we're just . . . *kids*. Playing at revolution."

It's midnight and I'm in bed, thinking. It's such a strange feeling when you see yourself clear, and all your little tricks are suddenly so transparent. Claire's right—the *angels* are where we belong right now, but I can't allow myself to hide away anymore. Right now the studio's more important than anything, but after then I'm not running away no more. Besides, there's nowhere to run.

Oh, I feel so bad about Sam. The only thing that helps is I didn't mean any harm . . . and I do love him, I'm just not *in* love.

**Wed., Nov. 29**
Only 2 days to go. When I walked into band practice tonight, Stace looked up from her fone. "What's up with Sam?"

"Why?"

"Cos he's just left me a message saying he ain't comin to rehearsals no more, but he won't let us down for the recording. Sounded dead upset."

"Yeah, well we're kind of taking a break."

Claire glanced at me, our eyes met. "I'm sorry, mate."

I sighed. "Yeah, me too."

## Thurs., Nov. 30

Bomb. This time they've blown up some junior environment minister's office. A crowd rocked the prime minister's car as he drove into an emergency debate in Parliament. I've just spent an hour on the fone to my parents telling them it's less than two weeks to go to the end of term and for them not to panic. Dad is really unhappy about me being here. He wants me straight home on the bus.

I sat on my bed and breathed deep, trying to control my panic. It keeps welling up, no matter what I do. My fone buzzed, and I shot up from my bed. Claire? Adi? But instead . . .

**V**FONE ciao amici... All is good here, we fight to keep the refugee help centre open, but the big news is Pulce. Vero, this dog is now the star of Sicily after he rescue 2 little girl from a sinking boat. evrywher I go the peope they cry Pulce mio! and giv him some eat. He now is molto fat. Ah, ah! Ṭano Adile x

I stared at it for ages, wishing like anything I was in Sicily right now. There it was an adventure. This is way too much like reality.

No! Just broke my A string. I'll just have to get myself down to the guitar shop in Waterloo before we leave tomorrow morning.

# December

## Fri., Dec. 1

I set off for the guitar store super early, but when I got to the subway, it was closed, the iron gates pulled shut across the entrance. There was hardly anyone around. Strange. I checked my fone in case I'd got the time wrong, but no. I turned toward the bus stop. A guy came out of his house and I stopped and asked him if the buses were still running.

He shook his head. "God only knows today."

"Why? What's going on."

He looked at me like I was crazy. "Get yourself indoors 'fore you find out for real."

I ran back to the dorm and pushed open Stace's door. She was already awake, hunched up over her station. She looked up, startled. "Oh, shit!"

"What?"

"There's a huge riot outside Parliament, started at midnight, they reckon half a million people. And now the gov's brought in the Territorial Army to back up the feds."

"They can't do that."

"They just did."

"But . . . how are we going to get to the studio?"

"Don't be stupid, mate, they've just shut the subway, stopped all the buses—and now they're closing the highways and the north and south circular."

I threw my bass down on the bed. "This is not happening! Not again. Why today?"

My fone buzzed. Mum. "Tell me you're on the bus up here!"

"No, I'm in the dorm with Stace."

"We're coming down to get you."

"I—I don't think you can."

"Who's to stop us?"

"Mum, they're blocking off the center of town and main roads in."

She started crying for real, and then suddenly Dad was on the fone. "This'll be all over in a day, those poor fools can't win against the army. So, Laura, you've got to stay indoors—and we'll get there as soon as we can. Don't do anything stupid, you hear me?"

I kept nodding, going *yes, yes* like that stupid back in the day Churchill dog.

Claire arrived a few minutes later and together we sat and watched rows of feds shoot tear gas at the rioting strikers. I'm so angry. Why today? Why, why? This was supposed to be our time, our 5 days—the whole reason why we're struggling to get by in this stupid, shitty town.

## Sat., Dec. 2

I must've fallen asleep on Stace's bed, cos I woke up to her going, "Guys, look at this! Total split in the city. The mayor and all the local councils have come out against the gov. They've taken over City Hall! And that's not all—a whole bunch of the Territorial Army has refused to fight, some of them have even come over to the strikers' side."

Claire sucked in a sharp breath. "This is civil war."

Suddenly there was a loud banging on the door. Stace ran down the hall and yanked the door open. Sam and Eman fell inside, gasping for breath. "Listen . . . there's been a raid on our uni hall . . . we just got out in time . . . The word is they're . . . going to sweep thru student dorms, specially the ones like this . . . y'know where they've put . . . people on . . . behavioral contracts. We got to get moving!"

Stace ran her hands thru her hair. "And go where? The roads are blocked, all our mates are in the same shit . . . and my aunt and Claire's parents are way over west."

"Kieran's," I said. "It's only a couple of Ks away and it's outside zone 1. Let's go now, before things get more locked down—they can't've blocked off all the back streets yet."

Eman shook his head. "I . . . uh . . . don't wanna . . . uh . . . run away. I say . . . uh . . . we go . . . to uh . . . City Hall . . . an' get . . . uh fightin'."

One of the dorm girls peered around the door. "What's going on?"

Stace spat. "Nothing. Just leave us alone." She turned to Eman. "First things first. Let's get out of here before we get into any fights, otherwise the only place we're going is the back of a pig wagon."

5 minutes later we ran down the dorm steps. I nudged Stace as we waited for the security gates to open. "Think that girl heard us?"

Stace shrugged. "Don't know. Anyway, don't matter, we only said Kieran's, not where. They'll never find us." She suddenly grinned. "Hey, we're finally busting loose, Brown!"

Even though it was only just light, there were already some people around on busy roads and at stations. We saw armed police patrolling, but no sign of the army. People seemed dead angry with anyone in a uniform, specially the police. At one point when we passed around the back of Waterloo Station, a group of smart city workers stood outside the locked subway gates, screaming at a line of officers. I stopped.

"I almost feel sorry for those guys. It can't be much fun being hated."

"Then don't be a fed," growled Stace. "I mean, I always used to try and be positive about them, it's kind of a shit job and I always thought all that *hate the pigs* bullshit was dead easy, obvious, y'know? But don't some of them ever think *this is a mistake, I'm protecting the wrong side?*"

Sam sighed. "Yeah, but thinking like that don't pay fed wages. The gov does."

Claire held up a hand. "C'mon, we need to concentrate, Lewisham police station's just up there."

We marched the last section to Charlton in silence, along deserted streets and past whole lines of closed-up shops, all with their shutters down, with me and Sam keeping as far apart as possible; like we needed this breakup on top of everything else.

And so here we are at Kier's. I just don't know what to do, I've got so many voices in my head. Dad, repeating *promise me, promise you won't go outside*—the *angels*—this isn't our fight, our place is in the studio—we're too young—Italy—the stink of the detention camp and the guards shouting—Tano, GPJ, Arthur, the girl in the camp who'd lost her family. . . . And meanwhile the madness grows. There are bits of central London just totally out of control. Feds, strikers, the UF, looters. How long can the strikers hold out? City Hall is now the center of resistance, with at least 100,000 people massed around it, spilling out along the South Bank. I watched as onscreen, the camera zoomed in on a fire raging out of control, a great spiral of smoke rising up over the skyline.

Eman jumped up. "How can . . . uh . . . we just . . . like . . . uh sit here an' . . . uh totally . . . uh watch this . . . ah . . . uh . . . happening? We got to . . . like . . . ah . . . get out there."

Stace glared at him. "And get battered as well? It's gone too far. This ain't something we can win, Eman."

"But look at these . . . uh people . . . there's other students out there . . . Who else is like . . . with me?"

Claire bit at her thumb, looked down, before dropping her head into her hands. "It's killing me being here, but *we're 19 years old*, mate. And we've already been thru this, twice, three times. Right?"

Eman shook his head.

**10 P.M.** Kier sneaked out to try and buy food, but came back almost right away. He leaned against the kitchen door, breath coming in big gulps. "There's police roadblocks on High Street, but people are starting to build their own barricades at the end of the residential roads . . . out of boxes and mattresses, rails, tables, chairs . . . you name it. I couldn't get us any food, though—only got as far as Cost-cutter before a patrol ordered me to get indoors." He tossed a flyer on the table. "This is everywhere."

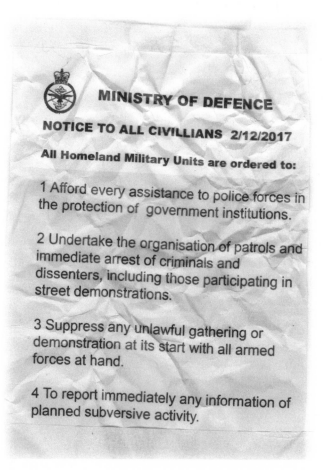

We read it in sick silence. Kieran looked around at us. "Come on, guys, I'll make us something to eat and then let's try to get some sleep. See what the morning brings."

An hour later we sat down to Kidney Bean and Couscous Surprise. Kier brought the casserole pan to the table, lifted the lid, and it smelled like the inside of a pet shop. No one picked up a fork, or went *oooh, great*, and Kier threw his hands up in the air. "Spoiled brats! Do I look like someone with well-stocked shelves? We'd better hope this is all over and soon cos it's canned bamboo shoots next. Then whitening toothpaste."

## Sun., Dec. 3

**9 A.M.** Nate's just called, his voice trembling. "Laur?"

"Nate?"

"I—wuz jus going home wid . . . my mates after a day on the streets. . . . We was walking past Liverpool Street station . . . it was some madness, security everywhere . . . there was dis boy, hoodie, sneakers . . . I noticed him, dunno why. . . . An' then 30 seconds later . . . the place just . . . blew up."

I squeezed the fone, tight.

"All I knew was a deep, deep *boom* . . . people screamin' all around an' a smell like burning hair . . . and then I saw his sneaker . . . right there in front of me. . . . His foot. Oh, God . . . I lay there, for ages I couldn't move . . . an' then I ran."

"Are you hurt?"

"Nah. Don't know how. Why him and not—"

"Nate, get yourself over here. Now. I'm at Kier's, next to where I used to live. Remember?"

"Yeah. I din't know who else to call . . . I need to be wid someone close."

"Do you want us to try and come and get you?"

"Nah. I'll be there, soon as I can, but it might take a couple hours."

"We'll be here. I promise."

When I locked off, the others were all awake. I told them the news.

Stace shook her head. "When is this gonna end?"

"What if it doesn't?" began Sam.

Stace wiped her hand across her face. "Cut it out, buddy."

Suddenly Claire screamed. "Oh, my God!" She pointed at the muted TV screen.

A line of tanks rumbling across Waterloo Bridge, military ships moving up the Thames, smoke hanging heavy as the sun rose over the city. Kieran put his hand to his mouth. "This is it. Not the territorials anymore. This is the real army. They're gonna crucify those poor bastards."

Dead silence in the room, then Eman slammed his fist into the wall. "That's it! I . . . uh . . . can't stay in . . . uh . . . here no more. I go on . . . uh . . . my own if I . . . have to."

I glanced around at the others. No words, then one by one they nodded.

"Even you, Kier?"

"Aye. Even though your parents will kill me." He blew out a sharp breath. "But otherwise, later, when it's all over, what'll we say? That we sat around a kitchen table and hid?"

It was like standing on the very, very edge. One step forward for a whole new reality. And then suddenly I felt this surge of excitement, fear, nausea . . . and I took the step forward into . . . what? I don't know and what's more I don't care. It's the strangest feeling. It's like I'm actually young again. I grinned. "OK, I'm in."

Stace cleared her throat. "Yeah, but what exactly are we gonna do? Run out there with Kier's hairdresser scissors?"

Kieran frowned. "No fighting! Unless we're forced to." He held up his hand. "All of you. Promise me you won't go looking for trouble." Honestly, he's so dramatic, so imagining himself as some superstar hunk in his Winnebago.

I shook my head. "But we can't go yet. I've just told Nate we'd wait up for him."

"How long, you reckon?"

I shook my head. "Don't know, but I'm not moving till he gets here. I'll stay on my own if I have to."

Kier laughed. "Chill it, Boadicea. There's plenty to do here till he comes. We're all gonna keep together."

So we went outside to where the streets were filling up with a steady stream of people. I suddenly spotted Mousy Woman, our old neighbor. She waved me over, squeezed me tight. "Are you here to help?"

I nodded. She pointed at a mattress that leaned against her front door. "Well, we're building barricades across the streets, the idea is to stop the army from having a free run."

"OK."

She patted a boy on the shoulder. "Then pick up a corner with

Jake here. He wouldn't go to his gran's like the others, insisted on staying here with me." She gazed down the street. "Well, your mum'd be proud of us, we're radical enough even for her now."

I forced a smile. Remembering a conversation I had with my hysterical mum an hour ago when I promised her I was going to stay locked inside Kier's living room. I got working with a mad group, about 20 of us—students, pensioners, housewives, kids—to build a line of barricades across the road until Nate finally appeared at about 1. Then our group all met at the flat before setting out together, our hearts beating loud as we turned the corner and left the safety of Kier's flat behind.

After half an hour, we'd only got as far as Greenwich, but we soon speeded up thanks to a bunch of stolen bikes from the park, courtesy of Sam and Nate. After that, we got all the way down to the Old Kent Road before we saw any real opposition, and even that was only a couple of police cars angled across the main road, with a sign in front of them. **STOP—ANYONE ENTERING THIS ZONE IS SUBJECT TO IMMEDIATE ARREST**

Kieran sighed. "This is where we separate the men from the boys. Everyone good to go on?"

We nodded.

"Nate, you, too? I totally understand if you're not up—"

Nate shook his head. "No, man, I'm sticking wid you guys all the way."

"Then everyone follow me. I've missed the last subway home so many times, I could walk these back streets blindfold."

20 minutes later we hit a dead end, roadblock after roadblock cutting us off from City Hall. Finally we joined up with a bunch of students, who told us about a new protest force massing in secret under the arches in Waterloo. By the time we'd worked our way over there, we were almost the last ones allowed in; the strikers had built a massive barricade to cut off the feds on the main road—and now

they were in the last stages of sealing up the smaller roads. As soon as we got inside, we helped to block up a couple of side streets, until after hours of hauling and stacking, the job was done and a young guy with a red armband called us all to attention with a megaphone.

Eman nudged me. "Uh . . . uh . . . I seen him before . . . he's . . . uh . . . from the **2**."

"Then why're we listening to him?"

"Cos . . . I guess like . . . uh right now . . . we uh . . . are . . . all as radical as . . . uh like them."

The man started to speak. "We've just heard that City Hall's been taken with force by the army." A murmur ran thru the crowd. He held his hand up. "We've also been reliably informed that early tomorrow they will spread outward in a bid to clear the city. This will reduce the numbers guarding the hall. For tonight we have successfully sealed ourselves off from attack from 3 sides and tomorrow at dawn, the plan is that we will take advantage of their dispersed forces and attempt to retake City Hall, approaching along the waterfront and through Borough Market. If we win, it will send the strongest message to all who are still fighting in London and across the country that we are not beaten. We are determined to use any means, any weapon, anything at our disposal to defend our freedom. We are not prepared to go down like dying dogs!"

The early twilight of winter is falling and I'm writing this in the last light, my fingers freezing. All of us have got our IDs pinned to the inside of our coats and a lawyer's number scrawled on our arms in pen. Behind us, the evening is lit up by a fire burning on the top floors of the Shell Building 2 blocks away. It's such a weird mix of crazy and normal. I'm watching a couple of old guys standing close by, drinking tea and chatting about the day, as if they were in their back gardens in the 'burbs. Meanwhile overhead, choppers are circling like black vultures. I look around at all the protesters, all totally ordinary people. Their faces scared, but determined. Lots of laughing and jokes. And then I look around at my friends. Stace narrows her eyes. "If we get thru this one, we are gonna record the demo of a lifetime."

Claire sits next to me, hugging her arms to her chest. Nate puts his arm round her. Kier warms his hands by a fire. "Tell me again why I left New York?"

"Cos you were bored."

"Oh yeah. Well I'm cured now."

Nate suddenly laughs. "But we ain't even got no weapons nor nothing. Dis the craziest shit I've ever done."

Sam looks up. "Nobody's gonna get hurt. The plan is to avoid the forces tomorrow. And they're not going to attack innocent people like us unless we make them."

Claire shakes her head. "You still don't really get it, do you? You still believe in the system, think it's on your side."

"Claire—"

"He's just a boy. He don't belong here with us, not really."

"Leave him alone!"

Sam hunches his shoulders. "Don't worry about it; it's true enough. None of you have ever really let me in, not after . . . him."

Kier spreads his hands. "Hey, come on . . . we've got enough going on without this."

Sam flicks him a bitter look. "Fine with me. When this is over, I'll be gone."

I glance at his face. What have I done, getting him involved in all this?

Messaged my parents, told them I'm lying low. Which is technically 100% true—sleeping outside under a dirty arch by Waterloo Station *is* about as low as you can go.

## Mon., Dec. 4

It's late afternoon and I'm grabbing half an hour inside a looted shop behind the striker lines. Sam's just come in, shaking. "We've got to

305

quit this now; it's insane. I just saw a guy with his brains spilling out of his head." And then he bent over the back of the cash register and puked.

I reached out, put my hand on his shoulder. "Mate, you've done enough now. Just stay here."

He turned, wiped his mouth. "I'm so scared."

I leaned forward. "So? Means you've not gone mad."

A flicker of a smile crossed his face. "I ain't so sure. Otherwise why am I still here with the psycho girls?"

I shook my head, grabbed him in a tight embrace. He's so lovely, still trying to joke to make *me* feel better. Anyway, just want to finish writing this, before I've got to go back out again.

After a long, long night, with only a few minutes' snatched sleep, we all gathered just before dawn, all totally ready to fight our way to City Hall. I looked around, maybe 5,000 of us. Pale, frightened, exhausted, but *there*. Feds were lined up along the main road and the day began with us hurling fistfuls of bricks at them. They began to charge us and we fell back, but then suddenly we figured out we outnumbered them. The plan was working—like the guy said last night, the forces must've been moved or redeployed overnight to other areas. We stopped moving backward, and then like a spring releasing, we charged! Screaming, shouting, hurling bricks. The feds falling back, scared, and then suddenly running, running away from us.

A group of kids jumped on top of a police van and set it on fire, and we all cheered and laughed before streaming onward toward Borough Market and down to the Thames. But by the time we reached the back of the market, a troop of soldiers appeared and chased us along the narrow cobbled streets, beating all they caught. Me and Stace ran into a tiny alley and crouched down for a moment, the sound of smashing windows all around, clothes, books, bits of looted stuff scattered along the street. In front of us a fed van lay on its side like some dead animal. We hugged each other tight, shivering like little kids, grinning. I've never felt so alive!

Suddenly there was a break in the fighting and a big group of us took the chance to move forward again, street by street, until finally we saw it. City Hall! Standing there like some monument in an ancient battle, smoke and fires raging all around, with thousands of protestors surging forward like a giant wave, smashing over massed lines of police, soldiers, horses, riot shields, and water cannons, our lines continually breaking up as people were clubbed, dragged, charged down. But for each one that went down, another took his place from the next row. Beside me, Claire burst into tears.

"Look at them . . . they're beating people half to death!"

We all stared, dumb. There was no way we could take back City Hall. The forces may have spread out across the city, but they'd left more than enough troops to keep control.

Our group stood there for a moment, unsure in the face of the opposition, when suddenly we were hit by a stinging, pounding, barrage of cold water that knocked us clean off our feet. We slithered and clawed at the ground to maintain our position, but then, from behind us, came the sound of rifle fire. Looking over my shoulder, I saw soldiers emerging from around the bridge. They were running directly at us, some pausing to shoot, sweeping the crowd before them. I pulled myself upright and started to run. I knew that if I fell, I'd be trampled in the forward surge of the crowd.

What followed is a blur. We'd got ourselves trapped to the left of City Hall, charged again and again by the feds, before they opened fire on us with rubber bullets. I felt a vicious punch in the back and

Eman fell down screaming, with a bright spurting gash on his neck. Everyone started running, bellowing, fighting to get free. A woman next to me was shot in the eye, the whole side of her face a swollen mass; another guy had the back of his head split open. Pure animal panic and fear all around.

But somehow we kept together. Nobody knew what to do, there was no plan, but we all moved as one. Everywhere there were troops we linked arms, formed a barrier, *resisted*. At one point I saw a group leap out from behind a barrier and charge a line of police horses, trying to tear the riders to the ground before they were clubbed down.

Unbelievable. I've never seen such courage, such a refusal to be beaten. I didn't knew people could be that strong. I felt so proud to be out there, to be part of it all.

No more time to write now.

Got to go again. Claire and Stace have just come in; they need my space.

Kier's flat. Midnight. We had to come back. About 3 hours ago what remained of our group huddled together behind a burned out truck in Bermondsey. We'd lost Eman and Kier. The situation was hopeless. By now City Hall was a military zone and they'd brought in huge water cannons and were blasting all the side streets to clear the rioters. All of us were cut, bruised, shot, exhausted. We couldn't go on anymore. It took us hours and hours to sneak back home, and we nearly got busted twice. Can't write any more now.

## Tues., Dec. 5

Oh, God—we dragged ourselves outside this morning to check on the street situation and then, out of nowhere—tear gas, sound bombs—soldiers, armored jeeps—troops everywhere. One minute all together, the next running, dodging, wildly scattering in all directions, desperate to escape. I ran blindly toward my old house—a

soldier barred the way, arms outstretched—and at the last second, I
dodged sideways, scrambling over railings, jumping down into
Arthur's basement garden. Landed, hard crunch of bone on concrete, then lay there, panting like a scared dog, waiting for him to
follow. I shrank into a corner . . . shielded my face . . . waiting . . .
but then . . . nothing. Sat there, fists clenched, still no one. Too
visible—I found plastic sheets in corner, dragged them over me,
curled up tight, hugged my knees to my chest. Waited for hours,
willing all to stop . . . the screaming and beating and shouting and
roar of engines to go away, to end.

And now, agony. My ankle. Made myself look. Foot at a weird
angle. Forced myself to stand on other leg, but no way to climb out,
walls at least 2 meters high. I yelled out for help. Footsteps, running.
I froze. Someone calling my name . . . Sam! I screamed out . . . suddenly he was there, reaching down thru the railings. He was still
inside Kier's flat when the soldiers came. Others are all gone, streets
totally dead, empty. He's gone to find something to get me out of
here. Got to stay calm, write slow, word after word, till he gets back.
Trying fone, see if any battery. More footsteps! But sound heavier
than Sam's. Going to check.

Shit! Nearly busted. Lifted my head to railing height, just as the
soldier stopped to check radio message. He was facing the other
way, but so close, could've reached out and touched him. Peered up
into his face. What was he thinking? Did he ever imagine he'd be
here, fighting his own people? Slowly I raised my fone.

15 minutes and counting. Come on, Laura. Keep writing, one
word, then the next . . . Sam's coming back, he promised. A bike
engine roars up the street. He's here! He's tying a rope round the
railings so I can climb out. I am so happy I'm crying. I'm gonna
be free!

## Sat., Dec. 16

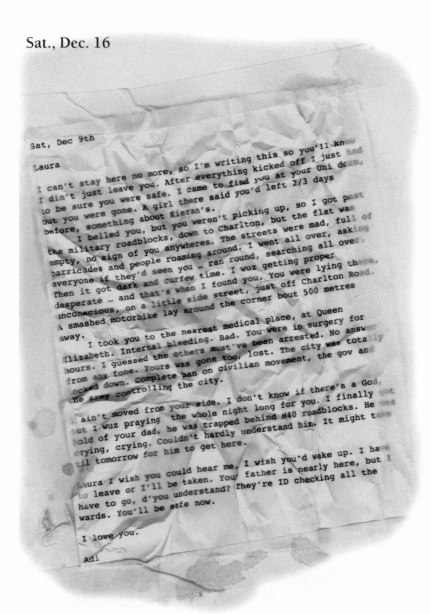

Sat, Dec 9th

Laura

I can't stay here no more, so I'm writing this so you'll know I just had to be sure you were safe. I came to find you at your Uni dorm, but you were gone. A girl there said you'd left 2/3 days before, something about Kieran's.

I belled you, but you weren't picking up, so I got past the military roadblocks, down to Charlton, but the flat was empty, no sign of you anywheres. The streets were mad, full of barricades and people roaming around. I went all over, asking everyone if they'd seen you — ran round, searching all over. Then it got dark and curfew time. I wuz getting proper desperate — and that's when I found you. You were lying there, inconscious, on a little side street, just off Charlton Road. A smashed motorbike lay around the corner bout 500 metres away.

I took you to the nearest medical place, at Queen Elizabeth. Internal bleeding. Bad. You were in surgery for hours. I guessed the others must've been arrested. No answ from any fone. Yours was gone too, lost. The city was totally locked down. Complete ban on civilian movement, the gov and the army controlling the city.

I ain't moved from your side. I don't know if there's a God, but I wuz praying the whole night long for you. I finally got hold of your dad, he was trapped behind M40 roadblocks. He was crying, crying. Couldn't hardly understand him. It might t til tomorrow for him to get here.

Laura I wish you could hear me, I wish you'd wake up. I have to leave or I'll be taken. Your father is nearly here, but I have to go, d'you understand? They're ID checking all the wards. You'll be safe now.

I love you.

Adi

I can't believe he came to find me.

Abingdon. Dad brought me back 4 days ago after they released me from Queen Elizabeth.

It's all so clear. Sam gunned the bike, we turned onto Charlton Road, ran straight into a military roadblock, but before the troops had time to react, Sam spun around, did a sharp cut down a side road—swerved, turned again, and we were out of there! Sam whooped, twisted the throttle full on, I clutched him as the bike jolted forward.

It was as if my mind had detached itself from my body and I was looking down on me from way above. I was lying in a driveway, half underneath a parked truck, I could see my arms and torso twitching. I saw soldiers running past, heard Sam's screams of pain as they kicked and beat him. I blacked out. After, when I came around again, I couldn't stop my body shaking. I've been scared before, in Sicily, in the detention camp, but somehow I'd always been able to control the fear. This time it was different. Now I knew what fear really was.

I didn't know why I'd escaped arrest before, I guess I must've been hidden by the truck. I knew I had to move, that the very soldiers who'd beaten him were my only hope. I was in too much shock to feel pain, but so weak that I didn't think I could move. I've never felt so alone. Just me, there. My chest was like it'd been crushed, blood was pumping from my shoulder. My left arm was numb, dripping red, but I could still move my right. Slowly, in agony, I pulled off my jacket, and bit by bit, I wrapped it tight around my left shoulder to try and stop the blood. Then I tried to get up and blacked out.

When I came around, I got up again and, holding my dead arm against my body, I turned and limped toward the main road. After a few meters, my vision went again and I had to sit down. All I could do was sit, slumped, till sight returned. Then I got up again, and forced myself to keep going, to focus on dragging each foot forward, left then right, again and again. I was so close, but all the time getting weaker and weaker, vision blurring with each step, my rests getting longer and longer until total black.

*   *   *

They beat Sam so bad he's still in intensive care. A 19-year-old boy. My fingers are trembling as I write this. I want to always be in shock, keep alive like this forever.

## Sun., Dec. 17

Global all-out strikes in Norway, Germany, Sweden, Spain, Brazil, Mexico, Venezuela, and China in support of the U.S. in London. Kieran got here late last night. He was released this morning, along with the others. They are all a mess, but OK. He sat by my bed, clasped my hand in silence, no words to say. I want Adi so badly, but I've got no way to get thru to him. All I can do is pray he's not hurt, not taken.

Memorial Service at Westminster Abbey at midday. 97 killed, over 12,000 injured, vigils for those still fighting for their lives. My family came into my bedroom and we watched the service together, in total silence, until a military band started to play "Amazing Grace" and the song caught and spontaneously spread out to the hundreds of thousands standing outside on the frozen ground. And then we all wept, Mum sobbing on Kim's shoulder, Kieran with his head on his arms, shoulders heaving.

## Tues., Dec. 19

The gov has fallen! After 2 days of bitter fighting in Parliament, the Opposition has forced a vote of *no confidence*. Those lying, cheating bastards who tried to beat their own people into submission are finished! The first I knew about it was when I heard the village church bells ringing out. The village has gone nuts, people dancing in the streets, letting off fireworks. Nobody can believe it's true. We won!

    I can't stop crying.

**Thurs., Dec. 21**

Stace came up to see me today, brought my bass and some clothes up from the dorm. Like with Kier, we didn't talk much, listened to some music together, quiet, but it was so good to have her near. She had to leave by late afternoon, but before she went, she reached down and pulled a postcard out of her backpack.

"I guess this belongs to you . . . when I went back to the dorm to get our stuff, it was lying there . . . so . . ."

I took the card, turned it over.

Oh, God. Tears started spilling down my face.

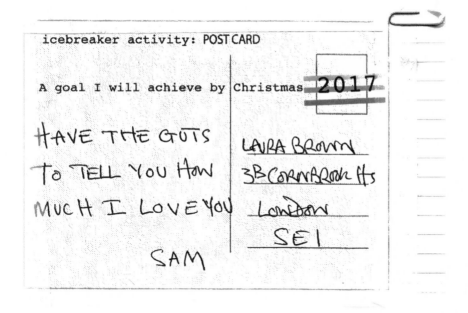

Stace shook her head. "It's not your fault, Laur!"

"Yes, it is! He was only there cos of me . . . and I didn't even love—"

"It's not all about you. He chose to be there. And don't you dare give up on him. Me and all the others have been to see him and when you're better, so will you. He's gonna pull thru, but he's gonna need you, more than before."

"What can I give him?"

She glared at me for a second. "I'm gonna let that one pass cos you're sick. But I'm giving you 2 weeks, and 2 weeks only to eradicate all traces of self-pity out of your system." She grinned. "One thing's definite—he's an *angel* for real now."

## Fri., Dec. 22

I woke up this morning and Mum was sitting in the chair by my bed, staring into space.

I tried a smile. "Hey."

She hardly moved.

"Mum?"

Suddenly she reached out, took my hand. "Twice in one year you've nearly been taken from me." Her face crumpled. "Twice!"

"What do you want? A medal? A crown?"

A pause—and then we both burst out laughing, big time.

## Sat., Dec. 23

I dread going to sleep, cos all I do is dream the same dream about Adi. I'm on a riot field and he's calling out for me to help him, but I can't find him, just hear his voice and I stumble about the twisted bodies and wreckage, but no matter what I do or where I go, I can't ever seem to get to him.

## Sun., Dec. 24

*Christmas Eve*

Just as night was falling, Dad came into my room. "Are you ready?"

"What for?"

"Yes or no?"

I sighed, but he looked so hopeful, like a boy. I nodded. "Yes, Dad."

He glanced toward the door and Mum and Kieran rushed in, laughing, and draped a blanket around my shoulders, then Dad scooped me up and carried me over to a chair by the window. Kim suddenly appeared, slid the pane back . . . and I leaned forward and gasped. The whole garden was alive with sparkling lights and candles—and there, down below, stood a group of about 20 little kids, shuffling in the cold. As soon as I poked my head out, they burst into "Silent Night, Holy Night," their frosty breath coming in little puffs from upturned faces, all lit by the soft light. It was about the most cheesy, tacky thing ever. Mum holding me tight, Dad's face pressed up against the window, Kieran warbling *All is calm, all is bright* by my side in such a weird high voice. I felt myself starting to giggle.

Kim pinched me. "That's the whole of the village of East Wing's electricity supply for the night. Smile and wave, baby sis."

Enough already. Tomorrow I get up.

## Mon., Dec. 25

Very, very, chilled Xmas day. As we sat down to eat, my dad suddenly burst out laughing and raised his glass. "We beat the bastards! We won! Here's to the first of many victories!"

Mum sighed. "Yes, but at what cost?"

Dad slammed his hand down on the table. "A high one, granted. But now we have to make it count. In the next election we bring in a government that does what *we* want and not what big business wants. We've proved we can do it!" He lifted his glass high. "To us."

Everybody jumped up and clinked glasses before forcing a sip of evil, evil carrot wine down their throats. I noticed Mum sloshing most of hers onto the floor under cover of the toast. She don't miss a trick, that woman.

It was later on, though, that I got the best present. A message.

**Wed., Dec. 27**

Waiting, waiting all day—and then, finally, as dark fell, a knock on the door. He's so thin . . . Mum burst into tears as soon as she saw him. She dragged him into the kitchen and forced him to eat a whole turkey leg, while we all gathered around the table and watched him do it, like he was an Xmas movie.

And then, later on, when we were alone, I felt suddenly so shy; such a strange feeling, like being with someone you've known forever, but a stranger, too.

"Adi, I can't believe—"

"Laur. Let's not talk tonight. Let's just be like we used to be. Please?" He pulled me to him and we fell into a kiss. The longest, deepest kiss of my whole life. It was like one of those deep, magical times that even when you're in it, you know you're going to remember always.

## Thurs., Dec. 28

I woke up this morning, with snow falling outside my bedroom window. I gazed at it for a moment, then suddenly I knew he was awake, too, watching me. Slowly, I turned, curled into his arms.

He pushed back a lock of my hair. "Laura, will you come with me?"

"With them?"

He nodded slowly.

Such a pain shot thru me, such a longing to stay like this forever.

"Babe?"

I shook my head. "No."

He sighed. "I love you. There's . . . only you for me."

"Me too."

"But you know I can't stay here, can't be with you like before."

"I know."

A tear welled up, slid down his cheek. "*Still.* After all you've been thru, you want to hide away like this."

"It's not hiding. It's the opposite. It's living it for real. Doing it without guns and bombs."

"And nothing changes! You think this gov would've backed down without us?"

"In the end, yeah. There were 4 million people on the streets. It was them, not you."

He groaned. "Are we gonna fight about this forever?"

"Maybe. I know for sure I can't change you, you're gonna go your own way, but I've got to do the same, too."

"How's that, then?"

"I—I don't have it all worked out . . . but it's deep inside me now. I won't let all that fighting be for nothing. The *angels* is gonna be my way."

"But . . . a band?"

I sat up. "You quit being so judgmental. I don't even have to justify it. *The Clash, Pistols, Minor Threat, Youth of Today*—they stand for themselves."

Adi threw up his hands. "But how is this gonna work? We can't be together . . . and we can't break up. We're a mess."

I felt my eyes start to sting and blur. "I don't know. I've given up on having answers."

"But you love me?"

"Yes . . . you stupid . . . bastard. Wish I didn't."

"Then how are we—"

I pulled him close. "You've got to stop now. We'll just do it as we go along. That's all we can do. Deal?"

We stared at each other, tears everywhere, and then both burst out laughing. How did we get ourselves into such a state?

## Fri., Dec. 29

He left this morning. I was standing at my bedroom window, staring out at the white, dead fields, when Claire called.

She shouted. "Log onto the *port* download chart, now!"

"Why?"

"Just do it, Brown!"

I turned, flipped on the monitor.

"Some bastard ripped it off from our Hackney Empire gig and released it as a downer, but who cares? Every protestor who was on the march is listening to our tune. Got it yet?"

"No, it's taking ages."

Down the fone, Claire screamed:

```
I see no freedom
I see only exploitation
Leaders growing fat
On the cheating of a nation.

If this is the standard then I defy it
If this is the price then I don't buy it
If this is advancement then I deny it!
```

And then the page loaded.

I gasped. Yes! Oh yes! Me and Claire sobbing, screaming, laughing. Number one!

## Sun., Dec. 31

I've got such a surge of hope. We've been given another chance, and there's no way we're letting this one slip thru our fingers. I'm lying here on my bed, my bass next to me—and one thing is crystal clear. A part of my life is over, the part where I tried to fit in, to keep it like it was before. I'm done with that shit. I don't know what the future will bring, and I don't care, anyway. Me, my family, my friends, the *angels*, the message, the fight. No bombs, no guns, no escape. All I want is a straight-up fight with all the crooked, thieving, lying, two-faced, cheating bastards. That's the only thing that matters to me anymore. Revolution!

After all that's happened this year, the fact that I managed to hold on to this diary is amazing. Who knows what the future holds; but if I should end up dead or in prison or something and this diary is found, I want to make sure that whoever finds it (at this point, probably a Yank since the U.S. seems to be marginally better off so far) is totally clear about everything. So here goes:

First off, Celsius and the Metric System. Really! It's hard to believe there are people who still don't know that 50 degrees is so bloody hot you'll get a seizure, go into shock, and get brain damage, if you survive at all. Well, Kier had a bit of trouble with conversions when he went to the States, but after batting his eyelashes at the hipsters in Brooklyn, he soon sorted it out! So check out my last diary for a detailed conversion explanation; or if you flopped maths, just head to a website like metric-conversions.org, which converts temperatures and other measurements for you.

**A&E:** Accident and Emergency—the emergency room at a hospital. But forget about being treated there nowadays. You could wait for weeks before anyone so much as looked at you.

**bougnol:** disgusting French word for immigrants from North Africa used by that obnoxious skinhead member of the Front

**chiller:** 10 carbon points. These are more valuable than hard currency. 1 carbon point is a cooler and 100 points is a cube.

**cotch:** to hang out or crash someplace, as in *Can I cotch here for a while?*

**flat:** an apartment, like my dodgy place in the Dox

**football match:** a soccer game—the *original* football, not the shiny, stop-and-start, covered-in-padding version they play in the States

**jack:** to take or steal, as in *He opened the fridge and jacked a beer.*

**locked off:** to disconnect a cell phone call. Lately, signals are so erratic that you almost never have a chance to lock off yourself; you just lose the call, which makes hanging up on someone when you're having a row bloody irritating.

**Molotov:** a homemade bomb usually thrown at riots, sometimes called a Molotov cocktail or Molotov bomb

**Morris men:** from an old English folk dance called a morris dance in which men dressed in silly costumes move around, hopping over sticks, swords, or even clay pipes laid across each other on the floor. Usually performed at festivals or fairs and generally regarded as weird and uncool.

**peg/pegging:** clothespin/pinning stuff on a clothesline—or in the case of my mum, pinning up a line of dried fish across our kitchen. *Sigh.*

**Red Arrows:** the Royal Air Force aerobatic team

**Reiki:** a kind of spiritual, holistic form of healing that's supposed to balance the body's life force energy through a laying on of hands. I could've used some Reiki many times this year!

**sacked:** fired from a job. You can "be sacked" or get "given the sack." You can also be "made redundant," which is just insulting, really.

**Somerfield:** a grocery convenience store chain. Very handy, as they're open from early in the morning until late at night seven days a week.

**squat/squatters:** a squat is an abandoned flat or apartment where impoverished "squatters" (like me at the Dox) crash illegally but rent free. I guess the idea is that you would squat on the floor of your illegal place; but normally you'd want to avoid contact with the floor, or any other surface for that matter.

**tagging:** a form of graffiti. Sam's tagging was brilliant.

**take the piss:** to mock or tease or totally diss

**tosser:** a jerk

**tuk-tuk:** a souped-up motorbike that looks like a three-wheeled taxi

**Uni:** university. In the UK, the secondary school system can take 13 years to complete. At the end of year 11, we take the GCSE (General Certificate of Secondary Education) exams in a range of subjects. (Some swots take as many as 10!) You can pack it in at that point and move on to a job or a vocational or technical college. Or you can stick it out for 2 more years and take A-Level (short for Advance-Level) courses and exams which are required if you want to get into a university. At university you can focus on your major (specialist subject) immediately, which means you can get your bachelor degree in 3 years.

And that's it, people. Anything else you don't understand, well, use your imaginations.

—L. B.